Not My Child

Kitty Neale was brought up in Battersea, a child born during World War II. She wrote gritty sagas for many years, drawing on her experiences of growing up in London. Her daughter, Sam, now carries on the Kitty Neale legacy. She lives in Spain.

Not My Child

Kitty Neale

ORION

First published in Great Britain in 2025 by Orion Fiction,
an imprint of The Orion Publishing Group Ltd.
Carmelite House, 50 Victoria Embankment
London EC4Y 0DZ

The authorised representative in the EEA is Hachette Ireland,
8 Castlecourt Centre, Castleknock Road, Castleknock, Dublin 15, D15 XTP3,
Republic of Ireland (email: info@hbgi.ie)

An Hachette UK Company

3 5 7 9 10 8 6 4 2

Copyright © Sam Michaels 2025

The moral right of Sam Michaels to be identified as
the author of this work has been asserted in accordance
with the Copyright, Designs and Patents Act of 1988.

All rights reserved. No part of this publication may be
reproduced, stored in a retrieval system, or transmitted
in any form or by any means, electronic, mechanical,
photocopying, recording, or otherwise, without the
prior permission of both the copyright owner and the
above publisher of this book.

All the characters in this book are fictitious, and any resemblance
to actual persons, living or dead, is purely coincidental.

A CIP catalogue record for this book is
available from the British Library.

ISBN (Mass Market Paperback) 9781398713727
ISBN (eBook) 9781398713734
ISBN (Audio) 9781398713741

Typeset at The Spartan Press Ltd,
Lymington, Hants

Printed and bound in Great Britain by Clays Ltd,
Elcograf S.p.A.

www.orionbooks.co.uk

For my mum

I'm so pleased that my mum got to read this book before she passed away. I'm going to miss her reading my manuscripts and approving them before I send them to my editor. Only a week before she passed, she told me, 'Have confidence in your work. You're a brilliant writer, better than me. Just don't rush your endings.' I'll be sure to always remember her advice!

Soon after my mum's death, I found this poem she had written. I'll treasure her words forever.

Tired. Time.

If I wasn't so tired I'd make my bed,
Make it cosy and plump to lay down my head.
If I wasn't so tired I'd clean and I'd dust,
But it all seems too hard, so I live with the fluff.
If I wasn't so tired I'd take on many tasks,
But my daughter is kind without being asked.
She looks after my roses, and mops up the mess,
While I lay on the sofa and feel truly blessed.

I know my life is short now, that it'll soon be time to go,
But I've many things to say and so much I don't know.
So many traumas in my life yet there's much happiness too,
Memories I treasure my darling girl, firstly giving birth to you.
We've been through so much together and I don't want it to end,
But my time is coming my baby, my daughter and my best friend.
I don't know where I'm going, but know my soul will never die,
I'll be watching over you and if there's a way to prove it, I will try.
If you don't sense me don't worry, I'll be right there by your side,
My love for you, a part of me, and my heart so full of pride.

Brenda Warren (AKA Kitty Neale) 1943–2024

RIP beautiful lady. Remembered with love, always xxx

I

London, 1923

'Try and keep your nose clean now, eh, Black.'

'I won't be sad to see the back of this place,' Cyril Black replied, grinning at the prison guard, revealing his missing tooth to the side of his mouth and the rest of his yellowed teeth.

'How long has it been this time? A year? I expect the missus will be pleased to have you home.'

'I doubt that my Florrie will have the bunting out to greet me,' Cyril scoffed, thinking of his hard-faced wife. Then leaning over the counter towards the guard, he winked and lowered his voice, 'But I know a lady who will be very welcoming,' he smiled, cheekily.

'Cor, you're not even out of the prison gates yet and you're already up to mischief. Just stay on the right side of the law.'

'I'll do me best, gov,' Cyril said with a tug on his flat cap.

It felt good to be back in his own clothes and out of the prison issue clobber. Cyril was thankful that at least he hadn't had to wear the broad arrow uniform that had been abolished the year before. And neither had his head been shaved. *Thank gawd*, he thought, pleased that at thirty-four years old, he still had a mop of thick, red hair and hadn't gone bald like his father had by his age.

Cyril stood outside of the prison and raised his face to the sun. He breathed in a long breath, expanding his lungs with *free* air. His liberty felt good, and he couldn't wait to fall into Jill's sexy arms and tumble into her bed. Granted, the delights that Jill offered would cost him a bob or two, but Cyril hoped she might waive her fees and pleasure him as a welcoming home gift. It was more than he could hope to receive from his wife. *The miserable cow*, he mused, shuddering at the idea of seeing Florrie's sour expression.

It took Cyril a couple of hours to meander across London. Nothing much had changed during his incarceration. Horses still pulled carts and delivery boys rode bicycles with baskets on the front, but he did notice that there seemed to be more motorcars on the road. An open top double-decker bus passed him, its carriage advertising Lipton's tea. *Cor*, thought Cyril. He could do with a decent cuppa and a nice hot meal. A woman on the top deck smiled down at him. Her hair was cut short, a new fashion that Cyril had heard about; *Flappers*. They were wild women, set on drinking and dancing, nothing like his Florrie who rarely cracked a smile.

As he cheerfully made his way towards home, Cyril kept his eyes peeled for any opportunities. He was a chancer and would readily steal anything that wasn't nailed down. Though after this last arduous stint in gaol, he had every intention of avoiding the long arm of the law. As he passed over the Albert Bridge that spanned the river Thames, he flounced into Battersea, his spirits soaring at the familiar sight of the run-down and overcrowded terraced houses. Most folk in the borough lived in poverty, but it was home, and Cyril had been born and bred in Battersea. At thirteen, he'd started work at Price's Candle factory alongside his father. But Cyril was bored by the mundanity of factory work and had instead turned to a life of petty crime to earn a decent living. Factory work had never suited him, and he'd soon discovered that stealing excited him. It made him feel alive. The high risk came with high returns... except on the occasions when he'd been caught by the Old Bill and hauled before a judge. Cyril shrugged. He'd be more careful in future.

Finally arriving at Jill's house, Cyril rapped on the shabby door. Stepping back, he smiled broadly as he felt his groin stir in eager anticipation. The woman had an ample bosom and firm thighs. He pictured her long, blonde hair cascading over her milky-white skin and tickling his face as she straddled him. But when the door swung open, Cyril baulked. Jill, who had been slim and pretty, now looked worn-out and slovenly. Her dishevelled hair was lank and greasy, and infected sores marked her once clear complexion. Cyril glanced, shocked at the sight of a baby in the woman's arms, wrapped in rags and quietly whining.

'It's about time you showed your face,' Jill snapped.

'I've been banged up for a year, love, you know that. I've only just got out.'

'Yeah, well, they should have hung you by your neck.'

'Come off it, sweetheart, that's a bit harsh. I thought you'd be pleased to see me.'

'I am. You can take this,' Jill barked, thrusting the baby towards Cyril.

'Whoa,' Cyril cried, throwing his hands in the air. 'I ain't come round here to babysit your sprog. You've obviously got your hands full... I'd best get off home to see the missus... take care, Jill.'

As Cyril spun on the heel of his worn boots and made a hasty retreat, Jill's shrill voice followed him.

'She's yours, you bloody fool. You left me lumbered wiv her.'

Cyril stopped. He could feel the blood draining from his freckled face. *A kid...* surely not. He already had a young boy at home, Jimmy, a smashing lad but spoiled rotten by Florrie. Two mouths were enough to feed. He wouldn't take responsibility for Jill's bastard too. And anyway, the woman was a whore which meant that the father could be any one of countless fellas.

'Do you hear me, Cyril Black?' Jill shrieked.

Cyril turned to face her. 'Yeah, I hear you. You reckon she's mine, do ya? I ain't being funny, love, but you've had more men in your bed than I've had hot dinners!'

'She's yours all right, look,' Jill said, sharply, and pulled back the rags from the baby to reveal her head.

Cyril gawped. The girl didn't have much hair, but she had a fine covering of ginger tufts, the exact same colour as his own and the same as Jimmy's.

'That's right, Cyril, look on. You and me both know that there ain't many blokes in these streets with red hair. And another thing, look at her thumbs...' Jill raised the baby's arm. 'See how short they are. Her thumbs are deformed, just like yours. You don't need no more proof. I'm telling you: the girl is yours.'

Swallowing hard, Cyril felt winded, as though he'd been punched in the stomach. This was the last news he'd expected to come home to.

Jill continued, 'I can't keep her. How am I supposed to work with her screaming the house down?'

'What do you expect me to do about it?' Cyril uttered.

'Take her. We're both starving. She'll be better off with you and Florrie.'

Cyril's eyes widened. He couldn't take a baby home to his wife!

'Don't look so worried, Cyril. Florrie's known for donkey's years that you've been regularly visiting me, and she's happy to turn a blind eye 'cos I see to your needs so that she don't have to. Stand up to the woman for once in your life.'

'But – but…'

'*But* bleedin' nothing! Either you take the girl, or me and her will end up in a workhouse.'

Cyril hung his head. He couldn't imagine a worse place to be. The workhouses were reputed to be even more dire than the gaols. Thinking fast, Cyril pleaded desperately, 'I could support you both… I'll give you money, enough for you and the baby to live on…'

'Don't talk daft, Cyril Black,' Jill spat, scathingly. 'You can barely keep a roof over Florrie's and Jimmy's heads, let alone look after another family. Anyway, I don't want the girl. Just take her.'

Before Cyril could protest further, Jill had thrust the child into his reluctant arms.

'Florrie will take good care of her,' she said, her voice softer. With a final sad glance at her daughter, she turned and stepped back inside, slamming shut the door.

Cyril stood stunned, holding his scrawny-looking daughter. He peered down into her sea-blue eyes, the same shade as his own, and he smiled tenderly. It was clear that the baby needed a good meal. 'It looks like you're coming home with me,' he cooed. 'Gawd help us both when my Florrie meets you.'

2

'You dirty, filthy, good-for-nothing git! You can take your bastard back to where you got it from. It ain't staying in my house and I ain't looking after it!' Florence Black screamed at her husband. She glanced with disgust at the wriggling baby on her kitchen table, shaking her head at the audacity of Cyril. 'You must have turned lunatic if you really believe that I'm going to take on that whore's child!'

'Please, love, I'm begging you. I know it's a lot to ask but the poor mite is hungry, and she needs us.'

'Out... go on... the pair of you can sling your hook. Go back to your slut and take the baby with you. It ain't welcome here and neither are you.'

Exhausted, Florence slumped onto a kitchen chair and tucked a strand of dark hair behind her ear. She ran her hand over her face, fighting back tears. She'd been working two jobs to cover the rent and put food on the table. Cyril's return from gaol was supposed to be a welcome relief. In fact, she'd been counting down the days and had been looking forward to his homecoming to lighten the financial burden. But she hadn't anticipated that he'd walk through the door with another woman's child! Florence glanced again at the girl, hatred gnarling her empty stomach that growled with hunger.

Cyril stamped across the kitchen and clumsily gathered the baby. Then to Florence's surprise, he shoved the bundle at her.

'Feed her,' he ordered, his voice ominous. 'Then when you've done feeding her, give me a list of what you'll need for the girl. I'll have it by sun fall.'

Forced to hold the baby, Florence glared at her husband. 'She's yours. You feed her,' she said, pushing the baby back towards him.

Cyril's lips twisted in anger, and she could see that his temples were throbbing. Florence had only ever seen him in this much of a rage the once before. It had been when his father had backhanded his mother in front of them both on Christmas day. Florence recalled how she'd stood back, aghast, as Cyril had grabbed his father by the neck, almost strangling the life out of the man. Though her husband rarely lost his temper, when he did, he could be dangerous. Snapped back into the present, Florence's pulse quickened and her heart began to race. Still, she wouldn't back down and accept the child into her home.

'I'm warning you, woman,' Cyril growled through gritted teeth. 'You'll do as I say!'

'Oh yeah,' Florence taunted boldly, 'and what if I don't?'

'Then you'll see my fist in your hateful mouth! Don't push me, Florrie. Me and the kid are staying whether you like it or not. This is *my* house and you're *my* wife.'

'Your *wife*! Huh, was you thinking about *your wife* when you made *that*?' Florence asked, flicking her eyes towards the baby who was still in her arms, gurgling unhappily.

7

'If you had been a proper wife instead of turning your back on me every night, I wouldn't have needed to visit Jill. But all of that is by the by now. That child doesn't have the energy to cry. Feed her. You'll take care of her as our own. Is that clear?'

Florence pursed her lips. She wanted to tell Cyril to go and take a running jump, but she could tell by the tone of his voice that he wasn't going to accept any nonsense from her. He wasn't often a violent man, though he'd grown up taking aggressive beatings from his father and had watched him regularly attack his mother. Cyril had always vowed that he'd never be anything like the man his father was, yet she knew he struggled to contain his anger, instead masking it with a cheeky character. She'd pushed him in the past to the point where he'd snapped and punched a hole in the door or cracked his knuckles whacking the wall. He'd blacked her eyes a couple of times, but only after she'd driven him to it. And on this occasion, she had a feeling that if she didn't comply, she'd likely feel the brunt of his fists again.

'I said, *is that clear?*' Cyril repeated, seething.

Florence lowered her eyes and nodded.

'Right you are. Tell me what you need for the baby.'

Florence sighed. She'd need a list of things as long as her arm, but she also needed her larder stocking and Jimmy had no shoes on his feet. Many of the neighbour's children went barefoot, but summer was coming to an end and the boy couldn't be expected to walk to school in the cold with no shoes. Florence wanted better for her son. She'd hoped that the little she was earning from mending clothes and cleaning would be boosted now that Cyril was home. Instead, she'd have to give up her job to look after a whore's child and

Cyril would be concentrating his efforts on acquiring stuff for the baby rather than for her and Jimmy.

'Does it have a name?' Florence asked, trying her utmost to contain her resentment.

Cyril looked blank.

'She *must* have a name,' Florence pushed.

'Penny,' he finally answered. 'Her name is Penny Black, just like the stamp.'

3

Later that day, Cyril was pleased with his work. He'd managed to pinch nearly everything that Florrie had requested, including the perambulator that was laden with the stolen goods. He walked smugly down his street, greeting the neighbours and doffing his flat cap at Mrs Whetstone in number seventy-nine. The old woman had been widowed for over twenty years; her husband killed in the Boer War. Cyril had been devasted by his death. The man had been like the father that Cyril had always wanted: kind, gentle and caring. Unlike his own dad who had battered him for everything from using the last sheet of newspaper to wipe his backside to accidently smashing the teapot. Even when Cyril had tried his best to be the perfect son, his tyrannical dad had found an excuse to violently punish him.

'Welcome home, lad,' Mrs Whetstone smiled warmly. 'What's the perambulator for? Are you going to make a cart for Jimmy?'

'No, Mrs Whetstone. This 'ere pram is for my daughter,' Cyril grinned. It felt peculiar to say *my daughter*, but he found himself beaming with pride. He'd always wanted a girl, though with Florrie being such a cold fish, he'd never thought that there would be any chance of one.

'Your daughter?' Mrs Whetstone parroted, sceptically.

'Yeah, that's right. Penny. Penny Black. Ah, you wait 'til you meet her, she's the spit of me.'

'When was she born?'

'About three months ago, I reckon.'

'And Florrie?'

'What about her?' Cyril asked.

'Well, I know that Florrie didn't have a baby three months ago.'

'She'll be a good mum.'

'You're a scallywag, Cyril, a bad boy,' Mrs Whetstone admonished with a smile, wagging her gnarled finger at him. 'But I shall look forward to meeting Penny. Be sure to bring her down to see me. I suppose I'd best get knitting.'

'Will do, and when I bring her to see you, I'll bring you some wool an' all,' Cyril replied with a wink. He often dropped stolen gifts in to the old woman who always gave him a friendly telling off yet readily accepted the presents all the same. With her salt and pepper hair smoothed into a bun, a shawl always across her shoulders and long, high-necked black dresses that swept the ground, the woman put Cyril in mind of a Victorian schoolmistress.

Back indoors, Cyril pushed the pram into the kitchen and glanced around for his daughter. He was delighted to see her sleeping soundly on the table, lying in a drawer from his bedroom cupboard, and now wrapped in a clean blanket. Jill had been right in what she'd said about standing up to Florrie. He'd spoken firmly to the woman, and she'd already proven herself to be a good mother to Penny.

'Where's me boy?' Cyril asked, looking forward to seeing Jimmy.

'He'll be home soon. He went to my mum's after school.'

'Good, I can't wait to see the lad. Now, how's my girl?'

'Settled,' Florence answered brusquely.

His wife had once been a fine-looking woman, but she'd let her figure go. Luckily for Florence, she was big boned with broad shoulders and wide hips. It meant she carried her extra weight well. And with her olive skin, black hair and dark eyes, Cyril had thought his wife to be exotic... until she'd open her nagging mouth.

'I've managed to get just about everything on the list... and this...' Cyril reached into the perambulator and pulled out a silk umbrella, delicately printed with a bamboo and lotus design. 'This is for you, my lovely,' he grinned, hoping that the fancy gift would appease his wife.

Florence looked at the umbrella he offered and scoffed.

'I thought you'd like it,' Cyril said, his feelings hurt.

'What do you expect me to do with it, eh? I need food in my cupboards and clothes on Jimmy's back, not a posh brolly. As if I could use something like that round here. I'd be a laughing stock, you fool!'

His ungrateful wife had always been harsh with her words, and a year of his absence hadn't softened her. Rage rose through Cyril's chest. He whipped off his flat cap and threw it down angrily onto the table.

'I ain't been home more than two minutes and already I've had enough of your lip, Florrie. I've a good mind to shove this brolly up where the sun don't shine,' he shouted.

Florrie marched towards him, her face just inches from his. Her dark eyes blazed with fury as she said quietly, 'I'm warning you, Cyril. If you lay even one finger on me, I won't ever again care for *your* child.'

Cyril sucked in a long breath. His wife had him over a barrel and she knew she had the upper hand. If he wanted his daughter to be well looked after, then he'd have to toe the line with Florence and go back to doing her bidding.

The door flew open wider and six-year-old Jimmy ran in. 'Dad!' he exclaimed, wrapping his small arms around Cyril's legs.

Cyril ruffled the boy's ginger hair. Peeling Jimmy's arms from around him, he said, 'Stand back, let me take a look at you.'

Jimmy stood rod-straight, grinning.

'Cor blimey, Son, I swear you've grown another foot.' Cyril held his hand up, showing his palm to the boy. 'Go on lad, punch it. Give it all you've got. Let's see how hard you can hit.'

Jimmy pulled back his elbow and hit Cyril's hand.

'Good one, Son, but don't tuck your thumb inside your fist,' Cyril instructed.

Hearing a noise, Jimmy turned and looked at the drawer sitting on the kitchen table. Dashing over, he peered inside. 'Who's this?' he asked.

'That's Penny, your sister,' Cyril answered.

'My sister?'

'Yes, lad. You're a big brother now which means you've got to always look after Penny. You'll do that, won't you, Son?'

'Yes, Dad. Where did she come from? Did you buy her from a baby shop?'

'Enough questions,' Florence snapped. 'Upstairs, to your room.'

'Aw, but I want to see my—'

'Upstairs! Now!' Florence interrupted.

'Do as your mother tells you,' Cyril added. 'But tomorrow, you can have the day off school and come out with me.'

'He'll do no such thing!' Florence barked.

'Oh, come on, love. It'll be good for me and him to spend some time together. I ain't seen the boy for ages.'

Florence looked derisively at her husband. 'You should have thought about that before you went and got yourself banged up.' Then, turning back to her son, she said softly, 'Up to your room, Jimmy. I'll call you when dinner is ready.'

Jimmy sloped off and Florence closed the door behind him. Her eyes narrowed, and she warned quietly, 'You'd better not get up to any of your tricks tomorrow. I won't allow Jimmy to go out pinching with you.'

'No, Florrie, I wouldn't,' Cyril lied. But he had every intention of teaching the boy the skills of being an artful thief. After all, such talents might come in handy one day for Jimmy.

4

Florence roughly shoved a bottle into Penny's mouth and the girl at last stopped crying. For over two weeks now, day and night, the crying had been relentless. The only time that Penny was quiet was when she had a bottle in her mouth. The endless bawling had worn down Florence and her bitter resentment towards the child had increased tenfold.

'Where's Dad?' Jimmy asked as he came into the kitchen, rubbing his tired eyes.

'Gawd knows. I reckon he's staying away to avoid all the racket that this one makes.' Florence frowned when she noticed the dark circles that ringed Jimmy's blue eyes. 'Did Penny keep you up last night?' she asked.

'Yeah, a bit,' Jimmy replied.

'You can stay at your gran's tonight and over the weekend, if you like?'

'Nah... I don't like the man who lives upstairs in Grandma's house. I want to stay here with my sister.'

Florence placed the baby back into the drawer that was used for a cot and then gently grabbed Jimmy's arm. Crouching down and holding the boy squarely by the shoulders, she looked deeply into his eyes. 'Listen to me, Jimmy,' she said, her tone serious, 'Penny isn't really your sister. You're not to have anything to do with her. I don't want to see you playing with her or talking to her. Do you understand?'

Jimmy looked confused and his young brow furrowed.

'We don't love Penny. We don't even like Penny. She's a wicked, horrible child, so I want you to stay well away from her, all right?'

Jimmy nodded.

'Good. You're my best boy, Jimmy. You'll do as I say, won't you?'

Again, the boy nodded, but Florence didn't think that he looked convinced.

'Your dad doesn't know that Penny is evil and even if I told him, he wouldn't believe me. But she is evil, Jimmy. She's got the devil inside her. That's why you must keep away from her. But like I said, your dad wouldn't believe me so you mustn't mention any of this conversation to him. We wouldn't want to upset your father, eh?'

Jimmy shook his head, his eyes wide and his skin deathly pale.

'It's all right, don't be scared. Penny can't hurt you and I'll always protect you. Just ignore her. Don't look at her. Pretend like she's not even there. I promise you, Jimmy, she's bad down to the core but she'll never, ever get past me to hurt you.'

'Gran said she's a bastard... what's a bastard?'

'Its another word for evil, but it's not a word that you should say. Just stay away from Penny. Now, remember, this is our secret. Off you go, or you'll be late for school.'

As Florence heard the front door close behind Jimmy, she

looked down at the baby who was just about to start crying again. An horrific thought struck her. She was tempted to put a pillow over the girl's face and shut her up for once and all. 'No one would ever know,' she whispered. 'Babies die all the time.'

Penny kicked out her skinny legs, then pulled them up to her stomach. Her face turned purple as her small lungs bellowed an ear-piercing scream.

'SHUT UP!' Florence yelled. 'Just shut up for one bleedin' minute!'

Feeling at breaking point, her head thumping and tiredness swamping her aching body, Florence walked to the sink and picked up a towel, which she carefully folded into four. Her heart felt as though it would pump out of her chest as she crept towards the baby. Gripping the towel in both hands, Florence lowered it towards Penny's face. Her mouth felt dry with fear, but without any doubts, she callously placed the towel over the baby's face. As she held it down, Penny instantly fell quiet. Florence closed her eyes, bile burning the back of her throat. *Die*, she silently urged, *die*.

'Hello, love. Where's my two favourite girls?'

Cyril's voice reached her ears followed by the sound of his heavy boots thumping along the passageway. Florence gasped, quickly pulling away the towel from Penny's face. She peered at the child, relieved when she saw her draw in a desperate breath and then begin to screech.

'Cor, there's nothing wrong with her lungs, eh,' Cyril smiled as he came into the kitchen.

'She never flippin' shuts up,' Florence spat.

'She'll grow out of it.'

'You better not have been with one of your tarts all night, Cyril. I won't bring up another one of your bastards.'

'Don't be like that, love. I've been out grafting.'

'Grafting, eh? So, where's the spoils of your night's work?'

"Ere,' Cyril answered, and threw a pocket full of coins onto the table. 'That should pay the rent for four weeks and buy Jimmy a pair of shoes. Any chance of a cuppa?'

Florence quickly gathered the coins and squirrelled them away in an old tea tin. 'The kettle's on. I'm popping out to see my mum.'

'The witch,' Cyril mumbled under his breath.

'Yeah, well, you can call her what you like but you should be grateful to her. If it weren't for my mum, me and Jimmy might have been doing a midnight flit. Thanks to mum, we've still got a roof over our heads and we ain't got to share the house with any other families, unlike most folk on this street who are packed into stinkin' rooms. Mum helped me to keep me standards up. She deserves your gratitude.'

'I've paid her back every penny that she lent you, and some.'

Florence rolled her eyes, unimpressed.

'Can't you feed her or something?' Cyril asked, throwing a look towards Penny.

'She's been fed and changed,' Florence replied. Then going into the passageway, she grabbed her coat from the newel post. Back in the kitchen, pulling it on, she said to Cyril, 'I'll see you later.'

As she walked towards the front door, Cyril called, 'Ain't you forgotten something?'

Florence sighed before shouting back, 'She's your daughter. Can't you look after her for a change?'

Cyril was in the passageway now. 'Men don't look after kids, and anyway, I've got work to do. Take her round to see the witch with you. The fresh air might do her good.'

Florence trudged back into the kitchen. Reaching into the drawer for Penny, a wave of guilt washed over her. Thank goodness Cyril had come home when he had. If he hadn't, Penny would be dead and Florence would have the girl's blood on her hands. She reasoned that it had been a moment of madness which endless sleepless nights had driven her to. Though deep down, truth be known, she longed for the child to die.

5

'It's only me, Mum,' Florence called as she kicked the front door closed behind her. Walking into her mother's crammed room with Penny in her arms, her mother looked up from an armchair.

'I wish you wouldn't bring that bastard here,' Lou grumbled.

'And I wish I didn't have to, but what choice do I have?'

'You can divorce him. It's legal now. As a woman, you've the right to divorce Cyril on the grounds of adultery. That new prime minister, Baldwin, he'll be ringing in the changes, you mark my words.'

'Don't be daft, Mum. A wife can't file for divorce on adultery.'

'Daft, am I? What's this say then?' Lou asked, handing a newspaper to Florence and pointing at a small article.

Florence put the newspaper to one side and laid Penny on the small sofa beside her. 'I don't care what the paper says, I couldn't divorce Cyril. It's not what women do round here, and I wouldn't know how to go about it. So I ain't doing it.'

'Why not? When he's not behind bars, he comes and goes like the wind. You'd be better off without him.'

'No, Mum, I wouldn't. He ain't always home, sometimes disappearing for weeks on end, but he always sees me all right. I only just managed to scrape by when he was sent down the last time and I would have been homeless if you hadn't've of helped. I need him, which means I have to put up with *her*.' Florence peered coldly at Penny. For once, the girl wasn't screaming.

'He takes liberties. I wouldn't stand for it. Your father, God rest his soul, he never even looked at another woman, let alone bring his bastard home to me.'

'Dad was a good man.'

'He was, and he hated Cyril. If the Spanish Flu hadn't killed him and he was still alive today, I reckon your father would have strung Cyril up by his whats-its by now.'

Florence smiled. Her father had made no secret of his dislike for Cyril. He'd believed in hard work, and he never broke the law. But his death had left Lou almost destitute. Luckily, the quick-witted woman had turned to hawking for a living and now sold her wares three times a week on the streets around Lavender Hill and Clapham Junction. Lou would peddle anything from bundles of watercress to baskets of kindling. It didn't earn her a fortune, but the woman led a simple life. And though Lou would never admit it, Florence was sure that her mother made a side income from shoplifting to order.

'By the way, Mum, can you mind your language in front of Jimmy. He asked me what a bastard is.'

'I'm only speaking the truth. Jimmy's old enough to understand.'

'He's only six, Mum.'

'Old head on young shoulders, that one.'

'Not half,' Florence guffawed, proud of her clever young man.

'I've made him some rock cakes. If he ain't coming round to see me, you can take them home with you. Go and wrap them up and make us a cuppa while you're in the kitchen.'

'Jimmy said that he doesn't like Ned upstairs. That's why he's not been round.'

'I can't say I blame him, I'm not keen on the fella either and I don't trust him.'

'Why, what's he done?' Florence asked. She had always thought that Ned seemed nice enough, albeit he could be moody sometimes. He lived with his wife and three young boys in the two rooms upstairs in the shared house. His wife had explained to Florence that Ned hadn't been the same since he'd returned from fighting in the Great War, and that his moods were often dark. The woman had apologised on her husband's behalf, saying that if he was in one of his sulks, he didn't mean to be impolite. Florence hadn't taken much notice. After all, many soldiers had come back from fighting in Europe as changed men. She supposed that they were lucky to come home at all.

'I'm sure he's watching me when I use the privy,' Lou whispered.

Florence wanted to laugh but refrained from doing so. She couldn't imagine why anyone would want to spy on her mother. The woman was past sixty and extremely plump. A liking for bread and dripping or sugar on bread had widened her hips to the point where she only just managed to sit comfortably in the armchair. Her once dark hair was now thin and white. And with her weather-beaten face and drooping eyelids, Lou might have once been a beauty, but she hadn't aged well.

Lou looked disgruntled. 'I'm telling you, he's watching me in the privy, but I can tell by the look on your face that you don't believe me.'

'I do, Mum, but what makes you think he's watching you?'

'Shush, keep your voice down. These walls are paper thin, he'll hear you... There's a hole been made in the privy door. It wasn't there before. Go and see for yourself if you don't believe me. I swear, Florrie, every time I come out the privy he's there, loitering in the backyard.'

'Loitering?'

'Yes. He tries to make out he's tending to his tomatoes or something, but I know he's watching me. And look,' Lou whispered, pointing up. 'There's a hole in the ceiling an' all, right above my bed.'

Florence searched the ceiling, but she couldn't see any holes. 'There's nothing there, Mum, just flaking paint and damp patches.'

'Get on my bed and you'll see it. It's small, but it's there.'

Florence climbed onto her mother's single bed and laid back, peering upwards. When her eyes fell on a small hole, she sat bolt upright.

'You've seen it. See, I haven't lost me marbles yet,' Lou said.

'It's an old building, Mum. Just because there's a hole, it doesn't mean that Ned made it.'

'He did, I'm telling you. I'm always getting the feeling that I'm being watched. It's him. He ain't right and he sends a shiver down my spine, like someone's walking over my grave.'

Her mother had never liked confrontation, though the

woman had ruled over Florence's father. 'I'll have a word with him,' Florence offered.

'There's no point, he'll only deny it.'

'Maybe, but at least he'll know that we're on to him. Is he home now? He works nights, doesn't he?' Florence asked.

'Yeah, he's home. His wife took the boys out early this morning. I ain't heard her come back yet.'

'Good.'

'What will you say to him?'

'I'll tell him to pack it in, the dirty so and so!'

With that, Florence marched up the stairs and knocked heavily on Ned's door. When the extremely thin man pulled it open, Florence was shocked to find him wearing only a pair of trousers, his top bare.

'Hello, Florrie. What can I do for you?'

'You can stop peeping at my mum!'

'Er, sorry, I don't know what you mean,' Ned argued.

'I've seen the hole in her ceiling, and she tells me there's one in the privy door too. Peeping on old ladies is wrong, Ned, and very disturbing.'

'I haven't been doing anything like that, honestly.'

Florence could see in his eyes that Ned was lying. 'Get the holes mended or I'll send my Cyril round, and he'll have more than just a few words with you.'

Ned looked down at his sockless feet.

'I mean it. I've a good mind to report you to the police ... and to the landlord!'

'No, please don't do that,' Ned blurted. 'I'll fill in the holes right now, I promise, and I'll never look at the woman again.'

'You'd better not! It's disgusting, Ned. What would your wife say if she knew about what you've been doing?'

'You – you won't say anything, will you? I promise to mend the holes.'

Florence pursed her lips. 'All right, Ned, I'll keep quiet so long as you get straight on to it and keep your eyes off my mother.'

The man nodded and looked humiliated.

Florence shook her head as she walked away. She couldn't imagine why Ned was interested in her mother, but she felt assured that the man's shame about his perverted actions had put a stop to his spying and peeping.

As she made her way back down the stairs, Penny's cries echoed through the house.

'If you can't keep her quiet, then take her home,' Lou moaned.

'She never blinkin' stops,' Florence huffed.

'Put a drop of whisky in her bottle. That oughta calm her.'

'Hmm,' Florence said, scooping the screaming child into her arms. 'That ain't a bad idea. Anyway, I've had a word with Ned. You won't be getting any more bother from him.'

'Thanks, Pet. What did you say?'

'Nothing much. I threatened to tell his wife and that seemed to do the trick.'

'I should think so an' all.'

'Shush,' Florence seethed in Penny's ear, rocking her from side to side.

'I can't hear meself thinking straight with her bawling,' Lou grumbled again.

'I'll get her home and give her a feed.'

'Remember what I said. Shove a drop of the hard stuff in her bottle. It'll her knock her out for the night, and looking at the state of you, I would say that you need a good night's sleep.'

'Yeah, I will, Mum, thanks. I'll see you soon.'

To Florence's relief, the fresh air outside quietened Penny. As she pushed the perambulator towards home, Mrs Potter from three doors up bustled out of the corner shop, dragging a young child in each hand and a basket over her arm.

'Oh, Mrs Black, nice to see you. How are you?'

Florence plastered on a smile. Mrs Potter knew everyone's business and enjoyed a good gossip. Florence had no doubt that that she and the bastard baby had been the latest topic of conversation on the streets of Battersea.

'I'm fine, thank you, Mrs Potter. You've got your hands full, I see.'

'These two should be at school but they've both got impetigo. Don't come too close, I'd hate for the baby to catch it. How is she?'

'She's well,' Florence replied curtly, her hackles rising and her back stiffening. She hated the idea of being spoken about. When Cyril had lumbered Penny on her, he'd done a good job of showing her up in front of all the neighbours.

'I must say, Mrs Black, you deserve a medal for what you've done.'

'Eh?' Florence mumbled.

'Taking on that child like you have. You're a saint. I don't think I would have been as accommodating.'

Florence shrugged. She hadn't had a choice.

'We've all been saying what a heart of gold you've got. That baby is lucky to have you.'

'She needed a mother,' Florence replied, suddenly lapping up the adulation.

'Well, she landed on her feet with you, Mrs Black. You're a good woman and we all admire what you've done. So charitable. Like I said, you're a saint.'

Florence smiled. So, the gossip about her and Penny had been favourable. 'I'm not a saint, Mrs Potter. But I couldn't see the poor girl left unwanted and without a home.'

'I admire you, I really do.'

After thanking Mrs Potter and promising to call in soon for a cuppa, Florence marched home with her head held high. *A saint*, she smiled, *a heart of gold*. She liked the idea of being well thought of for her good deed. Though glancing into the pram, her smile changed into a scowl as she looked contemptuously at the sleeping baby. Florence knew she could never hold any affection towards the child. *Never.*

Two days later, Florence flounced towards her mother's house, proud to be receiving looks of admiration from her neighbours. *Yeah, that's right*, she thought. *Look at me, caring for this bastard child.* It had come as a great relief to discover that she wasn't being talked about as a fool for taking on the baby of her husband's whore.

Gathering Penny from the perambulator, she walked into her mother's room.

'You've brought her with you again,' Lou grumbled with a tut.

'I can't leave her at home by herself.'

'Where's Cyril? Don't tell me he's got himself a job, 'cos I know there's no chance of that happening.'

'He's busy.'

'Out nicking stuff again, I suppose,' Lou said with disdain.

'Yes, Mum, out nicking stuff again. He got Jimmy a smart coat and look at this lovely scarf.'

'A scarf won't pay the rent, my girl.'

'It's paid, Mum. We're doing all right.'

Lou sniffed.

Florence thrust Penny towards her mother, urging, 'Hold her, and I'll put the kettle on.'

'I'll do no such thing. She ain't my flesh and blood and she ain't yours neither. Shove her over there on the sofa where I can't see her.'

Florence sighed. She couldn't blame her mother for shunning Penny. Changing the subject, she asked, 'Did Ned fill in the holes?'

'Yes, but there's a new one in my door. Look, can you see it?'

Florence walked closer to the door and studied it. 'The dirty sod!' she gasped.

'And he keeps coming into the kitchen and stands there staring at me. He don't say nothing. Just stares. It's peculiar.'

'I should think it is. What's his game?'

'I don't know, Florrie, but I don't think he's right in the head. I reckon that he's got that shell shock or something.'

'Shell shock or not, I'm not having this, Mum.'

Placing Penny on the sofa without any regard to the baby's safety, Florence stamped towards the door.

'What are you going to say to him?' Lou asked.

'I'm going to warn him off.'

'Leave it, Florrie. Let Cyril deal with him.'

'Ned don't scare me, Mum. He's a skinny weed and I'm going to give him a piece of my mind!'

Florence marched up the stairs, hoping that Ned's wife

28

would be home. It was time that the woman knew what a pervert she was married to. Hammering on the door, Florence shouted Ned's name.

He yanked open the door, looking irritated.

'You've been spying on my mum again and making her feel uncomfortable when she's in the kitchen.'

Ned stared blankly at her.

'I warned you Ned. I let you off the hook last time, but I'm not giving you any more chances. I want a word with you wife. Is she home?'

Ned didn't answer, his steely eyes fixed on hers.

'My Cyril will be paying you a visit and I've a good mind to go the Old Bill an' all.'

Ned's scraggy face glowed bright red, and his hard eyes narrowed. His lips set into a grim line, and he hissed, 'If you open your mouth and tell anyone, I'll sneak down in the middle of the night and put a knife through the bitch's heart.'

Florence felt her blood run cold as she suddenly realised that the man was unstable. Fear snaking through her veins, she quickly turned. Hurrying down the stairs, she burst into her mother's room. 'Pack your stuff, you're coming to live with me,' she blurted.

'What's going on?' Lou asked, looking bewildered.

'He's mad, Mum. You're not safe here.'

'Eh? Come off it, Ned's a bit peculiar but he's harmless. I'd only have to blow on him and he'd fall over.'

'Mum, I'm not arguing with you. Just get your things together. We're leaving.'

'What's he said?'

'That he'd sneak down in the night and kill you. There, satisfied?'

'He what?'

'You heard me. Come on, Mum, please. We've got to get out of here.'

Seeming to sense the need for urgency, Lou pushed her large body out of the chair, telling Florence, 'There's a bag under my bed, pull it out.'

As Florence got down on her hands and knees, Penny burst out crying and at the same time, she heard a knock on her mum's door. 'Don't answer it,' she warned.

Lou stood, her hands on her head, appearing alarmed. 'Do you think it's Ned?' she mouthed, silently.

Florence nodded.

The door knocked again, louder this time.

'What shall we do?' Lou asked, trembling.

Florence gulped, her heart racing. Ned didn't have the build of a strong man, but she feared he'd have a knife. 'The window,' she whispered, pointing towards it.

'I can't get out of there!'

'You'll have to, Mum.'

'No, you go. Get help.'

'I'm not leaving you.'

A loud thud shook the door. Florence's heart leapt as it dawned on her that Ned was kicking it in.

'Go, Florrie, fetch the police,' Lou urged frantically.

Another thunderous kick. The door frame splintered. Florence knew that one more kick would bring the door crashing in. She ran to the window and lifted the sash. Sticking her head through, the street was quiet, but she shouted out, 'HELP! Help us! Fetch the police!'

Hearing the door fly open and her mother scream, Florence snapped her head around and looked behind her. She was horrified to see Ned holding a long knife towards her mum. Beads of sweat trickled down the man's neck and over his pumped, protruding veins.

'Leave her alone!' Florence shrieked. 'Get out!'

Ned didn't take his eyes off Lou. Glaring menacingly at the old woman, he mumbled, 'I should have killed her back then.'

Florence edged slowly forward. 'Please, Ned, don't hurt my mum,' she pleaded.

'She tortured me for two years!' he yelled, his face crumpling as tears streamed down his face. 'I didn't have the strength to kill her then, but I have now.'

'Ned, I don't understand... my mum hasn't known you for two years. You only moved in a couple of months ago.'

'Her name's not Lou! She's Erna Meyer... a German bitch!'

'No, Ned, no, you've got it wrong. Lou is my mum. She's never been out of Battersea, let alone to Germany.'

'Liar! Liar! Liar! I know who she is. Shut that baby up!'

Florence scooted to the chair and picked up Penny which seemed to pacify the girl. 'Please, Ned, tell me what happened to you,' Florence asked, hoping to buy some time. 'What was you doing in Germany?'

Ned's eyes drifted upwards. It was clear to see the pain in his face as he must have been recalling his memories.

'Tell me, Ned. You were a Tommy in the Great War, wasn't you?'

He nodded.

'Were you captured?'

'Yes. I didn't want to surrender. I ain't a coward. But a bomb exploded. I was buried alive in mud and dirt. When I was dug out, I found meself surrounded by half a dozen Hun. I thought the Kaiser's men were gonna run me through, you know, with their bayonets. But they didn't. God, I wish they had've killed me there and then.'

'You were a hero, Ned. I can't imagine how terrifying it must have been for you. What happened next?'

'I don't know... interrogation, torture. They stripped me of everything, even cutting me finger off for me wedding ring... I remember being piled onto a train carriage, crammed in, starving, thirsty and wounded. Blokes died in that carriage, they died standing. I was taken to a camp and then into forced labour... her... Erna Meyer... I worked on her farm from morning 'til night, digging, digging, digging, digging. My back... it ached so bad I was grateful for the whippings. The stinging took away the ache.'

Ned turned slightly and Florence saw the ghastly criss-cross of scars across his shoulders and spine.

'She did that to me!' he spat. 'That spiteful bitch beat me every day for two years. She made me eat horse shit... and now it's my turn to make her suffer.'

'Ned, listen to me,' Florence said firmly. 'What you went through was ghastly, but she is not Erna Meyer. Lou is my mum. I swear, I'm telling you the truth.'

'Liar!' Ned screeched, lurching towards Lou.

Lou stumbled backwards and fell onto the armchair. Florence jumped forwards, trying to stand between Ned and her mother. She waved her arm hard, hitting Ned's, hoping to knock the knife out of his hand, and instinctively she held Penny away from him. Everything happened so quickly. Florence felt a blow in her ribs and found herself falling sideways towards the window. Her mother cried out. As Florence regained her posture, she screamed in terror when she saw Ned plunging the knife into her mother's stomach, jabbing her again and again. Blood seeped across the pale blue material of her mother's dress as the woman's cries turned to a light whimper.

'Stop!' Florence screeched in horror. 'Get off of her!'

Ned, panting hard to catch his breath, stood over Lou's lifeless body, his face contorted with hatred. 'She got what she deserved.'

Florence stared in shocked terror. 'You've killed her,' she muttered. 'You've killed my mum!'

As Penny cried in Florence's ear, three uniformed policemen bundled into the room, presumably alerted by the desperate screams. Ned dropped the bloodied knife. Florence wasn't sure what happened next, she felt dizzy and everything became a blur. Her mother was dead, stabbed to death in front of her. And all the while, Penny bawled and bawled and bawled.

6

Cyril couldn't pretend that he'd ever cared for Lou, but he felt awful that she'd been killed in such an abhorrent way. And poor Florrie had witnessed the whole attack but had been unable to stop it. Thankfully, his wife had kept Penny safe. The thought of anything untoward happening to his daughter sent a shudder through his body.

'Jimmy was right,' Florence said quietly.

Cyril looked across the kitchen table to his wife who was sat opposite with her head in her hands.

'What did you say, love?' he asked, gently.

'Jimmy was right. He said he didn't want to stay at my mum's 'cos he didn't like Ned. How does a six-year-old know, eh?'

'I don't know, maybe Ned said something to him.'

'Apparently not. Jimmy said it was just a feeling that he had. I should have listened to him. I should never have confronted Ned. I should have just moved my mum here and she'd still be alive now.'

'You can't blame yourself. Ned was deranged. He went through hell as a prisoner of war. It messed with his head.'

Florence shrugged. 'I won't rest until that lunatic has his neck stretched on the gallows.'

Cyril didn't know what to say to offer his wife any comfort. He fancied a half a pint of ale, but it felt wrong to leave Florrie alone so soon after Lou's funeral. The woman had been put in the ground just hours earlier. 'I hope Penny won't remember anything of that day,' he thought aloud.

'Of course she won't,' Florence barked. 'But I'll never forget it. If I didn't have that child in my arms, I might have been able to do more to stop Ned.'

Cyril decided to keep his mouth shut and his thoughts to himself. Whatever he said, his wife would jump down his throat. He dared not mention that he'd had a drink with Ned the day before he'd murdered Lou. The man had seemed all right at the time, even laughing when Cyril had cracked a joke. They'd done a bit of business together. Cyril had sold Ned a knife that he'd stolen from a butcher's shop on the Northcote Road. He could feel himself breaking into a cold sweat as he thought about it. That knife, the one he'd wrapped in hessian and tucked inside his jacket pocket, the knife he'd slipped under the table to Ned in exchange for a few pennies, it was the same knife that had brutally killed his mother-in-law.

'You look like you could do with a drink,' Florence said. 'Go on, bugger off. You don't have to sit here with me. I'm not in the mood for company.'

'Are you sure?' Cyril asked, secretly crossing his fingers under the table.

'I said so, didn't I. I'd rather be alone. Jimmy's in bed and your precious daughter is sleeping. I'm going to pull out the tin bath and have a soak.'

'All right, love, you do that. I'll leave you in peace, but I won't stay out late.'

Cyril smiled to himself as he walked out of the front door. He knew it was his duty to be with his wife in her time of sorrow, but she'd given him permission to leave. Now he could have a drink without feeling bad, though he felt guilty over the secret he harboured about the murder weapon.

As he sauntered down the street, Mrs Whetstone called out from her doorstep.

'Cyril Black, where do you think you're going?'

'Florrie wants to be by herself.'

'Well, I suppose grieving is a private matter. It was a good turn out today for Lou's funeral.'

'Yeah, I reckon it was.'

'Come inside a minute, lad, I've got something for you.'

Cyril, though eager to get to the pub, would never disappoint Mrs Whetstone. With a sigh he followed her indoors and into her cosy front room. He stood, impatiently waiting with his hands shoved into his pockets, as Mrs Whetstone slowly rummaged through a drawer in her sideboard.

Eventually, she turned to face him with a long wooden box in her hand.

'I've been waiting for the right time to give you this,' she said, holding the box out.

'What is it?' Cyril asked.

'Open it and see.'

Cyril carefully lifted the lid to see a collection of stamps inside.

'They belonged to Mr Whetstone. I doubt that they're worth much, but I think some of them are quite rare. He would have wanted you to have them. But will you promise me something, Cyril?'

'If I can.'

'Promise me you'll take good care of them, and you'll never sell them.'

'Oh, Mrs Whetstone, I can promise that all right. In fact, I'll do better than that. I'll add to the collection. I'll see if I can get a Penny Black stamp in honour of my girl.'

'That would be smashing. Mr Whetstone would have been ever so pleased. He'd always planned on getting a Penny Black. It was the first sticky postage stamp ever issued, and would you believe, it came out on the first of May 1840, my birthday. That's why Mr Whetstone had been so keen to collect one.'

'You're never eighty-three years old!'

'No, you daft bugger, of course I'm not, though my bones feel it,' the old woman grumbled. 'I was born twenty years later, but on the first of May.'

'Well, I'll see what I can do about adding a Penny Black to the collection.'

'Mr Whetstone always said that you were the son he never had.'

'I was fond of him.'

'And he was of you. And that's why I feel I have to say this to you, lad... change your ways. I know your father wasn't much to look up to, but aspire to be more like Mr Whetstone. He was a grafter and an honest fella. It wouldn't hurt you to follow in his footsteps. You're a family man and you're all Florrie has now.'

Cyril was taken aback. 'I provide well for my wife and kids,' he said, defensively.

'Sometimes. But what about when you're in gaol? You're not as good at thieving as you think you are. If you were, you wouldn't keep getting caught.'

'That's not fair, Mrs Whetstone, I've just been unlucky a few times, that's all.'

'Well, lad, I hope you won't be unlucky when the police find out that you stole the butcher's knife that killed Lou.'

Cyril's eyes widened. 'How... how do you know?'

'I saw you pinch it. I must admit, it tickled me at the time, but when I heard that Ned had stabbed Lou with a butcher's knife, I knew it was the one you'd stolen.'

Cyril hung his head, shame burning him.

'Don't feel bad, though let this be a wake-up call. Every action has a consequence. Keep out of trouble's way by staying on the straight and narrow.'

Cyril nodded. 'I'll try, Mrs Whetstone.'

'No, lad, I don't think you will. I just hope you never come to regret the choices you make. You've a good heart, Cyril, even if you are a rascal.'

Cyril gently kissed Mrs Whetstone's papery cheek. 'Thank you,' he said with affection, and holding the box of stamps aloft, he added, 'And I'll treasure this.'

Ten minutes later, wearing his best suit and waistcoat, Cyril threw open the door of the Prince's Head pub to be greeted with the familiar smoky atmosphere and the smell of old beer. Making his way across the room towards the bar, he smacked his lips together, looking forward to a quiet drink.

'How do, Cyril,' the landlord greeted. 'Sorry to hear about Florrie's mother. That was a bad turn. Terrible.'

'You can say that again. We had the funeral today.'

'I heard. Weren't you in here with Ned the night before the murder happened?'

Cyril shifted uncomfortably from one foot to the other. 'Er, yeah, I saw him in here.'

'I always thought there was something odd about the fella, but I never imagined he'd do what he did.'

'Same here.'

'One minute he'd be laughing and joking, the next he'd be in the blackest of moods. I'm telling you, Cyril, I've seen plenty of men come back from the war with shell shock, but it never occurred to me that Ned had been so badly affected.'

'Yeah, I know what you mean.'

The landlord placed Cyril's usual half pint on the painted countertop. 'On me, mate. And pass my condolences to Florrie.'

Cyril gulped down his drink quicker than he would have liked to. But with all eyes on him and hearing titters and whispers from the corners of the pub, Cyril couldn't wait to get out. He had no doubt that everyone in the borough was gossiping about the heinous murder of Florrie's mother. But he hoped that no one other than Mrs Whetstone knew of his unintentional part in it.

After a nod to the landlord, Cyril hastily left the pub. Outside, the early evening air had a nip in the breeze. He stood for a moment, wondering what to do next. The thought of going home didn't appeal, especially considering the solemn mood that Florrie was in. As his mind turned, he heard a familiar woman's voice.

'I've been looking for you,' Jill purred.

Cyril's heart sank when he set eyes on her leaning against the outside wall of the pub. She'd lost weight. Her coat was pulled tightly around her skinny body, and he noticed that she didn't look any better than the last time he'd seen her.

'What do you want?' Cyril asked, coldly.

Jill sashayed towards him. She ran a finger down the side of his face, asking, 'How's my girl?'

'Penny is fine, no thanks to you.'

'I knew Florrie would take good care of her. So, you called her Penny. That's nice, the name suits her.'

'I hope you're not thinking about having anything to do with her, 'cos I'm telling you, Jill, you've got no chance.'

Jill smiled. 'She's Florrie's child now. Maybe one day, when she's a young woman, you might want to tell her about me.'

'What, that her real mother was a whore who didn't want her? No, Penny will never know anything about you.'

Jill shrugged. 'So be it.'

Cyril tugged on the edge of his suit jacket, eyed Jill up and down with disdain, and stamped away.

'Wait, Cyril, I'd like a word,' Jill called.

'You've had one,' Cyril replied over his shoulder, keen to get away from the woman.

'It's about Lou... and the knife.'

Cyril stopped, his blood running cold. Spinning to face Jill, he spat 'What about it?'

She strutted towards him with a wicked grin that Cyril wanted to slap off her face. 'I've heard that the police are looking for information about where Ned obtained the knife from,' Jill said.

'That's right. Do you know anything?'

'Oh, yes, Cyril, I know *everything*. You'd be surprised what men tell me when they've got their pricks out.'

'What have you heard?' Cyril asked, his heart racing.

'Well, I know it was you who stole the knife and then you sold it to Ned. Some might argue that you encouraged Ned to murder Lou. After all, you never liked the woman.'

'That's ridiculous!'

'Is it? Is it really, Cyril?'

'Gossip, that's all you've got.'

'Actually, it's a bit more than gossip. See, the butcher whose knife you stole, he comes to see me twice a week. The man always brings me a big, fat, juicy sausage,' Jill said, licking her lips seductively. 'He knows you stole his knife. He saw you do it, but before he had a chance to go the police, Lou was killed. Of course, he's reluctant to admit that it was *his* knife that was sunk into Lou, after all, it might be bad for his business... but I've got nothing to lose.'

'Wh – what are you saying?'

'I'm saying that I could be persuaded to keep my knowledge to myself... for the right price.'

'You're blackmailing me?' Cyril asked.

'Blackmail isn't a nice word. Let's agree that I'm going to keep a secret and you're going to reward me for doing you a good turn.'

Cyril could feel his stomach knotting with anger. 'How much?' he snapped.

'I ain't a greedy woman. Five shillings a week.'

'No... I can't afford it.'

'Fine,' Jill answered and turned to walk away, adding as she went, 'I'm sure the police will want to have a word with you. And good luck explaining yourself to Florrie.'

Cyril grabbed hold of the back of Jill's hair and yanked her towards him. Pushing his face against her cheek, he hissed 'If you open your mouth, I'll cut your bleedin' tongue out.'

Jill smirked though she winced in pain. 'I've had bigger men than you threaten to do a lot worse. You'll have to do more than that if you want to scare me into silence... or pay up, of course.'

Cyril released his grip and roughly pushed her away. His fists clenched at his sides; it was all he could do to stop himself from slamming them into her smug face.

'Come and see me tomorrow, Cyril... with the money. If you don't, Florrie and the police will hear how you gave Ned the knife that killed Lou. It doesn't look good, does it?'

Cyril's mind raced as he watched Jill walk away. He couldn't possibly raise enough money to buy Jill's silence. And even if he could, he guessed she'd likely keep rising her price. *Christ*, he thought, the Old Bill would lock him away for this and throw away the key. He never plunged the knife into Lou, but he knew that the police would somehow stitch him up for his involvement. And Florrie... she was already difficult to live with. Once his wife discovered that he'd sold Ned the knife that killed her mother, then he knew that she'd make his life a living hell.

There was only one solution. Cyril would have to disappear.

7

Battersea, 1926
Three years later

Cyril hopped off the tram at Clapham Junction, his cap pulled low, hoping that he wouldn't be recognised. It had been three years since he'd left the borough, only briefing returning once a month to slip money under his wife's door. On his last visit, he'd seen Penny waddling up the street to watch a group of boys playing marbles. The toddler hadn't known him, but the sight of his daughter had made him realise how much he'd missed his family. Though he'd made a new life for himself in Hackney and had a good woman in his bed, a part of him longed to see Penny and Jimmy growing up. But Cyril had come to accept that it would never be safe for him to return to Battersea. And he knew that Florrie wouldn't leave the place without an explanation. He couldn't own up about the knife that had been used to murder Lou. Florrie would never forgive him. This, missing his children, was his penance.

As he bought a newspaper from a street vendor, he felt a tap on his shoulder. Panic coursing through him, he turned and was relieved to see Mrs Whetstone, still wearing the same long black dress.

'Cyril Black, well I never! It is you, isn't it?' the old woman exclaimed, squinting her eyes as she studied his face.

'Hello, Mrs Whetstone.'

'Are you home for good, lad?'

'No, just a quick call to drop some cash off to Florrie. How is she, Mrs Whetstone?'

'Why don't you knock on your door and ask her for yourself? I'm sure your wife will have plenty to say,' the woman chuckled.

'Yeah, I'm sure she would an' all. But I can't stay.'

'Florrie told everyone that you'd vanished off the face of the earth without an explanation or nothing. Course, we all assumed you'd been sent down again and was in Pentonville or Wandsworth gaol. So, if you ain't been serving time, where have you been and why can't you come home?'

Cyril sighed. 'It's a long story, Mrs Whetstone.'

'Well, make it shorter, lad. At my age, I ain't got time for long stories.'

'But I bet you've got time for a cuppa, eh?' Cyril asked, flicking his head towards a small café.

'You're buying,' the woman smiled.

Cyril was surprised to notice that Mrs Whetstone now walked with a stick and had a large hump at the top of her back. She'd aged a lot in three years. He pondered what else had changed.

'I see you've coloured your hair,' Mrs Whetstone remarked as she sat at a table inside the café.

'The red stood out too much for me to go unnoticed in Battersea.'

'So, lad, why do you need to go unnoticed? What trouble have you landed yourself in?'

'It was that butcher's knife, Mrs Whetstone.'

'What about it?'

'Someone else other than you knew about it. She tried to blackmail me. She threatened to tell the police and Florrie. The woman demanded a price that I couldn't pay.'

'Hmm, I see.'

'I had no choice. I had to have it away on my toes.'

'This woman... how did she know about the knife? I never told a soul, Cyril, I swear.'

'I know you didn't and thank you. The woman, the one blackmailing me, she and that butcher were *friends*. He told her that he'd seen me steal his knife. She even tried suggesting that I'd *given* Ned the knife and encouraged him to kill Lou!'

Mrs Whetstone's rheumy eyes widened. 'Oh, lad, you really did get yourself mixed up in the most terrible crime, all quite innocently I'm sure.'

'If I'd had any notion of Ned's intentions, I'd never have sold him that knife. I wish I'd never pinched it in the first place, the bother it's caused me.'

'Well, if it's any consolation, I can tell you that as far as I know your name has never been linked to that knife, so you're in the clear. This woman, she must have kept her mouth shut. Who is she? Do I know her?'

Cyril ordered two cups of tea from a pretty young waitress and asked for two slices of rhubarb flan. Once alone again at the table, he leaned closer to Mrs Whetstone.

'Jill, the brass from up Queenstown Road. It was her.'

'Archie's girl? The blonde one?'

'Yeah, yeah, that's her.'

'Oh, lad, you've no reason to worry about her no more... she's dead.'

'Dead?' Cyril repeated.

'Yes. Dead and buried at least two years ago. I heard she died of syphilis, but Archie swears blind that it was a weak heart that killed her. Mind you, you can't blame the man for trying to protect his daughter's reputation.'

'Syphilis?' Cyril parroted.

'Yes, is there an echo in here?'

'Sorry, it's just a bit of a shock.'

'Oh, lad, you didn't, erm, *spend time* with Jill, did you?'

Cyril felt his cheeks burning. 'Once or twice,' he answered, cringing.

'You silly boy! You'll need to see the doctor. But that aside, it's safe for you to come home now. It's been safe for the past two years,' Mrs Whetstone chuckled.

Cyril interlocked his fingers behind his head, his mind spinning. 'Do you think Florrie would have me back?'

'I'm sure that you could charm your way back into her good books. But why didn't you take Florrie with you when you ran away?'

'I don't know. I was scared of being found out, I suppose. Once I'd settled down, I did think about sending for her, but I couldn't think of a plausible reason to give her. You know how she can be, like a dog with a bone. If Florrie had got even a sniff that I was fibbing to her, she would never have dropped it.'

'I see your point.'

'I hope I can win her round now. Wish me luck, Mrs Whetstone.'

'I wish you all the luck in the world, lad. You're going to need it with Florrie!'

★

Florence turned to look out of the window that overlooked the backyard. Her legs had turned to jelly and she had to hold on to the sink to steady herself. She thought she'd seen a ghost at first, but no, her husband had breezed through the door and now stood in her kitchen with a soppy grin on his face. 'You've got some nerve,' Florence scathed, her back to the man. 'Waltzing back in here after three years. No word from you, nothing.'

'I sent money,' Cyril protested.

'Am I supposed to be grateful?'

'No, love, I didn't mean it like that.'

'Who is she?' Florence demanded.

'Who?' Cyril asked.

'You must have been living with some slut these past years. I know you, Cyril Black, you won't have been alone.'

'There's no one, love, I swear.'

'I don't believe you,' Florence spat, spinning around to glare at her husband. 'Why did you leave?'

'I, erm, I had the Old Bill breathing down my neck. They were setting me up for a robbery that I didn't do. I didn't want to leave you and the kids, but if I'd stayed here, they would have sent me down for years. At least by running off, I could still send you money. I couldn't have done that from prison.'

'You could have told me!'

'I know, love, and I should have. But I wanted to spare you the worry.'

Florence didn't believe a word that her husband spouted. 'Why are you back now? Your tart chucked you out, I expect?' she asked, expecting more lies.

'I've told you, there ain't anyone else, Florrie. I've missed you and the kids. Please, forgive me. I'm sorry.'

'That's it, is it? Three years, not a dickie-bird from you, you say you're sorry and you think that everything is back to normal. No, Cyril, I won't put up with it. You dumped that bastard child on me and then left me on the day of my mother's funeral! I'll *never* forgive you, never!'

Cyril looked defeated but Florence wasn't finished with him yet. 'And another thing... that bastard's slut of a mother died of syphilis! My God, Cyril, you might have it and if you've passed it on to me, I swear, I'll cut your balls off and shove 'em down your throat!'

'I ain't got nothing wrong with me, and let's face it, Florrie, you can't catch a disease by being laid in bed with all your clothes on and with your back to me!'

Florence pursed her lips and kept them tightly shut.

'Look, love, neither of us has been perfect. You rejected me after Jimmy was born. I never moaned or complained that I weren't getting my rights as your husband, did I? But a man has needs, Florrie, and I didn't want to pester you, so I went to Jill. But I always came home to you, didn't I?'

'Sometimes, Cyril, not always. You'd be gone for days, weeks, even months at a time.'

'I never left you short though.'

'That doesn't make it all right!' Florrie argued. 'And this time... three years... You shouldn't have bothered coming back.'

'You don't mean that, Florrie.'

'Yes, I do,' she fibbed. Cyril had hurt her deeply and broken her heart, but she still wanted the man, though gawd knows why. But she'd never tell him. Neither of them had ever said those three words: I love you. In fact, Florence was sure that Cyril had never loved her and never would.

Cyril edged closer with his arms outstretched. 'Please, sweetheart, let's start again, eh?'

Florence wanted to feel the strength of his strong arms around her. She wanted him to stay, to make her feel safe and to support her. But her heart had hardened, and she wouldn't allow herself to show him that she was vulnerable. Throwing her nose in the air, she sniffed. 'All right, you can stay, but on the sofa. Jimmy will be pleased to see you. He asks about you all the time. I've not known what to tell the boy. Don't lie to him, Cyril. You've made a fool out of me. Don't do the same to our son.'

'Understood. And Penny, where is she?'

Florence swallowed hard, suddenly remembering that she'd locked Penny in the half-empty coal bunker. The girl had slept on the floor in front of the fire in the front room, yet Florence had told her that she was forbidden from sleeping anywhere except for on the floorboards at the top of the stairs. Penny had needed punishing for her defiance. With the sight of Cyril shocking Florence to her core, she'd forgotten about the three-year-old girl in the coal bunker. And she knew that Cyril would think her punishment was too severe. 'Penny is, erm, playing in the backyard. Go and sit down in the front room and I'll bring her to you. I don't want you wandering into the yard and scaring the girl. After all, she doesn't know who you are.'

Thankfully, Cyril accepted her explanation. After closing the kitchen door behind him, Florence slipped into the yard and lifted the lid of the coal store. She heard Penny crying softly.

'Stop your tears and come with me,' she ordered sharply.

Penny looked up, squinting her blue eyes against the sunlight. As Florence picked up the girl and pulled her out of the bunker, she realised that Penny was filthy, covered in black coal dust. 'Look at the state of you,' she moaned. 'You are going to meet your father. You are not to tell him that I lock you in the coal bunker. If you do, you'll get the stick across the back of your legs. Understood?'

Penny nodded and her eyes welled with more tears.

After wiping a damp cloth across the girl's face and washing her hands at the kitchen sink, Florence ushered Penny into the front room. 'She's been playing with the coal,' Florence smiled. 'The naughty little imp; she's made her dress all dirty.'

'Hello, Penny,' Cyril smiled, his eyes full of adoration.

It irked Florence. She'd never seen her husband look at her or Jimmy with that look of love in his eyes.

'I'm your Daddy,' he said softly. Then patting his knee, he offered, 'Come and sit down.'

Penny, looking puzzled, climbed onto Cyril's knee.

'Aren't you a pretty angel, even when you're all grubby,' he cooed, and tickled her ribs.

Penny giggled.

It should have been a sweet scene to observe, but the sight of it left Florence feeling sick to her stomach. After all, the girl was a bastard and the daughter of a whore. Florence felt dirty and contaminated in the girl's presence. Everything about the child repulsed her and though she'd tried to be kind, Florence repeatedly found herself treating the girl harshly and with contempt.

'Put her down now, she needs to get cleaned up,' Florence instructed.

'You heard your mum, off you go now,' Cyril smiled at his daughter as he placed her back on her feet.

Florence cringed. She detested being referred to as Penny's *mum*. She didn't look at the girl as her own daughter and knew she never would. Penny was a constant reminder of how, since Jimmy's birth, her feelings had shut down. Soon after Jimmy had been born, Florence had become anxious and tired all the time. At first, she'd put it down to being a new mum, and her own mother had told her that the feelings would pass. But now, nine years later, she still felt numb, and the only feelings that touched her were ones of anger and annoyance. Even loving Jimmy was all an act. She cared for the boy, but she'd never bonded with him. She knew that's why she spoiled him so much; it was out of guilt because she didn't love him as she thought she should. And as for Cyril, she couldn't bring herself to allow him to touch her in bed. Unfortunately, her lack of emotion had driven her husband into the arms of another woman and Penny was the bitter consequence.

'Dad!' Jimmy exclaimed when he rushed into the room.

'Hello, Son,' Cyril grinned.

Jimmy threw his arms around his dad's neck. 'Are you staying? Please stay, Dad, please.'

'Yes, lad, I'm staying. Cor, look at the size of you, you're almost as tall as me!'

Jimmy turned to his sister excitedly. 'See, Penny, I told you he'd come home. This is our dad.'

'Get away from her,' Florence snapped, instantly regretting the harshness in her tone in front of Cyril. Thinking quickly, she added, 'Penny has been playing with the coal and she's all mucky, I don't want Jimmy's clothes getting dirty too.'

'I can see where my money has been spent,' Cyril said, eyeing his son's smart clobber.

'I won't send him to school looking like the other ragamuffins round here,' Florence defended. She then turned to Jimmy, saying tenderly, 'There's half a mutton pie in the larder for you. Wash your hands and help yourself.'

Jimmy dashed off, leaving Penny standing in the middle of the room, her eyes following her brother's wake.

'Any pie for me and my girl?' Cyril asked.

'Penny has already eaten,' she lied. In fact, Penny hadn't eaten since yesterday evening when Florence had begrudgingly given her a thin slice of bread and half a cup of milk. 'I'll make you some dinner soon, but first I need to get Penny changed into a clean dress.'

Grabbing the girl roughly by the arm, she dragged her up the stairs. At the top on the landing, Florence saw Penny's makeshift bed in the corner; nothing but a thin blanket folded neatly on the bare floor. She felt sure that Cyril wouldn't allow his daughter to sleep on floorboards, so she quickly picked up the blanket and took it into Jimmy's room.

Crouching in front of the child, she warned, 'If you tell your dad anything about where you've been sleeping, or the coal bunker, or the chores you do or the stick, I promise you, Penny, he will send you to the orphanage. You don't want that, do you?'

Penny, her innocent blue eyes wide, shook her head.

Florence hauled Penny to a small wooden crate in the corner of her bedroom. The crate held all the girl's clothes; two dresses, one jumper and one cardigan, a coat and a pair of shoes for best. 'Change your dress,' Florence ordered as she carelessly yanked Penny's dirty one over the girl's head.

As Penny slipped into her clean clothes, Florence glanced at her double bed, her mind turning. She supposed she'd have to tolerate the girl sleeping in it with her tonight.

'You can go downstairs now but remember what I told you. Keep your ugly mouth shut.'

Florence knew in her heart that her cold, harsh treatment of Penny was wrong, cruel even, yet she couldn't help herself. *The girl brings out the worst in me*, she thought, quickly justifying her actions by reminding herself that Penny was the unwanted child of a whore. Though with Cyril home, she'd have to be more lenient and be gentler with the girl. It wouldn't be easy to pretend to care for her, but she would try, in front of Cyril at least.

8

Battersea, 1927
One year later

Cyril looked at his wife's swollen stomach in awe. He still couldn't believe that she was in the family way. After all, he'd only had his way with her on the one occasion, when she'd allowed it after a few bottles of stout to see in the New Year.

Florence arched her back, holding her side. She looked uncomfortable and Cyril wondered if the baby was coming sooner than expected.

'Are you all right, love?' he asked, panicking slightly.

'You'd better send for Mrs Hawes,' Florence replied, lowering her huge body onto one of the kitchen chairs.

'Oh, my gawd, I'm on me way,' Cyril blustered, running towards the front door.

He heard Florence call after him, 'Slow down, me waters haven't even broken yet.'

As Cyril hurried down the street to fetch the local handywoman, Mrs Whetstone waved from her doorstep to gain his attention.

'You've got the wind up your arse, lad,' she chuckled.

'I'm on me way to fetch Mrs Hawes.'

'Is the baby on the way?'

'Yeah, I reckon. Do us a favour, will you go and sit with Florrie?'

'Of course,' Mrs Whetstone answered, pulling her shawl tighter around her shoulders as she shuffled off. 'And don't worry, lad. Mrs Hawes is the best woman for the job and a lot cheaper than the midwives and doctor.'

Cyril's heart raced. He couldn't remember being this excited when Jimmy had come along. But, he recalled, he'd been away at the time, earning some pennies fencing for a shoplifting gang over Chelsea way. He'd returned home a week later to find Florrie with a boy in her arms. And it had been Mrs Hawes who'd seen his son safely into the world.

Finally reaching the handywoman's house, he hammered on the front door. Mrs Hawes pulled it open with a young child on each hip, her strawberry blonde hair poking out from under a cloth cap.

'Where's the fire?' she asked.

'Eh?'

'The way you were banging on my door, I'm assuming there's some disaster somewhere... either that or your wife has gone into labour?'

'Yeah, yeah, it's Florrie, the baby, come quickly,' Cyril blurted.

'All right, keep your hair on. She's only having a baby, she ain't doing nothing special. I've had eleven of the little blighters, you know, and my old man went about his business as usual with each one of them.'

Cyril tried to stay calm, but he wished that Mrs Hawes would have some sense of urgency about her. 'Please, hurry,' he coaxed.

'Lily, bring my bag and come and take your sisters,' she called over her shoulder. Then turning back to Cyril, she said, 'One minute,' before pushing the door closed with her foot.

Cyril tapped his heel anxiously. Moments later, the door opened again, and Mrs Hawes emerged in a crisp, white apron and her hair scraped under the cap.

'Lead the way,' she said, gesturing with her hand.

Cyril walked at quite a pace.

'Slow down. I'll be puffed out before we get to your house,' the woman moaned.

'She will be all right, won't she, Mrs Hawes?'

'I should say so.'

Cyril wanted to run but he walked the five-minute journey in silence beside the handywoman. When they reached home, he rushed through the front door and found Florence sitting where he'd left her, sipping on a cup of tea, and Mrs Whetstone at the stove.

'Sorry, I think it might have been a false alarm,' Florence said, and then winced. 'Or maybe not,' she added, rubbing underneath her large belly.

'Cup of tea, Mrs Hawes?' Mrs Whetstone offered.

'Got anything stronger?' the woman asked.

'There's a bottle of port in the cupboard,' Florence said, pointing.

'You can wet the baby's head once it's been born,' Cyril ordered firmly, 'and not before.'

'And you can clear off and leave us to it,' Mrs Hawes instructed. 'You've done your bit nine months ago. You won't be needed now.'

'Will you watch Penny?' he asked Mrs Whetstone.

'She'll be fine, lad, and so will Florrie. Do as you're told and bugger off.'

Cyril threw a look at Florence as his wife's face crumpled in pain. The women were right, this was no place for the father of the baby to be. Making a hasty exit, he headed towards the Prince's Head pub for an early celebration.

Mrs Hawes had helped Florence up the stairs to her bedroom while Mrs Whetstone had taken Penny into the front room. Four hours later, worn out and hoping that it would be over soon, Florence began bearing down.

'That's it, Florrie, push like you're having a big toilet, not from the front, mind, but from the back,' the handywoman encouraged as she massaged Florence's stomach. 'This is your third, ain't it?'

Florence nodded. She was glad that Mrs Hawes had forgotten that she hadn't birthed Penny and that a whore had. The woman had helped most of the babies in the borough be born. It was no wonder that she couldn't remember them all.

'Two kiddies already, eh. You're old hat at this, you don't even really need me.'

'I do,' Florence panted. 'Argh!'

'Go on, girl, push. I can see the head, that's it, keep going.'

Florence gritted her teeth and cried out in pain as she pushed with all her might.

'There's the head.'

'Is it all right?'

'Yes, I should say so,' Mrs Hawes smiled, her hands in between Florence's legs as she supported the baby's head. 'Come on little one,' she said, looking at the baby being born, 'are you going to hang about there all day? Come on, out you pop, it's time for you to meet your mother.'

Another agonising pain gripped Florence as she pushed her child into the world.

The sound of her baby's cry came as a huge relief.

After Mrs Hawes had wiped the child's face, she announced, 'You have a beautiful daughter,' and handed Florence the baby.

Florence peered down at the pink and wrinkled girl, hoping that a mother's love would rush into her heart and overwhelm her. But just as no feeling had come when Jimmy had been born, neither did it when she stared at her newborn daughter.

'Have you decided on a name?' Mrs Hawes asked.

'No, not yet.'

'Well, whatever you call her, she's a lovely lass and you did really well.'

'Thanks,' Florence mumbled. Her dark eyes fixed on the baby as she studied her delicate features. It was impossible to tell yet if the child would have red hair like her father and Jimmy, but Florence hoped she wouldn't. Jimmy had taken a lot of ridicule at school for his ginger locks, some even accusing him of being Irish. Florence had an empty heart; nonetheless, she wanted the best for her daughter. And, by God, she'd ensure that Cyril put this girl's needs before those of that whore's child. Whatever it took, Florence wanted Penny well and truly pushed out of Cyril's affections.

9

Three weeks later, Florence dutifully put the baby to her breast, grimacing at the pain. She'd rubbed egg whites on her cracked nipples and let it dry, but it hadn't alleviated the discomfort. As her daughter suckled, she heard Cyril return home. He swaggered into the front room, proudly waving a piece of paper.

'There you go,' he said, grinning, 'it's official. Little Annie has been registered and here's her birth certificate. Look, it says right here, Annie Black. Cor, Florrie, you've done us proud.'

Florence glared at her husband. He might be happy, but she was far from it. The past three weeks had given her nothing but sleepless nights and had left her feeling sore down below and with heavy, aching breasts. 'Don't you ever touch me again, Cyril Black. Do you hear me? Never!'

'Aw, love, I know it's been hard work for you, but Annie is the most beautiful thing I've ever seen.'

Penny wandered into the room. The sight of her instantly infuriated Florence.

'Come and see your little sister,' Cyril insisted, scooping Penny into his arms. 'She's becoming quite a little pudding.'

'Take her away,' Florence demanded. 'I'm feeding Annie and I don't want you and her gawping.'

Cyril rolled his eyes at Penny and smiled at the girl. 'Come on, let's leave your mum to get on with it.'

'I'm not her mum,' Florence mumbled with contempt, but not clearly enough for Cyril to hear.

Looking back down at Annie, Cyril was right. The girl was a beauty with a mop of dark hair and big, blue eyes, and she was gaining weight well. Florence was glad that her daughter was destined to grow up prettier than Penny. Ten-year-old Jimmy had been mesmerised by his youngest sister, though he'd asked some awkward questions about why Penny was treated differently to Annie. Florence had explained that though he and Penny looked alike, Annie was his full blood sister which made her far more special. And then she'd carefully reminded him that Penny had the devil in her which is why he wasn't allowed to be nice to her and why she needed punishing. Florence was glad that her son seemed to accept her explanation.

Placing Annie on her shoulder, Florence gently patted her back until her wind came up. 'I don't feel normal, Annie,' she confessed. 'I should love you, but I can't feel anything. But never mind, eh. Your dad loves you and so does Jimmy. And your gran, if she were alive, she would have loved you very much,' Florence whispered and dashed away a tear. 'Look at me, silly fool. I'm always crying when no one is watching.' And as she thought of her dearly missed mum, images of Ned sticking a knife into the woman's stomach flashed through Florence's mind. Night after night, the horror of that day would haunt what little sleep she got. And though her mother's death had been years ago, each day she'd replay the last moments of the woman's life. *If only I wasn't holding Penny, I might have saved my mum*, she thought, resenting the girl's existence even more.

Later that day, Cyril nudged his son and reminded him, 'Don't tell your mum where that chocolate came from.'

Jimmy smiled. 'I won't, Dad.'

They'd just pinched several bars from a sweet shop in Wandsworth. Now as they headed down Battersea Rise, Cyril said, 'It's never a good idea to nick things from your local. If you're going to go out on the steal, go out of the borough. We don't want to do a bad turn to our neighbours, right, lad.'

'Right, Dad.'

'Now, shove them bars of chocolate in your pocket and you can sell them for a few pennies in school tomorrow.'

'I'd like to give one to Penny. She never gets much.'

'I'm always treating the girl,' Cyril said, surprised at his son's remark.

'Yeah, but Mum takes it from her.'

'What do you mean?' Cyril probed. He had noticed that Florence was strict with the girl, but his wife insisted it was for Penny's sake so that she didn't turn out like her whore of a mother. Cyril couldn't argue with that.

Jimmy didn't answer, so Cyril asked again, 'Son, what did you mean when you said that your mother takes away Penny's treats?'

'Nothing,' Jimmy answered, sheepishly.

'You must have meant something,' Cyril pushed.

'I dunno,' Jimmy shrugged. 'It's just... Mum is mean to

Penny, and she makes me be mean to her too. I don't want to be mean to Penny, and when Mum ain't looking, I'm nice to her.'

'What does she make you do?'

'Stuff.'

'What stuff?' Cyril asked, his voice strong.

'Honest, Dad, I don't want to do it, but Mum makes me.'

'All right, lad, you're not in trouble. Just tell me what your mum makes you do.'

'She ... she makes me pinch Penny sometimes, and spit at her.'

'Your mother wouldn't do that!'

'I'm not lying, Dad. Mum said that the devil is in Penny and that she's evil. When you're not home, Penny has to sleep on the floorboards on the landing and she's not allowed to eat with us. I feel sorry for Penny, she never gets any sweets or nothing.'

Cyril could feel his temples throbbing and his fists clenched into tight balls as his temper flared. He'd had his suspicions that Florrie wasn't treating Penny well, but what Jimmy had told him came as a shocking revelation.

'I'm telling the truth, Dad, really I am.'

'It's all right, Jimmy, I believe you.'

'Mum said you wouldn't. She said I wasn't to tell you 'cos you'd never believe that the devil was inside Penny.'

'There's no devil inside your sister, lad. If the devil lives anywhere, then he's with your mother!'

'Please don't tell Mum. She might whack me with the stick that she hits Penny with.'

'Your mother hits Penny with a stick?'

'Yes, and she puts the strap across Penny's legs. It's horrible,

Dad, I hear her crying when Mum beats her. I wish Mum wouldn't do it, and I wish she wouldn't put Penny in the coal bunker too. Penny told me it scares her.'

Cyril had heard enough. He knew Jimmy was telling the truth and his blood boiled. Granted, Penny wasn't Florrie's flesh and blood, but he struggled to understand how a woman could be so cruel to a defenceless young girl. *I'll give Florrie a taste of her own medicine*, he thought, stamping along the street with Jimmy trotting to keep up.

'Dad, please don't tell Mum,' Jimmy begged.

'Trust me, Son, your mother is *never* going to hurt Penny again, and she won't be punishing you neither.'

When they reached home, Cyril's temper was flaring. He pushed open the front door so hard that it nearly snapped off its hinges.

'Son, get Penny and go down to Mrs Whetstone,' he instructed.

Jimmy's face had drained of all colour, and he looked terrified.

'It's all right, lad, just do as I say. I need to have a word with your mother.'

Cyril waited until he saw Jimmy come out from the front room. The worried-looking boy held Penny's hand and pulled her towards the front door. Cyril forced a smile and nodded his approval to his son.

When the front door closed, he pounded along the passageway towards the kitchen, ready to confront his wife. Throwing open the door with gusto, he saw her sitting at the kitchen table, looking tense and pulling hard on a cigarette. Florence always kept a cigarette in her apron pocket, but he rarely saw her smoking.

'You 'orrible cow!' he ground out. It was all he could do to stop himself from putting his hands around the woman's neck and throttling the life out of her.

Florence, staring down at the table, said coldly, 'She's dead.'

'Who's dead?' Cyril asked, flummoxed.

'Annie. She's upstairs in her cot, and she's dead.'

Cyril's anger quickly turned to panic. He turned and ran back along the passageway towards the stairs, all thoughts of cruelty to Penny gone from his head. *Annie... dead...* Surely Florrie must be mistaken!

His wife's voice followed him. 'It's no use. Her lips are blue.'

Taking the stairs two at a time, Cyril burst into the bedroom and dashed to the side of the cot. Peering down, his brain tried to fathom what he was seeing. Little Annie, his angel, swaddled in blankets, looked as though she was sleeping. But her skin had mottled, and her lips were indeed blue.

Nervously, he reached into the cot and gave Annie a gentle shake. There was no reaction from the baby. Then, picking her up, he held her small face to his ear, praying that he'd hear the quiet sounds of her breathing. Annie's skin felt cold against his cheek. He waited, holding his breath, silently willing the girl to breathe.

'No, no, no,' he cried, grief stabbing at his heart. 'Come on my angel, breathe, sweetheart, breathe.'

When there was nothing, Cyril unwrapped the blankets, shocked to discover her floppy limbs. He studied the baby's chest, hoping to see even the faintest of rise and falls. It was still.

Holding her lifeless body close to him, tears began to roll down his ruddy cheeks. 'My angel... my beautiful, sweet angel...'

10

Annie's funeral took place in late September on a cool, crisp day. Her tiny coffin had gone into the ground in a plot close to Florence's mother's grave. As Florence passed Lou's headstone, she stopped for a moment.

'Look after her, Mum,' she whispered. 'Annie is with you now.'

She felt Jimmy slip his hand into hers. 'Do you think that Gran and Annie are in heaven together?' he asked.

'Yes, Jimmy, I'm sure they are. Your gran will take good care of our Annie.'

Florence looked around for Cyril. She spotted him standing at the gates of the churchyard with Mrs Whetstone, both waiting for her. Cyril didn't appear impatient, but he held a look of contempt towards her. Florence thought he'd been glaring at her in that way since Annie had died. She wondered if he blamed her for their daughter's death.

Joining them, Mrs Whetstone said, 'Cyril's never done an honest day's work in his life, but at least Annie didn't have a pauper's grave.'

Florence nodded. She was grateful that they could afford

a proper funeral for Annie. After all, it was the last thing that they could do for their child.

Cyril walked on ahead, his hands shoved in his pockets and his head down low. Jimmy and Penny ran to catch up with him, leaving Florence to stroll slowly with Mrs Whetstone.

'I had five children with Mr Whetstone and buried all of them before their fifth birthdays. I know the pain you're going through, Florrie,' the old woman sympathised.

But Florence didn't feel any pain. Her heart wasn't breaking into two. She felt numb. Angry, but numb. Her stomach twisted at the unjustness of it. Annie had died yet Penny had lived. It didn't seem right. She couldn't understand why. She'd taken good care of Annie. Was God punishing her for being unkind to Penny?

'Cyril isn't taking it well,' Mrs Whetstone added. 'Men ain't as strong as us women. They say that we are the weaker sex, but it's not true.'

'I think he blames me for Annie's death. But I took good care of our daughter.'

'Of course you did and I don't think he blames you, Florrie. He's just upset and taking it out on those he's closest to, that's all.'

Florence wasn't convinced and felt sure that her husband was holding her responsible for their daughter's demise. She gazed ahead and saw a man talking to Cyril. She supposed the fella was offering his condolences, but then she noticed that Cyril appeared agitated. The colour had drained from his face, and he looked around him, suspicion in his eyes.

'Who was that bloke talking to Cyril? Do you know him, Mrs Whetstone?'

'Can't say I do.'

Cyril marched on and Florence didn't give it any more thought.

Back at home, Mrs Whetstone insisted on coming in and making cups of sweet tea for everyone. Florence didn't have the energy to protest.

'Sit yourself down and rest,' Mrs Whetstone instructed. 'I've sent Jimmy and Penny to my house for a packet of biscuits and a tray of jam tarts. I'll bring you a plate with a nice cuppa.'

Florence nodded, but she hoped the old woman wouldn't stay for long. Sitting back on the sofa, she could hear Cyril banging around upstairs and wondered what he was doing. Then she heard his heavy boots thumping down the stairs and into the kitchen. Straining her ears, she listened to the sounds of muffled voices. Rising to her feet, Florence edged closer to the door and eavesdropped on the conversation between her husband and Mrs Whetstone in the kitchen.

'Why are you leaving?' Mrs Whetstone asked.

'I can't stay here,' Cyril replied. 'But please, promise me you'll look out for Penny.'

'Yes, lad, of course I will. Florrie thinks you blame her for Annie's death. Do you? Is that why you're leaving?'

'No, Mrs Whetstone. Florrie took good care of Annie… but she's cruel to Penny and that's why I want you to look out for the girl.'

'I've never seen her being cruel to Penny.'

'Florrie's sly with it.'

'Surely that's all the more reason for you to stay?' Mrs Whetstone challenged.

'As much as I want to protect Penny, if I stay, I'll end up swinging by the neck for murdering me wife. Honestly, I don't know for how much longer I can contain meself. I ain't said nothing to Florrie, not in the light of Annie's death, but I can't stand to look at the cow for a minute longer. Me blood is boiling, and I know I'll end up doing something that I'll regret for the rest of my life!'

'There's more to it, lad. I know you. Who was that fella you were talking to on the way home from the church?'

Cyril sighed. 'I did something, something stupid, and pretty soon I'm gonna have the Old Bill banging me door down.'

'Oh, Cyril, what have you gone and done now?'

'I ain't proud of it... it was a mistake... I jumped a bloke and robbed him... Mr Studder who owns the big furniture shop near the Junction. Only the silly bugger wrestled me, and he fell over in the scuffle and bashed his head on the kerb. He was out cold, I thought he was dead. Turns out, that bloke I was talking to warned me that Mr Studder has woken up in the hospital.'

'And he knows it was you who put him there?'

'Yeah, I reckon.'

There was a moment's silence, and then Mrs Whetstone said, 'All right, lad, it sounds like you leaving is for the best. I'll do what I can to protect Penny.'

Florence stepped into the passageway as Jimmy and Penny came through the front door and Cyril emerged from the kitchen. She saw that he was carrying a bag stuffed with his clothes.

'Going somewhere?' she asked, sarcastically.

Cyril's eyes were raging, his temples throbbing. He shoved past her. Then lowering himself down to Jimmy's level, he took hold of the boy's hand.

'I've got to go away for a while, Son. Promise me that you'll take good care of your sister?'

'Don't go, Dad, please don't go,' Jimmy begged.

'I have to. But I need to know that no matter what your mother says, you'll look after Penny. Do you think you can do that, Jimmy?'

Jimmy glanced at Florence with fearful eyes.

'Don't look at her, Son, look at me. Can you take care of Penny and make sure that no one ever hurts her?'

Jimmy nodded.

'Good boy. You're the man of the house now. Take care, lad.'

After pulling Penny to him and holding her tight, Cyril then stood tall and threw a hateful look over his shoulder at Florence. 'Take care of the girl and I'll send you money. But if I hear otherwise, then you'll not get another ha'penny out of me,' he seethed, before heading out of the front door.

Jimmy began to whimper.

'Pack it in,' Florence ordered. 'You heard your father, you're the man of the house now. Men don't cry!'

Jimmy sniffed as Mrs Whetstone edged past Florence and towards the front door.

'I hope you're proud of yourself,' the old woman said quietly, and tutted. 'Everyone in these streets thinks that you're an angel for taking on another woman's child. Little do they know about what you're *really* like.'

'It's none of your business, you old bag!' Florence retorted.

'I'll be watching you,' the woman warned.

'Get out of my house and don't ever cross my doorstep again!'

Mrs Whetstone turned to the children. 'You know where

I live. Don't be shy, little ones. If *she* ever hurts you, then you must come to me.'

Penny stared, Jimmy nodded and squeezed his sister's hand.

Florence marched along the passageway and rudely eased the old woman out of the front door before slamming it shut. She turned to Jimmy and asked, 'Did you say anything to your father about how I treat Penny?'

Jimmy, his chin jutting forward, nodded.

'Well, I'm very disappointed in you, Jimmy, and I hope you're happy now. I warned you that your father wouldn't believe you, and see, I was right. Thanks to you, he's left. Good work, Son, good work.'

She saw unshed tears in her son's eyes. Florence knew it wasn't fair to blame Jimmy for his father leaving, but she hoped it would teach the boy a lesson and he wouldn't defy her again. 'Go to your room. Tomorrow is a new day, and we'll start afresh from then. It's just you and me now, Jimmy, but we can get through anything together.'

'And Penny,' Jimmy quipped.

Florence glared at the girl, and muttered, 'God help you.'

11

Battersea, 1933
Six years later

Ten-year-old Penny cowered in the corner of the kitchen, holding her hands over her head and hoping that her mother wouldn't whack her with the stick that she held threateningly over her.

'What have I told you about cleaning the privy?' Florence seethed. 'I want it cleaned every day. Did you clean it this morning? No, you didn't.'

'I – I – I was going to do it next,' Penny whimpered.

'Stand up straight,' Florence snapped.

Penny swallowed hard as she rose to her feet.

'Now get out in the yard and clean the privy. Then once you've done that, you can put the sheets through the mangle.'

Penny scampered past her mother, her skinny legs running as fast as they would carry her. Through the back door and into the yard, the cold, biting February wind cut through her thin dress that hung off her small frame, making her shiver. Her teeth chattered as she opened the wooden door to the privy, the stench from inside overwhelming her and turning her stomach. It always smelled awful after Mr Peck had used it. The man rented the shed at the end of the yard that had once been used by Penny's dad as storage. Now Mr Peck sat in the wooden hut all day, sawing and sanding, making cabinets. He lived in a room in a house in the next street and he also paid the rent on his parent's home as well as supporting his sister and her two children. The cheap rent that Florence offered him for the use of Cyril's shed suited Mr Peck. But Penny wished that he wouldn't use the privy twice a day.

Penny's small hand went numb as she wrang out a cloth in a bucket of ice-cold water. She heaved as she ran the cloth around the ceramic toilet bowl. Turning her face away, she caught her breath when she saw her mother standing in the doorway with her hands on her hips.

'You'd better be using the carbolic soap,' Florence demanded.

Penny nodded. Fear coursed through her trembling body.

'You've left the wet sheets outside. They're frozen stiff. Hurry up, girl, you'll never get through your chores at this rate.'

Penny scrubbed faster, aware that her mother had a scrutinising eye on her. She dared not miss cleaning even the tiniest of bits. She'd tried cutting corners once before which had resulted in her having her backside beaten. It had been so sore she hadn't been able to sit down for two days.

Tired and with hunger pains griping in her stomach, by two o'clock she'd finally finished her jobs for the day. Standing beside the hearth as the coal fire roared, Penny was grateful for the feeling of warmth on her bare legs. She stood ramrod straight with her hands behind her back and her head lowered while her mother closely inspected Penny's work around the house.

Florence came back into the room and Penny searched her face for any clue of if she'd passed the daily inspection.

'Satisfactory,' Florence finally remarked.

Penny half-heartedly smiled. *Satisfactory* had earned her a slice of bread and jam and half a cup of milk, her first meal of the day. But best of all, it meant that she had free time to play with her best friend, Katy, who lived next door. Though Katy would be at school now but home in two hours.

'Hello,' Mr Peck called through the back door.

Penny saw her mother's demeanour immediately change. The woman looked in the mirror that hung over the hearth and patted her dark hair into shape. Then she pinched her cheeks to add a bit of pink colour. Her face softened and she smiled, something that Penny rarely saw.

'Just a moment, Mr Peck. Take a seat, make yourself at home, I'll be with you in a tick,' Florence called, coquetry. Then, her face stern again, she hissed at Penny, 'Stay out of my way for the rest of the day.'

Penny nodded, pleased to be given such an order, though she wasn't sure what she'd do with herself until Katy came home from school.

She heard the kitchen door close and then the sound of her mother's laughter. Mr Peck always made her mum laugh, and he'd make Penny giggle too. The man did magic tricks and had mysteriously made a farthing appear out of her ear! Of course, Penny hadn't been permitted to keep the farthing, her mother had promptly confiscated it. But for that moment that she'd held it, Penny had felt as though she was the wealthiest girl in the world.

Sitting on a low wall that skirted the front of the house, Penny enjoyed feeling the winter sun on her face, though she felt cold down to her bones. Her mother wouldn't permit her to wear her coat to play out in. The coat was saved for special occasions and was only worn when Penny accompanied her mother anywhere. She swung her thin legs, the backs of her shoes kicking the bricks behind her. Then, looking down the road to where Mrs Whetstone had lived, Penny recalled some of the fond memories she held of the woman. Mrs Whetstone had been a kind lady who'd died shortly after having a stroke. Her door had always been open, and she invariably had a bowl of boiled sweets on the table that Penny had been allowed to help herself to. Penny remembered how one day, her mother had found the empty sweet wrappers in her pocket and then she'd been banned from going outside for a fortnight. Penny missed Mrs Whetstone. A new family had moved in shortly after Mrs Whetstone's funeral. They seemed nice, though the young boy of about her age was forbidden to play with her. Penny thought maybe it was because she smelled. The week before, some other kids on the street had followed her to the shop when she was running an errand for her mother. The boys had chanted a horrid poem. Penny's lips downturned as she recollected their words:

Penny Black, lives in a sack. Hold your nose, 'cos her stinky clothes, smell of cack, rotten Penny Black.

Penny raised her arm to her face and sniffed herself. She thought she could detect a faint whiff of the privy, but was it just her imagination? After all, she couldn't possibly smell of cack because her mother made her wash her dress every other day.

Half an hour passed. She chewed on her already well-bitten

fingernails while she sat on the wall and waited for Katy. She drew in a long breath, bored. Then a thought struck her. Maybe she could pop into the shop where Jimmy worked. Her mother had told her that she was never to disturb Jimmy at work, but Jimmy wouldn't tell tales on her, especially to their mum.

Skipping along the street, Penny soon came to the small men's outfitters. Sixteen-year-old Jimmy worked as an apprentice, a job he said he hated. He'd voiced his opinion several times at home, saying that he'd rather be a labourer like his mates. But Penny had overheard their mum telling him that there was no future in labouring, and he'd always be poor. She'd told him to stick at the job with his Jewish boss, and one day he'd be a fully trained tailor.

Penny pushed open the door and popped her head through. She saw Jimmy arranging ties in a drawer behind the glass-topped counter. Scanning the shop, she couldn't see Jimmy's boss or any customers.

'Coo-ee,' she called, smiling broadly at her brother.

Jimmy lifted his head and smiled back warmly, then gestured for her to come in.

'Where's your boss?' she asked quietly.

'Upstairs. He'll be down soon, so you can't stay long, Munchkin.'

'I won't. Mr Peck is in the kitchen with Mum, so she told me to stay out of her way for the rest of the day.'

'That's a blessing, isn't it?'

'Yeah, I suppose. But why can't I go to school like Katy?'

'I don't know. Mum says it's because you're too skinny and scrawny, small for your age, and you'll get easily picked on, especially with your ginger hair. She reckons she keeps you off school to protect you.'

'Only 'cos she wants me to be her skivvy,' Penny pouted.

'Never mind, you're practising your three R's, aren't you?'

'Yes, Jimmy,' Penny said, proudly. 'I've finished all the work you set me.'

'In that case, I'd better prepare some more lessons for you. You're a clever girl, Munchkin. You'll be reading, writing and adding up numbers better than me soon.'

Penny gazed at her brother lovingly and asked him the same question she'd asked many times before. 'Jimmy ... why is Mum nice to you but wicked to me?'

She was disappointed when she got the same answer as always, and Jimmy replied, 'Mum says she is strict with you to make you into a good girl.'

'But I *am* a good girl.'

'Yes, Munchkin, you are. Now, clear off before my boss comes down and catches you in here.'

Penny sloped out of the shop and slowly ambled back to her street. She wasn't sure how much time had passed, but she hoped Katy would be home soon. Hopping back onto the wall outside her house, she looked along the street, waiting to see her best friend. After what felt like forever, she finally spotted Katy, whose long blonde hair whipped around her face in the light breeze.

'Hello, Penny, have you been waiting for me?' Katy asked.

'Yes. I wish I could come to school with you.'

'So do I, but you wouldn't be in the same class as me.'

'Why not?' Penny asked.

'Because you're ten and I'm only six.'

'But I'm only a little bit bigger than you.'

'That doesn't count. Wait here, I'll ask my mum if I can come out and play.'

Penny nodded and watched Katy run into her house. She liked Katy's mum. She thought that Gladys Darwin was a sweet lady, and often wished that the woman was her mother. Mrs Darwin had a two-year-old boy and another baby on the way. Katy was hoping for another brother.

Katy soon skipped out carrying two paper bags of ha'penny sweets. 'One for me and one for you,' she smiled, handing a bag to Penny. 'Mum said I have to be home by sunset, but we can go over the park. I'd like to see the new power station,' she said enthusiastically. 'The two chimneys are so tall, I reckon they must touch the clouds!'

'Jimmy told me that Battersea Power Station will supply London with electricity, and it was built on the Thames because it's easy to get coal barges to the building and they use the water from the river for cooling,' Penny said, proudly imparting her knowledge.

'I'm a bit scared of electricity. Are you?'

'No, I don't really know what it is.'

'Me neither. My school has got electricity. It turns on the lights, but we're not allowed to touch the switches. I hope my dad doesn't get electricity in our house. The gas lights can't give you an electric shock!'

Penny wasn't sure what an electric shock was, but she didn't like to ask and make herself look stupid. 'Come on, I'll race you to the park,' she said instead.

Running and laughing, they soon reached the gates of Battersea Park. Sitting on a bench together that overlooked the boating lake, Penny glanced at her legs that were almost purple from the cold.

'The houses here are ever so big. Do you ever wish that you lived in a big house?' Katy asked.

'I don't know,' Penny answered, her mood serious. 'I wish your mum was my mum, but I never think about living in a big house. Why? Do you?'

Katy nodded and looked away.

'But your house is nice. You've got your own bed. I haven't got a bed or nothing.'

'I don't want a bed.'

'Why not?' Penny asked. 'I bet it's warm and comfy.'

Katy's face paled. 'If I didn't have a bed, my dad couldn't get in with me.'

'Your dad gets in your bed... hasn't he got his own bed with your mum?'

'Yeah, but when he comes home from the pub, he gets in with me.'

Penny giggled.

'It's not funny,' Katy cried. 'He hurts me.'

'How? Does he roll over on you when he's asleep?'

Katy shook her head and clammed up.

'What's wrong, Katy?' Penny asked, confused.

'Nothing,' Katy answered, staring down at the ground. 'I'm not supposed to talk about it. You won't tell anyone, will you?'

'Tell anyone what?' Penny questioned.

'Nothing. Forget about it. Come on, I'll race you to the big oak tree.'

Penny began running, giggling with glee as she chased behind her best friend. Moments like this were rare and, for a short while, Penny could forget about her unhappiness at home.

★

Later that evening, Penny slipped into Jimmy's room.

'Hello Munchkin. Has Mum given you any dinner?' he asked.

'Yeah. I had a baked potato.'

'Has she hit you today?'

'No. She was going to because I hadn't cleaned the privy, but she didn't.'

'Good. You'll tell me if she does?'

'Yes, Jimmy. She hardly ever hits me anymore.'

'I reckon that talking to I gave her must have sunk in. And you'll tell me if she doesn't feed you?'

'She always feeds me after I've finished my chores.'

'That's not good enough, Penny. She should give you breakfast too.'

'I don't mind.'

'It's no wonder you're so small and skinny for your age... but you're still the prettiest girl in Battersea.'

Penny smiled. She loved her brother so much she thought her heart might burst. 'Me and Katy went over the park today.'

'Sounds fun.'

'It was... but...'

'What is it, Munchkin?'

'Can I ask you a question?'

'Don't you always,' Jimmy chuckled.

'Did my dad love me?'

'Yes, Penny, of course he did,' Jimmy answered, opening his arms wide. 'Come here, Munchkin,' he said, wrapping them around her. 'Our dad loved us both. He left because he didn't love Mum. Why are you asking about him?'

Penny shrugged. 'I dunno. Katy said her dad sometimes gets into her bed. I suppose it made me think about mine.'

Jimmy's eyes widened and Penny thought they might pop out of his head.

'Has Katy's dad ever touched you?'

'No,' Penny answered emphatically, shaking her head. 'He doesn't even talk to me.'

'Are you sure?'

'Yes,' she replied, worried, and her bottom lip began to quiver.

'It's all right, Munchkin, don't get upset.'

Penny sat on the edge of Jimmy's bed and looked down at the floorboards. She wished she hadn't said anything to Jimmy now, especially as Katy had told her not to tell anyone. But Penny had never kept things from her trusted brother.

'I want you to stay away from that man. You're never to go into Katy's house when he's at home. Is that clear?'

Penny swallowed hard and nodded, though she didn't understand why Jimmy seemed so agitated.

'I mean it, Penny. Never, ever go near that man or be in that house with him, all right?'

'All right, Jimmy,' she said. Her brother was always right. If he said to stay away from Katy's dad, then Penny would make sure that she did.

12

Battersea, August 1939
Six years later

Sixteen-year-old Penny dropped the thimble that covered her small finger. As she leaned forward to look for it on the kitchen linoleum, her mother walked into the room. The woman seemed flustered, and Penny wondered what was bothering her.

'Haven't you finished mending that coat sleeve yet?' Florence asked, abruptly.

'Almost.'

'Well, hurry up, girl. I won't get paid until it's repaired and returned!'

'Sorry, I'm working as fast as I can.'

'Don't answer me back!' Florence barked. 'Just get the job done.'

Penny found the thimble and placed it back on her finger before pushing the needle and thread through the thick material. Six mornings a week Penny sewed, mending the clothes of the wealthier folk in Battersea for a few pennies that her mother demanded for her keep. And once her morning sewing duties were completed, Penny had to attend to the house chores while her mother would return the mended clothes and collect new orders. Those few hours in the afternoon away from her mother's watchful eye and sharp tongue were blissful for Penny, even though she spent most of her time cleaning. But today, instead of pulling on her coat and issuing her orders to Penny, Florence sat at the kitchen table with a worried expression.

Penny kept her head down and concentrated on stitching the coat, but she covertly glanced at her mother. Something was unsettling the woman, though she dared not ask what the problem was.

The back door opened and Mr Peck stuck his head around. 'Good morning, ladies,' he greeted, cheerily. 'Can I trouble you for a cup of tea?'

Florence, who normally behaved quite flirtatiously in the man's presence, barely raised a smile.

Looking concerned, he stepped into the kitchen, and asked, 'Is something wrong, Mrs Black?'

'Yes, Mr Peck, something is very wrong indeed. I've just been speaking to Mrs Darwin next door, and she tells me that Katy and her younger brothers are going to be evacuated out of London. You know what that means, don't you?'

Mr Peck removed his hat and placed it under his arm. 'Yes, Mrs Black,' he answered sombrely, 'war with Germany is imminent.'

'Hitler and his troops have invaded Poland. This is the beginning of the end!'

'That's rather dramatic, Mrs Black, if you don't mind me saying. Poland is a long way from Blighty and so is Germany. I don't think we've any need to panic yet.'

'Is that right? So why have half the houses down this street been issued with bomb shelters and why are the kids carrying gas masks to school, eh? This war ain't going to be like the Great War, mark my words, Mr Peck. We'll be seeing the Nazi planes above our heads, and gawd help us all 'cos it might be the last thing we ever see before a bomb lands on us or we're poisoned with gas!'

Penny's mind raced. She'd heard her mother's alarming words, but she was thinking about Katy being evacuated. Where to? And for how long? She couldn't bear the thought of her best friend moving away!

'Please may I be excused?' she asked.

'Yes, get out of my sight,' Florence snapped.

Penny saw a sympathetic look on Mr Peck's face before she hurried out of the kitchen. Dashing through the front door, she then ran to Katy's school. The children were in the playground on their lunch break. Penny pushed her face to the fence, curling her fingers around the cold, metal railings as she peered through, searching for her friend.

'Katy,' she called, jumping up and down and waving, 'Katy, over here.'

When Katy saw Penny, she skipped over. 'Hello, what are you doing here?'

'Is it true? Is your mum sending you out of London?'

Katy nodded. 'Yes, I was going to tell you later. My brothers are going to live with my Aunt Sis but there ain't room for me an' all, so Mum said I have to be billeted. I don't know where I'm going or who I'm going to live with, but I can't wait to go.'

'I want to come with you.'

'You can't, Penny, you're sixteen. It's only kids being sent away.'

Penny could feel tears welling in her eyes, and cried, 'I don't want to stay here with my mum, not without you.'

'I wish you could come with me too, but I don't think you'll be allowed.'

A teacher rang a bell which he held in his hand, and all the children began to form orderly lines in the playground.

'I have to go, but I'll see you after school,' Katy said, before running off to join her classmates.

Penny sniffed back tears. With a heavy heart she traipsed to where Jimmy lived just several streets away. Her brother would still be at work, but he never locked his door. Jimmy's room had always felt like a safe haven for Penny. A place where she could relax and talk freely. It was only Jimmy who truly understood how awful Penny's life was. Unfortunately, she didn't get to hide in Jimmy's room as often as she'd like to, thanks to her mother's unreasonable rules.

Pushing open the front door of the scruffy house, Penny walked into the passageway, careful to avoid the hole in the floor where four floorboards were missing. She wrinkled her nose at the awful smell that wafted from the shared kitchen. Jimmy had told her that the waste-pipe was blocked. In his room on the first floor of the three-storey dilapidated building, Penny sat on the edge of Jimmy's bed and looked around. The place was a mess, as usual. She sighed and began tidying things away, just as she always did whenever she visited. She was glad to keep busy, it stopped her mind from wandering to the upsetting news of Katy moving out of Battersea.

Once the room was spick and span, Penny sat down again and immediately her thoughts returned to Katy. She hadn't realised how much time had passed until Jimmy breezed through the door.

'Hello, Munchkin,' he smiled, always pleased to see her.

'You're filthy,' Penny exclaimed, surprised to see Jimmy's boots covered in mud.

'I've got a new job,' he explained, 'working on a building site over Nine Elms way.'

'Another new job, blimey, Jimmy, you change your jobs more than I change my bed sheets!'

'You know me, Munchkin, I get bored easily.'

'Mum reckons that you're like Dad. She said you'll never settle anywhere.'

'Yeah, well, Mum says a lot of things. How's she been treating you lately?'

'You know, the same. I wish I could get a job and leave home like you have.'

'There's nothing stopping you.'

'Huh,' Penny scoffed. 'Apart from the fact that I haven't got anything that proves my name or my age. Look at me... no one would believe I'm sixteen. I look like Katy who's only twelve. And even if I did get a job, Mum said she'd find out where I was working and haul me back home. I wouldn't mind, but she only keeps me in the house so that I can be at her beck and call and do all the skivvying.'

'It's not easy for you and it never has been.'

'It's not fair, Jimmy. I've had no schooling except for what you've taught me, I've never had a birthday and I don't even know when it is! Why won't Mum tell me when I was born?'

Jimmy had taken off his muddy boots and placed them in the corner of the room. Coming to sit beside Penny on the bed, he took her hand in his.

'The truth is,' he said softly, 'Mum doesn't know when you were born, not exactly.'

Penny looked at him, perplexed. 'How can she not know? She gave birth to me.'

'That's just it, Penny... She didn't.'

'I – I don't understand.'

'I've never told you this, but I should have... I remember the day when you turned up. You just appeared. I'd got home from school and there you were, sleeping in a drawer on the kitchen table. Dad told me you were my sister and said that I had to look out for you. I just accepted it. I was too young to know where babies came from. But now, well, I know you never grew in Mum's stomach.'

Penny snatched her hand away, questions flying through her mind. 'Where did I come from?' she asked.

'I don't know.'

'So, you're not my brother?'

Jimmy nudged her ribs. 'Er, look at the colour of our hair. There's no doubt that I'm your brother.'

'But Mum ain't my mum?'

'No, she's not. We've got the same dad but not the same mum.'

Penny's thoughts raced. This news had come as a shock, but she wasn't hurt by it. 'I suppose it explains a lot. That's why she's always been so horrible to me. She hates me, Jimmy, and now I know why!'

Jimmy placed his arm across her shoulders and gave her a gentle squeeze. 'I'm sorry I never told you before now. But I didn't want to upset you.'

'I'm not upset, well, not about that. I'm glad she's not my mum. Do you know who my real mum is?'

'No, Munchkin, not a clue. Dad would know, but I doubt we'll ever see him again. Are you sure you're all right?'

'Yeah, I think so, but I'm really upset about Katy. She's being evacuated out of London, and I can't go with her because I'm too old.'

'You could easily get away with being the same age as Katy. I reckon mum keeping you short of food for all those years has stunted your growth. You could lie about your age?'

'How? I've no proof.'

'You have,' Jimmy smiled, mischievously. 'You just have to find it.'

'What do you mean? What proof do I need to find?'

'Annie's birth certificate. Do you remember our sister? She was born when you were about four years old. She didn't live long, just a few weeks, but Dad registered her birth. I'll lay money on the odds that Mum has still got the birth certificate somewhere.'

'I don't remember her, but Mum often says that she wishes I'd died instead of Annie. Oh, Jimmy, you're a genius,' Penny said, leaping to her feet with hope soaring through her heart. 'Do you really think I could fool people into believing that I'm twelve years old?'

'I'm sure of it, Munchkin.'

Penny leaned forward and planted a big kiss on Jimmy's cheek. 'I must go. I'm off to search the house for Annie's birth certificate and I've a good idea of where to look.'

'Wait, Penny, before you dash off, there's something I need to tell you.'

Penny looked at her brother, concerned to see the worried expression on his face. 'What is it?' she asked.

'This war that's coming with Germany... fit, young men will be needed to fight the enemy... and I've, erm, I've signed up.'

Penny gasped. Blinking back tears, she cried, 'No, Jimmy, no,' and ran to him. Dropping onto her knees in front of her dearly loved brother, she grabbed his hands. 'Please, Jimmy, don't do it. I couldn't cope if anything terrible happened to you!'

'It's all right, Munchkin. I'll get proper training so I'll know what I'm doing. Anyway, I won't have a choice. Chamberlain will be bringing in conscription, just like the government did during the Great War. But I'll be fine, Penny, I promise. Won't you be proud of me when I'm wearing a soldier's uniform?'

'Oh, Jimmy, I'll be as proud as a peacock,' Penny cried. 'But I wish there wasn't going to be a war.'

'Me too, Munchkin,' Jimmy sighed, 'me too.'

When Penny arrived home, she sneaked through the front door and was glad to hear her mother's laughter coming from behind the closed kitchen door. Mr Peck had obviously lifted the woman's mood and he had stayed to have his dinner. The smell of meat stew made Penny's stomach growl with hunger, but while Mr Peck was keeping her mother entertained, it meant that Penny could hunt for Annie's birth certificate.

Creeping up the stairs, Penny snuck into her mother's bedroom. She knew exactly where to search. In a mahogany dressing table, she carefully pulled open the middle drawer. Her pulse raced. If her mother caught her snooping, there would be devastating consequences! She came across a small box which she knew contained her gran's wedding ring. Lifting it out of the way, Penny found an envelope. *This must be it*, she thought, her heart pounding. Carefully peeling back the flap, she pulled out the contents and unfolded the piece of paper. Her hands trembled as she quickly read the elaborate writing written in black ink.

Annie Black.

This was it! Quickly placing the empty envelope back in the drawer and the small box on top, she quietly pushed the drawer shut and sneaked out of her mother's bedroom and into her own. Sitting on what had once been Jimmy's bed, Penny glanced again at the certificate before shoving it into her pocket. Looking up, she whispered, *'Thank you, Annie. You've saved my life, dear sister.'* Now she could leave London with Katy. As she dreamed of a very different future, Penny vowed to never return to live in the fearful shadow of the woman who, thankfully, wasn't her mother. She'd never again have to see the wicked woman who had raised her with the most spiteful of hands.

13

The following afternoon Penny stood at the front room window, peering up the street, desperate for Katy to return from school. When she saw her friend, her stomach flipped with delight and she rushed outside.

'Look what I've got,' Penny announced, waving the important document in front of Katy.

'What is it?'

'Let's go indoors and I'll tell you,' Penny grinned, fit to burst with excitement.

Katy threw her gas mask in the corner of the room and pulled off her coat. 'Come on then, spill the beans,' she urged.

Penny explained, 'It's a birth certificate for Annie Black, my sister who died when she was a baby. Annie was four years younger than me. You know what this means, don't you?'

'No,' Katy answered, her brow creasing.

'It means that I can be evacuated with you! I'll pretend to be Annie Black. Jimmy reckons that I could easily pass for twelve.'

Katy's face broke into a broad smile and she jumped up and down, squealing with glee.

'What's all this noise about?' Gladys Darwin asked, coming into the room with two tall glasses of water.

Katy turned to her mother, her face a picture of joy. 'Penny can come with me when I move away!'

Mrs Darwin didn't appear convinced. 'Oh, I don't think so, dear. Penny is too old to be evacuated.'

'Penny is, but *Annie* isn't,' Katy said with gusto.

'Who's Annie?' the small-framed woman asked.

Penny stepped forward and handed Mrs Darwin the birth certificate. 'She was my sister. She died but look at her date of birth. She would have been the same age as Katy is now.'

Mrs Darwin thought for a moment, and then she asked, 'So, you're going to pretend to be Annie?'

'Yes.'

'Does your mum know about this, Penny?'

'No, she'd blow her top ... and by the way, from now on, my name is Annie.'

Mrs Darwin huffed as she handed the birth certificate back to Penny. 'Oh, dear, it's not as simple as that. Your mum will have to register you to be evacuated. You can't just turn up with that and then hop on the next train out of London.'

'But ... my mum won't register me ... you know she won't.'

'I know, I'm sorry.'

Katy jumped up and down again. 'You could register Penny, I mean *Annie*. Please, Mum, say you'll do it.'

'Oh, I don't know about that,' Mrs Darwin replied, and gulped.

'Please, Mum, you know how horrible Florrie is to Penny. This is her chance to get away from her. It might be the only chance she ever gets!'

'Katy is right, Mrs Darwin. I'm almost like a prisoner next

door. The only time my mum lets me out of the house is when she wants to be alone with Mr Peck. I can't bear it, and it will be so much worse when Katy leaves. I'm begging you, please do this for me,' Penny pleaded with forlorn eyes.

Mrs Darwin held out her hand. 'Show me that thing again,' she demanded.

Penny was quick to hand over the birth certificate.

As Mrs Darwin examined it, she shook her head. 'I don't know about this. I could get into serious trouble with the authorities.'

'No one would ever know,' Penny urged. 'I'm not registered anywhere. As far as the authorities are concerned, Penny Black doesn't exist. That's how my mum managed to keep me off school. But Annie Black, she was a real person. It says so there in black and white. Please, Mrs Darwin, my life is a misery next door and I'd miss Katy something terrible... please?'

Mrs Darwin blew out a long breath through her thin lips. She was a slight woman with wispy fair hair who wouldn't say boo to a ghost. Penny feared that the woman wouldn't have the guts to do something so brazen. So she was over the moon when Mrs Darwin agreed to help.

'All right, I'll do it. But we'd all better hope that Florrie never finds out about this!'

Penny stood alongside Katy and Katy's fretful mother in the queue to register for evacuation. She could see that Mrs Darwin was a nervous wreck, and she feared the woman would back out of the lie.

Luckily, in the mayhem, Mrs Darwin wasn't asked too many questions. Much to Penny's relief, Katy's mum managed to convince the middle-aged woman administrator that Penny, or *Annie Black*, was her niece and had recently moved in with her following her sister's untimely death. She explained to the administrator that Annie hadn't yet joined the local school but would have very soon, only Operation Pied Piper had scuppered their plans.

Mrs Darwin was given a Ministry of Health leaflet which outlined what kit Annie would need to carry: a handbag or case containing the child's gas mask, a change of underclothing, night clothes, house shoes or plimsolls, spare stockings or socks, a toothbrush, a comb, towel, soap and a face-cloth, handkerchiefs and, if possible, a warm coat or mackintosh. Each child should bring a packet of food for the day.

As they made their way back home, Mrs Darwin hurried them along, tutting, then saying, 'I can't believe we got away with that!'

'I'm ever so grateful, Mrs Darwin,' Penny said. 'Thank you.'

'We're not in the clear yet and I won't relax until you're on the train tomorrow.'

Penny noticed that Mrs Darwin was clammy with nerves and the woman's hand shook when she handed Penny the leaflet.

After reading it, Penny mused aloud, 'I don't know how I'm going to sneak out in the morning without my mum noticing.' Biting on her bottom lip, she added, 'And I don't have a case.'

Mrs Darwin, a kind but weak woman, offered, 'I'll get your kit ready with Katy's.'

'Would you? I can't thank you enough, Mrs Darwin.'

'It's no bother. Then all you have to worry about is getting to the assembly point at the school. But for Christ's sake,

Penny, be careful. I could do without Florrie knowing about my part in this.'

'I promise, Mrs Darwin, I'll never let her know that you helped me,' Penny assured her.

Mrs Darwin feared her own shadow, and Penny guessed that the woman felt intimidated by Florence. And Katy's sweet mother wasn't the only one who feared Florence's wrath – so did Penny! She knew that if her so-called *mother* caught her in the act of running away, she'd face the harshest of punishments and the limited freedom she had now would be further restricted. Life wouldn't be worth living.

14

At half-past five the next morning, and following a sleepless night, Penny tried to behave normally but her heart raced with anticipation. When she came down the stairs, she was greeted by a pile of clothes on the kitchen table that were waiting for repair. Quickly sifting through them, she pulled out an elaborate black dress embossed with red embroidery. She'd never seen a dress so exquisite and would normally take a moment to dream of herself wearing it. But not today. Penny had far more pressing matters on her mind. Picking up her scissors, she cut a small hole in the embroidery, and then she placed the dress to one side and began mending a smart, white shirt which had two buttons missing. Her hands trembled as she pushed the needle through the fabric. Swallowing hard, Penny tried to calm her jangled nerves as she waited for her mother to rise from her slumber. And right on cue, at eight o'clock, Florence came into the kitchen.

'Is that all you've done this morning?' the woman grumbled, as she inspected the pile of repaired clothes in a basket by Penny's side. 'What about that dress?'

'I, erm, I'm sorry, but I will need a reel of red cotton to finish the dress' Penny explained, fearfully.

'Why? The dress only needs the hem taking up. Black cotton will suffice.'

'I – I, er, I noticed a small hole here, in the embroidery,' Penny said, pointing to the deliberate damage.

'Give it to me,' Florence snapped, snatching the dress. After closely examining the small hole, she threw the outfit back at Penny. 'You're bleedin' useless! I suppose I'd better go and buy some red cotton when the shop opens, but in future make sure your cotton stocks are in order. This isn't good enough. Slovenly, that's what it is, slovenly.'

Penny nodded. Her ploy to get rid of her mother was going to plan.

Continuing with her work, her mind raced as she watched the minutes slowly ticking by.

Florence marched back into the kitchen, now wearing her coat. 'I expect to see the rest of that work completed by the time I return,' she barked.

Penny waited with bated breath until she heard the front door close. But then a knock on the back door startled her. Looking over her shoulder, she saw Mr Peck through the window. Of course, he'd be here for his cup of tea before starting work in the shed at the end of the yard. *Bugger*, Penny thought, she hadn't considered Mr Peck in her getaway plan.

'Good morning, Penny,' the man said, stepping into the kitchen. 'I see you're hard at it, as usual.'

'Plenty to do,' Penny replied, forcing a smile.

'Well, even the middle-class folk can be frugal with their money. They wouldn't be wealthy if they were spendthrifts. I suppose it's more economical to have their clothes repaired rather than buying new garments, and it's nice to see that you've a good pile there to keep you busy. Though why the folk on the better side of Battersea can't do their own mending like the rest of us do is beyond me. Still, it's honest work for you and keeps the pennies rolling in.'

'Would you like a cup of tea, Mr Peck?' Penny offered.

'Is your mother not here? She normally sees to my tea in the morning.'

'She's popped out to buy some cotton. I'm happy to make you a cuppa, if you like?'

'Oh, no, thank you, Penny. I wouldn't want to keep you from your work. I'll get on with mine for now, and I'll call in later when your mother is home.'

Mr Peck doffed his hat at Penny before closing the back door behind him. At last, Penny was alone. Acting quickly before her mother returned, she hurried up the stairs to her bedroom. Her heart thumped hard and fast as she gathered her coat, a dress and a small black and white photograph of Jimmy. Then glancing out of the window, she looked up and down the street. When there was no sign of her mother, Penny ran back down the stairs and out of the front door.

Sprinting as fast as her legs would carry her, it only took Penny a few minutes to reach Katy's school. She was both pleased and hugely relived to see Katy and her mum waiting outside the gates.

'You made it,' Katy gushed, throwing her arms around Penny.

'Yeah, but my heart is beating thirteen to the dozen. Mum went to the shop, but she'll be back any minute now and will find me gone. I'm terrified that she'll come looking for me.'

Mrs Darwin handed Penny a small case. 'Don't worry

about that now, dear. I'm sure this is the last place that she'll think of to look for you. Let's get you tagged and out of here.'

'Tagged?' Penny questioned.

'Yes,' Katy said. 'We have to wear tags on our coats with our names and what school we go to. Don't forget, your name is *Annie*.'

Penny's mouth felt dry with nerves and her legs were shaking. Her head spun, making her feel dizzy, and she worried she might faint. Concerned that she might be found out as a fraud was nothing compared to how much Penny feared the notion of her mother finding her!

Ushering them towards waiting buses, Mrs Darwin reminded them, 'Now girls, remember, I've packed you both a sandwich.' It was obvious that Katy's mum was fighting back tears. 'Please write soon and look after each other,' she added, holding a handkerchief to her nose. Then, grabbing Katy's hand, she sobbed, 'You'll be safe now. You know what I mean, don't you?'

Katy nodded, looking sullen.

'Be good girls.'

As Penny boarded the bus, she looked over her shoulder to take a last glimpse at Mrs Darwin. The woman was openly crying. Penny would forever be grateful to Katy's mum, but she wondered what Mrs Darwin had meant when she'd told Katy that she would be safe now. Had she meant from the German bombs? Penny didn't think so, but Katy had seemed to understand.

By the time the bus had arrived at Clapham Junction railway station, Penny's nerves had settled a little and she began to finally believe that she was getting away from a life of servitude and misery. Busloads of anxious and excited children piled into the train station. A lady from the Woman's Voluntary Service had told Mrs Darwin that trains were leaving London stations every nine minutes, all of them stuffed with evacuees, and the trains would continue leaving until nine o'clock that night. Penny couldn't begin to imagine how many children were fleeing the threat of Hitler's bombs to safety in the countryside, but she knew it must be thousands or even millions. Some children were crying and being comforted by volunteers who'd been roped in to help with the mass evacuation. Others looked frightened at the idea of being separated from their parents, but some, like her, were clearly excited and looking forward to an unknown adventure.

Penny stood next to Katy on the train platform amid hundreds of children and many pregnant women who stood waiting for the next train too. She felt Katy's sweaty hand slip into her own.

'Are you scared?' Katy asked.

'No, I'm excited,' Penny fibbed a little. She was scared, scared of her mother turning up and dragging her home. She wouldn't feel assured until she was on the train and it had pulled out of the station.

'I was all right at first, but now I'm terrified,' Katy sniffed. 'I'm so glad you're with me.'

'What are you terrified of?' Penny asked.

'Where we might be going and who we might be staying with.'

'Look at it this way... whoever it is that takes us in, they can't be any worse than my mum,' Penny reassured her friend.

'That's true, I suppose. And nothing can be as bad as my dad.'

'What do you mean?'

'Nothing,' Katy quickly replied.

Come on, Penny willed, hoping that the train would arrive soon. She kept expecting to see Florence's face looming out from the crowds and feel the woman's wicked grip around the scruff of her neck.

'Look, Penny, here it comes,' Katy squealed, pointing towards a cloud of steam that billowed from the approaching train.

'I'm Annie, not Penny,' she whispered in Katy's ear.

'Oh, yeah, sorry.'

As the train pulled beside the platform, Penny found herself being moved along with the organised crowd. This was it. She was finally about to embark on a journey of happiness, and relief flooded over her. Thanks to Mrs Darwin's out-of-character bravery, she was about to be free of Florence and her domineering ways.

Penny gazed out of the window as the scenery changed from soot-covered, crammed-in buildings to rolling green fields. She'd never been on a train before or outside of Battersea, let alone out of London. She couldn't have imagined that anything could look so beautiful as Kent did. Even Battersea Park wasn't as green as this! And for the first time, she saw sheep and cows grazing in meadows.

'Isn't it wonderful!' she exclaimed, her eyes wild as she turned to her friend.

'It's smashing, Penny, really smashing!'

'Shush,' Penny whispered, 'call me Annie.'

'Oh, yes, sorry, *Annie*,' Katy whispered and giggled. 'It's going to take some getting used to!'

'For me an' all. When that woman from the Voluntary Service called out *Annie* Black, I didn't answer at first.'

'I need to go to the toilet,' Katy mumbled.

Penny peered out of the window again, mesmerised by everything she saw. Odd looking round buildings with tall, pointed roofs, thatched cottages with large gardens, blue streams, not with grey, murky water flowing like that in the Thames.

After a short while Katy returned to her seat, saying, 'The lady from the Voluntary Service said that those round, funny-looking buildings are oast houses.'

'What's oast?' Penny asked.

'I dunno, but I also heard her telling someone that we're nearly at our destination.'

Looking back out of the window, drinking in every new sight with wonder, Penny couldn't wipe the smile off her face. A new life beckoned, and she hoped she'd never see Florence Black again. Though she'd miss Jimmy and imagined him at the army basic training camp. *He'll have the time of his life*, she thought, pushing away her fears of what could happen to him once his training was completed. Today was going to be a happy day. She wouldn't worry about Jimmy. There'd be time soon enough to think about her brother, but certainly not today.

Later that afternoon, after arriving at a rural train station in Kent, many of the children, including Penny and Katy, were led to a church hall. Eagerly awaiting news of who they would be staying with, the minutes slowly turned into hours. Sitting on their small cases, bored, tired and hungry, some of the younger children were becoming fractious.

A guardian from the Women's Voluntary Service who'd accompanied them on the train cleared her throat before making an announcement.

'Apologies for the delay. There appears to have been a small mix-up, but you will all be moving on shortly.'

Another woman came to stand by her side. She had a clipboard in her hand and a pen in the other and began calling out the names of some of the children.

Penny heard her name.

When the woman had called about twenty-five of the children, she instructed, 'Come with me.'

Penny and Katy exchanged a panicked glance.

'She didn't call my name,' Katy stated, worriedly. 'Oh no, I hope they ain't going to take you somewhere without me!'

'Wait here,' Penny instructed.

Rushing over to the woman as a group of children gathered around her, Penny pushed her way through the small crowd.

'Excuse me, Miss,' she said, and tugged on the woman's jacket.

The woman looked at Penny's name tag that was pinned onto her coat. 'Yes, Annie, how can I help you?'

'You called my name to come with you, but you didn't call my friend.'

'What is your friend's name?'

'Katy. Katy Darwin.'

The woman looked at her clipboard, her eyes scanning down the list. 'I'm afraid your friend's name isn't on this list. But fear not, she will be allocated a place very soon.'

'No, Miss, you don't understand. Me and Katy are best friends. We live next door to each other. We have to go to the same place, together.'

'I'm sorry, sweetie, but we've had to separate brothers and sisters. So, you see, we can't possibly arrange for friends to stay together.'

As Penny was about to beg and plead to be allowed to stay with Katy, another billeting officer approached and said to the first woman, 'I need two children older than ten years of age. A late placement has just become available.'

Penny was quick to push her hand in the air and interrupted. 'Me and Katy,' she blurted, 'we're both twelve. Please, can me and Katy take the placement?'

The first woman smiled. 'It's your lucky day, Annie. I'll cross you off my list. Off you go with Mrs Porter. Fetch your friend and no dilly-dallying.'

Penny didn't stop to thank the woman. She rushed over to Katy and, grabbing her own case, she urged, 'Come on, hurry. Bring your case. They've found us a place together and we don't want to miss it!'

Mrs Porter marched across the church hall with Penny and Katy following. Outside, in the cool, evening air, she pointed towards a grumpy-looking man sat on a cart behind a horse.

'That's Mr Gaston. You'll be going with him to his farm.'

Katy's eyes widened and Penny could see that her friend was afraid. The girl didn't trust men, especially men she didn't know.

Mrs Porter must have seen the anxious look on Katy's face and offered some soothing words. 'Don't worry, Katy. I know that Mr Gaston doesn't look very welcoming, but Mrs Gaston and her two children are at the farm, and they are looking forward to meeting you.'

This seemed to appease Katy and she smiled at Penny.

Hand in hand, the girls walked to the cart and helped each

other climb on. Penny had never ridden on the back of a cart before. Already, her new life was proving to be one of thrilling experiences.

Mr Gaston, his face weathered and his head hunkered down into his broad shoulders, kept his eyes straight ahead. His voice was a low rumble when he commanded the horse, 'Gee up.'

Penny looked at Katy, and they both shrugged.

'Say something to him,' Katy whispered in Penny's ear.

'How do you do, sir?' Penny ventured.

Mr Gaston said nothing.

'I'm Annie and this is Katy, my best friend.'

'I know who you are,' the man replied, gruffly.

'Is your farm far from here?'

''Nough chit-chat. Save it for Mrs Gaston,' he answered.

Though Mr Gaston came over as surly and aloof, Penny wasn't bothered by his brusque manner and she didn't feel at all threatened by him. She assumed it was just the way he was. But she hoped that Mrs Gaston would be more friendly than her husband.

15

Clara Gaston pulled off her dressing gown, shuddered with the cold, and slipped into bed beside her husband. 'It's chilly tonight,' she said, and then, snuggling closer to him, she asked quietly, 'What do you think of the new girls, Will?'

'I don't. It's not my job to think,' Will Gaston replied.

'But you must have noticed how thin Annie is. She's skin and bone, bless her.'

'I'm sure you'll soon fatten her up.'

'And Katy, well, isn't she a nervous little mouse,' Clara mused.

'I've not heard her speak yet, but Annie makes up for it.'

'I like them, and I think that Rosemary does too. But I'm not sure that Basil is very keen. I reckon he was hoping that we'd get two boys instead of girls. I hope they all end up rubbing along nicely together.'

'I'm sure they will. Get some sleep, woman. I've got to be up at sunbreak to see to the cows.'

Clara rolled over in the bed and pulled the covers up to her chin. ''Night, Will,' she said, knowing that sleep would evade her. Thirty-seven-year-old Clara had suffered with insomnia for as far back as she could remember; worries keeping her awake until the small hours. Will had told her that she fretted needlessly, but now with war imminent, she had cause for concern.

'Stop thinking about the Hun,' Will said.

'I'm not.'

'Yes, you are.'

'How do you know what goes on inside my head?' Clara asked.

'Because I know you, woman. Switch your thoughts off and rest. Whether we go to war with Germany or not, you laying there awake and worrying about it won't change the outcome.'

Clara sighed. Her husband knew her so well. Though no matter what he said, she couldn't stop her thoughts from troubling her. And she couldn't pretend that the war wasn't going to happen. After all, she had proof of it in the form of two malnourished young girls sleeping under her roof. Chamberlain's government wouldn't have evacuated the children from the cities of Britain if he didn't think that there was a genuine risk to their safety.

It proved to be a long and restless night for Clara. Before the dawn broke, she quietly eased herself out of bed, careful not to disturb Will, and then she crept down the stairs of their ragstone farmhouse.

In the kitchen, the embers of the previous night's fire still glowed in the large hearth. Throwing on some kindling and several lumps of coal, she used the bellows to encourage a roaring fire. Clara wanted her guests to feel warm in their new home, especially as they didn't have enough flesh on their bones to protect them from the cold. And though they'd both turned up in coats, Clara had noticed that Annie's was too short in the arms and didn't reach around her front. They'd be sure to need their coats today. Glancing out of the window, the sun rising brought a pale pink hue to the sky, and a ground frost made the gravelled path outside glisten in the early morning light. It was going to be another frigid morning.

Will's voice behind her startled Clara.

'I hope I won't have to wake Basil again,' he grumbled.

Since leaving school, their fifteen-year-old son worked alongside his father on the farm, but Basil hadn't taken well to the job. Will called him lazy. Clara preferred to think that the lad was cut from a different cloth and made for better things. She knew that Basil would have liked to have moved to London. He'd said that he wanted to work for the British Broadcasting Corporation. The young man had a fascination with television sets. Clara had never seen one. She assumed that watching a television screen must be similar to the cinema. She'd only been to the picture house twice in her lifetime. The moving images unnerved her. Pulling on an apron around her waist and tying it at the back, Clara frowned as she thought about television sets.

Will pulled out a seat at the large and chunky kitchen table. 'What's bothering you?' he asked as he studied his wife's face.

'Nothing. I was just thinking that even if we could have afforded a television, and if we had electricity, I'd still refuse to allow one of those things in my house. I mean, if I can see the people on the television screen, then they must be able to see me too!'

Will chuckled. 'No, Clara, I'm sure they can't. You thought the same about the wireless. As I explained, you can hear them, but they can't hear you.'

'I'm still not convinced about that! You'd better not be sneaking that contraption into the house. I'll thank you to keep your wiry thingy in the barn.'

Will smiled.

'There's boiled eggs in the larder and bread that needs toasting over the fire. Help yourself.'

'I'm to fix my own breakfast now, am I?'

'Yes, Will, and I'm sure you'll manage. I've got to get today's bread in the oven and collect fresh eggs and get the chickens fed, all before the girls wake up.'

'They looked worn out yesterday after all that travelling. I shouldn't think they'll be up early.'

'Even so, I want them to wake up to a hearty breakfast.'

'Yet your husband has to make his own.'

Clara kissed the man on the cheek. 'You're big enough to look after yourself from time to time,' she said, and then whooped when she felt him slap her backside. At forty, Will was only three years older than her, yet he had the virility of a man half his age.

As Will cut two thick slices of bread, he said, 'You'd better wake Basil up. If I have to go up to his room, I'll chuck a bucket of cold water over him. I'm sure he'll appreciate your more gentle approach.'

'Ha, talk of the devil,' Clara said when she saw Basil trudge into the kitchen. Her son, who now towered over his father at nearly six feet, looked tired and still half-asleep. His knitted jumper hung off his wiry frame, but Clara thought that working hard on the farm would fill out his chest and broaden his shoulders. And as his trousers were a good two inches too short, it showed that the lad was still growing. *You'll be a heartbreaker one of these days*, Clara thought, admiring his good looks. With strong cheek bones and dark hair that flopped over one hazel eye, Clara could imagine her son as a movie star. And she thought he must have got his good looks from his father. The boy had Will's colouring, so different from her light brown hair and grey eyes.

'Liven up, lad,' Will encouraged. 'I want more work out of you today than you did yesterday.'

Basil breathed in a long breath, then said, sardonically, 'Great.'

'And no lip,' Will added. 'I suppose a smile and a bit of enthusiasm would be too much to ask for?'

Basil threw his father a blistering look. Then reaching for the coffee pot, he moaned, 'It's cold.'

'Your mother's not made any yet, so that'll be your first job of the day. And I'll have a strong cup when it's done.'

'Great,' Basil repeated.

Will looked at Clara. 'See what I have to put up with all day,' he said with a roll of his eyes.

'Cheer up, Basil,' Clara smiled. 'I realise that working on the farm isn't where your heart is, but for now, with war likely, this farm is the safest place for you to be.'

'If you say so.'

'I do, and thank your lucky stars that you've got a home that is out of danger's way. Look at those two young girls upstairs, ripped away from their parents and sent to live with strangers. I don't think you realise how fortunate you are.

And talking of the girls, please show them some kindness. You were quite rude last night.'

'I wasn't rude. I just didn't feel in the mood to talk to them.'

'Well, I'd appreciate you making more of an effort. Tell him, Will.'

Will turned to his son. 'You heard your mother, make more of an effort.'

'You didn't make much effort with them,' Basil spurted at his father, accusingly.

'Oi, less lip. Just do as your mother says.'

Clara removed the bread from the warming drawer of her range stove and placed it in the oven. She was looking forward to the mouth-watering aroma of the baking bread wafting around the house. She couldn't imagine anything more welcoming to greet her guests. She was pleased that it was Saturday. Work on the farm continued seven days a week, but the school wouldn't be open until Monday. That meant that Annie and Katy had a couple of days to find their bearings and settle in before joining school with Rosemary. And because Annie and Katy were the same age as her daughter, Clara was glad that they would share a classroom together. But one thing worried Clara which she kept to herself. She'd heard disturbing tales about London children: pickpocketing, fighting and even drinking alcohol. From what she'd seen so far, Clara was sure that they were nice girls, but she was aware that they were likely on their best behaviour last night. She hoped that what she'd been told about Londoners was just idle gossip and that Annie and Katy wouldn't lead Rosemary into any trouble.

★

Penny's eyes flickered open. It took her a few moments to remember that she wasn't in Jimmy's old bed, and she didn't have to rush down the stairs to begin mending clothes.

Stretching out her legs and toes, Penny appreciated the clean cotton sheets and soft feather pillows. She'd never slept in such a comfortable bed, even if she was sharing it with her friend.

'Are you awake?' Katy whispered in her ear.

'Yeah, are you?' Penny laughed.

'I'm busting for the loo.'

'Go then,' Penny said.

'I'm too scared. Will you come with me?'

'There's nothing to be scared of here. You'll be fine.'

'Please,' Katy insisted.

'Come on then,' Penny said with a sigh, reluctant to get out of the cosy bed.

As Penny slipped her feet into her ill-fitting shoes, Katy put on her plimsolls.

'It's cold,' Penny advised, 'we'll need our coats.'

The heavy curtains were pulled closed, leaving the room in darkness. Penny felt around for her coat, hoping she wouldn't disturb Rosemary. She had no idea what the time was, but she was sure she could smell fresh bread, and her stomach rumbled.

'I heard voices from downstairs. I think that Mr and Mrs Gaston are up and about,' Katy said quietly. 'Do you think we should wake Rosemary?'

'No, she'll wake when she's ready.'

'Are you sure it's all right for us to go downstairs to use the privy?'

'Of course. Mrs Gaston said that we're to treat the place

like home. I'm sure she'd rather you used the privy rather than wetting the bed.'

Katy smiled. 'Yeah, you're right. I don't know how I've held it in for so long. I was dying for you to wake up and come with me.'

'Come on then, we'd better get you to the crapper pretty sharpish.'

The bedroom door creaked as Penny pulled it open. She glanced over her shoulder and saw that Rosemary was beginning to stir.

'Good morning,' the girl chirped as she sat up in bed.

'Sorry,' Penny said. 'We didn't want to disturb you, only Katy really needs the loo.'

'You'd better hurry then,' Rosemary said, stretching her arms over her head, and yawning.

Penny went down the stairs first with Katy closely following. The delightful smell of baked bread twitched Penny's nose. She had a feeling that she was going to enjoy staying at the Gaston's farm, though she wasn't convinced that Basil Gaston wanted them there. When she'd first met him last night, she'd been struck by his handsome features. But the young man had been moody, seeming to sulk at their presence. *Oh well*, Penny thought, and assumed that Basil must take after his father. She wasn't going to allow a surly young man to spoil her new life, especially as Rosemary and Mrs Gaston were the nicest people she'd ever met!

'I've never seen a privy with three seats,' Penny exclaimed as she sat down to poached eggs with thick slices of warm bread, slathered in butter made on the farm.

Mrs Gaston poured tea from the biggest teapot that Penny

had ever seen, and looking under her pale lashes, the woman smiled. 'Rest assured, I never sit next to Mr Gaston in the privy,' she said, pulling a disgusted face.

Katy giggled.

Nauseating memories of having to clean the privy twice a day shot through Penny's mind. She wondered if she'd be forced to do the same on the farm, and asked, 'Will we have chores to do?'

'Yes, we all muck in here. Farm work isn't an easy life, but you'll be rewarded with plenty of fresh, clean air and good, wholesome food.'

'These are the best eggs I've ever tasted,' Katy said, her mouth full.

'What chores will we have?' Penny asked.

'You can make your own bed, for one, and put your sheets in the laundry every fortnight. Rosemary washes the dishes after dinner, so you can help her with that.'

'Many hands make light work,' Rosemary added.

'And what else?' Penny asked, dreading that she might hear the word *privy*.

'Well, now that there are four of us ladies, perhaps we can share the floor-sweeping duties? Have you ever swept floors before?'

'Annie did *all* the cleaning at home,' Katy announced.

Mrs Gaston looked surprised. 'Did you, Annie?'

Penny could feel her cheeks burning red as she slowly nodded her head.

'Was your mother poorly?'

Before Penny could answer, Katy piped up, 'Her mum's 'orrible. She made Annie do *everything*.'

Penny discreetly elbowed her friend in the side, hoping

that the nudge would mute her. Since being too afraid to go to the toilet alone, Katy had found her voice and was disclosing information that Penny would rather she didn't.

'Oh dear, Annie, that doesn't sound very pleasant. I hope you find life a little easier here.'

Penny saw a genuine kindness in Mrs Gaston's eyes and sympathy too. 'Thank you,' she said, 'I already love it here.'

'I'm glad to hear it. And as for chores, there's always lots to do on the farm. I'd appreciate a hand churning the butter or collecting eggs from the hens. There's bread to make daily, pies to bake and apples to pick to make the pies. But your schooling is more important than chores.'

'You'll really like my teacher,' Rosemary said.

'I'll be going to school?' Penny asked, surprised. *Of course*, she thought. *They think I'm only twelve years old.*

'Yes, on Monday, you'll be going to the same school as Rosemary.'

'Annie's never been to school,' Katy informed them.

Penny could feel her jaw tighten as all eyes around the table fell on her.

'What, *never*?' Rosemary asked.

Feeling uncomfortable, Penny shook her head.

Mrs Gaston gently asked, 'Can you read and write, Annie?'

'Yes, my brother taught me.'

'Proficiently?'

'What does that mean?'

'Can you read and write well?'

'I think so,' Penny answered, her chin jutting forward.

'Good. Then you'll be just fine at school, and you will make lots of new friends. And talking of writing, have you got the postcards that were given to you before you left London?'

Katy nodded.

'Then I think you should write home and tell your parents where you are, and I'll pop them into the post office on Monday.'

Katy dashed up to the bedroom, soon returning with two white postcards. She pushed one across the table to Penny as she smiled at Mrs Gaston, saying, 'I can't wait to tell my mum that I'm on a farm!'

As Katy scribbled away, Penny stared down at her blank card.

'Do you need my help to write yours, Annie?' Mrs Gaston kindly asked.

Penny shook her head.

'If you'd rather that your note home remained private, I can give you an envelope to put the postcard in.'

'No, thank you ... I – I don't want to write home.'

'But you must tell your mother where you are.'

'She won't care,' Penny spat.

'I'm sure she would. But we can leave the postcard for today, and perhaps you can write it tomorrow. Now before anyone leaves the table, I'm going to inspect your hair.'

'Not the nit comb,' Rosemary whined.

'Yes, the nit comb' Mrs Gaston smiled.

'I ain't got nits,' Katy said proudly. 'The nit nurse came to our school last week.'

'Nonetheless, I'd like to check,' Mrs Gaston said firmly.

Penny had never seen a nit comb or had her hair checked. She kept her fingers crossed under the table, hoping that Mrs Gaston wouldn't find any nits. As the woman pulled the

Derbac metal comb through her tangled locks, Penny winced when her hair tugged on her scalp.

'Sorry, Annie,' Mrs Gaston said. 'Your hair needs a good wash and brush, but there aren't any nits. I must say, your hair is a wonderful colour.'

'Thank you. My brother, Jimmy, he's ginger too.'

'Well, it suits you, Annie. Now, Katy, it's your turn for inspection.'

Penny watched Mrs Gaston being as gentle as she could with Katy's hair. Already, Penny was fond of the woman. But she didn't believe that her ginger hair suited her. She'd have liked blonde hair like Katy's. And she wished she was pretty like her friend too. But she wasn't. Her mother said she was an ugly girl, and Penny believed it to be true.

'And you're all clear too.'

'I told you I would be. Thank you, Mrs Gaston,' Katy grinned.

'I think you should both call me Clara. Help Rosemary with the dishes and then the day is your own. Feel free to explore, but don't wander too far away from the house.'

'And we must stay out of Dad's way,' Rosemary added. 'He doesn't like to have girls hanging around him when he's working.'

Penny happily washed the plates while Katy dried them and Rosemary put them away.

'We're a good team,' Rosemary chirped. 'I like you being here.'

'You're our new best friend,' Katy replied.

'Come on, I'll show you the bridge over the stream at the end of the yard. We can play Poohsticks.'

'What's Poohsticks?' Penny asked.

'You've never heard of Poohsticks?' Rosemary said, sounding astonished.

The girls shook their heads.

'It's a game from a book, *The House at Pooh Corner*. Winnie the Pooh plays it with Christopher Robin. They race sticks under the bridge. It's such good fun but Basil won't play with me anymore.'

'Put your coats on,' Clara ordered. 'And try to stay dry. Rosemary has a habit of falling into the stream, and I already have enough washing to tackle.'

Penny had skipped rope occasionally in the past and played hopscotch several times with Katy, and five jacks. She'd shared games of marbles with Jimmy when their mother hadn't been watching. But she'd never felt as carefree as she did now. And though she thought that she was probably too old to play Poohsticks, she knew she'd enjoy the game all the same. It was liberating to live the life of twelve-year-old girl. She was having the childhood she'd missed out on. All thoughts of war, of her mother and of endless sewing and cleaning were pushed to the back of her mind. As she pulled on her ill-fitting coat, Penny beamed with delight. This was the happiest moment of her life.

16

Clara's mind was troubled. She couldn't stop thinking about what Katy had divulged over breakfast. Piecing the sparce information together, it seemed that poor Annie had been used as a slave under her mother's rule. Clara had hidden her shock, but she'd been appalled to hear that the young girl had never been schooled. Something was very much amiss in Annie's London house and Clara pondered what effect this may have had on the girl. Though she had to admit, Annie seemed to be a well-rounded and confident child.

As she rolled out pastry, Clara glanced up and out of the back window. It warmed her heart to see the girls skipping back from the stream, their pale faces now rosy cheeked. Rosemary was laughing and revelling in the company of her new friends. It struck Clara how her daughter looked a picture of health compared to Annie and Katy. She was at least four inches taller than the girls, and twice as wide to boot. And Rosemary's chestnut hair glistened in the sunlight, a stark contrast to Annie's red but dull hair and Katy's lack-lustre wispy blonde curls. But if Clara had care of the girls for a long enough time, she felt sure she would be sending them home in tip-top condition. Though the thought of Annie returning to live with her mother twisted Clara's stomach.

'Mum... Mum...' Rosemary called as she bounded through the front door. 'Katy won at Poohsticks. Can we have lunch, please?'

'Yes, your dad and Basil will be here for food soon. Go and wash your hands, you too, girls.'

Clara turned up the heat under the vegetable soup she'd prepared and placed a block of cheese on the table next to the bread. Stretching her neck to look out of the window and towards the fields, she saw her husband trudging home with Basil a few steps behind. Clara sighed. Her son looked as miserable as sin. But as she'd said to him, working on the farm was the safest place for him to be, at least until they knew if Germany would withdraw from Poland. Unfortunately, war looked likely, so the best that they could hope for was a rapid victory.

'Strong coffee,' Clara said, handing Will a cup when he came into the kitchen. Basil was still removing his muddied boots at the front door.

Rosemary, Annie and Katy came in too, larking around and laughing, each taking a seat at the table, and then Basil joined them. Clara dished out large bowls of the nourishing soup.

'Help yourselves to bread and cheese,' she offered, pleased to see that her meal was being hungrily devoured.

'This is delicious,' Annie said.

'There's more in the pot if you'd like some.'

'Thank you, I think I will. What's this?' the girl asked, holding a small, green floret on her spoon.

Clara again had to hide her astonishment. 'That's broccoli,

Annie. I grow it in my garden. Perhaps you'd like to have a look after lunch?'

Annie shoved it into her mouth. 'Yeah, I'd like that. What else do you grow?'

Basil looked over his soup bowl, his eyes boring into Annie with disdain. 'Stop talking with your mouth full of food. It's disgusting and it's bad manners,' he said, with an air of superiority.

Clara saw Annie's cheeks redden. She threw an admonishing look at her son, and then tried to make her guest feel better. 'Don't worry, Annie. I'm afraid we are quite the sticklers for manners around the table. You'll soon learn.'

'Yes,' Rosemary agreed. 'No elbows on the table and chew your food with your mouth closed. No talking with food in your mouth either. And we're supposed to clear our plates and then ask to be excused, but Basil never asks.'

'I'm not a child,' he argued.

'There's too much talking and not enough eating,' Will barked.

The table fell quiet, all but for the noise of spoons lightly scraping in ceramic bowls. Clara broke the silence. 'Who'd like a slice of warm apple pie?' she asked.

Rosemary stuck her hand up. 'Me,' she said.

'Yes please,' the girls chorused.

'Save ours for later,' Will instructed. 'There's work needs doing before the sun sets. Come on, lad.'

Scraping back his seat, he tapped Basil on the shoulder, and the pair of them headed towards the door.

'Take no notice of Basil,' Rosemary said in a hushed voice. 'He's nice, really, you'll see.'

Clara nodded. 'He is. I don't know what's got into him lately.'

'He ain't happy working on the farm,' Rosemary said.

Clara's eyebrows rose. 'I beg your pardon, young lady.'

'What?' Rosemary asked.

'*Ain't* is not a word!'

'But Annie and Katy say it all the time.'

'Yes, because they are Londoners and that's how folk from London speak. But you're not, so please use your words correctly.'

'Sorry. We'll try to speak better,' Annie said, obviously keen to please.

'There's no need and there's nothing wrong with how you speak. Colloquialism is perfectly suited for where you are from. But I'd rather that Rosemary didn't try to copy you.'

'Mum wanted to be a teacher before she married my dad. She reads a lot of books, and she uses big words sometimes,' Rosemary explained, with a smirk.

'I'd like to read more books,' Annie stated.

'Then you must see if I have any that you think you'd enjoy. What about you, Katy?'

'No, thanks. Reading is boring.'

'It expands your mind,' Clara stressed.

Katy shrugged and didn't appear at all interested. But Clara was pleased that Annie had shown an interest in reading. And she was sure that the girl would find something to pique her interest in the small library that had once been the boot room.

'Can we go back to the stream?' Rosemary asked.

'Yes, after you've done the dishes.'

Annie waited until she'd finished chewing the food in her

mouth before she spoke. 'I'm whacked, I'd rather have a look at your books than go to the stream, if you don't mind?'

Clara was thrilled. 'Of course I don't mind. We'll take a stroll around my vegetable garden and then I'll show you the library. In fact, Rosemary and Katy can do the dishes. Come with me, Annie.'

Outside, Clara took great pride in showing off her home-grown vegetables, and she readily answered all of Annie's questions. The girl had a probing mind and soaked up information like a sponge. She thought it was such a shame that Annie had missed so much school as the youngster was clearly as bright as a button.

Meandering past the cabbages and spinach, Clara spotted a cheeky rabbit who appeared to have taken a liking to her carrots. She'd never hurt the cute creature, but she picked up a big stick and held it above her head, ready to frighten off the animal.

'Get out of there,' she yelled, wielding the stick threateningly.

It was then that she noticed that Annie had cowed down and was holding her hands up defensively.

'Goodness, I'm sorry, Annie, I didn't mean to startle you.'

Annie, trembling, stood straight and brushed herself down.

Clara thought that Annie's reaction was unusual, and it suddenly dawned on her that the girl may have been beaten in the past.

'Did your mother hit you with a stick?' she asked directly.

Annie's face paled.

'Oh, my poor girl. I promise, no one here will ever hit you. Mr Gaston and Basil might seem a tad grumpy, but their barks are worse than their bites. You're safe here, Annie.'

'She's not my mother.'

'The lady who raised you?'

'Yeah. Florence, the 'orrid cow. A couple of days before I arrived here, Jimmy told me that she's not my mum.'

'Oh, I see. Did she adopt you?'

'I dunno. Jimmy reckons me dad brought me home one day and that was that. No wonder my *mum* never liked me. I reckon she hates my guts.'

Clara swallowed hard. She didn't know what to say. Searching for words that she couldn't find, she instead suggested, 'Shall we have a look in the library now? It's quite nippy out here.'

Inside, Annie selected *The Secret Garden* by Frances Hodgson Burnett.

'A good choice,' Clara commended.

When Annie retired to the bedroom to read the book, Clara fought to hold back tears. She adored children and felt sick at the idea of that vile woman beating little Annie. Children were supposed to be loved, nourished and educated. Florence had failed on all three points and had acted in the most depraved way possible.

Drying her face with a handkerchief, Clara's mind turned. War hadn't yet been declared, but she was already dreading the day that she'd have to send Annie back to London.

17

On Sunday morning when Penny opened her eyes, she beamed with joy. Carefully sliding her hand under the pillow, she pulled out the book that Clara had allowed her to read. Penny only had a few pages left and was eager to know how the story panned out, yet she didn't want the book to end.

Pulling back the wool blankets, she threw her legs over the edge of the bed.

'Where are you going?' Katy asked quietly.

'To sit downstairs so that I can read in the light. It's too dark up here.'

'You're as mad as a box of frogs.'

'You don't know what you're missing,' Penny swooned, holding the book to her chest.

As she crept down the stairs, voices drifted from the kitchen. Penny recognised Clara's soft tones.

'I can't begin to imagine what the girl has been through.'

'It's none of our business,' Mr Gaston remarked.

'It is so. I am Annie's guardian while she's here, so that makes it my business.'

'Just don't get too attached to the girl.'

'Why not?'

'She'll be damaged and you've enough on your plate without trying to fix a broken girl.'

'But that's just it, Will. She's not broken. She should be, but she isn't. It proves that Annie has a strong spirit.'

'Even so, whether the girl is broken or not, she'll still have to return to London, and none of us knows when that might be. I know you, Clara. If you start getting too involved with her, you'll struggle to send her back to Mrs Black.'

'It's too late, Will, I'm already involved. And I don't know how I'm going to fight it, but come what may, Annie will never return to that cruel woman.'

Penny padded quickly back up the stairs and into the bedroom.

'Change your mind?' Katy asked.

'Yeah, it's blinkin' freezing.'

'Go back to sleep, it's still dark outside.'

Penny closed her eyes, but the conversation she'd just overheard kept replaying through her mind. *Damaged. Broken.* They were the words that Mr Gaston had used. Clara had disputed what he'd said, but had the man been right? After all here she was, at sixteen, pretending to be a child. She was a fraud, and was she taking advantage of Clara's compassion and generosity? Isn't that what a damaged and broken person would do? Lie ... be someone they're not for their own gain?

'Stop fidgeting,' Katy moaned.

A tear fell from Penny's eye and soaked into the pillow. Maybe she should own up and tell Clara the truth about who she really was. She knew it would be the right thing to do, but it was a risk, and Penny worried she might lose her new-found freedom. *I can't go back to Florrie*, she thought, her head spinning.

The notion of living back there made Penny's heart pound hard with fear. But she couldn't continue to live a lie either.

Penny was quiet all morning, wrapped in her conflicting thoughts. When Katy had asked her what was wrong, Penny had fibbed and said she felt a little off colour. She'd said the same to Clara too but had now decided that enough lies had been told. It was time to come clean. Only a damaged and broken person would continue to live with the identity of her dead baby sister.

Sitting around the kitchen table, Penny glanced at the others. Katy was shelling peas while Rosemary scraped potatoes. Clara was filling pans of salted water ready to be heated on top of the stove. She'd promised them a big Sunday dinner with a cut of quality beef and all the trimmings to go with it, but as was expected on the farm, everyone had to muck in. And while Mr Gaston and Will tended to the cows, the ladies prepared the food.

Penny stared at the clock sitting on a shelf in a large Welsh dresser that dominated one side of the kitchen. As the hands approached eleven-fifteen, she drew in a long breath, ready to make her confession. But doubts crept in. She didn't want this homely life to come to an end. Though no matter what the outcome of her revelation, Penny knew she could never return to Florence. She planned on carving out a life for herself away from the woman's suffocating grasp. It wouldn't be easy. She had no idea how she'd support herself. And Penny wasn't even sure what she should do first: find a home or find a job? Either way, she had no clue of where to start! But Penny would worry about that later. First, she had to muster all the nerve she had and tell Clara the truth. It was the least that the good woman deserved.

Pulling her chewed-down thumbnail from her mouth, Penny's pulse raced. 'Erm... there's, erm... there's something I need to—'

The kitchen door burst open, bringing with it a waft of cool, fresh air. Basil stood, holding on to the frame, panting to catch his breath.

'We're at war!' he announced.

'What?' Clara asked.

'I was in the barn with Dad's wireless. The prime minister, Chamberlain, he just made an announcement. Britain has declared war on Germany!'

Penny saw Clara's knuckles turn white as she gripped the towel that she was holding.

'But it's Sunday,' the woman said, inanely.

'What difference does that make?' Basil asked.

'I – I don't know. It just doesn't seem right. Does your father know?'

'No, I don't think so,' Basil answered.

'Fetch him, Son, and make haste. We should all be together at a time like this.'

Basil ran off, leaving the door wide open.

'What do we do, Mum?' Rosemary asked. Her hazel eyes, the same colour as her father's and Basil's, were wide with fear.

The blood had drained from Clara's face, but the woman masked her obvious fear with a smile. 'I don't know what to do, but your father will. Just... just sit tight and carry on scraping the potatoes. There's a good girl.'

Clara pulled out a seat at the table and lowered herself onto it. Penny could see that the woman was shaking and watched as Clara hid her trembling hands under the table. They all sat in silence, quiet with their own thoughts and fears.

Mr Gaston eventually thudded into the kitchen. 'So, it's happened then. What do you need me back here for?' he asked his wife.

'We're at war, Will. I don't know what to do.'

'Do as you're doing, woman. We all knew it was only a matter of time. I don't know why you're looking so surprised.'

'I didn't want to believe that it would ever really happen.'

'There's nothing we can do about it. The hens will still lay, and the cows will still need milking… and I'm looking forward to a nice bit of roast beef.'

Clara sighed and pursed her lips. A new look of determination set on her face. 'You're right, I'm making a fuss about nothing,' she said as she rose from the seat and smoothed down her apron. 'I'm just glad that Basil isn't old enough to be a soldier and I'm thankful that we're all together.'

Penny liked Mr Gaston's no-nonsense approach. You knew where you stood with the man. His straight-talking had eased the tension.

'Will the Nazis bomb Britain now, Dad?' Rosemary asked.

'I couldn't say, but it makes no odds what Adolf sends our way, because like I explained, I've still got work to do which isn't getting done while I'm stood here talking to you.'

With that Mr Gaston turned to leave and grabbed Basil by the arm. 'Stay here,' he ordered, his voice hushed. 'Look after them, Son.'

Penny met Basil's deep-set eyes. She couldn't read them like she could read Clara's, but she was sure that he was just as afraid as she was. No one knew what was coming or how this war would end, but Penny decided that now wasn't the right time to own up to her deception.

18

On Monday morning, Clara gave each of the girls a cannister with snacks and a raw potato.

Penny looked curiously at her spud, and asked, 'What's this for?'

Rosemary explained. 'My school doesn't have a proper kitchen, so we all take in a potato and the dinner lady bakes them in the oven for our lunch.'

Clara began ushering them out of the front door, 'Hurry, you don't want to be late on your first day. Rosemary normally walks to school alone, but I shall be coming with you today. Please ensure you come home together.'

Penny felt a bag of nerves. She was looking forward to her first day at school, but a niggling voice in her head kept reminding her that she was a damaged, broken phoney. And at sixteen, she had no right to be in a classroom!

Clara hurried the girls along the winding country lane, and she offered some thoughtful words to Penny. 'You may feel a little overwhelmed today, Annie, which is perfectly normal. But try not to worry. Rosemary will look after you.'

Penny gulped. She was on the verge of telling Clara

everything. A lump of raw emotion caught in her throat. 'I shouldn't be here,' she croaked, fighting back the urge to cry.

'You've every right to a proper education.'

Penny looked down at the gravel track, and at her scuffed shoes that pinched her toes. As she placed one foot in front of the other, she found the courage to admit the truth. 'No, you don't understand… I'm not who I say I am.'

As Penny spoke, a truck tooted its horn several times. To allow the truck to pass, Clara and the girls were forced to push themselves against the bushes that lined the narrow lane. The truck roared past, but its horn and rattling engine had drowned out Penny's words.

'I've never seen a motor vehicle along this lane. If this is a sign of the times and of things to come, then you'll have to take the wider road to the village.'

'Aw, Mum, that's the long way round. It will take us twice as long to get to school,' Rosemary moaned.

'Then you will have to leave twice as early. I'm sorry, Rosemary, but I don't want you walking this lane any longer. It's too dangerous.'

They turned a corner and, on the edge of a small village, the school building loomed ahead. Penny was lagging a small way behind and Katy paused, waiting for Penny to catch up.

'Is something bothering you?' Katy asked, her face etched with concern.

Penny nodded. 'I feel awful about lying to Clara. She's such a nice person. She deserves to know the truth.'

Katy's eyes widened. 'No, you can't tell her! You mustn't!'

'I have to, Katy.'

'But if she knows the truth, she might send us back to Battersea!'

'There's no need for her to send you back. It's me who isn't who I say I am.'

'But I've lied for you. She won't let me stay if she can't trust me. Please, Penny, don't tell her. I – I can't go back to my mum's house. I won't!'

Penny saw that Katy's eyes were wide with fear and filling with tears. 'What's wrong? Why can't you go home?' she asked, perplexed.

Katy bit on her lip, her brow furrowed.

'What is it, Katy?' Penny pushed.

'Do you remember years ago when we were in the park, and I told you about my dad getting into bed with me?'

Penny wracked her brains. 'Yes, I think so.'

'He still does… and… and… he hurts me.'

'What do you mean?'

'I'm not supposed to tell anyone. He says he loves me and it's what dads do to their girls. But I hate it, Penny! I hate it!'

Penny stood stunned, unsure of what to say. Katy didn't need to explain the sordid details. Penny understood enough about the birds and the bees to know what Mr Darwin was doing to Katy. Her heart broke for her friend. Penny had never had a dad, so she couldn't say for sure if all dads did it to their girls, but she was sure that Mr Gaston never climbed into bed with Rosemary, and she instinctively knew that it was wrong.

Clara's voice broke into her thoughts.

'Come on, girls, keep up.'

'Please don't tell anyone,' Katy whispered urgently.

'I won't, I promise.'

Rosemary skipped towards them. 'Hurry up,' she smiled. 'And don't look so scared. You're going to love my school.'

Until this moment, Penny hadn't considered the consequences that the truth might have on Katy. After all, her friend had gone along with the lie. They had both deceived Clara, and Penny feared that the woman would be mortified. Penny had never understood why Katy was so keen to get away from home. After all, Mrs Darwin was so sweet and caring. But her friend had never seemed happier than she'd been these past few days and now it all made sense. It occurred to Penny that admitting she wasn't twelve-year-old Annie Black could ruin Katy's new life and shatter her friend's happiness, sending her back to the clutches of her disgusting father. Penny wasn't prepared to do that to the best pal she'd ever had. So for now, to protect Katy, she thought that maybe it was best to keep quiet.

That night, Clara lay in bed with a smile on her face. She felt Will drape his arm across her stomach and nuzzle her neck.

'Are you all right, my darling?' he asked.

'Yes, why wouldn't I be?'

'I know what a little worrier you are, and this war, well, the reality of it must have sunk into your head by now.'

'It's awful, Will, I can't lie. I keep thinking about the young men who will lose their lives, and then I feel terrible for being grateful that I won't be mourning Basil's death. Life is so unfair. Mothers in Britain and Germany will be burying their boys. Is it wrong that I'm thankful that my family won't have to make such a sacrifice?'

'You can't think like that.'

'I try not to, and most of the time I'm too busy to think. The girls are a good distraction. They help to keep me sane.'

'Ha, they drive me mad,' Will chortled. 'They never stop talking.'

'I know, the house is much louder than it used to be, but it's nice to hear laughter in such dreadful times. I found it ever so quiet today when they were all at school and I missed them.'

'Each to his own. I'm glad to be out on the farm all day and away from them. But you're right, it is nice to see Rosemary so happy.'

'She loves having them here.'

'Well, I hope she doesn't get too used to it. I reckon the war will be over by Christmas and then you'll have to send the girls back to where they came from.'

'Possibly,' Clara said.

Will pushed himself up on to his haunches. His face was serious in the darkness as he looked down at Clara. 'You can't keep them. You do realise that they will have to leave at some point, don't you?'

'Maybe,' Clara answered, her mind turning. 'I'm sure Katy will want to go back home to her mum, but I don't think that Annie will, and the woman isn't even Annie's real mother!'

'Makes no odds, the law is the law.'

Clara sighed heavily and turned her face away. She felt Will's large and calloused hand on her cheek as he tenderly pulled her face back to him.

'I know you've always wanted a big brood,' he said, tenderly, 'but it didn't happen for us. We've got two great kids; you can't add to our lot by taking a child who doesn't belong to us.'

Clara sighed again. She knew she should be grateful for what she already had. 'You're right, I've always wanted at least six children, but Basil and Rosemary are wonderful. I couldn't wish for better children, and I'm blessed to have them.'

Will's hand ran up the inside of her thigh and his eyes darkened with lust. 'We could keep trying for another,' he said huskily.

Clara was happy to try though she knew it would never happen. One of them wasn't very fertile and she assumed it must be her husband, who was an only child. She'd come from a family of twelve children, seven who'd survived childhood.

As Will climbed on top of her, Clara could feel her passion rising, and all thoughts of war and of keeping Annie on the farm left her mind.

'I love you, Clara,' Will whispered.

As she writhed her hips beneath him, Clara raised her arms above her head and gripped the iron headboard to keep it from banging against the wall. 'I love you too,' she gasped, giving way to bliss. And though she doubted they were making a baby, Clara held on to the hope that one day, before her body became too old, another child would grow in her womb.

19

'Are you looking forward to school again?' Clara asked at the breakfast table.

Penny had accepted that she'd have to continue to live a lie for Katy's sake, so she'd made the most of being at school and had enjoyed every minute. 'I learned about the Kings and Queens of Britain, and about gas, liquids and solids,' she said with enthusiasm.

'When I spoke to your teacher yesterday, Miss Cottee said that although you are a little behind in most subjects, she feels confident that you will soon catch up. Jimmy taught you well.'

'Yeah, I reckon he did. Miss Cottee put a map of the world on the board, and I knew nearly all the countries.'

'Annie knew more than me,' Rosemary confirmed. 'And she knew that elephants live in Africa *and* India. I thought they only lived in India.'

'Jimmy had a small globe and he used to tell me about the different countries and the animals that live there,' Penny explained, proudly. She missed her brother and wished she knew where he was and how to write to him.

Clara suddenly looked concerned and placed her hand on

Rosemary's forehead. 'Are you feeling all right?' she asked. 'You're quite warm and you don't look well.'

'I feel sick,' Rosemary groaned. 'And my head hurts.'

'Right, back to bed for you, young lady.'

'No, Mum, please, I want to go to school.'

'Not in that state. Rest today and I'm sure you'll feel better tomorrow. Go on, off you go. I'll bring you some toast and jam and a cup of warm milk before I walk Annie and Katy to school.'

'See you later,' Rosemary said miserably to the girls as she trudged away with slumped shoulders.

Penny could see the worry on Clara's drawn face. The woman was an excellent mother who deeply loved her children, and it clearly upset Clara to see her daughter unwell. Florence had never cared when Penny had been poorly. It had been Jimmy who'd secretly looked after her. She recalled having an itchy rash all over her body. Large, red, swollen pimples had appeared, and her head had thumped with pain. Florence had still made her clean the house and do the washing, smacking a stick across her hands every time she'd scratched the irritating spots. Jimmy had sneaked a bottle of calamine lotion to her and dabbed it on the sore marks. He'd also slipped her cups of warm tea with sugar and had told her wonderful stories about the adventures of Peter Pan and the Lost Boys. Any thoughts of Florence always left a bitter taste in Penny's mouth, and she scowled.

Katy asked, 'Did you send my postcard to my mum?'

'Yes, Katy I did. I'm sure you'll be receiving a letter from her soon.'

Penny lowered her head and hoped Clara wouldn't press

the issue of her not writing home to Florence. Unfortunately, the woman did.

'I understand that there are problems for you at home, Annie, but you really must write to let Florence know where you are.'

'No, I can't,' Penny protested.

'I know you don't want to, but I will have to insist that you do.'

Penny's head shot up and she looked at Clara with imploring eyes. 'Please, please don't make me do it. I don't want her to know where I am.'

'She has a right to know.'

'No, no, please... she must *never* know.'

'Why not?'

When Penny didn't answer, Clara asked again, this time her voice firmer. 'Why don't you want her to know where you are, Annie?'

Penny remained tight lipped.

'Answer me,' Clara demanded.

Penny couldn't, but Katy burst out, 'Because Florrie will come here and then she will drag Annie back to Battersea with her!'

Penny glared at her friend.

'Is this true, Annie?' Clara asked.

Penny swallowed hard and nodded her head.

'Why would she drag you back home if she sent you away in the first place? That doesn't make any sense at all... unless... did you run away, Annie?'

Rubbing her clammy palms together nervously, Penny's heart felt as though it was going to beat out of her chest.

'Annie, tell me the truth. Did you run away from Florence?'

'Yes,' Penny finally answered with reluctance.

'How on earth did you manage to get billeted? I was under the impression that mothers had to register their children. What did you do, sneak on to the train with Katy or something?'

It was Katy who answered. 'My mum registered Annie because she knows how 'orrible Florrie is.'

'Did she, Annie? Did Mrs Darwin register you?'

'I ain't fibbing,' Katy insisted, sounding narked.

'I'm not suggesting that you are, I'd simply like to hear the truth from Annie. So, Mrs Darwin registered you, Annie?'

Penny nodded as her mind raced. Now would be the right time to reveal the fact that her name wasn't Annie and that she was sixteen, and not twelve. But she still feared that Clara would hate both her and Katy for their deceit. The woman had opened her home to them and had gone out of her way to make them feel welcome. If she knew that they had both lied, it would be a slap in the face for Clara to take.

Clara pulled out a seat opposite the girls, her face deadpan serious. 'Florence hasn't done right by you, Annie, and Mrs Darwin has been a witness to it. I can understand your reasons for wanting to be away from Florence, and I'm pleased that Mrs Darwin was able to help you. But listen to me carefully girls... give me your word that you will never tell anyone. I will keep your secret and so must you.'

'We promise,' Katy said. 'My mum said the same. I shouldn't have told you. You won't tell my mum that I said anything, will you, Clara? Only, Mum will go potty if she finds out.'

'Like I said, it will be our secret. Mr Gaston need never know, and neither do Rosemary or Basil.'

'Need to know what?' Basil asked. He'd walked into the kitchen and no one had noticed.

'None of your business,' Clara told him. 'Women's things.'

Basil didn't look convinced as he poured himself a cup of coffee.

'Anyway, what are you doing here? Shouldn't you be in the fields with your father?'

'Dad sent me back to get his wireless. He wants to keep up to date with the news. Where's Rosemary?'

'I've sent her back to bed; she's not feeling well.'

'She probably caught something off one of those,' Basil said contemptuously, indicating to the girls.

'Basil, that's enough!' Clara cautioned.

'I'm only speaking as I find. They're clean now because you made them have a good scrub, but you should have burned their rags.'

'I said, that's enough! Get out, and don't come back until you have a civil tongue in your mouth.'

Penny could feel herself cringing inside. Basil was suggesting that they were dirty. She supposed they were compared to Clara's standards. But hearing it said reminded her of the days when she'd been taunted by the other children in the street and called a *fleabag*, among other cruel names. Jimmy had stuck up for her and the bullying had eventually stopped. She wished Jimmy was here now. Her brother would put Basil in his place and wipe the smirk off the young man's face.

'I hope Basil hasn't upset you. He's ungrateful and doesn't realise how fortunate he is to have grown up on the farm. Sadly, Basil has no idea of the hardships that many families suffer. I shouldn't have to apologise for my son, I thought I'd raised him better than that. But I am very sorry.'

Katy laughed it off. 'He'd 'ave a right shock if he came to

see where me and Annie live. You could fit both our houses and the next-door neighbour's house into this one, and with room to spare! My mum always says that we ain't got much but we've got a roof over our heads, food in our bellies and hearts full of love. She reckons that's all you need in life, and anything more is wasteful.'

'Very wise words, Katy.'

Penny thought that Mrs Darwin's words were an excuse to accept poverty. 'I never want to feel hungry again,' she said, bitterly.

'Florrie never fed Annie properly,' Katy explained. 'Annie wasn't allowed round to my house very often, but when she was, my mum used to give her a dinner when she could, but we never had much either.'

'How awful for you,' Clara said, and spooned another serving of scrambled eggs onto Penny's plate. 'What about your fathers? You've never mentioned them.'

Katy clammed up and gazed down into her lap.

Penny quickly said, 'My dad left when I was very young. I don't remember much about him.'

'And yours, Katy?' Clara asked.

'He's a labourer,' Katy answered, tersely.

'Is he at home with your mother?'

Katy nodded. Penny tensed and saw her friend's eyes fill with tears.

'Oh dear, I'm sorry, Katy. I'm such a busybody and I should mind my own business. You must miss your dad very much.'

Sniffing back tears, Katy shook her head. 'I'm glad to be away from him,' she admitted.

'Oh, I see. Don't you get on with your dad?'

'No... I hate him! I hate, hate, hate him!' Katy screamed, pushing her chair back with such ferocity it toppled over. Katy fled from the room in a flood of tears, leaving Clara with her mouth hanging wide in shock.

'Goodness, what is all that about?' the woman mumbled.

'I'll see that she's all right,' Penny said, and hurried after Katy.

After searching for a few minutes, she found her friend huddled under a tree outside, her face streaked with tears and with a snotty nose.

'You need a hanky,' Penny said, softly.

'I miss me mum, but I don't want to go back to *him*, not ever!'

'It's all right, you don't have to, well, not for a while.'

'I wish he was dead.'

Clara came over. Wrapping her cardigan closely around her body, she folded her arms across her chest. 'Come back inside, Katy, it's chilly out here,' she urged.

Katy wiped her nose along the sleeve of her dress before standing up. 'Sorry,' she mumbled, avoiding eye contact with Clara.

Penny placed her arm across her friend's bony shoulders. She knew that Katy felt ashamed of what her dad did to her, and it was something that Katy had only recently admitted to. But she also knew that Clara was going to question Katy's outburst. 'Shall I tell her about your dad?' she whispered in Katy's ear.

Katy began to cry harder.

'It's all right,' Penny soothed. 'He can't get at you here,' she assured her, feeling hopeless.

Clara gently asked, 'Does your dad hit you, Katy?'

'No. He knocks me mum about, but he only hits me when I'm naughty. I'm never naughty, Clara, I swear. I'm not, am I, Annie?'

'You're not as naughty as me,' Penny smiled.

'So, what does your dad do that hurts you?'

Katy squeezed her eyes shut, as if trying to block out her heinous memories. 'I – I can't say,' she cried.

It was then that Penny saw a horrified look of recognition come over Clara's face. 'Come girls, inside,' she insisted, sounding flustered. 'Splash some cold water on your eyes, Katy, they look quite red and swollen. You don't want to go to school with swollen eyes, do you?'

In the warmth of the kitchen, Katy had stopped weeping now and went to the sink. Clara placed her hands on her hips and said in a strong voice, 'I think you are extremely brave young ladies.'

Penny could see that the woman was holding back her emotions and was on the verge of crying. It must have come as an awful shock for her to discover what Mr Darwin had been doing to young Katy.

'I'm so proud of you both,' Clara added, her voice breaking.

You wouldn't be proud of me if you knew the truth, Penny thought, guilt almost choking her. But after seeing Katy's outpouring of hate and fear and how much pain her friend was suffering, Penny was even more convinced that keeping her secret was the right thing to do. She couldn't risk Clara sending Katy back to live in Battersea. She just hoped that neither she nor Katy would slip up and let the cat out of the bag.

20

Nearly three months had passed, and there'd been no sign of Hitler's planes in the sky. People were calling the war a *phoney* war, and fears of bombs landing on civilians in cities had now abated.

Penny and Katy had settled in well to life on the farm. Even Mr Gaston cracked a smile at them now and again, though Basil was still stand-offish and often rude. His coldness didn't bother Penny. The love she felt for Clara and Rosemary far outweighed any bad feelings with Basil.

Skipping home from school, the girls fell into the kitchen in fits of laughter.

'What's so funny?' Clara asked, looking from one to the other, bemused.

'Katy needed the loo and couldn't wait until she got home, so she went behind a bush,' Rosemary chuckled.

'Katy, you didn't! That's not very ladylike.'

'Yeah, but you ain't heard the funny bit yet,' Penny giggled.

'Go on then, tell me, I'm all ears.'

Rosemary managed to contain her laughter and continued with the tale. 'Katy was, you know, doing her business, then all of a sudden we heard her screaming, and then she came running out from behind the bush with her knickers around her ankles. *A spider*, she screams, swatting at her face. *There's a spider on me.* Then, running in funny little steps because her knickers are still around her ankles, Katy tripped over and landed flat on her face in a pile of horse manure. You should have heard her, Mum, she swore really loudly, but I've never seen anything so funny in all my life.'

'I only said *flippin' 'ell*. That's not really a proper swear word, is it?' Katy added, looking alarmed.

'Oh, Katy, you'll need a bath and give me your clothes to wash. I wondered what that smell was.'

'She washed her hands and face in the stream,' Rosemary said, shuddering as she added, 'I put my hand in the water and it was freezing!'

'Well, a nice hot bath and a cup of warm milk will make you feel much better, Katy. And I suggest in future, you use the toilet at school before you leave.'

The girls looked at each other and started laughing again.

Clara smiled. 'Honestly, you three, you're inseparable and as thick as thieves.'

Linking their pinkie fingers together, Rosemary gushed, 'We pretend that we're sisters.'

'That's nice,' Clara beamed as she handed out biscuits.

Penny gratefully accepted the home-made biscuit, and as she thanked Clara, she noticed a peculiar look on the woman's face.

'Talking of sisters,' Clara said, 'you might be getting a new one soon... or a little brother.'

Penny's eyes widened and she gawped at Clara's belly.

'How?' Rosemary asked.

'I reckon your mum is having a baby,' Katy grinned.

'That's right, I am. But we won't get to meet your new brother or sister until the summer.'

While Rosemary and Katy squealed with delight and discussed whether they hoped for a boy or a girl, Penny stood, her eyes transfixed on Clara's slightly bulging stomach. She couldn't understand why Katy was so excited about the prospect of Clara having a baby. Didn't her friend understand the implications? She'd heard that babies were hard work and demanded a lot of attention. With a new one soon arriving, Clara would have her hands full, and it would be another mouth to feed. The woman might consider sending them back to Battersea!

'Calm down, girls,' Clara coaxed. She hadn't expected such a rapturous reception to her news. Will, of course, had been over the moon when she'd told him, but Basil had just shrugged and mumbled a comment about her being too old. She was delighted to see the girls so pleased.

'Can I name the baby when it's here?' Rosemary asked.

'We'll see,' Clara replied. Then pulling on her apron around her expanding waist, she remembered there was a letter in the pocket for Katy. 'This came for you. I think it's from your mother,' she said, handing the girl the envelope.

Katy ran to the table and sat down, ripping open the envelope with gusto. It was a pleasure to see the girl grinning happily as she read Mrs Darwin's words. But then Clara noticed that the colour drained from Katy's face and her eyebrows knitted together.

'No,' Katy cried, 'No, she can't! She can't do this!'

'What's wrong?' Clara asked, rushing to the girl's side.

'My mum... she said she's coming to take me home... she said *my dad* wants me back for Christmas.'

Clara scooped Katy into her arms and held her as she sobbed. She'd feared something like this would happen. Several evacuee children in the village had returned to their homes in London. Everyone seemed to think it was safe there now.

'Don't let her take me, Clara, please don't let her take me,' Katy begged.

Clara gulped. She didn't want to allow Katy to return to that horrendous man, but she knew that she was powerless to prevent it. 'I wish I could keep you here,' she said, trying not to cry in front of the girls. 'But if your parents are coming to collect you, I'm afraid there's nothing I can do to stop them.'

'Please... Don't let them in! Hide me. You can say that I ran away and you don't know where I am.'

'I can't do that, Katy. The police would be called to search for you.'

'I won't go... I want to stay here,' Katy sobbed.

'It's all right, Katy,' Penny soothed. 'I won't let you go back there. We'll run away together to a place where your dad will never find you.'

'No, you can't do that,' Clara said quickly, a cold feeling running through her veins. 'I'll write to Mrs Darwin. Perhaps I can persuade her to change her mind.'

'She won't,' Katy snapped. 'She always does *exactly* what my dad tells her to do. And if she doesn't, he gives her a good hiding.'

'Then I shall write to the authorities and explain that your home isn't a suitable or safe environment and I'll insist that you stay here.'

'Do you think they will listen to you?' Katy asked, hopefully.

'I'll make sure that they do!'

21

Nearly a week had passed since Katy had received the letter from her mother. Clara had written to Mrs Darwin and to the council and the police in Battersea, as well as her local Member of Parliament in Kent, yet she'd heard nothing back. Penny hoped that when they arrived home from school today, good news would be waiting for them.

A thin blanket of white snow covered the green meadows that flanked the lane from the school. The snow turned slushy under Penny's shoes, and she slipped a couple of times, almost losing her footing and toppling over. She was pleased when Rosemary linked her arm, and they supported each other in the treacherous conditions.

'Katy really doesn't seem herself,' Rosemary whispered.

'She's not. She's worried sick about having to go back home.'

'My mum's doing everything she can to keep Katy here.'

'I know,' Penny replied, grateful for Clara's help. She looked back to see Katy traipsing behind. 'Come on, slow coach,' she called to her friend.

They waited for Katy to catch up with them and then

Rosemary linked her arm through Katy's too, and announced, 'Sisters.'

'Sisters,' Penny parroted.

'It'll be all right, Katy. We'll stay together forever,' Rosemary assured her.

But Penny could see that her friend was tense with worry. The girl hadn't smiled or said more than a few words since receiving the letter from Mrs Darwin.

'I mean it, Katy,' Penny said through chattering teeth. 'If the worse comes to the worst and your mum still comes for you, then we'll run away together.'

'Would you really do that for me?'

'I said so, didn't I?'

'And I'll come with you,' Rosemary added.

'You can't,' Katy argued. 'You can't do that to your mum. She'd worry about you and be furious with me and Annie.'

'Katy's right,' Penny agreed.

'Then I'll hide you on the farm somewhere and I could sneak out food to you.'

'That's a good idea,' Katy said. 'At least me and Annie would be safe, and we wouldn't starve to death.'

Penny wasn't so sure and voiced her opinion. 'But we couldn't hide on the farm forever. And what about Basil? If he found us, he'd turn us in.'

Rosemary thought for a moment and suggested, 'I'd hide you where Basil wouldn't find you. He never goes down to the stream. There's that hollowed tree down there. We could make it nice and snug.'

'Oh, gawd, no, I couldn't hide in the tree,' Katy exclaimed, 'not with spiders!'

'And we wouldn't want you to get into trouble,' Penny said.

Hiding on the farm was out of the question. If Mrs Darwin was determined to move Katy back to London, then Penny knew that they'd have to run far, far away. But she hoped it wouldn't come to that. Instead, she prayed that there would be a letter waiting for them at the farmhouse. Surely someone must have listened to Clara's concerns. Though Penny had a terrible feeling that something awful was going to happen.

'It's so cold, I can't feel my toes,' Katy moaned.

'My nose has gone numb,' Rosemary giggled.

'There'll be a cup of something warm waiting for us,' Penny said, pulling on Rosemary's arm to hurry her towards home.

As they almost tumbled through the large gates and along the gravel drive, Penny spotted Basil coming out of the house. He stood for a moment and looked at them, a wicked leer on his face. Penny's heart began to thud. The feeling she'd had that something bad was going to happen intensified at the sight of Basil.

He turned to walk away, but Penny called his name.

'What are you doing?' Katy asked Penny, sounding anxious.

'I dunno... I think he's up to something.'

Penny gulped when Basil marched towards them, his eyes glaring at her.

'It looks like we're finally getting rid of at least one of you,' he sneered.

Penny frowned. 'What do you mean?' she asked.

'You'll find out,' he answered, and sauntered off.

'What's he on about?' Katy questioned. 'It's bad news, ain't it? My mum is coming for me. Oh, gawd, I knew this was going to happen!'

Rosemary yanked on Katy's arm. 'We don't know that for sure. Come on, let's go and ask my mum,' she urged.

Penny was first through the front door, with Katy and then Rosemary following. She rushed into the kitchen, looking for Clara. But as soon as she burst into the room, her stomach lurched when her eyes fell on Mrs Darwin sat at the kitchen table with a cup of tea in front of her.

Katy stood wide-eyed, her mouth agape. 'Mum,' she mumbled. 'You're not taking me back... Please, Mum, let me stay here.'

Mrs Darwin slowly rose to her feet. The woman looked pale and gaunt and had obviously tried to cover two black eyes with make-up. She nervously held her arms open towards her daughter. 'My goodness, you look a picture. I've missed you.'

Katy backed away, edging towards the door, and bumped into Rosemary who wrapped her arms protectively around her friend.

'I'm not going home, Mum. You can't make me.'

'Don't be difficult, Katy, and please don't make a scene in front of Mrs Gaston.'

Clara stepped forward, away from the stove, and tried to reason with the woman. 'I wish you would reconsider, Mrs Darwin. You can see for yourself that farm life suits Katy. She's thriving and she's doing well at school. Please allow her to stay, at least until we know for sure that the war has ended.'

Mrs Darwin appeared uncomfortable. 'I'm grateful for all you've done for my Katy, but her father has said that she's to come home for Christmas, so that's that.'

'But we're still at war with Germany,' Clara argued.

'You wouldn't think so. London is just as safe as here, which means it's time Katy comes back to where she belongs.'

'Mrs Darwin, please, I'm appealing to you as one mother to another. We both know that Katy is better off here.'

Mrs Darwin swallowed hard and turned to her daughter. 'Katy, get your things together. We don't want to miss the train.'

Tears rolled down Katy's anxious face and she trembled with fear.

'Mrs Darwin,' Clara said, firmly, 'I cannot allow you to take Katy back to an unsuitable environment. Need I make myself clearer?'

Mrs Darwin ignored Clara and brushed past Penny. Holding Katy by the shoulders, she looked into the girl's eyes. 'You *must* come home, Katy. Your father has said so. This isn't my doing. You understand, don't you?'

Katy's shoulders jerked up and down as her heart broke and she sobbed.

'If it was down to me, I'd let you stay here. I'm sorry, Katy, really I am.'

Clara rushed towards them. 'If you insist on taking Katy, then I will be forced to call for the police.'

Mrs Darwin looked over her shoulder at the woman. 'She's *my* daughter. The police won't stop me from taking her.'

Clara walked closely to the woman, whispering in her ear, 'I beg to differ. You will leave me no option other than speaking the truth and believe me, Mrs Darwin, I won't hesitate in telling the police exactly what Katy's father has been doing to her! I assume you know what I'm referring to?'

Mrs Darwin hung her head. 'I've had my suspicions, but my husband insists on me taking heavy doses of sleeping pills.

He ain't silly. I could never prove it but that's why I was so keen to have her billeted.'

'You knew?' Katy questioned, in disbelief, looking devastated.

'Not for sure. I hoped it wasn't true.'

Clara sounded hopeful, saying, 'Katy has found the courage to speak out about it. I think we should go to the police.'

'There's no point. It will be her word against her father's and the police won't believe her.'

'You don't know that,' Clara argued.

'Oh, but I do... the Old Bill didn't haul my husband down the nick when I told them what I thought he'd done to my girl. They didn't want to listen. It ain't none of their business, see.'

'You've been to the police?' Clara asked.

'Yeah, when he started going on at me to bring Katy home, I went down the station and all I got for me trouble was this from me husband,' Mrs Darwin said, pointing to her bruised eyes. 'It's a waste of time. The coppers don't want to hear the disgusting details. How do you think I got me nose broke, eh? Do you think I walked into a door? A copper told my husband that I'd been in and what I'd accused him of, so he knocked ten bells out of me.'

Penny was flabbergasted. She'd had no idea that Mrs Darwin had been aware of Katy's abuse and had reported her husband to the police. At least she'd tried to save Katy from the man, so why was she taking her back to him now?

'I'm sorry, I know it ain't ideal, but I've got to take Katy home and I need to leave or we'll miss the train.'

'Stay. Both of you, stay here,' Clara suggested, a ring of desperation in her tone.

'Eh?'

'Stay here with Katy. There's room for you here, Mrs Darwin. Neither of you have to go back to that man.'

'Huh, I wish it was as easy as that. But with respect, Mrs Gaston, you've no clue what you're talking about. I've got two young 'uns at home, see, boys. And if I don't bring Katy home, then I don't know if I'd ever see my boys again. I dread to think what harm might be done to them. I'm sorry, but I ain't got time for this. Katy, go and get your things together.'

'Perhaps I didn't make myself clear. I'm asking that you move in here with us and bring your boys too.'

'You made yourself clear, all right. But you don't know what my husband is capable of. He'd be on the next train out of London, and he'd go through this place like a dose of salts. I wouldn't bring that to your home, thank you all the same.'

'Please, Mrs Darwin, we can face him together, with Mr Gaston.'

'I know you mean well, but you're from a different world to me and mine. It's best you stay out of it and protect your own. My old man will kill me, and then what will happen to my boys, eh? Who'd look after them?'

Mrs Darwin began to try to usher Katy out of the door, but the girl held on firmly to the door frame.

'Collect your belongings or we'll have to leave without your stuff,' the woman urged.

Katy kept a grip on the frame. 'I'm not leaving,' she cried.

Her mother pulled on Katy's arm. 'Stop this, Katy, all you're doing is making it more difficult. Think about your brothers. Your father will do his nut if you don't come home with me, and you know as well as me that he'll take it out on Billy and Tim.'

'No,' Katy screamed, 'No!'

'Do you want to see them boys battered, Katy? Is that what you want, eh? Please, Katy. You only have to put up with him for a couple more years and then he'll leave you alone. Trust me, Katy, I know... My grandad did the same to me, but he lost interest when I got older.'

'I can't stand it, Mum... I can't...'

Clara butted in. 'I'm sorry, Mrs Darwin, but I cannot allow you to remove Katy from my home and take her back to that man!'

'I've no choice,' the woman answered sharply. 'Don't you think I've thought of everything... I even considered telling him that Katy had died. But he'd find out the truth and then what, eh? You don't know what he's like and I've got me boys to think about.'

Penny ran to her friend and threw her arms around her. With desperate eyes, she looked at Mrs Darwin. 'Please don't take her,' she begged. 'What he does to Katy, it ain't right!'

Mrs Darwin's face flamed red. 'You stay out of it, Penny,' she snapped. 'It's obvious that the pair have you have been mouthing off all about my private business. Have you told these good people everything, eh? Do they know that you're not *Annie* Black and you're sixteen, not a twelve-year-old?'

Penny gawped open-mouthed at Mrs Darwin.

'No, I thought not, you ain't told them, have you? Well, stay out of my business and I'll stay out of yours.' Then, angrier than she had been, Mrs Darwin took a firm grip of Katy. 'Come on, no more mucking about. We're going!'

Katy released her hold on the door frame and threw her arms around Penny. They stood clinging to each other, their tears mingling in the other's hair.

As Penny cried, she felt Mrs Darwin dragging Katy from her arms. They parted and Katy was pulled out of the front door.

Clara ran after them. 'This isn't right!' she screamed in desperation. 'You can't take her...' Falling to her knees on the doorstep, she held her apron to her face. 'Bring her back,' she screamed.

Penny felt helpless and stood in tears as she watched Katy walk away. Her friend threw a look over her shoulder and their eyes locked.

'I love you,' Penny mouthed.

She hadn't noticed that Mr Gaston had appeared until she saw him gather his wife from the floor and pull her into his muscular arms. As the man offered soothing words in his wife's ear, Katy disappeared out of sight. Penny's heart shattered, and as it did, the disturbing realisation hit her that Clara now knew her secret.

'One down, one to go, *Penny*,' Basil sneered as he barged past her, roughly knocking shoulders with her. 'You'll be next.'

22

Clara dried her eyes and sat at the kitchen table, welcoming the cup of tea that her husband had placed in her hands. She saw Rosemary hovering in the corner of the room. And though her daughter looked upset at the terrible scene she'd just witnessed, Clara couldn't deal with her now. 'Rosemary, go to your room.'

'What's going to happen to Katy?' the girl cried.

'I don't know. Please, do as I say and go to your room.'

'Why? What have I done wrong?'

'Nothing.'

'Go on, Rosemary, give your mum some time,' Will encouraged, gently.

Rosemary stomped off. Clara wanted to comfort her daughter, but she needed to be able to give the girl some reassurances about Katy's welfare, and as it stood, she couldn't do that.

Will pushed the kitchen door closed. 'I warned you not to get involved. Look at you, all worked up. You shouldn't be in this state, not in your condition,' he said, shaking his head.

'I'm all right, but I can't believe what has just happened.

How is a twelve-year-old girl allowed to live with a man that does God only knows what to her? Why hasn't the law stepped in? And the local authorities? Katy needs protecting, yet I've been ignored by all the people who should be protecting her!'

'It's out of our hands now.'

'What, that's it, is it? I'm supposed to get on with life and simply pretend I don't know that Katy's father will be in the girl's bed tonight. Can you live with that knowledge? I know I can't.'

Clara watched as Will ran his hand through his hair and paced back and forth. She knew his mind was turning. She hoped he would come to the only right decision.

Will eventually stopped pacing and leaned forward, placing the palms of his hands on the kitchen table. 'We've just sent a lamb to the slaughter. If no one else will save Katy from that pervert, then it's down to us.'

Clara sucked in a huge breath of relief. 'We've got to act fast, Will.'

'I know.'

'How... what do we do?'

'*We* don't do anything. You leave it to me.'

'But—'

'No buts, woman. I'll stop them before they get on the train.'

'You can't snatch Katy back. You'll be arrested for kidnapping!'

'So be it, and then I'll tell the police that if they had done their job properly in the first place, I wouldn't be having to do it for them!'

'Oh, Will, I'm not sure about this.'

'Have you got a better suggestion?'

Clara wrung her hands, thinking hard, and came to the same conclusion as her husband: the only way to protect Katy was to forcibly take the girl from her mother. And then another thought struck her. 'Where's Annie?' she asked, her eyes flitting frantically around the kitchen.

'I don't know.'

'Oh, Will, I've got to find her. She was so upset, and she'll think that she's in trouble.'

'Why would she think she's in trouble?' Will asked, perplexed.

'It's a long story, I'll explain later. But first I must find her.'

'No, you stay where you are. I'll go and look for her.'

'But you'll miss the train!'

'One problem at a time. If I miss the train, then I'll catch the next one to London. Even if I have to kick down Mr Darwin's door and barge through his house, you can rest assured that Katy will be coming home with me. Where do you think that Annie might have got to?'

'I've no idea, Will, but when you find her, please make sure she knows that she's not in any trouble with me.'

Basil ambled in, and Clara was disappointed to see the smug look on her son's face.

'Good riddance to them,' he said as he poured himself a cup of coffee.

Clara looked at her husband, but when Will didn't say anything to the lad, she barked at their son. 'Out of my kitchen. Now!'

'What have I done?'

'You may not have liked the girls living with us, but there's no need to be unkind. I'm ashamed of how you've treated those young ladies, ashamed and disgusted.'

'Those *young ladies* have spent months lying to you. They're the ones you should be disgusted with.'

'You heard your mother,' Will growled. 'Get out. Go and make yourself useful in the barn and pile the hay bales. I want them off the ground before they rot.'

Basil tutted before sloping off.

'What did he mean about the girls lying?' Will asked.

'I told you, I'll explain later. Please, find Annie and then see about saving Katy.'

Penny pulled her knees tightly to her chest and wrapped her arms around her legs. She'd run from the house in a panic and unsure of where to go, she'd hidden behind some bales of hay in the barn. *What a mess*, she thought. Mrs Darwin had not only ruined Katy's happy new life, but she'd spoiled Penny's too. Silent tears slipped down her cold cheeks. If she didn't get away from the farm soon, Penny imagined that Clara would be sending her back to London behind Katy!

Her ears pricked when she heard the barn door open wider, and she prayed she wouldn't be found before she had a chance to escape.

Hardly daring to breathe, Penny slowly climbed onto her knees and bravely sneaked a peek, poking her head just above the height of the bale. It was Basil, and he was forking hay up onto a low loft. Ducking back down, she hunkered lower. *Please go*, she thought, *please don't find me.*

Penny stayed as still as she could. Five minutes passed, maybe ten. Basil continued working quietly, getting ever closer to her hiding place. Fifteen minutes, perhaps twenty.

Mr Gaston's voice reached her ears.

'Have you seen Annie?' the man asked.

'Yes, she's behind those three bales over there,' Basil answered.

'For Christ's sake, Son, why didn't you tell me she was in here. I've been searching all over for her.'

'I didn't know you were looking for her... and her name is Penny, not Annie.'

'What are you on about?'

'Ask her.'

Penny's mind whirled. She knew there was no point in trying to hide any longer. Yet she couldn't seem to make her legs work and stand up on them.

'Annie,' Mr Gaston called. 'It's all right. Mrs Gaston said that you're not in any trouble.'

Penny chewed on her thumbnail.

'I told you, she's not called Annie,' Basil said. 'Her name is Penny.'

'Makes no odds. Whatever your name is, come home, pet. Mrs Gaston is worried about you. Out you come, there's a good girl.'

'She's not a girl, Dad, she's older than me.'

Mr Gaston lowered his voice to a low growl, but Penny could still hear him.

'Basil, I don't know what you're talking about, but will you please shut up. You're not helping, Son.'

Then louder again, he called, 'Come out, don't be scared. I just want to take you back to the house.'

Penny didn't feel that she could face Clara and she certainly couldn't face Mr Gaston. She regretted living her lie and wished she'd told the truth months ago.

She gasped when the highest bale was lifted away. Looking up, she saw Mr Gaston peering down at her. Her eyes were wet with tears. She wiped the back of her hand across her snotty nose.

'You must be freezing. Are you coming indoors for a hot drink?' the man asked, his voice softer than usual.

Penny nodded and tried to stand up. She felt dizzy and grabbed onto a bale of hay to steady her weak legs.

'It's all right, lean on me,' Mr Gaston offered, holding out his massive hand.

Penny couldn't meet his sympathetic gaze. She'd been outed as a liar and had never felt so ashamed.

'I'm all right, I can manage, thank you,' she sniffed, refusing the man's help.

As she came out from behind the bales, she saw Basil standing there, leaning on his pitchfork and smirking.

'I knew you weren't a kid,' he said, 'but you did a good job of convincing my mum and dad.'

'Basil,' Mr Gaston cautioned.

'She's taken advantage of Mum, of all of us. *Penny* is nothing but a dirty liar!'

'I'm warning you, Son. You've said enough.'

Penny tried to ignore Basil as she walked past him, but she could feel his accusing eyes boring into her. And to make matters worse, she had no defence. Everything that Basil said was correct, which made Penny feel even more terrible than she already did.

As she walked from the barn and towards the house with Mr Gaston by her side, she found the courage to speak to the big man.

'I'm sorry for everything.'

'I don't know what you've done or why, and I don't care. You can talk to Mrs Gaston.'

'I – I can't. I don't want her to hate me, and she will.'

'Clara doesn't have a bone in her body that knows how to hate. Don't get me wrong, she can be a little firecracker when she's upset, but she's not upset with you. She just wants you home, safe and sound.'

It's not home, Penny thought, not her home. She was only a guest in the Gaston's home, and, as everyone now knew, she was a guest who was there under false pretences.

23

'Where's Annie? Or whatever her name is?' Will asked when he came into the kitchen half an hour later.

'I sent her to her room with Rosemary. We had a good talk, and all is now as it should be.'

'Why the hell did she lie to us?'

Clara sighed as she buttered bread. 'Desperate people do desperate things. And let's face it, she's barely more than a child and she's no more mature than Rosemary.'

'Well, if what she says about what her life was like is true, then it's no wonder that she's like a twelve-year-old.'

'It is true, Will. She couldn't have made up the terrible things that she disclosed to me.'

'If you say so, but I don't know if we can believe a word the girl says.'

'I think we can, and I believe it will be best to start again with a clean slate. We're going to put everything right. *Penny* won't be attending school, and I'm going to help her find a job in the village. Here,' Clara said, and handed her husband a package.

'What's this?' he asked.

'Sandwiches for your journey.'

'I don't need sandwiches, woman. Food will be the last thing on my mind.'

'I know, but it made me feel better making them. Oh, Will, my stomach is in knots.'

'Don't worry, it will all be fine.'

'You don't know that! I'm so worried that you'll be arrested, or Mr Darwin will hurt you.'

'Have you seen the size of my fists?' Will smiled, 'and look at these chunks of muscle,' he said, flexing his biceps. 'I won't resort to violence unless I'm left with no choice. And if it comes to that, I promise you, Mr Darwin won't know what's hit him.'

Clara wrapped her arms around her courageous husband. Though years of farm work had built his muscles and he was as strong as an ox, Clara knew that he wasn't a fighter.

'There's a late-night freight train that passes slowly through the station. I'll jump on it and be in London by sunrise, hopefully sooner.'

'Please take care, Will.'

'Always. Basil will be in for his supper soon. I've given the lad instructions that he's to look after you and the girls.'

'Just so long as he's nicer to Penny.'

'We've had words. He will be. Right, I'm off and I'll be back tomorrow. Don't fret.'

Clara waved her husband off, proud of him for doing what was needed to protect poor Katy, but she was also sick with worry. Will had only been to London once before when he was a child. Somehow, he had to find his way across the city, navigating the run-down labyrinth of streets and contending with any nasty characters that he might encounter. And then once he found Katy's house, Will would have to deal with Mr Darwin and from what Clara had heard, the man sounded wicked and evil.

As her husband trudged through the farm gates, Clara's anxiety got the better of her and she called his name, ready to beg him to cancel his trip. But Will didn't hear her and carried on his way. She supposed it was for the best. After all, there wasn't anyone else who was rushing to rescue Katy. *Please, God, keep him safe*, she prayed. *And keep Katy safe too.*

24

Florence stirred in her sleep. A noise from next door had disturbed her, but she didn't take much notice of it. They were always rowing next door: Berty Darwin whacking Gladys Darwin, the boys crying, doors slamming. It wasn't a harmonious house and Florence had grown accustomed to the sound of angry fights through the thin walls. Though something was different this time. She sat up in her bed and listened carefully to the unfamiliar voice that seemed to be coming from the front door.

'I'm not going to stand here and argue with you, Mrs Darwin. Either hand the girl over or I'm coming in.'

Florence threw back the bed covers and rushed to her bedroom window. Looking down, she saw a large man standing on Mrs Darwin's doorstep, and though she couldn't be sure, she thought the man had jarred her neighbour's door with his foot.

'I'll have the Old Bill on you,' Mrs Darwin shouted.

'That's a very good idea. I'd be happy to wait for them to arrive.'

Florence raised the sash window. 'What's going on down there?' she screeched. 'There's folk trying to sleep up here!'

'Sorry, Mrs Black, the gentleman 'ere is just leaving,' Mrs Darwin called back.

'I'm going nowhere,' he growled, 'not without Katy.'

Florence baulked. She hadn't known that Katy was home. Pulling on her dressing gown, she charged down the stairs and out of the front door. The man standing on her neighbour's step looked much bigger and wider than he had from her viewpoint out of the window. She wondered who he was, though she wasn't very bothered. It was far more important that she got to speak to Katy. Florence was convinced that the girl would know of Penny's whereabouts.

Marching along her short path and around to Mrs Darwin's house, Florence stood behind the angry man and spoke to Katy's mother.

'Is that right that Katy's home?' she asked.

The woman nodded.

'Is she awake? I'd like a word.'

'No, she's not. You can speak to her in the morning. In the meantime, you can both bugger off.'

Mrs Darwin couldn't close the door because the angry man still had his foot in the way.

'I'll give you one more opportunity to bring the girl to me,' he said in a deep voice.

Florence sensed danger and stepped back, folding her arms across her chest. She couldn't imagine why the man would want Katy.

Mrs Darwin tried in vain close the door again. The large man shoved it wider open and stepped into the house. He almost lifted Mrs Darwin off her feet as he moved her to one side.

'I won't do you any harm, but don't get in my way,' he warned.

The man thumped along the passageway and up the wooden staircase with Mrs Darwin giving chase and tugging on the back of his jacket.

'No,' she cried, 'you can't take her!'

Florence could see that her neighbour was powerless to stop the man. And as there was no sign of Mr Darwin, she hurried into the cold and damp house, quickly following them up the stairs.

'Oi,' Florence shouted, 'get out!'

The man pushed open the first door on the landing. In the dim moonlight that flooded the bedroom, Florence glimpsed the two boys huddled together and whimpering in Mrs Darwin's bed.

He pulled the door closed and then opened the second one.

Florence stretched her neck to see inside and what she saw shocked her to her core. Her hand flew over her mouth, and she gasped.

Katy was sat in bed, trembling from head to toe, tears rolling down her face. And beside her, under the bed-covers, Mr Darwin was sat, bare-chested and holding a knife to the terrified girl's neck.

'Get out or I'll slit her throat,' Mr Darwin threatened.

'Please, Berty, don't hurt her,' his wife pleaded.

'There's no need for any of this,' the big man said calmly. 'I just want to take Katy back to the farm to keep her safe. No one needs to get hurt.'

'You ain't having her, she's my girl. Now fuck off!'

'Put the knife down, Mr Darwin.'

'Who the fuck do you think you are, eh? Forcing your way into *my* house in the middle of the night to take *my* daughter. Get out!'

'I won't leave without her, Mr Darwin. Come on, be reasonable, man. You don't want to harm Katy. You'll end up in gaol or swinging by the neck. Stop this madness. Just give me the girl and that'll be an end to it.'

'And what if I don't give her to you, eh? What you gonna do about it?'

'The police didn't listen to your wife, but I'll make bloody well sure that they listen to me,' the man hissed. 'I'll stand testimony that I saw you in her bed and you'll be charged with incest. That's not a popular crime, Mr Darwin. You won't have an easy time behind bars.'

'You can't prove nothing.'

The big man turned to Florence. 'Fetch the police,' he demanded.

Florence was still stood in shock with her hand covering her mouth. With her feet rooted to the ground, her eyes moved from the horrific scene in Katy's bedroom to the big man filling the doorframe.

'I need you to fetch the police,' the man repeated.

Mrs Darwin turned to Florence, her eyes wild with fear. 'No,' she begged, 'please don't bring the police here. Berty will see sense, won't you?' she asked, looking back at her husband. 'We don't want the police to cart you off, Berty. Me and the boys need you here. Please, Berty, let Katy come to me.'

Florence found her voice, and she said, shakily, 'Trust me,

Mr Darwin, you don't want to be banged up. My husband spent years in prison, he reckons they're dreadful places, nearly as bad as what the workhouses were like.'

Mr Darwin, after a few moments, slowly lowered the knife away from his daughter's neck.

'Come here,' the big man told the girl with urgency, holding his arms open.

Katy scrambled out of the bed and fled into his embrace.

It didn't go unnoticed to Florence that the child was naked from the waist down. She glared at Mrs Darwin in disgust. Then, placing her hand on the big man's back, she quietly suggested, 'Bring her to my house, she'll need clothes.'

Hurrying down the stairs, Florence threw a look behind her and saw Mrs Darwin had fallen to the floor in a heap. The sound of the woman's sobs left Florence's heart cold. She felt no sympathy for her neighbour. Gladys Darwin must have been aware of what her husband had been doing to Katy. *Disgusting*, she thought, wrinkling her nose, *an utter disgrace!*

25

Penny couldn't sleep. Instead, she lay in bed listening for Mr Gaston to return. As the sun broke and a sliver of light came in through a chink in the heavy curtains, she rolled over in bed to the empty space where Katy should be.

'Don't worry, my dad will bring her back,' Rosemary assured her. Then climbing out of her bed, she snuck in beside Penny. 'Do I call you Annie or Penny?' she asked.

Penny smiled at her friend. 'Well, my name is Penny, so I suppose you should use it.'

'And you're really sixteen?'

'Yeah, I am.'

'But I'm taller than you.'

'I reckon I'm small 'cos I didn't get fed well.'

'You're getting fed well now. Do you think you might grow?'

'I doubt it.'

'I wish you were still coming to school with me.'

'Me an' all, but I'm looking forward to earning my own money. And your mum is right, no more lies. It's a fresh start.'

'I'm glad my mum is letting you stay here. Can we still be sisters?'

'Yes, of course we can, but now I'm your *big* sister which means you have to do as I say,' Penny smiled.

The bedroom door opened and Clara came in. 'I thought I heard voices,' she said. 'You're awake early.'

'We didn't get much sleep,' Rosemary explained.

'Hmm, me too. Come down for your breakfast.'

Penny couldn't meet Clara's eyes. The woman had said that she didn't harbour any bad feelings, but Penny felt awful about her deception.

Downstairs in the kitchen, as Penny pulled out a seat at the table, she didn't look at Basil or acknowledge him, but she guessed that his judgemental eyes would be glaring at her. She squirmed, feeling uncomfortable. She tried not to let him bother her. After all, he was only a fifteen-year-old lad, yet he had the arrogance of a condescending man twice his age.

They sat in silence and as Clara prepared breakfast. Penny kept glancing out of the window, hoping to see Mr Gaston coming down the path with Katy in tow.

'I know we're all thinking the same,' Clara said, pouring tea for them. 'But we won't talk about it. Let's get on with our day as normal and try not to worry about your dad and Katy. I'm sure they will be home shortly.'

'I don't have to go to school, do I? Can't I wait for Dad?'

'You're going to school, Rosemary, and I'm taking Annie, I mean, Penny, to the village to see about finding her a job.'

'Please can I stay home?' Rosemary asked.

Basil spoke up. 'No, you can't. You'll do as Mum tells you.'

'What's it got to do with you?' Rosemary snapped at her brother.

'Dad left me in charge, I'm the man of the house when he's away.'

'Thank you, Basil,' Clara smiled, looking admiringly at her son. 'And as you're in charge, perhaps you'd like to suggest some jobs that you think Penny may be good at?'

Penny tensed, expecting Basil to say something scathing. So, she was pleasantly surprised by his reply.

'Cleaning. She's been doing it her whole life.'

'I agree, but I should think that Penny might enjoy a role other than a domestic one. She's a fast learner and confident.'

'But cleaning is all I know,' Penny interjected.

'I think you'd find shop work more interesting,' Basil said, his tone considered, then guffawed as he added, 'as long as you can see over the top of the counter.'

'Oi, I'm not *that* small,' Penny smiled back at him.

'Yes, you are. I could fit you in my pocket.'

'Well, I might be small, but I can pack a powerful punch.'

'Maybe you should be a boxer then,' Basil laughed. 'But I'd best keep quiet, because I wouldn't like to be at the receiving end of one of your punches.'

Penny's eyes locked with Basil's and she felt herself blush.

'It's nice to see you two getting along,' Clara chirped. 'And I agree, Basil, I think Penny would find shop work far more interesting than cleaning.'

'I'd love to work in a shop, but I don't think anyone would employ me.'

'You leave that to me,' Clara assured her.

Though worried about Katy, the affable exchange with Basil across the breakfast table had given Penny a warm feeling inside. She'd seen another side to him, and he'd even looked different too. She hoped they might become friends, but in the meantime, she'd keep her guard up around him.

Clara's head pounded and her stomach twisted into griping knots. Her eyes caught the clock again. She didn't expect Will to be home quite yet, but she hoped he was at least on a train out of London and had Katy with him.

Plastering on a smile, she handed Rosemary her cannister for lunch. 'Concentrate on your schoolwork. When you return home later, I'm sure you will find everything as it should be.'

Kissing the girl on the cheek, Clara stood in the doorway and waved her off to school. She found herself lingering on the step, looking along the drive in the hope of seeing Will.

'It'll be all right, Mum.'

Clara turned to see her son standing behind her holding a cup of steaming coffee. He seemed to have matured overnight and she thought he was doing a smashing job in his father's role.

'You're a good son,' she said affectionately. 'And it was ever so nice to see you and Penny getting on better. Thank you for making the effort.'

Basil shrugged. 'It's clear I'm going to be stuck here with her.'

'Yes, you are, and Katy too I hope. They've had rotten lives, Basil. We can't begin to imagine what suffering they've been through. It costs us nothing to show some kindness.'

'I don't like that they lied to us, but maybe if I'd walked in their shoes, I might have done the same.'

'Why the sudden change of heart?' Clara asked, curiously.

Again, Basil shrugged. 'I don't know. Seeing Dad go after Katy like he did, it made me think. He's a good man and he always does the right thing. I want to be like him.'

Clara could feel tears welling in her eyes.

'Are you upset, Mum?' Basil asked, looking concerned.

'No, not at all. It's this baby,' Clara replied, rubbing her stomach. 'I can't seem to keep a check on my emotions... I'm overjoyed to hear you talk like that, Basil, truly overjoyed.'

'Well, as Dad would say, *there's work needs doing*. I'll see you later.'

Clara's heart swelled with love and pride as she watched her son traipse off to the fields. The boy had become a man, and a fine young man at that!

Back in the kitchen, she held a warm towel on her forehead in the hope that it would relieve the thumping ache that boomed inside her skull. She knew that once she saw Will and Katy, the headache would dissipate and her stomach would settle down. She'd had no appetite at breakfast and hadn't eaten a morsel. Now a wave of nausea washed over her and she felt the room begin to spin.

Reaching out for a chair at the table, Clara's vision blurred. She made a grab for the back of the seat but missed. Swooning, she could feel herself floating away as she fell to the floor with a thud.

Penny inspected her reflection in the mirror. She'd smoothed her hair behind her ears and secured it with a clip on each side. And after scrubbing her face for three minutes, she looked clean and her skin glowed. *But you're still ugly*, she thought, repulsed by the image that stared back at her. She wouldn't allow herself to believe that anyone in the village would employ her, especially to work in a shop. Penny had learned that it was best to keep her expectations low. That way, she'd never be disappointed. *You're an ugly cow, you're useless and a liar*, she said in her head, full of self-loathing. She had no faith in herself, but she believed in Clara, and reminded herself that the woman had said that she'd find Penny a job. It gave her hope, and a flutter of excitement danced in her stomach.

Wearing a smart dress that Clara had given her (and she had adjusted it to fit), her shoes polished and her coat freshly laundered, Penny pushed away all thoughts of Katy. She had to focus. As Clara had instructed, *they were to carry on with their day as normal*.

Coming down the stairs, Penny hoped that Clara would approve of her appearance and the effort she'd made. 'I'm ready,' she announced as she flounced into the kitchen.

Her eyes scanned the room, looking for Clara. And when she saw the woman's legs on the floor behind the table, her heart leapt into her mouth.

'Clara!' she called, hurrying to the woman's side.

Blood had pooled on the tiles beside Clara's head, oozing from a nasty looking gash on her temple.

Quickly grabbing a towel that hung over the stove, Penny held it to the wound. 'Clara... Clara... Can you hear me?'

Penny sighed with relief when the woman groaned, thankful that Clara was alive.

'It's all right, lie still,' Penny said, and whipped off her coat. Gently lifting Clara's head, she slid her coat beneath. 'There, rest on that,' she said, her heart racing as fast as her thoughts. She had no idea what to do, or how Clara had ended up bleeding on the kitchen floor. But after a quick glance around, she thought that the woman must have bashed her head on the corner of the table.

'I'll fetch Basil,' she said, 'he'll know what to do.' But Penny was scared at the sight of so much blood pouring from Clara's head and she didn't want to leave her alone on the floor. Pressing the towel firmly against the cut, Penny saw Clara's eyes flicker open.

'You've had an accident,' she explained. 'And you've cut your head.'

Clara looked confused.

'Here,' Penny said, and grabbed Clara's wrist. Lifting up the woman's arm, she placed Clara's hand over the towel. 'Don't try to move. Just lie where you are and hold this towel on your head. Can you do that, Clara?'

Clara batted Penny's hand away and moved her head from side to side, agitated.

'Please, Clara, keep still,' Penny urged, trying to calm her. 'You're bleeding. Hold this on the wound,' she said, and tried again to place Clara's hand over the towel. 'You must stay still. I'm going to get Basil.'

Clara's eyes closed, and she nodded weakly.

'I'll be as quick as I can. Don't move.'

Penny jumped to her feet and raced out of the house and towards the fields. 'Basil,' she yelled as loudly as she could, 'Basil!'

She saw him in an adjacent field and, thankfully, he must have heard her cries because now he was running towards her.

'What's wrong?' he asked.

Penny, trying to catch her breath, grabbed the arm of his coat. 'Your mum… she's had a fall… come, quickly!'

Basil didn't stop to ask any questions and took off towards the farmhouse. Penny ran and tried to keep up with him, but her short legs couldn't keep pace with his long strides. When she finally reached the house a while behind Basil, she flew into the kitchen, dreading what she might find.

Basil had managed to sit Clara on a seat and was cleaning his mother's wound with a fresh towel and a bowl of water. 'She's all right,' he assured Penny.

'Oh, thank gawd. I thought for a moment that she was a goner,' Penny cried, her legs feeling shaky.

'Sit down, you both look as though you could do with a cup of tea.'

'I'll put the kettle on,' Penny offered, still breathless.

'No, you won't. I will,' Basil affirmed.

Penny was grateful to take the weight off her unsteady legs. She quite liked this *new* Basil. He reminded her of Mr Gaston. No-nonsense, but a caring man.

'I'm sorry to have given you a fright,' Clara said.

'What happened? Did you trip?'

'Er, yes, I think I must have.'

Penny felt a draught on her back and realised that the kitchen door had opened. She swivelled around in her seat to see Mr Gaston and, mercifully, Katy standing beside him.

'What's going on?' the man asked as his eyes went from the bloodied bowl of water on the table to the towel soaked in crimson and then his wife's hair, which was caked in her blood.

'I had a fall,' Clara explained, 'but I'm fine. Penny and Basil looked after me.'

Mr Gaston marched to his wife's side and studied the cut on her head. 'You'll have a bump to show off,' he said.

Penny scraped back her seat and ran to Katy. She threw her arms around her friend, but Katy stood rigid, her arms straight and tight to her sides.

'I'm so glad you're back,' Penny gushed. 'Are you all right?'

Katy didn't respond.

'She's had a shock,' Mr Gaston said, his voice soft. 'I think you should take her up to bed to get some rest.'

Penny took her friend's hand and gently eased her out of the kitchen and up the stairs. In the bedroom, she helped Katy to get undressed and flinched when she noticed that her friend had large blue and purple bruises on the insides of her thighs. Penny didn't mention it, and Katy remained silent. Tucking Katy into bed, she sat beside her and gently stroked her friend's hair. Penny had never seen Katy so traumatised. She realised that whatever had happened in Battersea, it must have been horrendous. But she'd never ask Katy about it. Some things were best left unsaid.

'Stop fussing, the pair of you. I've told you, I'm fine,' Clara insisted.

'You look as white as a sheet,' Will said.

'Drink your tea,' Basil instructed.

'Haven't you both got work to do?' she asked.

'Yes, but the cows can wait,' Basil replied.

'I'm not going anywhere until I'm convinced that you're all right,' Will added.

Clara tutted. 'Honestly, it's nice to know you care, but you're like a couple of old mother hens. Leave me be, I've got Penny upstairs if I need anything.'

'Are you sure?' Will checked.

'Yes. Go and see to the cows before you drive me to distraction.'

'It's all right, Dad. I'll see to the cows, and you can stay with Mum.'

'Thanks, lad, but I think your mother would rather I was out from under her feet.'

'Yes, I would,' Clara said, firmly. Then lowering her voice to a whisper, she asked, 'What happened in London?'

'You don't want to know. It wasn't nice.'

'You're probably right, I don't *want* to know but I *need* to know. Katy looked troubled, Will, I need to be aware of what I'm dealing with.'

Will glanced at his son. 'Off you go then, lad,' he said.

Clara reached for Basil's hand. 'No, Will, let him stay for a while. Basil is second in command on our family ship. He has a right to know too.'

Will raised his eyebrows. 'If you say so. But I'm not sure that it's things he should hear about.'

'Basil isn't a boy, Will, he's a young man and he needs to know that there are wicked people in this world and what horrid things those people are capable of doing.'

As Will told them the details of the night's events, Clara openly cried. 'That poor child,' she sniffed. 'But I'm grateful for small mercies. At least neither of you were seriously hurt. It could have been so much worse.' Her gaze went from her husband to her son, and she saw that Basil looked deathly pale. 'Are you all right?' she asked.

Basil nodded. 'I can't find the words. But I know I should have been nicer to the girls.'

'Yes, you should have been. But what's done is done. You can make it up to them.'

'I'll see to the cows,' Basil said solemnly, and walked away.

'I hope that wasn't too much for him to hear,' Clara whispered.

'It won't do him any harm. Like you said, he's a young man now and he's had a sheltered life. It's better he has some understanding of the darker side of life. We can't keep him wrapped up in cotton wool forever.'

Clara agreed but was distracted by the tugging sensation in her womb. 'Oh no,' she cried in panic, as the seat beneath her began to feel damp.

'What? What's wrong?' Will asked.

A sharp, cramping pain ripped through Clara's lower belly. It felt similar to the uncomfortable aches she had during her monthlies, only this pain was far more intense. 'Argh,' she cried, leaning forwards and wrapping her arms around her painful stomach. She knew what was happening. She'd seen two of her sisters suffer miscarriages.

'Oh, Will,' she sobbed, grief already filling her heart for the child she so desperately wanted. 'I... I think I'm losing the baby.'

26

It had been over two weeks since Mr Gaston had turned up at Mrs Darwin's house and taken Katy away. Florence hadn't seen the woman since, but today, on Christmas morning, she suspected that Mrs Darwin would knock on the door with a small Christmas cake. Every year for as long as Florence could remember, she would exchange niceties with her neighbour on Christmas morning. Mrs Darwin always brought a heavy fruit cake and Florence would offer a tray of suet mince pies.

Florence couldn't wait to see the woman, and she drummed her fingers impatiently on the kitchen table as she stared at the mince pies. *Some Christmas this is going to be*, she thought, missing Jimmy. The mince pies were all that was festive in Florence's home, and she wasn't looking forward to eating her Christmas dinner alone.

Hearing a quiet knock, Florence hurried along the passageway and forced a smile as she opened the front door. 'Merry Christmas,' she boomed.

Mrs Darwin looked as nervous as always. 'And to you,' the woman said, holding the cake aloft.

'Come in,' Florence offered, opening the door wider. 'Go through to the kitchen. You've got extra mince pies this year. There's no point in me keeping a load seeing as there's only me who will be eating them.'

In the kitchen, Florence gestured for Mrs Darwin to take a seat. 'Can you stop for a cuppa?' she asked, trying to sound as friendly as possible.

'Erm, no, sorry, not really. The boys are over-excited, I don't want to leave them for too long with their father.'

'Not to worry. You'll have a quick mince pie with me before you leave though, won't you?'

'Yeah, why not,' Mrs Darwin agreed.

Florence placed a pie on her prettiest china plate and handed it to her neighbour. 'I wish my Jimmy could come home for Christmas, but he's doing his bit in France,' she sighed.

'You must be very proud of him.'

'I am, but it's lonely without him, especially at this time of year.'

'I'd invite you round to mine, but you know how Berty can be.'

'Don't I just,' Florence replied, her lips set in a grim line.

'It's an odd Christmas this year for everyone. There's no midnight mass services being held on account of the blackouts. And there won't be a service at Westminster Abbey as most of the choirboys have been evacuated. Not that I'm religious. God's never done anything for me, and I don't have much to thank him for.'

As Mrs Darwin prattled on, Florence walked across the small room and closed the door. Leaning her back against it, she now had the woman trapped in her kitchen. Glaring at Mrs Darwin, she demanded, 'So, where is Penny?'

'I – I – I don't know,' Mrs Darwin answered, looking frightened.

'Don't lie to me. I know Penny is with Katy. That fella, Mr Gaston, the one who took your girl, I couldn't get anything out of him, but I knew he was trying to pull the wool over my eyes. So, I'll ask you again, where is Penny?'

'Honestly, Mrs Black, I swear I've no idea.'

Florence pulled out a writing pad and a pencil from the pocket of her apron. She marched over to the table and slammed the items down. Pushing the pad to Mrs Darwin, she threatened, 'Either you write down where Penny is, or I'll start gossiping to the old cronies on this street. And boy, oh boy, I've got plenty I can gossip about.'

'Like what?' Mrs Darwin asked, nervously.

'Like the fact that your old man took your daughter to his bed and you allowed it to happen. Cor, the old cronies would have a field day with that, and your name would be mud round here.'

'Please, Mrs Black, you wouldn't say anything, would you?'

'Not if you write down the address of where Penny is staying. And don't bother to deny anything, I can see straight through you.'

Mrs Darwin picked up the pencil with a trembling hand and scribbled down the address. 'Penny is sixteen. You won't be able to force her to come home, so why do you need to know where she is?'

'Mind your own,' Florence snapped. She knew she couldn't make Penny come home against the girl's will, and she didn't particularly want her back. But money was tight since Mr

Peck had said that he wouldn't need to rent her shed any longer. And Florence had a plan that she hoped would bring in some pennies.

Penny stood at the kitchen sink and peeled another potato to add to the pile she'd already done. The sun hadn't yet risen and it was dark outside. Everyone else in the house was still sleeping. But Penny wanted to get a start on preparing the Christmas dinner, though she was dreading cooking it. Her culinary skills weren't a patch on the delicious meals that Clara would produce. But since the woman had lost the baby, she'd taken to her bed in a state of mourning and Penny had been left to cook the dinners and clean the house. She didn't mind, and felt it was the least she could do. Today though, as it was Christmas, Penny believed that Mr Gaston, Basil, Rosemary and even Katy would much prefer Clara doing the cooking. Instead, they would all have to suffer another of Penny's undercooked or burnt offerings.

She smiled to herself, recalling the look on Mr Gaston's face at dinner yesterday. The man had pretended to enjoy the cottage pie she'd prepared, but Penny had later found it wrapped in newspaper with the vegetable peelings ready for composting. And he'd been very polite about the apple pie she'd attempted to make. She could kick herself now. She should have known that it was sugar added to the fruit and not salt! Still, with Clara laid up and feeling poorly, they were all mucking in, and no one was complaining, which was the way of Gaston Farm.

'Has Father Christmas been?' Rosemary asked as she bounded into the kitchen.

'Pack it in, you don't believe in Father Christmas, the tooth fairy or the Easter bunny,' Penny smiled. 'Good morning and merry Christmas.'

Rosemary leaned over the kitchen worktop and dipped her finger into a bowl of uncooked cake mixture. She wrinkled her nose at the gooey texture and quickly wiped her finger clean on a towel. 'I know I'm too old for Father Christmas, and I doubt we'll have anything in our stockings this year. Mum hasn't been herself. I don't know if she's even given Christmas a second thought.'

'You should know me better than that,' Clara said.

Penny was surprised to hear Clara's voice and turned to see the woman standing in the kitchen doorway. She was pleased that Clara had regained some colour in her cheeks and it warmed Penny's heart to see her smiling.

'Mum! You're up,' Rosemary exclaimed.

'Yes, I am. I couldn't miss my favourite day of the year and Basil's birthday.'

'Basil's birthday?' Penny quizzed.

'Yes, my brother was born on Christmas day which really bothers him,' Rosemary said with a roll of her eyes. 'He's convinced that he would receive more presents if he was born in July like me.'

'I don't know why he thinks like that,' Clara said with a shake of her head. 'Basil always gets twice the number of gifts that you get on Christmas day.'

'Not always,' Basil grinned, as he came into the kitchen. Kissing his mother on the cheek, he said warmly, 'Merry Christmas, Mum.'

'And happy birthday to you,' she replied.

'I still wish you'd timed it better so that I didn't have to share my birthday with Jesus.'

'At least you get a birthday,' Penny mumbled.

'I'm sorry, what did you say?' Clara asked.

'I said at least Basil gets a birthday. I've never had one.'

'You've never celebrated your birthday?'

'No, I don't know when it is.'

'Oh!' Clara said, then sounding flustered, she added, 'We shall have to remedy that. Do you have an idea of when you were born?'

'Some time in the spring, I think.'

'Lovely. I think May first should be your birthday. Would you like that?' Clara asked.

'Yeah, I would, very much.'

Mr Gaston strolled in. His ruddy cheeks made him look as though he'd already been on the port and brandy, though Penny had never seen the man drink.

'Birthday... did I hear that it's someone's birthday today?' he joked.

'Yes, Dad, it's Jesus's birthday,' Rosemary laughed.

'And mine,' Basil pointed out.

'Penny, pop upstairs and wake Katy, please. We have a family tradition on Christmas morning which I'd love to share with you both. And by the way, thank you for making a start on the Christmas dinner. Would you like me to take over?'

'Yes, yes please, yes,' Mr Gaston and Basil chorused.

Penny smiled. 'There's your answer.'

Dashing up the stairs, Penny couldn't wait to get back down to the kitchen and to the joyful atmosphere. She hurried into the bedroom and gently shook her friend. 'Katy... Katy... wake up, it's Christmas!'

Katy rolled over with her back to Penny and pulled the blankets over her head.

'Come on, Katy. Everyone is waiting downstairs for you.'

'I'm not coming down,' she grumbled.

'Please, Katy, it won't be the same without you. And you'll never guess what... it's Basil's birthday too.'

'Don't care. Leave me alone.'

Penny sighed heavily. Katy hadn't been the same since she'd retuned from Battersea. The girl had barely spoken and had withdrawn into herself. But what was most worrying was that Penny had seen several deep and sore-looking scratches on Katy's arms. She suspected that her friend had inflicted the injuries on herself.

Speaking gently but firmly, Penny appealed to Katy. 'The Gaston's have been so good to us. If you don't come down and join in their Christmas day, you'll upset Clara.'

Penny's words had worked. She was pleased when Katy huffed and angrily threw back the bed-covers. 'Thank you,' Penny said, trying to smile. She didn't like to see her friend in distress, but she wasn't sure how to help her recover from her dreadful ordeal.

Back in the kitchen, everyone was sat around the kitchen table.

'Please, join us,' Clara instructed. 'You know how excited I get about Christmas,' she smiled at everyone, 'Well, I couldn't sleep last night so I came down to prepare our game.' Then, once Penny and Katy were seated, Clara placed an egg in front of each person and one in the middle of the table. 'Basil, perhaps you'd like to tell the girls about our Christmas tradition,' she suggested.

With a soppy grin, he explained, 'We bang the egg on our head. The eggs, all but one, are hard-boiled. And whoever has the egg that isn't cooked is the winner.'

'The winner has raw egg on their head?' Penny confirmed.

'Yes, that's right,' Rosemary added. 'It makes your hair ever so shiny.'

'Does the winner win anything?'

'The right to lick out the bowl of Mum's special Christmas cake mixture,' Basil announced.

'It's delicious,' Rosemary grinned.

All eyes turned to look at the messy bowl on the kitchen side where Penny had been preparing the cake.

'Er, I think I'll leave it to the younger generation this year,' Mr Gaston said, pushing his egg away.

'Actually,' Basil grimaced, 'Maybe we can leave it for just the girls to play.'

Clara went to the cold storeroom and came back carrying a large, ceramic bowl. 'I hope you don't mind, Penny, but while I was down here boiling the eggs last night, I also took the liberty of mixing my cake recipe.'

'Thank gawd for that,' Penny said with a roll of her eyes.

'Right, I'm back in the game,' Mr Gaston chuckled. He picked up his egg and whacked it down hard on his head. 'Ouch,' he winced when it didn't smash.

'My turn,' Rosemary chirped, and closed her eyes and screwed up her face as she tried to crack her egg on her head. 'No mixture for me,' she said, glumly.

'Go on, Basil, have a go,' Mr Gaston encouraged.

'Ladies first,' he said, sweeping his hand towards Penny and Katy.

Katy didn't look to be having fun when she banged her egg on her head.

'Go on, Basil, you do it next,' Penny coaxed.

When Basil's egg didn't smash, she asked, 'I'm last, so does this mean I've got the uncooked egg?'

'Not necessarily,' Basil replied. 'It's between the egg in your hand and the one on the table.'

'What happens if my egg doesn't smash? Who is the winner?'

'Whoever is first to grab the egg on the table,' he snickered.

'Right, 'ere goes,' Penny grimaced.

Bang. The eggshell smashed and Penny could feel slimy, raw egg dripping down her face. 'Ew, yuck,' she giggled.

'Congratulations,' Clara said, and handed her a towel.

Penny gratefully accepted the towel and mopped her face as she asked, 'What happens to the hard-boiled eggs?'

'I make Scotch eggs. Nothing goes to waste. I'll get the mixture into a tin and then the bowl is all yours and you're allowed to devour it before breakfast.'

Clara was pleased that she'd made the effort to get out of bed to enjoy Christmas. It had taken her some effort, but after two weeks of wallowing in anguish, she'd decided that enough was enough and it was time for her to get on with life. She'd lost herself for a while, consumed in grief for her miscarried child, but she already had a family and they needed her. *It wasn't meant to be*, she thought, and doubted that she'd ever have another baby. But God had sent her two troubled girls instead, and Clara was determined to give them a special day.

As Penny cleared away the breakfast plates, Clara whispered in her ear, 'Thank you for taking care of everything. The house is spotless, and everyone has been well-fed.'

'I don't know about them being well-fed,' Penny chuckled.

'They ate, but no one enjoyed my cooking. I'm glad you're back on your feet, and everyone's bellies will be grateful an' all.'

'Is it time now, Mum?' Rosemary asked, clearly struggling to contain her excitement.

'Yes, it's time,' Clara answered. 'Follow me.'

Walking through to the large and rarely used living room, Clara watched the glee on the faces of her children. She noticed that Penny looked bemused but poor Katy didn't seem to care what was going on around her. 'Five stockings,' Clara announced, proudly pointing at the knitted red socks hanging on the hearth.

'You made one for me?' Will asked.

'Don't I always,' Clara replied. 'After all, you're the biggest child of all.'

Clara handed around the stockings, pleased to see the look of joy and bewilderment in Penny's eyes. She doubted that the girl had ever received a Christmas stocking before, a sad thought that stabbed at Clara's heart.

'A doll in an army uniform!' Rosemary shrieked. 'It's the best doll ever. I love her, thank you!'

Will stoked the fire and Clara sat in a comfy armchair beside the hearth.

'Oi, woman, you haven't got time to sit there on your laurels,' he joked. 'You've got work to do in the kitchen.'

'All in good time, it's still early.' Then looking at Penny, Clara said, 'And talking of work, we'll go down to the village after Christmas and see about getting you a job.'

'But not as a cook,' Basil laughed.

'God forbid,' Will added.

'Stop picking on Penny,' Clara warned, though she knew

everything was said in jest. 'You'd all be as skinny as rakes if Penny hadn't done the cooking.'

'Have you seen how loose my trousers are,' Mr Gaston said, smiling when he added, 'I'm only kidding, Penny.'

'It's true, I'm rubbish at cooking,' Penny agreed.

'We can't all be good at everything, and you're excellent with a needle and thread. If my husband insists that his trousers are loose, perhaps you could alter them and take them in on the waist.'

'There's no need for that,' Will said, patting his stomach. 'I've got a Christmas dinner to look forward to so I shall need room in these trousers.'

Clara glanced across at Katy. It worried her that the girl seemed disinterested in the festivities around her, instead looking glum sat in the corner of the room on a footstall. Clara felt awful. She'd selfishly spent two weeks in bed and had neglected Katy's needs. She wasn't sure how to reach through the dark cloud that surrounded Katy, but she believed that given some time, love and nurturing would drag the girl out of the mire.

'Well, the dinner won't cook itself,' she said, pushing herself up from the armchair.

'Wait there just one minute,' Penny instructed, and ran from the room.

'What's Penny up to?' Clara asked her husband.

'I've no idea,' he answered with a shrug.

Moments later, Penny came back carrying a pillowcase that appeared to be stuffed with several items.

The girl looked around sheepishly, her eyes going from one person to another. 'It's not much,' she said, 'but I hope you like them.' Reaching inside the pillowcase, Penny pulled out a small package wrapped in newspaper and handed it to Basil. 'This is for you. Sorry, if I'd known it was your birthday, I would have made you two gifts.'

Basil looked curiously at the present in his hand.

'Open it then,' Clara encouraged.

He ripped off the paper to reveal a hand-sewn wallet made from canvas, with *Basil* skilfully sewn on the front.

Penny looked embarrassed as she said, 'I heard coins jangling in your pocket. I thought you might like something to keep them in. I made it from one of the potato sacks.'

'Thanks, Penny, it's great, and clever too.'

'And this is for you, Rosemary,' Penny said, handing her friend a gift.

'Aw, she's beautiful,' Rosemary cooed, cuddling a small rag doll to her chest. 'I'm going to call her Penny.'

'*Penny* was made from some scraps of material I found in your mum's sewing box, and do you remember you lost a glove?'

'Yes.'

'Well, her hair is made from the wool of the other glove. One glove is no use to anyone, so I unthreaded the wool.'

Katy accepted Penny's offering but showed little interest in the peg doll with brown wool hair.

Mr Gaston smiled affectionately at Penny as he accepted his gift. As he carefully unwrapped the newspaper, he chuckled, 'I hope it's a pair of braces to keep my trousers up.' Holding a colourful, knitted scarf, he beamed, 'Perfect! Just what I need on these chilly mornings.'

'Oh, Will, it's lovely!' Clara gushed. 'And I'm glad to see all my scraps finally being put to good use. You're very talented, Penny.'

'Thank you,' Penny said, presenting Clara with her gift.

Tears welled in Clara's eyes as she ran her fingers over a delicate drawstring pouch, decorated with pretty pompoms and embroidered with delicate pink flowers. 'It's beautiful,' Clara said, choking back tears. 'I shall keep my best soap in it. I don't know where you found the time to make us these wonderful gifts, it must have taken you hours and hours.'

'I did it at night, mostly. I wanted to do something to say thank you, and … and … this is the best Christmas I've ever had!'

Clara thought so too, though she'd liked to have seen Katy smiling.

'I'll see to the cows,' Will said quietly.

Clara nodded and walked to the door with Will, but her eyes were on Basil who was gazing at Penny.

On the doorstep, Will wrapped his arms around Clara. 'I won't be gone long,' he promised.

'Make sure you're not.'

'I don't want to be away from you for more than a minute than I have to be.' As he unpeeled his arms, he stepped back. Studying her face, Will asked, 'What's bothering you? You look worried.'

Clara sighed. 'It's Basil,' she replied. 'I can see trouble ahead … he's got a crush on Penny.'

27

Florence looked angrily at the screwed-up paper on her kitchen table. She'd spent most of Boxing Day trying to pen a letter to Penny, yet all her attempts had failed. She wanted money from the girl, which meant her words had to be perfect. But Florence hadn't found the balance between desperation and persuasion and, so far, she didn't believe her letters to Penny had sounded convincing.

Dear Penny, she tried again, contempt flowing through her veins as she scribbled the girl's name.

As she thought carefully about what to write, she heard an unexpected knock on the front door. 'It had better not be carollers,' she mumbled. 'Christmas is over.'

Plodding along the passageway, Florence shuddered with the cold. She was wearing two cardigans under her coat and a woollen hat over her unkempt hair, but with no money for coal, the house was freezing and a chill had got down to her bones.

Pulling open the front door, annoyed that yet more icy air would waft into her house, Florence recoiled at the sight on her doorstep. Snarling, she spat, 'Cyril Black. What the bleedin' 'ell are you doing here?'

'Merry Christmas to you an' all,' he grinned, his arms open wide.

'It ain't Christmas no more, and you can bugger off to wherever you came from.'

'Ain't you even gonna offer your old man a cuppa? It's taken me hours to get here, and it weren't easy with the blackouts. Did you know that even Big Ben ain't lit up?'

'I couldn't care less about Big Ben or how difficult it was for you to navigate the dark. You shouldn't have bothered, Cyril, you ain't welcome.'

'Come on, Florrie, where's your Christmas spirit? 'Tis the season of goodwill and all that.'

Florence was about to slam the door in his face, but then a thought struck her. She was skint, but Cyril was rarely without a few shillings in his pocket. And even if he didn't have any money, she could probably talk him into pinching some coal for the fire. 'Are you 'ere on the cadge, Cyril? Because if you are, then forget it, 'cos I ain't got a pot to piss in.'

'Course I ain't here on the cadge,' he answered, 'I'm here to see how me wife and kids are faring.'

Florence didn't believe that he was sincere; he hadn't sounded convincing. Nonetheless, she was almost destitute and was willing to take desperate measures. 'I suppose you can come in for a while,' she said, pulling the door open wider.

'Cor blimey, Florrie, it's blinkin' taters in here,' he said, rubbing his hands together.

'If you want to warm up, you'll have to go and get some coal.'

'Ain't you got any?'

'No, Cyril, I haven't. Don't you think the fire would be alight if I had any coal? Do you think I'd be sat here in me coat if the coal bunker was full?'

'All right, all right, I'm sorry I asked.'

'Are you going to get some coal then?' Florence pushed.

'Where am I supposed to get coal from at this time of night?'

'The same place you've always pinched it from,' Florence suggested.

'Right,' Cyril sighed, turning back towards the front door. 'The lady wants coal so its coal the lady shall have.'

Tugging his flat cap, Cyril offered up one of his cheeky grins as he left. Florence's stomach flipped. She was surprised to find herself hoping that he'd soon come back, and not just for what he could provide her with. She hadn't seen him in years, and her old wounds had healed. The man was a scoundrel who had let her down more times than she could remember, even bringing a bastard child into their home. But seeing him now, that mischievous glint in his blue eyes and the soppy smile that had once melted her heart, she remembered the much younger man who she'd fallen head-over-heels in love with. *Don't be daft*, she told herself. *It's loneliness that's making you soft in the head, that's all.*

Penny sat quietly in the kitchen reading another of Clara's books. She was so engrossed in the fascinating story, unaware of Clara kneading dough, and she didn't notice when Basil ambled in and pulled out a seat beside her.

'Where's your dad?' Clara asked.

'He's listening to the wireless in the barn.'

'Go and tell him he can bring it inside.'

'But I thought you didn't trust it?' Basil asked.

'I didn't, but after listening to the King's Christmas Day message, I've decided that though I can hear them, they can't hear me through the wireless. I mean, it's most unlikely that King George is listening to anything that I have to say. He is such a wise man, and as he said yesterday, *a new year is at hand. We cannot tell what it will bring.* With Britain in the throes of war, I think we need to know what's going on in the world, and that wireless thingy will keep us up to date.'

Basil went to fetch his father, saying as he left the kitchen, 'At last. It's about time you became more modern, Mum.'

Penny looked up from her book. 'You'll be getting a television set next,' she teased Clara.

'Never, not for all the tea in China. Now, young lady, if you can tear yourself away from that book for more than two minutes, there's clean bedsheets that need putting on your bed.'

Penny cringed with embarrassment on behalf of poor Katy. For the past fortnight, night after night, Penny had woken to find herself laying in a damp patch where Katy had wet the bed. She hadn't mentioned it to her friend. Instead, Penny would discreetly strip the bed and wash the sheets before slipping them back on. But Clara had found Penny doing the laundering this morning and, after Penny had explained the situation, Clara had taken over the load.

'You look upset,' Clara commented. 'I know Katy isn't herself, but she'll come round in her own time.'

'It's not just the bed-wetting... I'm worried about Katy because I think she's hurting herself,' Penny admitted.

Clara looked shocked, and uttered, 'Oh dear. What is she doing to herself?'

'Scratching her arms until they bleed. She tries to hide it, but I think it's getting worse, and if I say anything she denies it. I don't know how to stop her.'

Basil returned, followed by Mr Gaston who appeared delighted to be allowed to bring his prized wireless indoors.

Clara leaned towards Penny and in a hushed voice she said quickly, 'We'll talk about it tomorrow.'

Rosemary skipped in, hugging her rag doll under her arm. '*Penny* wants a glass of milk and two biscuits, please,' she announced.

'Sit at the table then,' Clara instructed. 'And what about Katy? Is she going to come down from the bedroom too?'

'No, I asked her but she ignored me.'

'I'll try to persuade her,' Penny said, pushing back the chair. 'And if Katy comes downstairs, it will give me a chance to put clean sheets on the bed.'

Clara placed a steadying hand on Penny's shoulder. 'Actually, I shouldn't worry about the sheets; I think you should leave her be for now.'

Penny reckoned that Clara was probably right. It seemed the more they tried to talk to Katy, the more Katy withdrew.

'She'll be all right,' Basil said, sounding older than his years. 'We've got a few sheep that graze in the back field. Last spring, one of the ewe's struggled after birthing a lamb. She went lame but her lamb managed to suckle that night. The next morning, I went to check on them and found the ewe with her hind leg and ears missing. It must have been a fox attack. The ears are easy to take and make a nice snack for Mr Fox. I thought he might have got the lamb too, but I found her hiding in the hedgerow. She was terrified and trembling, bleating for her mother. It took a long time before I could coax the little lamb out of the bushes, and even longer to gain her trust to feed her. I had to back off and let her come to me, and she did, eventually. She's a bossy little madam now,' he smiled.

Penny thought for a moment. 'You're saying that we should let Katy come round in her own time?' she asked.

'Yes. She has to learn to trust again.'

Clara nudged her son in the ribs, saying, 'When did you become so smart?'

'With age comes experience,' he joked. 'And I'm sixteen now.'

'What exactly happened to Katy?' Rosemary asked as she dunked a biscuit into her glass of milk.

'Mind your own,' Clara said, brusquely. 'Suffice to say that Katy had an awful experience, and that's all you need to know.'

Penny turned to Basil. 'Thank you for sharing that story with me. I feel better now.'

'Good. I don't like to see you upset.'

He looked back at her with an intensity in his eyes that she'd never seen before, and it made her feel peculiar. Her stomach did somersaults, and quickly pulling her eyes away, Penny could feel herself flushing pink. She hoped that Basil hadn't noticed.

'Cor, my shoulder is aching,' Cyril moaned to Florence as he came in from the backyard.

'I'm not surprised after lugging that sack load of coal. You didn't put it in the bunker, did you?'

'No, I've left it outside the door.'

'At least we'll be warm tonight. I suppose you want a cup of tea now?'

'Yes please, love, and a bite to eat,' he answered, as he pulled out a seat at the table and plonked himself down. It had been a while since he'd been in Florrie's kitchen, but it still felt like home. And though there was a chilly nip in the air, it was a vast improvement on where he'd been living for the last two years: in prison, doing time on His Majesty's Service.

'There's not much grub in the larder, but Mrs Darwin made a nice Christmas cake. You can have a slice with your cuppa.'

'That'll do. I'll go out on the steal tomorrow and get us some food.'

'Are you planning on staying for a while then?' Florence asked.

'If you'll have me?'

'I suppose so, but you'll need to pay your way.'

'Don't worry, Florrie. I know you're on your uppers. I'll see you're all right.'

Florence placed a plate with cake on the table. 'Why have you come back?' she asked.

'It's Christmas… and we're at war… The truth is, I wanted to know how my kids are.'

'You're not bothered about me then?' Florence asked.

Cyril was sure he'd heard a note of disappointment in his wife's voice. 'Why do you say that?' he asked. 'Are you bothered about me?'

Florence looked away. 'Sometimes. You're often on my mind.'

My God, he thought, stunned. After all this time, Florence still had feelings for him, and he wondered if something about her had changed. She seemed softer, and he could see a glimmer of the woman he'd fallen in love with. 'I think about you a lot an' all,' he lied.

'Do you? Then why haven't you come home sooner?'

'I didn't think you'd have me back.'

'I might not yet. You'd better behave yourself,' she smiled.

Cyril couldn't believe his luck. He had assumed that he'd either have to use all his charms or battle with Florrie to get his feet back under her table, yet she was making it easy for him. 'How are Jimmy and Penny?' he asked.

'Jimmy signed up and is in France. I've only had one letter from him, he's not one for writing.'

'Cor, my boy, a soldier! It don't seem possible. He was only a nipper when I last saw him.'

'He's a good three inches taller than you now,' Florence smiled.

'I can't believe it, Jimmy in the armed forces, who'd have thought it.'

'Yeah, well, don't sound so pleased about it. I hate it, Cyril, and I've had many a sleepless night. He could be killed!'

'Huh, leave off, Florrie. You've heard everyone talking; this war, they're calling it a phoney war.'

'We'll see, but I hope you're right.'

'And Penny, how's my girl?' Cyril asked.

'She, erm, she moved away to the country with Katy. It's safer there.'

'She wasn't evacuated, was she?'

'No, don't be daft, she's too old for that. In fact, I was just writing to her.'

'That explains the paper everywhere,' Cyril guffawed. 'Tell

her I'm home. Tell her to come and see her old dad. Cor, she won't be expecting to hear that, eh.'

'No, I don't suppose she will.'

'And how have you been, my lovely?'

'Like you care. And don't *my lovely* me. You can stay, but you won't be in my bed.'

And there she is, thought Cyril, the bitter, sharp-tongued wife he remembered. But for now, until he got back on his feet, his old home in Battersea would do very nicely indeed. It meant he'd have to be nice to a woman he loathed, but it was better than sleeping rough like he had been since his release from prison. And in Battersea, he could avoid the debt collectors in North London who were vying for his blood.

Penny tucked the clean sheets under her arm. 'I think I'll turn in now,' she said to Clara.

Clara sipped a steaming cup of hot milk. 'Good night. Don't stay up too late reading that book.'

'I won't.'

'I'll be up soon,' Rosemary said. 'But I'm making the most of the Christmas break. As soon as I go back to school, Mum will be sending me to bed early.'

Penny padded up the stairs, passing Basil who was coming down.

'You off to bed?' he asked.

'Yes, good night.'

'Have sweet dreams,' he said.

Penny felt uncomfortable under his long stare and lowered her eyes. She couldn't be sure, but she thought that Basil had pressed against her unnecessarily as he passed her. He'd been so close that she could smell the mustiness of the farm on him.

At the top of the stairs, she looked back over her shoulder. Basil was standing at the bottom, peering up at her. She smiled awkwardly at him before making a hasty retreat to the bedroom.

Flinging open the door, Penny wasn't surprised to find Katy in bed. Her friend was facing the wall, which meant Penny couldn't tell if she was sleeping or not. Either way, the clean sheets needed to go on the bed.

'Katy,' she whispered. 'Are you asleep?'

Katy didn't stir so Penny gave her a gentle shake.

'Sorry, sleepy head, but you can't sleep on a bare mattress. I need you to get up so that I can put a sheet on the bed... Katy...'

Katy remained silent. Penny wasn't sure if her friend was really sleeping or just choosing to ignore her. 'Katy... wake up,' she urged, shaking her a little more vigorously.

When Katy still didn't respond, Penny suddenly became concerned. 'Katy,' she said, louder. 'Wake up!'

'What's wrong?' Rosemary asked, coming into the room.

'I can't wake Katy. Turn on the light.'

As Rosemary lit the gaslight and the room illuminated, the reason for Katy's silence became apparent. Penny stared in horrified disbelief. She could hear the ear-piercing screams of Rosemary that filled the room and bounced off the thick, stone walls. Over and over, Rosemary screamed.

'What's going on?' Basil asked, running into the room, sounding flustered.

Penny couldn't answer. Her eyes were fixed on the fresh red

blood that had soaked the bed-covers. Rosemary screamed louder.

'Jesus Christ,' Basil gasped.

Pushing past Penny, he grabbed Katy's arms. Blood pumped from a large wound across her wrist. 'Give me that sheet,' he demanded.

Penny stood, unable to move. She felt as though she was out of her body and watching the gruesome scene from afar.

Basil snatched the sheet from under Penny's arm. Holding two edges, he ripped a strip from the linen. As he wrapped the makeshift bandage around Katy's bleeding wrist, Clara came running in.

'Oh no, no,' she cried. 'Is ... is she alive, Basil?'

'Yes, I think so. Get Dad.'

Clara dashed away. Rosemary's screams had faded to a whimper. Penny still couldn't move.

Once Katy's wrist was bandaged, Basil reached for the small knife that Katy held limply in her other hand and shoved it into his trouser pocket. Then, grabbing at the sheet again, he ripped off another long strip. 'The blood is coming through,' he mumbled, and began wrapping the second strip over the first.

'Out of my way, lad,' Mr Gaston said. 'Let me see how much blood she's lost.'

Basil stood back, and Penny felt his hand stroking her arm. 'She'll be fine,' he said, his voice shaky.

Penny shrugged him away and snapped, 'So much for your lamb coming to you! I shouldn't have left her alone. I should have been with her!'

Clara placed her arm over Penny's shoulders, giving her a gentle squeeze as she whispered, 'This isn't your fault.'

Mr Gaston easily picked up Katy in his arms and began to carry her across the room and towards the door. 'I'm taking her to the doctor's house,' he said.

Clara grabbed a blanket from the bed and chased after her husband. 'Wait,' she called.

As Clara wrapped the blanket around Katy, Mr Gaston urged, 'Hurry up. She's lost too much blood and she's not in a good way.'

As Mr Gaston hurried to the stairs, Penny cried out after him, 'Please don't let her die! She's my best friend in the world. Please, please, don't let her die!'

28

8 January 1940

'Well, it's Coupon Monday today,' Clara announced as she sliced warm, freshly-cooked bread for breakfast. 'Bacon, sugar and butter will be rationed from now.'

'We've no need to worry about the butter,' Will said.

'We are luckier than most. But we do need sugar so I shall be going to the village today and using my ration coupons for the first time.'

'You can't go out in this weather!' Will said, nodding his head towards the window. 'Have you seen it out there?'

'Yes, Will, I have, and it's freezing. I can't remember a January colder than this one in my lifetime. Can you?'

'No, I can't say I can. I've kept the cows in and brought the sheep in too. If you insist on going to the village, I'll take you on the cart.'

'No, thanks, it's fine. I'll walk Rosemary and Katy to school and Penny is coming too. I'm hoping to find her a job today.'

'Jon Hamble's grandson has been conscripted so he's looking for someone to help him in the greenhouses.'

'Really? That's perfect! I think Penny will enjoy growing

bulbs and cut flowers. She's always shown a keen interest in my vegetable garden.'

'Jon won't be growing bulbs. He said he's changing his crops from flowers to potatoes and anything else that folk can eat.'

'Oh, well I suppose that makes sense. According to the Ministry of Food, there are going to be food shortages.'

'Did someone say food shortages?' Basil asked, pulling out a seat at the kitchen table.

'Don't worry,' Clara smiled, 'we won't have any shortages here.'

'Good. I'm hungry. Where are the girls?'

'Still in bed. I feel awful waking them when it's so cold, but I don't want Rosemary and Katy being late for school.'

'Is Katy ready to return to school?' Will asked.

Clara sighed. 'I don't know, but I think it will do her good. She's well enough, physically, though I'm not sure about her mind. Rosemary will keep an eye on her.'

After wiping her hands on her apron, she crept up the stairs and knocked lightly on the girls' bedroom door.

'We're awake,' Rosemary called.

Clara pushed open the door and found all three girls huddled in one bed.

'It's so cold, Mum.'

'Yes, it is, but it's nice and warm in the kitchen, so up you get.'

'Do we have to?' Rosemary asked.

'Yes, you do,' Clara answered. Then walking over to the bed, she sat on the edge and looked warmly at Katy, asking, 'Do you feel strong enough to go to school today?'

Katy bit on her bottom lip as she nodded. 'You won't tell anyone what I did, will you?'

'No, Katy. I promised you that I wouldn't mention it to anyone, and neither will Rosemary,' Clara assured. The poor girl had been distraught since her *accident*. She'd apologised profusely, terrified of being sent back to Battersea, and had begged Clara not to write to her mother. 'And I've got good news for you, Penny,' she smiled. 'So, come on, all of you, I want you downstairs in ten minutes.'

Florence placed a slice of toast on the table in front of her husband, smiling at him, though she'd rather have kicked his shins. The man had proved himself to be about as useful as a chocolate fireguard.

'Is that it?' he asked, gawping at his meagre breakfast.

Florence felt anger rising from the pit of her knotted stomach. Taking the *nice* approach with Cyril wasn't working, and now he had the nerve to complain. 'Food is being rationed from today. If you want more, then you'll have to get off your lazy backside and get out there and find us some.'

'Cor blimey, Florrie, you don't ask for much,' he said sarcastically. 'It's bleedin' arctic outside and I've got holes in me boots.'

'Then put some cardboard in them,' Florence answered without any sympathy. She'd hoped that Cyril's return would mean more coffers in her empty tea tin where she stored her money. But the bitterly cold weather had kept her husband indoors. 'And see about getting some more coal. We've already gone through that sack you brought home. I've burned all the wood that Mr Peck left in the shed and the table that was in Jimmy's room. I mean it, Cyril, I'll have no choice but to burn your bloody shed next.'

'All right, all right, I'll see what I can do.'

'Make sure you do. You're supposed to be paying your way, but all you're doing is eating *my* food. I've stretched it to just about as far as it will go, and I don't want to have to hide from the rent man again. Enough is enough. Either cough up some grub, coal and money, or you'll be out on your ear.'

'For gawd's sake, stop nagging! I said I'll see what I can do, so drop it will you!'

Florence bit her tongue and poured herself a cup of tea.

'Is there one in the pot for me?' Cyril asked.

As she slid a cup across the table to him, Cyril threw her one of his cheeky grins. There would have been a time when his smile would have melted her heart, but now it made her want to slap it off his face. She tried not to show her contempt and offered a smile back. After all, Florence had no desire or energy to go to work, but Cyril could be a good provider and she needed him as her cash cow.

'You've not heard back from Penny yet?' he asked.

'No. I've written two letters to her now,' Florence replied. She wasn't lying. She had written two letters to Penny, but she'd thrown both on the fire.

'I was sure she'd want to come home to see me,' Cyril mused.

'You walked out on her when she was only four years old. I doubt she even remembers who you are, so I don't know why you'd think that she wants to see you.'

''Cos I'm her dad.'

'A dad who left her with a woman who isn't her mother.'

'But Penny don't know that you ain't her mum.'

'Yes, she does. Jimmy told her.'

'Eh? Why would he do that?'

'I don't know,' Florence snapped, 'You'll have to ask him. But he ain't bothered writing back either. Face it, Cyril, your kids ain't interested in you... or me come to that.'

'Well then, my lovely, it looks like it's just you and me stuck together,' Cyril said, and held his cup of tea aloft, 'Cheers.'

'You can have my bit of toast,' she offered, pushing her plate towards him. 'It'll help to keep your strength up to battle the cold weather today.' Florence knew her husband well. She could tell that he held as much affection for her as she did for him – none. And she doubted that he'd stay for very long. He never did. But while he was under her roof, she planned on getting as much out of him as she could.

29

Two weeks later

Penny stamped her feet to get some feeling back into her toes that were numb with the cold. She cupped her hands around her mouth and blew onto her fingers that peeped out the ends of her fingerless gloves. It was bitter, even in the greenhouse.

Her boss, Jon Hamble, came in, wrapped up in several layers of clothing which made the man look twice his size. Penny liked Mr Hamble. He talked a lot, mostly about flora and fauna. He said he preferred his dogs to people, which Penny could understand.

'I must say, young Penny. When I first saw you, I was in two minds about giving you the job. I thought a little snip of a girl like you would struggle with the wheelbarrow and wouldn't have the fortitude to carry sacks of soil. But as it turns out, I was wrong. You're far stronger than you look.'

'I think my muscles are getting bigger,' Penny smiled.

'Unfortunately, unless this weather breaks and Britain thaws, all your hard work will go to waste. My crops are going to fail in this freeze.'

'Mr Gaston said he heard on the wireless that parts of the river Thames have frozen!'

'It's the wildlife I feel sorry for.'

Penny nodded in agreement. She knew that Mr Gaston had lost two cows and several sheep, even though his cattle had shelter.

'You should get yourself home,' Mr Hamble said. 'There's nothing much you can do today and it's far too cold to be working in here.'

'I don't mind the cold,' Penny protested.

'If I don't send you home, Mrs Hamble will give me a good telling off.'

Penny was keen to prove that she was a hard worker, but before she could protest further, a loud thud on the greenhouse roof startled her and she screamed.

'What on earth...' Mr Hamble uttered, looking up.

Penny's heart raced and her words tumbled out. 'Gawd, that made me jump. What was it? It's not the Germans is it? Are we being bombed, Mr Hamble?' she asked in fear.

Mr Hamble shook his head, 'No, no, it's not the Germans. It was a bird, frozen stiff and fallen out of the sky,' he said, sadly. 'That's it, young Penny. No arguments, you're to go straight home and I don't want you back here until the temperature has risen above zero.'

'But—'

'Off you go.'

Penny wrapped her scarf over her face and pulled her hat down low. The road to the Gastons' farm was iced over, so Penny walked along the snowy grass verge. She slipped a couple of times, grazing her knee and hurting her wrist. Thankfully, Jon Hamble's greenhouses were only a short distance down the lane from the farmhouse. Even so, it took Penny nearly an hour to reach home.

'My goodness, you're frozen through,' Clara exclaimed when Penny walked into the kitchen. 'I told you Jon wouldn't expect you in work today. The school is closed, and the village roads are pretty much impassable. I admire your determination, Penny, but I think you were silly to go out in this weather.'

'I know,' Penny replied, her teeth chattering and her body shivering.

'Warm yourself in front of the fire and I'll make you a hot drink.'

After several minutes, as the feeling slowly returned to Penny's feet, Basil ambled in, brushing ice from his hair. 'There's a storm coming,' he said gravely. 'The sky is black.'

'It can't get any worse than this, can it?' Clara asked.

'Dad said if it rains, it'll fall as ice, so yes, Mum, it can get a lot worse. Where's Katy?'

'She's in the snug.'

Basil promptly left, and Penny looked curiously at Clara. 'Why did he want to know where Katy is?' she asked.

Clara wiped her hands on her apron. 'Katy's been talking to Basil about how she feels. I think they've become quite close.'

'Have they? Why is Katy talking to Basil and not to me? I'm her friend.'

'Sometimes it's easier to be open with someone you don't know. Just be glad that she's not bottling up her feelings anymore.'

'Yeah, I suppose so,' Penny answered, but she couldn't help feeling a tad disgruntled. Though she wasn't sure if she was upset because her best friend had been confiding in someone other than her, or jealous of Basil and Katy becoming closer.

Mr Gaston came into the kitchen, his nose red and his fingers purple. 'Batten down the hatches,' he warned. 'This storm that's coming is going to be the worst we've seen.'

Penny gulped. She enjoyed her job at the nurseries and hoped the greenhouses would endure the weather. But it sounded as though the snow that was covering large swathes of Britain was going to fall as ice in the South. Heavy ice and glass weren't a good combination!

Cyril pulled open the kitchen drawers and cupboards in search of a box of matches to light the gas stove. Florence had thrown the last of the coal on the fire in the front room, and then she'd demanded that he chop down the shed to use as fuel. Unless they started burning their furniture, Cyril worried they'd freeze to death. At least they had gas on the stove, which wouldn't heat the whole house but would take the chill out of the air in the kitchen.

Cyril pulled a writing pad out of the drawer, hoping to find the matches. As he went to put the pad back, he noticed an address written on the open page. Gaston Farm in Kent. It dawned on him that it must be where Penny was staying. Ripping off the sheet of paper, he stuffed it into his pocket. If Penny refused to come to London to visit him, then he'd go to Kent to see her!

Florence came in from the backyard, her arms folded across her chest. 'It's so cold, the water in the privy is frozen.'

'Where's the matches?' Cyril asked.

'Here,' Florence answered, and pulled a box from her

pocket. 'What are we going to do, Cyril? We've hardly any food and only my furniture left to burn.'

'I can't go out in this, Florrie.'

'I know, it ain't safe. There's telephone poles down, trees fallen and the roads are like ice-skating rinks.'

'We'll just have to make do until the weather turns for the better. We can keep each other warm,' he grinned.

Florence threw him a scathing look. Cyril was relieved. He had no desire to cuddle up to his wife, but he had to keep her sweet for now. With nowhere else to lay his head, Cyril knew that he wouldn't survive if he was forced to sleep on the streets again. But now that he had Penny's address, a plan began to formulate in his mind. He needed the weather to break, and then that would be it, he'd be off on his toes and away from Florence.

Cyril smiled wryly to himself. A new life in Kent beckoned.

30

March 1940
Two months later

'Look at you,' Penny cooed at a small green shoot as she re-potted the seedling. 'You're growing up strong and beautiful.'

'So, Jon isn't the only mad one who talks to the plants.'

The voice startled Penny. Nearly jumping out of her skin, she spun around to see a rotund woman standing in the greenhouse.

'Sorry, I didn't mean to creep up on you. I'm Vera, Jon's wife, and you must be Penny?'

'Yes. It's nice to meet you, Mrs Hamble.'

'Vera will do. We don't stand on formalities here. Don't tell me Jon has got you calling him Mr Hamble?'

Penny nodded.

'We'll put an end to that!' Vera said as she waddled over. Eyeing Penny up and down, she added cheerily, 'Aren't you a pretty little thing.'

Penny didn't know what to say. No one had ever said that she was pretty. For years Florence had constantly told her that she was useless and ugly, and Penny believed it to be true. But she was just starting to think that maybe she wasn't useless, which was evident in the fledgling crops she'd grown. Though she still thought that she was ugly.

'Jon won't be at work today. That bombing of the Domala cargo liner off the Isle of Wight has got him all worked up, all those lost souls, God bless them. So, the silly old codger has taken it upon himself to go out recruiting for the Home Guard. He said he trusts you to look after this place in his absence.'

'I will, I promise.'

'I know you will. Jon only has good things to say about you. You've been a godsend. With our grandson in the Navy now, I don't think my husband would have coped without you.'

Penny could feel herself bursting with pride. 'Has Mr Hamble left any instructions of what he wants me to do today?'

'Nope. He said you're a sensible girl and will know what needs doing. I don't know how much Jon is paying you, but knowing him, it won't be much. You should push for a pay rise. He won't want to lose you, trust me,' she chortled.

'I'm, erm, I'm quite happy with my salary, thank you.'

'If you say so, but don't sell yourself short. Right then, I'll leave you to get on with it. Keep up the good work.'

Penny watched Vera Hamble walk away, toddling from side to side. She thought the Hambles seemed like a mismatched couple. Vera was round, with short legs and a jolly chuckle. Her mass of brown hair had been hidden under a scarf, and she'd worn the biggest pair of earrings that Penny had ever seen. Mr Hamble, on the other hand, was tall and slender. Though he was chatty, he was always serious. She had no idea of how much hair Mr Hamble had as she'd never seen the man without a hat on, but she suspected that he was probably bald.

Looking around the greenhouse, although there was no one else around, Penny never felt alone among her seedlings and cuttings. She'd read that talking to plants helped them to grow. Penny didn't know why speaking to plants encouraged growth, but she wondered if they could feel that they were loved and that's what made them sprout better. After all, she'd lacked love and she'd never grown tall. But she had noticed that her breasts were becoming fuller. This pleased her immensely because Penny longed to look like a woman instead of a child. If plants grew better when they were spoken to, Penny wondered if her breasts would too. Looking down at her chest, she whispered with hope, 'Grow, little ones, grow.'

Clara stretched her neck, looking through the kitchen window and along the drive, hoping to see Penny coming home from the nurseries. The girl often worked longer than her hours, but Clara didn't like the idea of Penny walking home in the dark. Though Will had reassured her numerous times that it was perfectly safe, it didn't stop Clara from fretting.

At last, she glimpsed the girl and breathed a sigh of relief. Putting the kettle on the stove, she knew that Penny would appreciate a cup of tea when she came through the door.

'You're late,' Clara said, sounding tart though she hadn't meant to.

'There was lots to do. Mr Hamble wasn't at work today and he left me in charge.'

'He must have a lot of faith in you. Jon's plants are his pride and joy.'

'I met Mrs Hamble today.'

'She's a merry woman,' Clara smiled, 'Quite different from her husband.'

'Yeah, I thought so too. She said I'm pretty.'

'And rightly so!'

'Do you really think so?' Penny asked, shyly.

'You're beautiful, Penny. You have the prettiest blue eyes, gorgeous high cheek bones, and the colour of your hair is so striking.'

Penny shrugged.

'Believe me, you are going to have men flocking around you and you'll have your choice of husbands. Choose wisely, Penny. Don't fall for anyone who doesn't treat you with respect.'

'Gawd, I've never thought about getting married.'

'There's no rush,' Clara said, her tone serious. 'This is your home. I don't want you to ever feel that you have to get married. You can stay here for as long as you choose.'

'Thank you. Where are the all the others?'

'Will is in the barn, Katy and Basil are in the snug listening to the wireless, and Rosemary is upstairs making a doll's house for *Penny*. She loves that rag doll; you made her the perfect gift.'

Penny half-heartedly smiled, and Clara wondered if the girl was smarting at the idea of Katy and Basil together again. Katy often accompanied Basil in the fields, the two had become close. Clara thought that Katy looked up to Basil like a big brother. But she'd noticed that Penny seemed pushed out and she thought that the girl might resent the attention that Katy was receiving from Basil. Though Penny needn't feel that way. Clara would never tell her, but she knew her son was holding a torch for her. And looking at Penny's face, Clara believed that Penny liked Basil too. But her son felt awful for the way he'd treated the girls, especially considering what had happened to Katy in Battersea and her almost taking her own life. Basil had gently reached out to the girl, not in a pushy way. And just like the motherless lamb in Basil's story, Katy had come to him in the same way as the baby lamb had. She'd learned to trust again.

Penny took her cup to the sink and rinsed it under the tap. As she looked up and through the window, she saw the figure of a man walking towards the house. The shadowy image appeared to be too short to be Mr Gaston, and he wasn't as wide either.

'There's a man coming to the door,' she told Clara.

Clara came to stand beside Penny and looked through the window too. 'He's probably a salesman,' she groaned, before going to the front door.

Penny knew that Clara would be diplomatic at shunning him away. The woman was well practised as they often had unwanted callers at the farm, hawking their wares. Pouring herself another cup of tea, Penny sat on a chair beside the large open fire and slipped off her boots. Holding her stockinged feet towards the flames, she rested her head back and enjoyed the warmth from the burning coals.

'Er... Penny...' Clara said, swallowing hard.

Penny opened her eyes, surprised to see the man standing just behind Clara.

'Penny, this gentleman is here to see you... he says he's your dad.'

Penny, stunned, stared at the rough-looking man. He had

the same red hair as her and Jimmy, but nothing about him was familiar. She'd often tried to remember her dad and had always assumed that if she ever saw him again, she'd instantly recognise him. But as she studied the stranger's face, her mind was blank.

'Hello, Penny. Look at you, all grown up. You ain't changed one bit,' the man smiled, showing his missing teeth.

Penny wanted to rise to her feet yet she remained sat, rooted to the spot.

'I bet this is a surprise, eh? 'Ere, I've got something for you,' he said, reaching into his pocket. 'It's a stamp... a Penny Black, like you. I named you after this stamp. What do you think, eh?'

Penny couldn't speak. Her mind raced but no words came.

'Erm, can I offer you a cup of tea?' Clara asked, politely.

'Cor, yeah, I'm parched. Any chance of a sandwich or something an' all?'

'Er, yes, of course. Please, sit down,' Clara offered, sweeping her hand towards a seat at the table.

As the man sat down, he grinned at Penny. 'You wanna see the look on your face,' he said. 'Me turning up out of the blue has blown your mind, ain't it?'

Penny managed to nod.

'Florrie wrote to you a couple of times to tell you I was back in Battersea. Didn't you get her letters?'

Penny shook her head.

'Oh well, I'm here in person now. That'll save you a trip to Battersea to see me, eh?'

'I – I – I don't remember you,' Penny mumbled.

'Well, I can't say I'm surprised. You was only knee high to a grasshopper the last time you saw me.'

Penny wasn't sure how to react to the man. She never believed that she'd ever see him again, though she'd spent years dreaming of him coming to rescue her from Florence. But he never did. He'd left her to be cruelly raised by a woman who wasn't her mother. 'What are you doing here?' she mumbled.

'I've come to see my girl, ain't I? I thought you'd be pleased to see me an' all.'

'I think Penny's had quite a shock, Mr Black,' Clara said, awkwardly, and handed him a cup of tea. 'It's a shame you didn't let us know that you were coming.'

'Like I said, Florrie wrote a couple of times.'

It suddenly dawned on Penny what he'd said, and as fear snaked through her veins she blurted, 'Florence knows where I am?'

'Yeah, course she does. She was disappointed when she never heard back from you, 'cos Jimmy hasn't written to her either.'

'Penny hasn't received any correspondence from Mrs Black, and she didn't want your wife to know where she is.'

'Why not?'

'Mrs Black has spent years treating Penny most unfairly. Penny ran away, and she didn't want to be found.'

'I see, you ran away, eh. Florrie didn't tell me that. And I don't suppose she wrote to you like she said she did, the lying cow. I'm sorry, love, I had no idea.'

'Yes, you did!' Penny spat. 'You left me with her, even though you knew she hated me!'

'No, love, it wasn't like that, I swear.'

'It was. Jimmy told me everything.'

'Look, I knew she weren't treating you right, but I thought

that Jimmy and Mrs Whetstone were looking out for you. I thought that once Florrie had been found out, she would change her ways and be half-decent.'

'You thought wrong!' Penny said, heatedly. 'You shouldn't have left me with her.'

'I couldn't take you with me, love. Blokes don't know the first thing about bringing up a girl. If I'd known...'

Tears of anger, disappointment and frustration welled in Penny's eyes. 'Why did you leave? You knew Florence was cruel to me, so why didn't you stay and protect me?'

'I couldn't, love. I was so angry with her. If I had stayed, I would have killed her and then I'd have been in the dock on a murder charge. I had to leave to save meself from hanging. And to be honest, I was on the run from the Old Bill. But I'm a changed man now and there ain't been a day gone by when I ain't thought about you.'

Penny didn't believe him. If he'd thought about her as much as he claimed, then why hadn't he come back to see her before now? She glared at him accusingly. 'Who is my mother?' she demanded to know.

'I suppose you have a right to know, though it won't do you any good. Your mother's name was Jill. A real beauty she was, just like you but with blonde hair. Cor, thinking about her takes me right back,' he chuckled.

'*Was*... is she dead?'

'Yeah. She's been dead donkey's years.'

'Is that why you took me, because my mum died?'

'Er, no, not really. Your mum, see, she was a working woman, and she couldn't look after you an' all.'

'What work did she do?'

'Jill was a, erm, an entertainer.'

'What was her whole name?'

'Jill Durrant. She was a smashing woman, and bloody resourceful.'

'Did she have any other children? Have I got brothers or sisters?'

'No, love. As far as I know you was her only child. But if you want to know if you've got any family on that side, her dad, Archie, I think he's still alive and living in Battersea. He'd be your grandad. Nice old boy, he is. I reckon he'd be chuffed to know he has a granddaughter.'

It was too much for Penny to take in. Her long lost father was sat just feet away. She hadn't expected to feel so much contempt for the man. And all the years she'd spent terrified of Florence and desperate to escape the woman, she'd had a grandad living nearby. Overwhelmed, she had to get away from the man who'd abandoned her. She fled the room in floods of tears. So many unanswered questions ran through her mind, but Penny hoped she'd never see her father again.

Clara looked on, dumbfounded. Mr Black was overly confident and thoughtless, and Penny didn't appear to be pleased to see him. The poor girl had only just settled in properly to her new life, and now her father had turned up unexpectedly and upset the apple cart.

'What did I say wrong?' he asked when Penny ran out of the kitchen.

'You didn't expect her to welcome you with open arms, did you?'

'I dunno, yeah, I suppose I did.'

'Mr Black, you left her with a woman who half-starved her and worked her like a skivvy. Penny was beaten into submission, kept away from school and made to work for no money of her own. I don't think she will thank you for that, do you?'

'Not when you put it like that. Gawd, I'm sorry I walked out.'

'It's not me who needs to hear your apology.'

'But she won't talk to me. You saw her, she's legged it.'

'Give her time,' Clara sighed. 'Are you staying locally?'

Mr Black's eyes roamed the large kitchen. 'You've got a big place here. Surely you can put me up for the night?'

Clara was taken aback. 'Oh, I, erm, I think we can manage. I'll have to check with my husband.'

'Yeah, you do that. I don't reckon he'd mind, seeing as I'm family, eh.'

Clara's eyes widened. The man really did have some nerve. She hoped Penny was all right, but thought it was best to give the girl some space to think.

'Another cuppa would go down a treat,' Mr Black said, pushing his cup towards her.

Clara went to the sink to rinse the cup and was grateful when she saw Will heading towards the front door.

'Excuse me,' she said, and hurried to meet her husband.

'Penny's father is here,' she whispered urgently as Will removed his boots.

'What?'

'In the kitchen. He turned up out of the blue. Penny is quite upset; she ran off crying.'

'I'm not surprised. What does he want?'

'He says just to see her. And he's asked to stay for the night.'

'I hope you told him to get on his bike.'

'I wish I had, but he put me on the spot.'

'Oh, Clara, don't tell me that you've agreed he can stay?'
'Yes, sorry.'

Will sighed deeply. 'All right, but only for one night. If he wants to be around to make amends with Penny, then he can stay with Joan Savage, she takes in lodgers. Where's Penny?'

'I don't know, in her room, I expect.'

'All right, you see to him and I'll check on Penny.'

Clara returned to the kitchen and was astounded to find Mr Black frying himself two eggs.

'That sandwich only just touched the sides, I could eat an horse. I didn't want to put you to any trouble, so I've made meself at home.'

'As I can see.'

'Was that your husband I heard?'

'Yes.'

'I'd like to shake the man's hand and thank him for taking in my girl and giving her a nice place to live. Is she working, Penny? Does she have a job?'

'She works at the nurseries along the lane.'

'Is she on a good wage?'

'That's her business, Mr Black, you will have to ask Penny.'

'Right you are. Got any salt for me eggs?'

Clara placed the salt pig beside the stove, narked at the audacity of the man and suspicious of his motives. Asking about Penny's salary had raised Clara's hackles. She wanted to believe that the man was genuine, but she feared that Mr Black wanted money from his daughter. And she hoped that Penny wasn't foolish enough to give him any.

31

Cyril woke up on the sofa and yawned. *Cor,* he thought, *this is more comfy than Florrie's lumpy one!* And he knew he could soon get used to it. From what he could see, Penny had landed on her feet at Gaston Farm. His girl seemed to be doing all right for herself, and Cyril hoped that if he played his cards right, then he could have the easy life on the back of his daughter's good fortune. But first he had to win her round.

Soft voices reached his ears. He could tell the household had risen, and he supposed that he should join them and charm his way into their affections. After all, they'd clearly taken Penny on as one of their own. And as her father, Cyril hoped he'd be welcomed too.

'Good morning,' he bellowed as he strolled into the kitchen.

The room fell silent, and he noticed that all eyes were on him – except for Penny's. His daughter was sat with her head down and was chewing her thumbnail.

'Cor, fancy waking up to the smell of baked bread. It beats the stench of London. All this fresh, country air ain't 'alf given me an appetite, I can tell you.'

'We are just about to have breakfast, Mr Black, if you'd like to join us?' Mrs Gaston kindly offered, though Cyril could see she felt uncomfortable.

'Thank you, I would indeed,' he replied. 'And please, call me Cyril.'

'Penny has the same colour hair as you,' Rosemary piped up, to be quickly shushed by Mrs Gaston.

Cyril nodded to the girl, and then he smiled at the man of the house. But Mr Gaston wasn't as friendly as his wife and glowered back at him. He hadn't seen much of Mr Gaston last night, so now he took the opportunity to get into the farmer's good books. Leaning across the table with his arm outstretched, Cyril offered the man his hand to shake. 'Thank you for what you've done for my girl,' he said, trying to fill his words with sincerity.

He wasn't surprised when Mr Gaston snubbed his handshake, and he realised that he'd have to try a lot harder to gain the man's trust. 'It's a fine place you have. Penny's a lucky girl.'

'This place is what hard work gets you, and I wouldn't say that Penny is lucky, far from it.'

He didn't like Mr Gaston and he sensed that the feeling was mutual. The man was patronising and obviously thought that he was a cut above Cyril. Anger simmered, rising from his chest. But Cyril knew he had to swallow it down if he was going to make a good impression on the Gastons.

'I've heard that farm work is tough. You must be made of stern stuff, Mr Gaston. If I had me hat on, I'd take it off to you.'

Mr Gaston's response was no more than a grunt and Cyril guessed that he was going to be a hard nut to crack. Still, when he'd been in prison, he'd charmed tougher men than

Mr Gaston which had saved him from receiving a few good pastings. He felt sure that they'd be the best of mates soon.

Mrs Gaston broke the tension, asking, 'I trust you slept well?'

'Like a log. In fact, I had the best night's kip I've had in ages.'

'What are your plans?' Mr Gaston inquired.

'Well, seeing as I've come all this way to see my girl, I was hoping to stick around for a while and spend some time with her. We've got a lot of catching up to do.'

Mr Gaston sniffed. 'You'll find decent, clean lodgings in the village with Joan Savage. She charges a fair rate.'

'Ah, well, the thing is, I'm a bit strapped for cash at the moment. But you good people won't mind me kipping on your settee, will ya?'

'Yes, Mr Black, I will mind,' Mr Gaston said, abruptly.

'You're not going to throw me out, are you? Me and Penny ain't had a chance to have a proper chat yet. I won't be no bother. You'll hardly even notice that I'm here. What do you say, Mr Gaston? You'll give a fella a chance, won't you?'

The man didn't answer which Cyril took as a good sign. At least, he hadn't said *no*. 'How's my girl this morning?' he asked, directing his question at his daughter. 'Have you got over the shock of seeing me yet?'

Cyril wasn't happy when Penny ignored him. Trying harder, he said softly, 'I hope you'll give me a chance to say how sorry I am, and to make it up to you. 'Cos I am, love, I'm really sorry.'

When Penny kept her head down, Clara intervened. 'Time is a great healer, Mr Black. Penny will be leaving for work shortly. Perhaps it would be better if you left her be, for now.'

Cyril wanted to bark at the woman and tell her to poke her nosey beak out, but instead he smiled and mumbled, 'Thanks.' He had no intention of backing down from plying for Penny's forgiveness. With no coins in his pockets and reliant on the generosity of the Gastons, Cyril needed money and he needed it soon!

Later that morning, Penny found herself telling her seedlings her woes and was glad to get her worries off her chest.

'I told Clara that I didn't want to see him again, but Clara said that apart from Jimmy, my father is the only *real* family I have, and she reckons I should give him a chance. I'm not sure. I don't know what to do. I can't feel any love for the man, he's like a stranger to me. But Jimmy always said our dad has a good heart. Has he? I don't know. Gawd, I wish he hadn't shown up!'

'You know how to break a fella's heart.'

Penny spun around to see her dad standing there. She cringed as she realised that he must have heard her taking to the plants about him.

'Sorry, love, I wasn't eavesdropping, but I couldn't help overhearing. Clara's right, you know. You should give me a chance. Let me prove to you that I can be a good dad, albeit better late than never, eh. Look, I know it sounds daft, but there's a war on. None of us knows the future and life is too short to hold grudges. Let's be friends, eh, what do you say?'

Penny gulped, her heart telling her one thing and her head another.

'I know I ain't been there for you, but I am now. I'll never let you down again, my girl, cross me heart an' all that. The biggest mistake I ever made was walking out on you and

Jimmy. I'm not asking you to forgive me, I'm just asking that you let me back into your life.'

Penny bit on her bottom lip as her mind turned, her emotions in turmoil. She'd longed to see her dad again, but she hadn't expected to feel so bitter towards him. Though she knew, if she turned her back on her dad now and sent him packing, it would be something that she'd probably forever regret. 'If you really want to be my dad, then you'd better grab that watering can over there and give me a hand watering these plants.'

'I've never wanted to water plants more. But I must warn you, I ain't got green fingers.'

'Good,' Penny grinned. 'If you had green fingers, I'd be sending for the doctor!'

They chatted easily, the hours ticking by. Penny learned that her dad had spent quite a few years behind bars, and she believed him when he said that he was going straight now. She'd been fascinated hearing his stories of prison life, it had sounded horrendous though she laughed often because the way her dad told a tale was very amusing. She realised that her dad and Jimmy shared the same sense of humour. She also learned that her mother had died from a weak heart and had looked sad when she'd given Penny up.

'Do you think she wanted to keep me but couldn't?' Penny asked.

'I'm sure of it, love. She was happy to know that I'd called you Penny. And talking of which, here's that stamp, the Penny Black.'

Penny looked curiously at the black stamp printed with Queen Victoria's head.

Her dad explained, 'I was given a stamp collection once, it had belonged to a man who I was very fond of.'

'Mrs Whetstone gave you the collection, didn't she?' Penny asked.

'Yeah, that's right. How do you know that?'

'She told me.'

'Oh, right. Well, I promised the old girl that I'd always take care of her husband's stamps and that I'd add a Penny Black to the collection. But I messed that up an' all 'cos I ain't got the collection now. But I said I'd get a Penny Black, and I did, so here it is. You will look after it, won't you?'

'Yes, I will, and thank you.'

'King George has been collecting stamps since he was a kid, and so does President Roosevelt. I reckon that the stamp might be worth a few bob, and one day, it'll be worth a lot more than it is now.'

'I'll never sell it.'

'I said that about the collection that Mrs Whetstone gave me, but you have to do what you have to do. Anyway, I'll leave you to get on with your work. See you later, love.'

Penny waved off her father, filled with a new sense of optimism. She wished she knew how to contact Jimmy so that she could write to him. Jimmy never spoke badly of their dad, and Penny felt sure that her brother would be thrilled to know that his father was back.

'We get on rather well,' she whispered to one of the plants. 'In fact, I quite like him. I'm upset that he walked out on me, and I'm not sure that I've forgiven him yet. But that's enough about my dad for today. Mr Hamble is still on a recruiting drive for the Home Guard, so I've got lots to do and don't have time to stand around chatting to you,' she smiled.

Penny enjoyed her work, but she couldn't wait to get home later to spend more time with her dad. And she hoped that the Gastons would come to like him too.

Florence trudged back from the factory where she'd just secured a job. With men leaving their positions in their droves to join the armed forces, the workplace was crying out for women to fulfil the roles. But Florence wasn't looking forward to starting work the next week. It was a depressing thought, sitting for hour after hour on a bench in a large noisy room, packing small metal screws into boxes. She didn't relish the notion of taking orders from anyone either. And she was tired, so tired. But Florence had no choice. Cyril had been gone for three nights now and she knew he wasn't coming back. She wouldn't miss him, but she'd miss his money! And though the factory paid a fair wage, less than that of a man doing the same job but decent nonetheless, she wouldn't earn enough to keep up the rent payments on her two-bedroomed house. At least she had a few days to get her life in order before starting at the factory.

As she turned onto her street, she bumped into Mrs Darwin.

'Good morning, Mrs Black,' the woman greeted her, nervously. 'I've just done a bit of shopping. It's not easy to make the rations stretch.'

'And I've just found meself a job,' Florence replied, her lips set in a grim line.

'Oh, that's nice.'

'No, it ain't, but beggars can't be choosers.'

'Is, erm, is Mr Black all right?'

'He's buggered off again, and good riddance to him. I'll be

moving out an' all. There's a room for rent three streets away. It'll do me. I won't be needing all my furniture, so you're welcome to offer me a price for anything.'

'Oh, erm, thank you, but I don't think so. Berty hasn't had much work on lately, money is tight.'

'Suit yourself. My stuff is good quality, you'll be missing out.'

Mrs Darwin shrugged. 'I'm sure, but I can't buy what I can't afford.'

'Have you heard anything from Katy?'

'No, and I don't expect I will. I thought about sending her a Christmas card, but then decided against it. She's better off where she is, and away from – from – her ... dad.'

Florence understood. She knew it couldn't be easy for the woman, but Mrs Darwin only had herself to blame. Granted, Florence was the first to admit that she hadn't been a good mother to Penny, but she would *never* have allowed a man to hurt the girl in the vile way that *Berty* had harmed Katy. Just the thought of the man's name turned her stomach. 'I'm not pleased about having to give up my home, but I shan't be sad to get away from your husband. Living next door to him, knowing what he did to that poor child, it makes me feel sick,' she spat, speaking her mind.

Mrs Darwin's face turned beetroot red, and she looked as though she was about to burst into tears.

'I've kept your filthy secret, but now that we're not going to be neighbours, I'm sorely tempted to open me mouth.'

'You wouldn't! Please, Mrs Black, I'm begging you ... for Katy's sake.'

'Katy ain't here, and you and me both know that she won't be coming back.'

'Mrs Black, please... I wouldn't be able to walk the streets, and, please, think about my boys...'

Florence hadn't intended to use her knowledge against Mrs Darwin. But seeing how desperate the woman was to preserve her *family* secret, Florence could see an opportunity. 'I'll keep quiet – for a price.'

'A price? What do you mean?'

'You can pay me to keep me mouth shut. I can't say fairer than that.'

'But, I've already told you, I don't have any money.'

'You'd better find some, or all of the borough will know about you and that disgusting husband of yours.'

'Please,' Mrs Darwin cried, 'please don't do this. I've got two boys to feed!'

'Yeah, well, I've got meself to think of. I don't like what I'm doing, but I ain't going to feel guilty. This ain't a patch on what you allowed your old man to get away with.'

'I can't pay, Mrs Black, I haven't got anything!'

'So you keep saying. I'll be knocking on your door tomorrow evening. Pay up or face the consequences. It's up to you.'

Florence's heart was pounding. She'd never been so daring! Blackmail was an ugly word, but incest and rape were uglier.

32

The next day, after laundering Cyril's clothes, Clara pegged them to the washing line. She hoped they would dry before Will returned to the farmhouse. Her husband was already peeved about the man sleeping on their sofa, and the sight of Cyril's worn-out clothes on the line would likely tip Will over the edge.

Back in the kitchen, Clara placed a large pot of stew in the oven, and then went to the windowsill for her wedding ring. She always removed it before doing the washing. *That's odd*, she thought, searching the ledge for her ring. *I always leave it in the same place*. Rummaging in the pocket of her apron, it wasn't there either. Clara began to panic. The wedding ring had belonged to Will's mother. She hoped it hadn't been knocked off the windowsill and lost forever down the plug hole. Will would be ever so upset, and so would she!

Leaning over the sink and peering down the plughole, she couldn't see anything glimmering. She began frantically examining the kitchen countertops and floor, but she knew her search would be fruitless. Clara had always been vigilant with the ring; she couldn't believe she'd been so careless.

Cyril came into the kitchen, sniffing the air as he said, 'Something smells nice. What's for dinner?'

Distracted, Clara didn't answer.

'Are you all right?' Cyril asked.

'Have you seen my wedding ring? A thick, gold band. I'm sure I left it on the windowsill.'

'No, I can't say I have. I'll help you look for it.'

'I've searched everywhere! It's not here.'

'Are you sure you took it off?'

'Yes. I never do the washing with my ring on.'

'Perhaps you forgot,' Cyril suggested.

Clara huffed and stood with her hands on her hips, annoyed with herself. 'Maybe. It's the only explanation. If it came off with the washing, it'll be gone. I tipped the water down the drain that goes to the stream.'

'I'll go and take a look. You never know, you might be lucky.'

Clara was grateful for Cyril's help, though she doubted the man would find the ring. She wasn't looking forward to breaking the news to her husband. Will's mood would likely go from bad to worse.

Penny closed the front door and crept up to her bedroom, hoping to avoid seeing anyone. She'd had a rotten day at work, and all she wanted to do was curl up with her book and block out the world.

Rosemary was adding the finishing touches to the doll's house she'd made for *Penny*, her rag doll. 'What do you think?' she asked.

'It looks amazing,' Penny replied, trying to sound cheerier than she felt.

Kicking off her shoes, Penny picked up her book and sat with her legs tucked beneath her on the bed. She began reading while Rosemary hummed softly in the background, sewing tiny curtains for the windows of her doll's house.

Turning the page of her book, Penny realised that none of what she'd read had sunk in. Her mind was elsewhere, and she couldn't push away the troubles of her day.

The door opened and Clara popped her head through. 'I thought I heard you come home. What are you doing up here?'

'Reading,' Penny answered.

'Your dad's downstairs. He's waiting in the kitchen for you.'

'I'll see him later.'

Clara came further into the room. 'Oh, Rosemary, that's looking wonderful,' she said, admiring the doll's house.

'Thanks. I've nearly finished it.'

Then, sitting on the edge of the bed, Clara asked, 'Are you all right, Penny?'

'Yeah.'

'You don't seem yourself. Has someone upset you?'

Penny could feel tears pricking her eyes and fought to hold them back.

Clara turned to her daughter. 'Rosemary, would you mind giving us a few minutes alone, please? Katy is in the snug, why don't you join her?'

Rosemary didn't question her mother and skipped off merrily.

Penny closed her book and placed it beside her before chewing nervously on her thumbnail. She hadn't done anything wrong, but she didn't think that anyone would believe her.

'I can see you're upset, Penny. Do you want to talk about it?'

'No, not really.'

'You should. We all know the consequences of bottling up our feelings.'

Penny didn't need reminding of the day when Katy had cut her wrist. The memory of finding her friend soaked in blood would stay with her forever. But it had taught them all a lesson; it was better to share their feelings, no matter how bad they might be. 'I know I lied when I first came here, but I'm not a thief,' she blurted.

'No, Penny, of course you're not. Has someone accused you of something?' Clara asked.

'Yeah... well, sort of... Mr Hamble thinks I stole his delivery money. I didn't, Clara, I swear I didn't. I'd never do nothing like that!'

'It's all right, calm down. Start from the beginning and tell me exactly what's happened.'

Penny drew in a long breath. 'Mr Hamble ain't been at work for the past few days. He's left me to get on with things. Then today, he came in after lunch and was pleased with all my work. But then we had a delivery arrive, and when Mr Hamble went to pay the fella, he said that three shillings were missing from the pot. I never took the money. You believe me, don't you?'

'Yes, Penny, I believe you. Did Mr Hamble accuse you of stealing the three shillings?'

'Not exactly, but I know he must think that I took it. He was looking at me differently, I could tell what he was thinking.'

'But he never accused you?'

'He didn't have to. He made a point of saying that he knew exactly how much cash was in the pot and he said he *never* makes mistakes when it comes to money. I know he reckons I stole it. Oh, Clara, I feel terrible.'

'Your conscience is clear, so you have nothing to worry about.'

'He's going to sack me, I'm sure of it. How can I prove that I'm innocent? I'm the only person other than Mr Hamble who has access to the pot. If Mr Hamble hasn't made a mistake, and I didn't take the money, then where's it gone?'

'And you're sure no one else has access to the pot?'

'Yeah, I'm sure. The only people who've been in the nursery are Mrs Hamble and my dad.'

Clara took hold of Penny's hand, and said firmly, 'You have nothing to worry about. Come downstairs and have some dinner. I promise you, Penny, you will *not* be losing your job.'

Florence stood next to the front room window and watched for Berty Darwin to go out to the pub. When she saw the man walking off with a roll-up in his mouth, she threw on her coat and marched next door.

After knocking on her neighbour's door three times and being ignored, her patience was wearing thin. 'I know you're in there,' Florence shouted through the letterbox. 'Open up.'

Mrs Darwin pulled the door open just a crack. 'I haven't got any money,' she said in a hushed voice.

'Yet your old man has got money to spend in the pub.'

'He holds the purse strings. I asked him for some, I lied and said the boys needed new clothes, but he wouldn't give me none.'

'That ain't my problem. You've had all day. You could have pawned something.'

'Pawned what? I ain't got nothing worth pawning.'

'Your wedding ring, your husband's bicycle. Like I said, it ain't my problem. But now *you* have a very big problem, 'cos I'm off to see her at number forty-eight. What's it that everyone round here calls her? Oh, yes, *the bellows of Battersea*. You and me both know that anything I say to *old bellows* tonight will be public knowledge in these streets by the morning.'

Gladys Darwin's face drained of colour. 'Please, Mrs Black, give me one more day to get you the money. I'm begging you.'

Florence thought for a moment. She supposed it was better to have the promise of some cash rather than shouting her mouth off just yet. 'One day,' she growled. 'Or I'll blab.'

Back indoors, Florence carried on with packing her belongings. She was sad to leave her home and blamed Cyril. Opening the kitchen drawer, she found the writing pad and noticed that the page with Penny's address had been ripped out. *The sly git*, she thought, guessing that Cyril had taken it, and she assumed that he'd gone to try his luck in Kent.

Grabbing a pencil, Florence sat at the table poised to write to Penny. She decided that it was about time the girl found out a few home truths, and Florence wouldn't be shy with the facts. She had no doubt that Cyril would have spun a web of lies, but Florence would soon put Penny straight. Smiling cruelly, she could picture the girl's face as she'd read the letter. Oh, how Florence wished she could be a fly on the wall!

33

Clara's sleep had been intermittent at best, and when she woke in the morning, she gently nudged her husband.

'Urgh,' he groaned.

'I'm not sure about this, Will. What if Cyril turns nasty?'

Will sighed and opened his eyes as he sat up in the bed. 'You leave him to me.'

'But what if I'm wrong about him?'

'You're not. I haven't trusted him from the off. It's too much of a coincidence that since he's been here, money has gone missing from Penny's workplace and so has your wedding ring. It's him. We know he's been in and out of prison for petty theft. A leopard doesn't change its spots.'

'Poor Penny will be so upset. She's growing fond of her dad.'

'It's better she knows sooner rather than later. What sort of father would risk losing his daughter her job? He's here for one thing only, and that's for what he can get.'

'I know, you're right. He asked me how much Penny earns. I suspect he'll be coaxing her wages from her too.'

'Then we'd better get on with the plan.'

Clara agreed, but her stomach was twisting in knots and she felt sick.

In the kitchen, she tried to act normally and hide her nerves. Rosemary was full of the joys of spring and chatting about school. Katy was quiet, as usual, and showing Will a drawing she'd made of the cows. Penny sat chewing her thumbnail as though she had the weight of the world on her young shoulders. The girl was upset now, but she'd be devasted when her father would be outed as a thief. Clara pursed her lips. She felt awful for setting up Cyril, but she knew it was the right thing to do.

Will threw her a discreet look and winked. That meant their plan was in place. Clara knew that her husband had left several coins on the table near the front door. He'd drilled through one of them, so if someone helped themselves to the money, a search would be instigated and the stolen coins easily identified.

Basil wandered into the kitchen, frowning.

'Good morning,' Clara said, trying to sound bright. 'You're not looking very happy.'

'Have you seen my wallet?' he asked. 'The one that Penny made me for Christmas.'

Clara's heart leapt. She was sure that Cyril must have taken it. 'No, I can't say I have. Where did you last see it?'

'I thought it was in the pocket of my coat, but it's gone. I must have dropped it in the fields.'

Will suddenly jumped to his feet, and Clara could tell by the thunderous look on his face that her husband was furious.

'That's it, I've had enough of this,' he shouted.

'Will, please,' Clara implored. She didn't want a scene in

front of the children. No one knew how Cyril Black would react to the accusation of being a thief.

'No, Clara, I'm not putting up with this any longer. Basil has worked hard for his money. I won't have *that* man coming into *my* home and stealing from us!'

Cyril appeared bewildered. 'What are you saying? You reckon I've pinched Basil's wallet?' he asked.

'And my wife's wedding ring and money from the nurseries,' Will barked.

'Well, I'm insulted, I am. I thought you were good people, but good people don't go around accusing folk of crimes they ain't done.'

'Let's have a look, shall we?' Will bellowed and stamped out of the kitchen.

Clara ran to keep up with her husband who'd stormed into the lounge where Cyril had been sleeping. The man's bed was still on the sofa, the blankets bundled at the end.

Will began grabbing at Cyril's clothes that were piled in the corner of the room. As he went through the pockets, Cyril pushed past Clara.

'Get off my stuff,' Cyril growled.

'Why? Have you got something to hide?'

'No, I bleedin' ain't. But you've got no right to touch what's mine.'

Will ignored the man and continued searching Cyril's belongings.

'You won't find nothing 'cos I ain't stole a bleedin' thing from you lot.' Then turning, he glared at Clara. 'This don't look good in front of my girl. Thanks. Thanks for flippin' nothing!'

Clara watched wide-eyed as Cyril marched out of the room.

'There's nothing here,' Will hissed, throwing a pair of trousers angrily to the floor. 'Where's he hidden it?'

'Oh, Will, we might have just made a terrible mistake!'

'Don't be fooled by him, Clara. He's a thief and he's manipulative with it.'

Penny had heard the raised voices from the lounge. She looked around the table. Basil, Rosemary and Katy were gawping back at her, stunned. She could see in their eyes that they all believed her father had stolen from them.

'He hasn't pinched anything!' Penny cried out. 'My dad wouldn't do that to us,' she insisted.

Pushing back her chair, Penny dashed from the kitchen and towards the lounge. She saw her father hurrying through the front door, but he didn't see her.

Mr Gaston's voice carried from the room. 'I'm telling you, Clara, that man doesn't care about Penny. He's out for what he can get.'

Penny felt as though someone had stabbed her through the heart. Mr Gaston had to be wrong. After all, her father had promised that he'd go straight, and she believed him.

Chasing out of the door after him, she stood, her eyes searching through the morning darkness, hoping and praying that her father hadn't left Gaston Farm. When she spotted a shadowy figure going inside a small outbuilding to the side of the house, relief flooded over her and she ran to catch up with her dad. The bicycles were kept in the building, and she assumed her dad was going to take one to ride away from the Gastons'. *I have to stop him*, she thought, hoping that she could talk him into staying. She was sure an apology from Mr Gaston would change her dad's mind about leaving.

As Penny hurried into the outbuilding, she saw her dad crouched on the floor prying open a loose floorboard. She stepped back into the shadows and watched silently. It was obvious that he'd hidden something under the boards. Tears were already falling down her cheeks and disappointment engulfed her heart. She hadn't wanted to believe Mr Gaston. She'd defended her father to Basil and the girls. But there was no denying what Penny was witnessing.

Her father reached through the floorboards and, in the dim light, Penny saw him pull out a small, sack cloth. He emptied the contents onto the floor: a gold ring, three shillings and the wallet she'd made for Basil. Gathering his stolen stash, he shoved the wallet and the ring into his jacket pocket and the coins into his trousers. As he turned to make his exit, Penny stepped in front of him.

'How could you?' she asked. 'After everything they've done for you... for me, too. How could you do this to us?'

'Oh, love, it's not what you think.'

'Mr and Mrs Gaston have been kind to you. I – I – I can't believe you'd steal from them!'

'I need the money and they've got plenty.'

'You stole from Mr Hamble too! I could get the sack because of you,' Penny sobbed, her heart breaking. 'Mr Gaston was right. You don't care about me... you never have.'

'That's not true, love. You're my girl, and I think the world of you.'

'Give me back everything you stole,' Penny demanded, stretching out her hand towards him.

'I can't do that, love. Sorry, but I'm going to need this to help me on my way.'

'I won't let you leave with things that don't belong to you.'

Her dad smiled as he stepped towards her. 'You're a good kid, Penny. Remember, always look after that stamp I gave you.'

'I suppose the stamp is stolen too.'

'Yeah, and I did time for pinching it, so I've paid my dues on that stamp which is all the more reason for you to treasure it. I'll be seeing you, love.'

Cyril went to walk around Penny, but she jumped in front of him. 'I want Clara's ring and Basil's wallet,' she demanded.

'Get out of me way,' he said, his tone fierce.

Penny stood firmly with her feet apart, her shoulders back and her chin jutting forward. 'No. I won't get out of your way, not until you give back what ain't yours to take!' she said, defiantly.

Penny yelped when her father roughly pushed her to one side. She stumbled on a wooden crate, lost her footing and fell to the floor. Landing awkwardly, pain shot down to her fingers and up her arm. 'Argh,' she cried, wincing.

Her father looked down at her. 'Sorry, I didn't mean to do that, but you shouldn't have got in my way. Take care, love. You'll be all right. You're set for life here.'

'Dad!' Penny shouted. But he was gone, and he'd taken the stolen goods with him.

Penny cradled her aching wrist, but the pain in her arm was nothing compared to the agony ripping through her heart.

'Penny!' Basil exclaimed, rushing to her side. 'What have you done?'

'My dad... he's leaving... chase after him, Basil. He's got your wallet and your mum's ring.'

Basil gathered Penny in his arms and gently pulled her to her feet. 'Let him go. You're more important. Let's get you back to the house. It looks like your wrist might be broken.'

Penny knew it was broken, and so was her heart. 'I'm so sorry about my dad.'

'Hey, don't be. It's not your fault. But when that wrist is healed, you can make me another wallet, if you like?'

Penny smiled through her pain. 'Yeah, I would,' she said, gazing up at Basil's caring eyes. She didn't have the guts to tell him, but he had just become her hero. As her arm throbbed and her heart broke, she felt a peculiar sensation of butterflies fluttering in her stomach. *Just like the lady in the story I'm reading*, she thought. The main character in the book had fallen in love and had described fluttering in her stomach and a racing pulse. *Oh gawd*, Penny panicked, *I've fallen in love with Basil!*

34

July 1940
Four months later

Penny was now over seventeen and a couple of months earlier, with her wrist in plaster, she'd enjoyed her first official birthday party. Vera Hamble had bought her three different shades of light-coloured lipsticks. Penny wore one every day and felt quite grown-up. Of course, Rosemary wanted to wear it too, but Mr Gaston forbade it. Her little sister would often join Penny in the nurseries after school and help with watering the plants. Katy, on the other hand, still preferred her own company or Basil's.

'It's so hot in the greenhouse today,' Rosemary moaned.

'I know, it's sweltering. The coldest winter on record feels like it's a long way behind us now, though it was only six months ago,' Penny replied, remembering the frozen bird that had fallen out of the sky and hit the roof of the greenhouse.

'Do you think Mr Hamble will give me a job here when I leave school?'

'You're only thirteen, you've got another year to go until you can leave school.'

'I know, but I like working here with you.'

'I thought you wanted to be a nurse. Have you changed your mind?' Penny asked.

'Hmm, I'm not sure. If I do nursing, I'd probably have to move away from home.'

'Ah, I see your point. But you could come back and visit us.'

'It wouldn't be the same... What's that noise?'

Penny strained her ears and could hear a low, rumbling sound that was becoming louder and louder. 'Oh my gawd!' she mumbled, looking skyward through the glass overhead.

Her eyes fixed on a fleet of silver-grey aeroplanes about a thousand feet above, their wings glinting in the summer sun.

'Is it the Germans?' Rosemary asked, fearfully.

Penny's heart raced as she realised that it was, and judging by the direction they were flying, she thought they must be heading for London.

More planes appeared, this time coming from the other direction. The Royal Air Force swooped in, and Penny could hear the crackling of gun fire.

'RUN!' she shouted, grabbing Rosemary's hand.

Penny dragged Rosemary out of the greenhouse and towards the lane that would take them home, her heart pounding hard with fear.

'What's happening?' Rosemary asked, sounding terrified.

'It's a dog fight right above us. Just keep running. We'll be safe at home.'

The roaring of the planes' engines and the booming of their guns seemed to follow Penny all the way to the farm. Shrapnel fell around them as they raced home. Rounding the gates, she saw Clara on the doorstep, gripping the hem of her apron, her face pale. And from behind the house, Penny could see Basil and Mr Gaston sprinting from the fields.

When Clara saw Penny and Rosemary, she frantically waved her hands. 'Hurry, girls,' she cried, 'Quickly, run!'

Penny yanked Rosemary along, desperate to reach the safety of the farmhouse. When they arrived at the doorstep, Clara threw her arms around them and held them both tightly.

A terrific boom blasted through the air. Penny looked up and saw the wing of a plane fluttering in the sky like a piece of paper. A trail of black smoke followed the stricken plane as it plummeted towards the ground.

'It's one of ours,' Basil panted. 'It's a Spitfire.'

'It looks like it's going to come down just west of the village,' Mr Gaston said, struggling to catch his breath.

A thick plume of smoke billowed into the sky as the ill-fated aircraft hit the ground.

'We should help,' Basil suggested, 'The pilot might be alive!'

'How can you help?' Clara asked. 'You won't get there in time.'

'Bikes,' Basil said, and ran towards the outbuilding.

Penny ran after him. 'Wait for me,' she called, 'I'll come with you.'

'Basil ... Penny ...' Clara called as the pair pedalled hard, racing along the gravel drive towards the gates. 'Come back!'

'Your mum is calling us,' Penny shouted to Basil who was pedalling faster than her.

'I know.'

'Are you sure we should go?'

'Yes!'

Penny's bicycle was smaller than Basil's. It was an old one

that had belonged to Rosemary and Mr Gaston had fixed it up for Penny to learn to ride. She hadn't long mastered the skill and wobbled as she struggled to keep up with Basil.

Along the lane, left and then right, up a small hill and down the other side, Penny could hear the planes battling above but dared not look up. They passed a small woodland and out into an open stretch of fields.

Basil's bike skidded to a screeching stop and Penny caught him up. She gasped at the destruction before her eyes. The British plane had come down in a cherry orchard. A long path of blackened dirt had ripped through the field. Tree upon tree had been torn from its roots. Scattered small fires burned and smouldered among the twisted metal and molten aluminium. There was no crater, and nothing resembling a plane. And sadly, there was no pilot either.

An ambulance tore up to the scene along with three army vehicles. Penny turned to look at Basil who was staring at the wreckage.

He saluted. 'Thank you for your service, sir. God rest your soul.'

Penny couldn't speak, her vision was blurred with unshed tears.

'That's what I want to do,' Basil stated with an air of determination, 'I want to join the Royal Air Force and fly planes.'

Clara had sent Will in search of Basil and Penny. Now she stood at the kitchen window, peering through and willing them to come home safely.

'Do you think the pilot survived?' Rosemary asked.

'I shouldn't think so.'

'Why didn't the German bombers drop their bombs on us?'

'They were trying to get to London where they'd cause more damage.'

'Do you think the airmen could see us from up there?'

'I've no idea.'

'I wonder what it's like to fly.'

'Rosemary, go and sit in the snug with Katy, please. I don't think she should be alone after that. It's been quite a shock for us all.'

'Katy doesn't like me sitting in the snug with her because she likes to listen to the wireless and says I talk too much.'

'Then sit quietly and listen to the wireless with her,' Clara instructed.

As Rosemary ambled away, Clara was pleased to see Will returning with Basil and Penny walking beside him, both pushing their bicycles.

'The pilot didn't make it,' Will said miserably when he came into the kitchen.

'Tell them, Basil, tell your mum and dad what you told me,' Penny urged.

Clara looked at her son. 'What?' she asked.

'I want to join the air force,' he said.

'You're only sixteen, you're too young.'

'I'll be seventeen this Christmas and then I can join.'

Clara gulped. 'Only with our consent, and I'm sorry, Basil, but I shan't give it.'

'Please, Mum, I really want to fly planes.'

'You've just seen what happened to that poor pilot. Can you imagine what his family will have to go through? No, Basil, I won't allow you to join the RAF.'

'Dad?' Basil appealed.

'I'm with your mother on this, Son. Anyway, I need you on the farm. You're in a reserved occupation. You won't need to sign up with any of the armed forces.'

'But I want to! I want to fight the Nazis... I want to protect my family and my home!'

'I appreciate your sentiments, Basil, but your dad's right. You're needed here. The country needs farmers just as much as it needs soldiers, sailors and airmen.'

'Fine. But you can't stop me once I'm eighteen.'

'Let's hope the war is over by then,' Will said.

'And that we are victorious,' Clara added. She could feel a headache coming on and pinched the bridge of her nose with her finger and thumb. It was probably caused by the stress of seeing the Luftwaffe in the sky above her home. The war had seemed a long way away, but with the Germans just across the English Channel in France, and their air force flying over Kent in their droves, it had suddenly become very real and too close for comfort. 'That plane could have come down on our house,' she thought aloud. 'We all could have been killed!'

Stumbling backwards, Will quickly pulled out a chair from under the table and eased Clara onto it. 'It was a one-off, a fluke. We'll be all right here,' he assured her.

Clara felt sick with nerves. 'I do hope you're right, Will. But I don't think it's the last we've seen of the German air force.'

Even their remote farmhouse no longer felt a safe place to be.

35

August 1940
Five months later

Clara stuffed a letter into the pocket of her apron, her stomach turning with disgust.

'It's a scorcher today,' Will said, wiping his brow on the back of his forearm as he came into the kitchen. 'What's for lunch?'

'Bread, cheese and pickles. Where's Basil?'

'He's stopped to look at the planes flying over.'

'I can't hear any?'

'No, they're about a mile east of the marshes. It looks like the RAF are doing a great job of holding the Luftwaffe back. Basil said he saw a couple of our boys doing victory rolls in the air.'

'They're so brave, but I can't bear to watch the dogfights. Every plane that comes down breaks my heart when I think of the mothers of the young pilots. I wish Basil would change his mind about wanting to fly.'

'Don't worry, it'll be a while before he's old enough.'

Clara placed a plate of food in front of her husband and sat opposite him at the table. 'Penny's had another letter,' she said, shaking her head.

'From Florence again?'

'Yes. I feel awful keeping them from her, but I can't see that giving the letters to Penny will achieve anything.'

'What does Florence say this time?'

'Just the same as all the others. Rambling and full of hate. Nasty things about Penny's mother being a prostitute and dying from syphilis. I don't understand why she keeps writing to the girl.'

'I think she must be mad. Florence seems obsessed with going out of her way to make Penny's life a misery. You're doing the right thing in destroying the letters before Penny sees them.'

Basil came through the door with gusto, his handsome face sun-kissed pink. 'I saw a British plane shot down! The pilot turned the plane upside down in mid-air, got out of the cockpit and parachuted down. I think he's landed on the marshes. Wow, it was amazing!'

'I hope he's alive and well,' Clara said.

'I'm sure he is, Mum. If he'd been closer, I would have gone to help.'

'I wish you'd stay out of it.'

'What if it was me lying injured in a field somewhere? Wouldn't you want the locals to help me?'

'Yes, but there are plenty of other people available to help. There's no need for you to get involved. It's dangerous!'

'How?' Basil asked.

'Well, would you still run to rescue a German pilot?'

'Yes, and I'd hold him prisoner until the army arrived.'

'See, that's exactly what I mean. Will, have a word with your son. Explain to him that the Germans will have guns and will think nothing of putting a bullet in him!'

'You heard your mother,' Will said. 'No chasing after downed German pilots, all right?'

'All right,' Basil agreed, with a roll of his eyes.

With that sorted, Clara gave Basil his lunch and her mind wandered to the letter in her apron. She thought about writing back to Florence to tell her to stop sending letters, and she'd give her a piece of her mind at the same time. But if Will was right and Florence was mad, then appealing to the woman would be a waste of time. She'd just have to continue to intercept the letters and hope that Penny would never get to the post before her.

Florence was sat on the edge of her bed. Looking down, she stamped her foot heavily three times on the floorboards. 'For gawd's sake, shut that child up!' she shouted.

The constant crying from the baby in the room below was grating on her. She didn't like the mother, a feeble woman who rarely left the house. Florence had no idea where the father was, she assumed he'd been conscripted. But, she supposed, at least the mother kept the shared kitchen clean, though the cleanliness didn't deter the bugs and vermin that infested the run-down building. The only thing that Florence could find to not complain about was the reasonable rent.

Huffing, Florence was worn out after her day working at the factory, but she knew she wasn't going to find any peace at home. Grabbing her handbag, she stomped down the stairs and out of the front door.

It was a warm evening, the summer sun still high in the sky. Florence traipsed to the street she'd recently moved from, her heart heavy. She missed her old home, the space and the privacy. A new family had moved into the house now, and they'd bought several pieces of her furniture. Florence had welcomed the money, but after forking out for new shoes that were suitable for work and a wireless for her room, the extra cash hadn't lasted long.

Florence hoped Mrs Darwin's husband was at the pub and knocked on the woman's door.

Gladys Darwin looked surprised when she opened it and saw Florence. 'I'm not due to pay you until tomorrow,' she muttered.

'I know, but I thought I'd collect early.'

'I ain't got any money. You'll have to come back tomorrow.'

'You never had anything last week. How is tomorrow going to be different from today, eh?'

'I – I – I'll get you the money. I just need more time.'

'I reckon you're trying to fob me off. But I ain't going away and neither is your sickening secret.'

'I promise, I'll have something for you tomorrow. Please, Mrs Black, I'm doing my best. I can't give you what I ain't got.'

'You need to find yourself a job.'

'I can't. Berty won't allow me to work.'

'Then you need to speak up for yourself. There's a cleaning job going at the factory. It's only a couple hours in the mornings. It would suit you down to the ground, and I can put the good word in for you.'

'You'd do that for me?'

'No, Mrs Darwin, I'm doing it for me. But we'd both have a few extra coins in our purses.'

'Berty leaves me short, I could do with the extra cash. But I really don't think he'll stand for it.'

Florence shrugged. 'I suggest you talk him round, 'cos if

you can't keep up with your payments to me, then I'll have no reason to stay quiet. Speak to him when he comes home. You know where to find me.'

Florence heard the door close as she walked away with a wry smile on her face. She didn't know why she hadn't thought of this sooner. Helping Mrs Darwin find work was worth it for the added cash she'd be able to extract from the woman. And she knew that Mrs Darwin would put her earnings to good use. They would both be better off. She didn't feel bad; she was doing the woman a favour.

A cool breeze blew, which Florence was grateful for. She wasn't in any rush to get back to her room and slowed her pace. But when she saw *the bellows of Battersea* walking towards her, Florence wished she'd hurried home so she would have dodged the busybody. The white-haired woman would no doubt impart a stream of gossip which Florence had no interest in. Now, almost face-to-face, there was no avoiding the old crone.

'Hello, Florrie, how are you, deary?'

'I'm fine, thanks, Doris.'

'I was sorry to hear about your Jimmy. How is he getting on? It can't be easy for him.'

Florence looked at the woman, perplexed. 'What do you mean?' she asked.

'Getting injured. I heard he's lost his sight. Is that right?'

'Jimmy … injured …'

'Yes, Mrs Dunbar told Helen who told me that Cathy in the next street, her son, Sam, he was caught up in the blast with Jimmy. They went to the same field hospital. Sam wrote to his mother and said that his injuries weren't too bad and he was going back to join his unit, but Jimmy was being shipped home. I was wondering how he is 'cos no one has seen him.'

Florence stared blankly at Doris, her head spinning.

'You don't look well, Florrie, are you sure you're all right?'

'Er, yeah... I've got to go,' she answered, and walked around the woman.

'See you, deary. Give Jimmy my best.'

Jimmy... lost his sight... It couldn't be true, could it? Maybe if he couldn't see, that was why she hadn't received any correspondence from him. After all, he couldn't write if he was blind. A sob caught in Florence's throat. She wanted to gather her son in her arms and reassure him that she'd always look after him. But she had no clue of his whereabouts. And no idea of how to contact him. *My dear, sweet boy*, she thought, her womb lurching as she imagined him hurt. She'd always cared for Jimmy but had known that the numbness she felt in her heart wasn't normal. Yet now, hearing that her son had come close to death had evoked powerful emotions in Florence that she'd never expected. At last, she could finally feel a mother's love.

36

It was a lazy Saturday afternoon and Penny was enjoying a long glass of water as she sat in the shade under a tree.

Rosemary skipped out of the house and ran across to join her. 'Will you come to the stream with me?' she asked.

'What, now?'

'Yes. Mum is busy making Katy a birthday cake, Katy is listening to the wireless as usual, and I'm bored.'

'I suppose so,' Penny smiled, and held out her hand. 'Give me a pull up,' she said.

'Heave-ho,' Rosemary laughed, tugging on Penny's hand.

'Go and fetch Katy. It'll do her good to get out in the sun for a while.'

'She won't come,' Rosemary replied. 'I've already asked her.'

'Go and ask her again and tell her I said she *must* come with us.'

Rosemary dashed off, minutes later returning with Katy following.

'Come on then, I'll race you,' Penny smiled as she ran off towards the stream.

When they reached the hollowed tree near their favourite spot, the girls fell into the long grass in a heap of giggles. Even Katy was laughing. Penny lay down, enjoying the warmth of the sun on her face and the grass tickling her arms. She gazed up at the blue sky, studying the small puffs of white clouds that slowly moved across. 'That looks like a duck,' she said, pointing up.

Rosemary lay beside her. 'It's changing into an elephant,' she said, her eyes following the same cloud.

Katy was sat on a fallen log. 'It's so peaceful here,' she mused.

'Until the Germans fly over,' Penny commented.

'I love seeing the planes!' Rosemary piped, enthusiastically. 'Basil has been teaching me the names of them. I can recognise nearly all of them now!'

'Are you becoming a tomboy?' Katy asked.

'No, but I'm getting too old for dolls. I should be thinking about getting married.'

Penny sat bolt upright. 'Married, at your age... no, Rosemary, you don't need to be thinking about that yet!'

'If you had to marry someone, who would it be?'

Penny knew exactly who she wanted to marry, but she couldn't admit it to her sisters. 'I don't know,' she fibbed.

'What about you, Katy?'

Katy shrugged.

'If you had to choose someone to marry or you'd die if you didn't, who would you choose?'

Penny could feel herself blushing as she thought of Basil.

'Tell us, Penny, who?' Rosemary pushed.

'I don't know, Basil, I suppose.'

'My brother!' Rosemary spat.

'Yeah, well, I don't really know anyone else.'
'Do you like Basil?'
'Of course I do, why wouldn't I?'
'Do you love him?'
'Oh, Rosemary, that's a silly question.'
'No, it's not. You do, don't you? You love Basil.'
'No, pack it in,' Penny said, embarrassed.
'You're going bright red. It's true, you love Basil!'

Penny couldn't stop herself from smiling. 'Yes, it's true. I love him so much, but please, don't say anything to him.'

'It's all right, I won't tell him. Lots of the girls in my school like him too. But I hope he marries you because then we will be *real* sisters.'

'Can you hear that?' Katy asked, looking skyward.

'Oh no,' Penny whispered. There was no mistaking the droning sound of approaching German aircraft. The Luftwaffe were a constant threat and relentless in their ambition to bomb London. The battle for control of the skies over Britain had become a daily occurrence which terrified Penny.

'Look, there they are,' Rosemary cried, jumping to her feet and pointing upwards over the direction of the nurseries.

Penny's pulse quickened when she realised how close the planes were, and they were flying far lower than she'd seen before. 'Hurry!' she screamed, ushering Katy towards her. 'We must get home.'

'Let's get a closer look,' Rosemary squealed excitedly, and ran through the long grass towards the lane.

Penny called after her, 'No! Rosemary... Come back!'

When Rosemary continued running in the direction of the planes, Penny turned to Katy. 'Run home, as quick as you can. I'll have to chase after Rosemary.'

Katy nodded, her eyes filled with panicked tears.

'We'll be all right. Go,' Penny said, giving her friend a gentle push.

Once Penny was satisfied that Katy was on her way home, she took off after Rosemary, silently cursing the girl. Rosemary, like Basil, showed no fear of the fights in the sky. In fact, the opposite was true. The sight of enemy aircraft and the RAF planes always thrilled the pair of them. *Lunatics*, Penny thought, running as fast as she could.

The sound from above was deafening. Engines roaring and guns popping. Penny screamed when a plane swooped down. She ducked, covering her head with her arms.

'Rosemary!' she shouted. 'We've got to get out of here!'

Rosemary stood in the middle of the lane, her neck cranked back as she peered up at the warring planes.

Another aircraft came in low, a German with a British plane on his tail. Penny felt a whoosh of air as they flew over the top of her.

Rosemary spun around and looked along the lane at Penny. 'Did you see that?' she called, an awestruck smile on her face.

Penny ran towards her. They were still a good twenty feet apart. 'Come on, Rosemary. We're going to get hurt if we stay here,' she urged. As she drew closer to her friend, terror filled her body when she saw a German plane flying towards them, his nose down. Penny stopped, staring at the face of the enemy as his plane roared up behind Rosemary. 'GET DOWN!' she screamed.

As Rosemary began to turn towards the plane, bullets thudded along the lane, throwing dirt and stones into the air. Penny threw herself to the ground and covered her head. The noise of the engine thundered past.

Daring to steal a look, Penny peeped up. 'NO!' she cried, scrambling to her feet, then running towards her friend. Her legs felt weak and gave way. She stumbled, falling to the ground, but kept her eyes fixed on Rosemary. Trembling, she crawled some of the way, before managing to clumsily stand again. 'Rosemary!' she shrieked, 'Rosemary!'

The girl was lying motionless on her back, her eyes closed. Penny dropped to her knees beside her. 'Rosemary... Rosemary...' she said, afraid to touch her. She looked to see if Rosemary's chest was moving, praying that she'd see it rise and fall. There was no movement. If Rosemary was still breathing, then it was only barely.

Blood oozed from a wound on her stomach, and from her thigh too. Penny knew she had to stem the bleeding, but she feared it was too late and her friend was dead. Her hand hovered above Rosemary's blood-soaked dress as she willed herself to press down on the bullet hole.

'My belly is burning...' Rosemary groaned weakly.

Penny couldn't believe it! Rosemary had opened her eyes and spoken. 'You've been shot. It's all right, you're going to be all right.'

'Burns... feel sick...'

'I'm going to press down on the wound. This might hurt,' Penny warned. Her hands shook as she lowered them towards Rosemary's stomach. But it was then that she noticed that the wound on Rosemary's thigh was pumping out blood at an alarming rate.

Without hesitation, Penny clamped her hand over the hole. Rosemary's skin felt clammy, and Penny could see her friend was sweating profusely.

'Cold... so cold...' Rosemary whimpered.

Blood gushed out from under the sides of Penny's hand and through her fingers. She pushed harder, but she couldn't slow the bleeding.

'My Poohstick is beating yours,' Rosemary said, thrashing her head from side to side.

Penny knew her friend was delirious, and her shallow breathing was becoming more rapid.

Penny yanked off her skirt and wrapped it around Rosemary's thigh, yet the wound continued to bleed and showed no sign of slowing. She knew that Rosemary was losing too much blood and could see her friend was dying.

'Rosemary... Rosemary... talk to me. Please, Rosemary, talk to me,' Penny begged, tears rolling down her cheeks.

Rosemary's head lolled to one side, and she looked at Penny. As Penny gazed back at her friend, she saw no fear, but she could see Rosemary's soul leaving her eyes.

'Cold...' Rosemary murmured, before falling into unconsciousness.

Penny leaned over her friend, pulling her into her arms and holding her lifeless body close. 'I'll keep you warm,' she sobbed, gently rocking back and forth, 'you're my sister, I'll always keep you warm.'

'Where are they, Will?' Clara asked frantically as she looked through the kitchen window. 'Katy said that Rosemary ran off to chase the planes and Penny went after her. They should be home by now!'

'I'll go and look for them,' Will replied, gravely.

'I'll come with you, Dad,' Basil said.

Clara saw Penny coming through the gates at the end of the drive. 'Here they are!' she declared and rushed out of the kitchen and towards the front door. Throwing it open, she ran along the drive towards Penny. *Where's her skirt?* She thought, then panic set her heart racing when she realised that the girl was covered in blood!

Running towards her, she could see that Penny was shivering. It was a hot summer's day, so she realised that the girl was shaking from shock. 'Oh, good lord, where are you hurt? Where's Rosemary?' she asked hysterically.

Penny stared blankly at Clara, her face tear-streaked.

'You're bleeding, Penny. What's happened?'

Penny didn't answer. She appeared unable to speak.

'Where's Rosemary?'

Will and Basil now flanked her.

Clara turned to her husband. 'She's in shock and she's bleeding, but I can't see where from.'

'That's not her blood,' Basil said, grimly.

'Oh my God, Rosemary! Where's Rosemary?' Clara screeched. She grabbed Penny's shoulders. 'Where is my daughter?' she screamed.

Penny, her eyes staring wildly, shook her head. 'I – I – I tried... I tried to stop the bleeding...'

'Where is she?' Clara demanded.

Penny slowly raised her arm and pointed.

'I'll find her,' Will assured. 'Basil, take Penny and your mother inside.'

'No, Will, I'm coming with you,' Clara cried, and ran towards the lane.

She felt Will's hand grab her arm.

'No, Clara, go inside.'

'My girl, Will... I must find her!'

'Go with Basil and Penny,' Will ordered.

'Come on, Mum,' Basil encouraged.

Clara yanked her arm free of her husband's grip. She had to find Rosemary and raced out of the gates.

Will was beside her. 'Please, Clara, leave this to me.'

'She's been hurt, and she needs me!'

Running along the lane towards the nurseries, Clara saw a bundle on the ground in the middle of the lane a short distance ahead. She knew it was Rosemary and stifled a scream. Will must have seen their daughter too. He could run faster than Clara and was in front now, racing towards Rosemary.

As Clara caught up, she saw her husband look down at their daughter. Clara hoped he'd give her a sign that Rosemary was all right, but instead he threw his head back and yowled, a long and arduous cry.

'No...' Clara mumbled, shaking her head as she ran faster, 'No...'

Will saw Clara and raced towards her. Gathering her in his arms, he pulled her close. Clara fought to free herself.

'No, Clara, don't look,' he warned, gripping his arms tightly around her and turning her around to face the opposite direction.

'Let me go!' Clara screamed. 'Rosemary... Rosemary...'

'She's gone, Clara... she's gone.'

Clara knew it was true, but she didn't want to accept it. She could feel the life draining out of her and thought she might faint. 'No, Will, no... she can't be dead... let me see my daughter,' she sobbed.

'Don't, Clara. Please, I'm begging you, don't look.'

Clara peered into her husband's wet eyes. 'I must,' she wept. 'I must see my beautiful girl... Please don't leave her there all alone, I need to be with her.'

Will lowered his head and released his hold on her.

'It's all right, darling, Mummy's here,' Clara called through her tears as she walked unsteadily towards Rosemary. She couldn't believe that Rosemary was dead. Her child was always so full of life and joy. The bloodied mess on the ground couldn't be Rosemary. It was, Clara knew it was, but her mind continued to deny it. Wiping away her tears, her jaw tense, she forced one step in front of the other.

Clara gazed down in horror, wailing. It was Rosemary, but the dead girl didn't look like Rosemary. Her legs felt as though they were going to give way and she almost collapsed beside her precious daughter, but was vaguely aware of Will supporting her. 'Why?' she howled, 'Why? She's just a child, for Christ's sake... a child!'

Will pulled her to him and Clara buried her face in his chest, her agonising grief unbearable. 'I want to die too,' she cried. 'Oh, God, I can't take this... please... let me die too.'

37

September 1940
Two weeks later

In Battersea's Bolingbroke hospital, Florence sat beside her son's bed and reached for his hand. But Jimmy quickly pulled away and avoided any eye contact.

She felt awful. Florence wanted to help Jimmy and make him understand that his injuries, though life-changing, weren't the end of the world. But Jimmy had sunk into a deep depression and had shunned Florence. Now, he was refusing food too and the doctors had warned her that Jimmy would have to be committed to an asylum.

'Please, Son, you're making matters worse for yourself,' she sighed.

Jimmy closed his eyes, and Florence knew she was wasting her breath. It had been two weeks since she'd discovered that he was in the hospital and during that time, she'd observed his mood rapidly declining. Her once handsome and cheerful son was now damaged and had lost his zest for life.

'You're lucky to be alive, Jimmy. Others haven't been as fortunate. You'll learn to cope without your arm and the doctor said you'll get some sight back in one eye. But if you don't eat they'll put you in an institution, and believe me, Son, that's the last place you want to be.'

Florence's heart broke as she gazed lovingly at her boy. She wished he'd allow her to help, but Jimmy seemed to have given up on life. 'I've got to go,' she said, reluctant to leave his side, 'and I'll be back tomorrow. Please, Jimmy, don't give up. For my sake, try and buck yourself up, eh?'

No amount of begging and pleading got through to Jimmy. So, out of desperation, Florence had come to a decision. With little money in her purse, she headed to Gladys Darwin's house. But this time, she wouldn't demand blackmail money. Instead, she'd ask the woman to lend her the train fare to Kent.

Rounding a corner, Florence's stomach flipped when she thought she saw a familiar figure walking into the Battersea Tavern pub. *It can't be him*, she thought, though the man had looked remarkably like Cyril. But her husband hadn't stepped inside that pub since the landlady had caught him with his hand in the cash till. She shouldn't be surprised if it had been Cyril waltzing into the pub. Florence knew her husband well and supposed that he was brazen enough to try and charm his way back into the landlady's good books. One thing could be said for sure about Cyril Black: the man had audacity!

Pushing open the door to the pub, Florence peered through the smoky room. The landlady, Winnie Berry, was at a table near the door collecting glasses. She grimaced when she looked up and saw Florence.

Folding her arms across her ample chest, Mrs Berry glared. 'Can I help you?' she scowled.

'I thought I saw Cyril come in.'

'Huh, he's not likely to show his face in here, and if he did, he wouldn't be welcomed.'

'Right you are. Good day, Mrs Berry.'

As Florence went to leave, she heard the landlady call.

'Wait... Florrie...'

Florence turned. She'd once been good mates with Winnie, but Winnie's husband had put a stop to their friendship. Florence had never known why the man hadn't approved of his wife's choice of friends. And she'd never understood why Winnie had allowed her husband to dictate his rules to her. Florence suspected that Brian Berry was knocking Winnie about, but if he was, Winnie had never admitted to it.

'I was sorry to hear about Jimmy,' Winnie said, her face softer. 'I can't imagine what you're going through. I know I'd be devastated if something like that had happened to my David. If there's anything I can do?'

Florence swallowed hard, fighting back tears. 'Thanks,' she uttered.

'Do you fancy a cuppa?' Winnie offered. 'Rachel can look after the bar for a while.'

Florence nodded, 'I could do with one.'

In the small kitchen at the back of the pub, Winnie put the kettle on to boil. 'It's been a while since you've sat at that table,' she smiled.

'Yeah, a good fifteen years or so.'

'How's Jimmy doing?' Winnie asked.

'Not good. His injuries are healing well but his mind is sick. He's refusing to eat. I feel like I'm watching him slowly die.'

'Oh, love, I'm sorry to hear that. He's been to hell and back, but I'm sure Jimmy will get better soon.'

'No, Winnie, I don't think he will. He doesn't want to live. He won't talk to me. I don't know what to do,' Florence sniffed, and pulled a handkerchief from her handbag. Dabbing at her tears, she added, 'I've lost me job 'cos I'm spending so much time at the hospital. I'm skint, and if I don't pay me rent, I'll be homeless an' all. How can I bring Jimmy home if I ain't got a place to call home? And you've probably heard that Cyril has vanished off the face of the earth again. It's all such a bleedin' mess.'

'I did hear about Cyril. There ain't much that passes me by behind that bar. And I'm sorry to say that you won't find him in Battersea. Len told me that Cyril was around a couple of weeks ago and was boasting about moving to a posh pad up the West End somewhere.'

Florence rolled her eyes. 'Knowing him, he's probably hoodwinking someone, a fancy tart no doubt.'

'It ain't fair that you've been left to deal with this by yourself. I wish I could help, Florrie.'

'You can,' Florence said, shifting uncomfortably in her seat. 'I hate to ask, but if you could lend me the train fare to Kent, that would be a great help and a weight off my mind.'

Winnie placed a cup of tea on the table for Florence. 'I can stretch to that. Are you going to visit Penny?'

'I'm hoping to persuade her to come back to Battersea. She might be able to get through to Jimmy.'

'I wouldn't count on Penny coming back.'

'Jimmy needs her. Why wouldn't she?'

'It's none of my business, Florrie, but you know I speak as I find, and, well, Penny's got nothing to thank you for.'

'You're not a stupid woman, Winnie. You know I didn't give birth to the girl. I don't feel any guilt about the way I treated Penny. I did my best, but it's impossible to feel any affection for the bastard of a whore.'

'It wasn't her fault, Florrie. I've heard shocking stories about what went on in your house, but that's all in the past now. I hope for Jimmy's sake that Penny can put it behind her.'

Florence felt offended and stood with her chest puffed out and her lips pursed. 'If you can lend me that money now, I'd better be going. As it is, I won't arrive in Kent 'til this evening.'

'Yes, of course... and, erm, good luck, Florrie.'

Penny sat beside her friend in the snug and placed her hand on top of Katy's. 'Are you all right?' she asked, gently.

Katy shrugged. 'It's not the same here anymore.'

'I know,' Penny sighed. 'That's why I'm sitting in here with you. I can't bear to see Clara so upset.'

'It's 'orrible. Basil never smiles and he's more determined than ever to join the air force. Mr Gaston works every hour of every day in the fields. And Clara cries all the time. I miss Rosemary. I wish she was still alive.'

'I know, me too.'

'I feel like I'm walking around on eggshells, and you must feel that way too.'

'I do,' Penny agreed, 'but the family need time to grieve.'

'We're not Rosemary's family, are we?'

Penny thought before answering. 'Yes, we are. Family is what is in here,' she said, and held her hand to her chest. 'Rosemary was our sister.'

Katy shrugged again and looked away. 'She wasn't though, not really. And... and...'

'*And* what?' Penny asked.

'And I don't think that the Gastons want us here anymore.'

Penny had felt the same but had pushed her fears away. She'd felt she was intruding on the family's anguish. But worse, she thought that they blamed her for Rosemary's death. No one had said anything to make her feel that way. It was just something she saw in their eyes.

'I'm right, ain't I? We're in the way,' Katy said, woefully.

'I don't know. But we can't go back to Battersea.'

'I'm *never* going back.'

'Don't you miss your mum?' Penny asked.

'No. I did, but then I learned in school about sacrifice. I realised that my mum put my brothers before me. She sacrificed me for them. I *hate* her for that. And she should have protected me from my dad, but she didn't.'

Penny had thought the same about Gladys Darwin, though she'd kept her thoughts to herself. The woman hadn't bothered writing to Katy either, which made Penny believe that she didn't care about her daughter at all. 'We've got each other, and we always will have,' Penny assured her friend.

'That's not true. I'll be all alone when you marry Basil.'

'*Marry Basil*... what are you on about? I'm not going to marry Basil.'

'Yeah, you will. You love him. You said so when we were at the stream. I don't blame you. Basil is nice.'

Penny had forgotten about those carefree moments before the Luftwaffe had come. The only memories of that fateful day were too upsetting to recall, though the images of Katy's last minutes haunted Penny's sleep.

'Who could that be?' Katy asked, when they heard someone knocking on the front door.

Penny pushed herself up from the comfortable sofa. 'I'll go. Clara won't want to see anyone.'

When she pulled open the heavy front door, Penny blinked hard and fast several times, hardly believing her own eyes. She thought about slamming the door in the woman's face, but found herself rendered to the spot, unable to react.

'I'm here about Jimmy,' Florence announced, unsmiling.

Penny stood staring, her jaw hanging wide.

'You'll catch flies in your mouth if you don't close it. Did you hear what I said? I've come all this way for Jimmy. Ain't you going to invite me in?'

'What about Jimmy?' Penny managed to ask, her stomach twisting in knots.

'He's been injured and sent home. I'm not going to talk about it out here in the dark.'

Penny's heart hammered as she stood to one side and allowed Florence over the threshold. 'Go through there,' she said, indicating to the snug.

Following the woman into the room, Penny was desperate for news of Jimmy.

Katy looked up and when she saw Florence, she leapt to her feet. 'What's she doing here?' she asked in disbelief.

'Jimmy's been hurt,' Penny explained, her mouth dry with nerves.

Florence's eyes flitted around the room. 'Hello, Katy,' she said curtly.

'Is Jimmy all right?' Penny asked.

'Where are your manners, girl?' Florence snapped. 'I'd expect you to offer me a cup of tea.'

Penny could feel herself shrinking under Florence's hard stare. 'I'll, erm... I'll put the kettle on.'

'I'll do it,' Katy whispered, and scooted out of the room.

'The pair of you have done very nicely for yourselves,' Florence remarked, 'very nicely indeed.'

Penny was sure that she could hear a hint of jealousy in Florence's voice. 'Please, tell me how Jimmy is,' she pressed.

Florence sighed and sat down on the sofa where Katy had been seated. Clutching her handbag on her lap, she finally answered, 'Jimmy's not in a good way. He's lost an arm and the sight in one eye. He's badly scarred an' all. But he'll live, only he doesn't want to.'

'What do you mean?'

'He's refusing food. If he doesn't eat, the doctor said Jimmy will have to be sectioned or he'll die.'

Penny gasped, horrified to hear of her brother's suffering and his devastating injuries.

'I need you to come back to Battersea and talk some sense into him. He won't listen to me. Perhaps he will listen to you.'

'Do you think he will?'

'I don't know, but I wouldn't have come all this way if I thought I was wasting my time. We'll leave first thing in the morning.'

'But—' Penny muttered, her mind racing.

Florence interrupted, 'Don't question me, Penny. Jimmy needs you, so you'll be with me on the next train to London.'

Penny didn't protest. She wasn't brave enough to argue with Florence. The woman was formidable, and Penny had the scars to prove it. Anyway, if Jimmy needed her, then she was prepared to rush to his side.

Katy came in carrying a tray. The cups rattled in the saucers as the girl's hands trembled.

'I'm going to London to see Jimmy,' Penny explained to her friend.

Katy looked sad but said nothing and quickly left the room.

'Have you got any money?' Florence asked.

'Some,' Penny replied. She was frugal with her earnings and had saved quite a bit.

'Good. We'll need money. Bring all you have.'

Penny nodded. She'd do anything for her brother, even returning to Battersea with Florence. But she vowed, as soon as Jimmy was well enough she'd be coming back to Gaston Farm. To home. And away from Florence Black forever.

38

'Brace yourself,' Florence warned. 'He's not a pretty sight. You might not recognise him. That's him in that bed over there.'

Penny looked to where Florence was pointing, and then walked through the hospital ward, her eyes fixed on her dear brother. She was lugging her bag of spare clothes, as they'd come directly to the hospital from the train station. Penny was keen to see Jimmy, though she was dreading finding what state he'd be in. She prayed it wasn't as hopeless as Florence had portrayed. As she approached Jimmy's bed, her heart dropped. Her brother looked just as bad as Florence had warned, worse in fact.

Plastering on a smile that hid her sorrow, Penny stood beside Jimmy's bed. She wouldn't have known the man behind the dressings was her brother if Florence hadn't pointed him out.

'Hello, Jimmy,' she said, holding back tears. 'It's me, Penny.'

Jimmy had one eye covered with a gauze patch and his head wrapped in a thick bandage. He narrowed his other eye and squinted at her. 'Munchkin?'

'Yes, Jimmy, it's me.'

'You shouldn't have come,' he said, gloomily.

'Aren't you pleased I'm here?' Penny asked, her eyes threatening to cry.

'No. I'd rather you didn't see me looking like this,' he said, turning away to face the ceiling.

'Well, I must say, you're not looking your best, but you're still a sight for sore eyes. Oh, Jimmy, I've missed you so much!'

He didn't answer.

'We've got a lot to catch up on. I wish I'd known where to write to you. I was desperate to tell you about my job, and more besides. Anyway, how are you feeling?'

Jimmy laid still on his back, staring upwards.

'Please, Jimmy, talk to me. Haven't you missed me too?'

Nothing.

Penny glanced at Florence, feeling helpless.

'Told you,' Florence silently mouthed.

'Oh, Jimmy, this isn't like you. I hate seeing you so down in the doldrums. It's ever so upsetting.'

'Go.'

'Go where?'

'Back to where you came from.'

'No, Jimmy, I won't. I'm staying here in Battersea until you get better.'

'I won't get better,' Jimmy hissed. 'I'm not going to grow a new arm, or a new eye to replace the one I've lost. And I won't grow new skin to cover these ugly scars. This is it, Penny, this is as good as it gets!'

Penny wasn't sure how to respond, but she was relieved that he was at least talking. 'You're alive, Jimmy, that's what's important.'

'Is it? I'd rather be dead.'

Finding herself surprisingly angry, she raised her voice, 'How dare you! I've just watched my very good friend be buried in a hole in the ground. I held her as she died in my arms, Jimmy. I saw the life leave her eyes and there was nothing I could do to save her. She was thirteen years old, and she had her whole life in front of her. But a German pilot mowed her down. He killed her in the dirt. That pilot didn't just destroy her life, he also destroyed the lives of all who loved her. I can't stand by and watch you do this to yourself, Jimmy. Life is too precious to throw away.'

'Nice speech. I'd give you a round of applause if I had two hands to clap with,' Jimmy sneered sarcastically.

'See, he's lost an arm and an eye, but there's nothing wrong with his mouth!' Florence snapped. 'All the more reason for him to eat something.'

Penny couldn't hold back the tears any longer. 'Oh, Jimmy,' she cried. 'Please don't die. I couldn't cope with losing you.'

'Go, the pair of you.'

'No. I'm not going anywhere. I'm going to be here by your side every day. If you want rid of me, then you'll have to eat. But until you do, I intend to be your biggest pain in the backside.'

Jimmy shook his head, looking exasperated.

'Right, I hope you're comfortable, because I'm going to give you a day-by-day account of everything that's happened since I last saw you. I'll start with Poohsticks... Oh, and if you want me to shut up, which I'm sure you will soon, then you'll have to have a bowl of soup to quieten me.'

An hour passed. Penny talked incessantly, and each time she thought that Jimmy might be falling asleep, she gave him a gentle shake.

Two hours went by.

'Visiting time is over,' Florence said quietly.

'Thank gawd,' Jimmy moaned.

'I've only just started,' Penny smiled. 'There's so much more to tell you. I can't wait to come back tomorrow morning!'

'God, no,' Jimmy whined. 'You reckon a bowl of soup will shut you up?'

'Yep.'

'Get me one. Anything for a quiet life.'

Florence rushed off to the nurses' station, returning minutes later with a smiling matron.

'Here you are, Lance Corporal Black: chicken soup. And there is plenty more if you would like seconds.'

'Lance corporal, eh?' Florence remarked, proudly.

'It's no big deal, and it means nothing now,' he said.

Penny grinned broadly as she watched her brother spoon the broth into his mouth. She tried to ignore the bandaged stump on the end of his shoulder. Most of his head was covered, but she could see that some of his ginger hair had burned away. Deep reddish-purple scars marked his cheek and down his neck. He looked very different to how he had when she'd last seen him, but he was still her brother and she loved him intensely

'All gone,' Jimmy said, lifting his empty bowl for her to see. 'Will you shut up now?'

'Yes. Thank you,' she smiled, tears of happiness welling in her eyes.

'Don't start blubbering, Munchkin,' Jimmy warned.

'I'll see you tomorrow,' she sniffed. 'And I promise to just sit here quietly.'

As Penny walked alongside Florence through the streets

of Battersea, she looked around at the familiar sights. She hadn't been away for long, though it felt like she'd lived in Kent forever. Nothing in the borough had changed, yet it all felt very different. The houses seemed smaller and more tattered. The streets looked narrower. The people appeared pale and gaunt. The place lacked colour and seemed to be grey. She missed the undulating green fields and the wildflowers coloured all the shades of the rainbow. And mostly, she noticed how thick and foul the air felt in her lungs.

They walked in silence which suited Penny. She preferred it when Florence didn't speak. The woman unnerved Penny and had the power to reduce her to a quivering wreck with only a few spiteful words.

When they reached where Florence now lived, Penny climbed the stairs behind her. In the room, Florence peered through the window and out onto the grubby street. 'As you can see,' she said, turning around and sweeping her arm across, 'it's cramped in here. There's nowhere for you to sleep. And I can't bring Jimmy here.'

Penny's eyes roamed the small room. She'd known that Florence had moved address, but she'd assumed that the woman still rented a house.

'You said you've got money?' Florence checked.

'Yes, a bit.'

'Then here's what we'll do. You'll rent us a house. I'll stay home to look after Jimmy, and you can go to work. There's plenty of jobs going in the factories.'

'I, erm, I wasn't planning on staying in Battersea,' Penny dared to say.

'Why are you here then?'

'To help to get Jimmy back on his feet.'

'And then what, eh? You're going to bugger off back to Kent, I suppose?'

Penny bit on her bottom lip and nodded, too afraid to speak.

'You selfish cow!' Florence boomed. 'How do you expect me to look after Jimmy *and* put a roof over our heads? I can't go out to work and leave your brother all day to fend for himself. No, that won't do. So you'll have to stay in Battersea and get any foolish notions about going back to the farm out of your thick head. Is that clear?'

Again, Penny nodded, but her mind was racing. She'd promised Katy that she'd be back soon. And she enjoyed her job in the nurseries. Working in a factory held no appeal at all. Clara required help too, with the cooking and cleaning. The woman was barely coping since Rosemary's death. And Basil. Her heart ached at the thought of never seeing him again.

'First things first. I owe Winnie Berry the money for the train fare to Kent. You can pay her back and then we can get on with moving. There's a house available on our old street. I've made enquiries, the rent is affordable and it's in a decent state. You can leave your bag here for now. We'll call in to the Battersea Tavern and see about getting the keys for the house.'

Penny wanted to cry. She wanted to run back to Clapham Junction and flee on a train to Kent. But she had to stay for Jimmy. Her brother, her only *real* family, he needed her now. And Penny wouldn't let him down.

39

Over the course of a week, Jimmy regained some strength and his mood lifted. Though none of them were under any illusion of the challenges he would face ahead. On the day of his discharge from the hospital, Florence stood on the other side of a curtained screen around Jimmy's bed, her heart breaking as she heard him groaning with frustration. Even the simplest of tasks, like buttoning his shirt, were now almost impossible for him to do alone.

'Can I help?' Penny offered through the curtain.

'No,' Jimmy barked.

'Leave him be,' Florence whispered. 'He's got to learn to do these things for himself.'

Florence couldn't wait to get him home. She'd asked Penny to clean the house from top to bottom, and she had a delicious pot of stew ready for him. His room, though sparsely furnished, had two extra blankets on the bed and Florence had been careful to avoid hanging any mirrors. She found it difficult to look at Jimmy's disfigured face. He didn't need reminding of how his good looks had been burned away.

Outside the hospital building, Jimmy appeared apprehensive.

'It's a smashing day,' Florence said, trying to bolster him up. 'You'll enjoy the walk home.' But she had a feeling it would be anything but enjoyable for Jimmy. She could see people staring at him, some in horror, others with sympathy. She knew the gawping looks were making Jimmy feel uncomfortable and self-conscious.

An old man with a bushy white beard and short, bowed legs saluted as they passed him in the street.

'Gawd bless you, lad,' the old man said.

Florence could see that Jimmy wasn't sure where to look or what to say.

'Come on, Son,' she encouraged, linking his one arm and gently pulling him along.

'Do you know him?' Penny asked.

Jimmy shook his head.

'The old boy was showing his gratitude,' Florence said. Then changing the subject and distracting Jimmy, she added, 'Penny is starting work on Monday.'

Jimmy gave a slight nod.

'I'm going to be a factory girl,' Penny smiled. 'You'll be pleased to hear that the hours are long which means you'll be getting plenty of peace and quiet away from me.'

It worried Florence that her son wasn't interested in a conversation. He seemed tense. She hoped that he'd relax at home and feel happier away from the gawks of strangers.

Clara worked mechanically, unpegging the clean laundry and folding it before putting it into a basket. But every chore was an effort. She wandered up to Katy's bedroom with fresh linen and hesitated outside the door. It wasn't really Katy's bedroom. It was Rosemary's room and Clara hadn't been able to step inside since her daughter's tragic death.

A tear slipped from her eye. She hugged the clean sheets close to her chest and threw her head back. *Oh, my darling girl.* Clara wept, her heart shattered. From the moment she woke until her eyes closed to sleep, Clara could think of nothing apart from Rosemary. And it was agony. It hurt so much that Clara had wanted to end the pain. But then she'd thought of Basil and Will and had known she couldn't put them through anymore anguish than they were already suffering. So she struggled on with life.

She wasn't ready to see Rosemary's empty bed, or the beautiful doll's house her daughter had skilfully made. She placed the fresh bedding on the floor outside the room and hurried back down the stairs, running, as if trying to escape her memories.

Standing at the sink, Clara poured herself a glass of water. As she drank and glanced out of the window, she saw a large flock of birds take off from a tree. And then the low rumble of incoming airplanes hummed ominously in the air.

A rage rose within Clara. The man who'd put the fatal bullets into Rosemary's body was flying over her house! *Nazi child murderers*, she thought bitterly, hoping that each one of the German pilots would be shot down out of the sky and killed. If she'd had a gun, she would have gone outside herself and fired at the bastards!

The planes were flying high. Clara could see them glistening against the backdrop of the clear, blue sky. She'd never seen so many of them before. Her eyes widened as she watched one hundred, two hundred, or maybe more aircraft flying from France towards London. She craned her neck, searching for the RAF, but she couldn't see any British planes.

Oh, good Lord, she thought, *they're going to get through!*

'Mum... Mum...' Basil shouted as he came racing through the door. 'Have you seen how many planes are in the sky?'

'Yes, hundreds!'

'I can hear the ack-ack guns in the distance, but there's no sign of the air force shooting them down.'

'I know. Those planes are going to be over London soon. God help them. God help all the folk of London, and God help Penny.'

The air raid siren wailed over the rooftops of London, its up and down cry carrying the warning of impending danger.

In the kitchen, Florence didn't want to admit that she was scared or that her heart was beating thirteen to the dozen. Instead, she drew in a steadying breath and fixed on a brave face. 'I reckon we should take cover under our beds,' she suggested to Jimmy.

'You can, but I'm staying right where I am,' he slurred, and poured himself another glass of port.

'Please, Son, if you won't get under your bed, at least get under the table, eh?'

Jimmy ignored her request and knocked back the glass of alcohol.

'Take it easy, Jimmy. You've only been home for an hour, and you've already gone through more than half of that bottle.'

'Can't a man enjoy a quiet drink by himself?' Jimmy grumbled.

Florence reached for the bottle. 'If you want another, you'll have to get under this table with me.'

Jimmy went to snatch the bottle from her, but already drunk, his reactions were slow and Florence quickly pulled her arm back.

Penny had been in the privy and she burst in through the back door. 'There's flippin' loads of them!' she said, looking terrified.

'Scrim the windows,' Florence instructed, and began rummaging through an unpacked box. 'We should have done this when we moved in. I'm sure I've got some here somewhere that the landlord dropped off.'

'There's no time!' Penny shrieked.

Florence found the roll of three-inch gummed brown paper and handed it to Penny. 'There's plenty of time. Or would you prefer to have shards of glass flying through the house? Wet it first, then stick it from corner to corner over each window.'

Florence could see that Penny was shaking with fear. 'Hurry,' she shouted at the girl. 'Don't just stand there!'

She noticed that Jimmy had slyly got his hands on the port, and was now drinking it straight from the bottle. But with the threat of Hitler's bombs about to land on them, Jimmy being drunk was the least of her concerns.

Penny was at the sink, attempting to moisten the glue on the roll of brown paper, but the girl was making a right pig's ear of it.

'You're making it too wet,' Florence snapped. 'Give it here,' she said, and roughly pushed Penny aside.

The deafening noise from the German planes and the

nearby anti-aircraft guns firing skyward from Battersea Park made the roof shake and the windows rattle.

'It's too late to worry about the windows,' Florence moaned just as a thundering boom blasted close by. Her body tensed with fear as she felt the floor vibrate beneath her feet.

Penny screamed. Jimmy chuckled.

Florence dived under the table. Grabbing Jimmy's leg, she urged, 'Please, Son, get under here with me.'

But Jimmy kicked her off as Penny scrambled under and sat beside her. The petrified girl hugged her knees to her chest, staring wildly. Florence looked scathingly at her. She didn't want to despise Penny any longer, but she couldn't quash the hatred in her heart.

As bomb after bomb exploded around them, shattering the windows and filling the air with brick dust, Florence prayed that God would spare them. *If you must take a soul*, she said in her head, *then take Penny.*

40

March 1941
Six months later

Will came through the kitchen door sighing heavily. 'Here they come again,' he tutted. 'I don't now how London is still standing. The Luftwaffe are relentless.'

Clara could hear the planes some way off. 'Penny talks about it in her letters. She calls it the Blitz. It sounds horrendous. She's so brave. I don't think my nerves could take it. I wish she could come home.'

'I know, me too.'

Turning away from Will so that he couldn't see the tears in her eyes, she whispered, 'The house is so quiet now and I think Katy is lonely.' Her grief simmered close to the surface, but, feeling that she had to be strong for her husband, Clara tried her best to supress her heartache. She saved her tears for when Katy was at school and Will was in the fields.

'Basil would be sorry that he's not here,' Will chuckled. 'I think he'd take a fancy to Mary.'

'She is very pretty. Perhaps you could get Katy out in the fields with the Land Girls, I think she'd enjoy it.'

'Katy is more than welcome to help on the farm, but it's hard work, as I'm sure Mary and Bet will testify.'

'They seem to manage.'

'Bet is as strong as an ox. She's got muscles bigger than me!' Will scoffed. 'She's from a farming family; she understands the nature of the work. Mary tries, but I think she's struggling. The girl was sat in front of a typewriter before joining the Land Army. She's been complaining about calluses on her hands.'

'Well, she's doing her best and I'm grateful for them. The farm was too much for you to cope with after Basil left. We should never have given our permission for him to join up at seventeen. I wish I hadn't allowed you both to talk me into it.'

'He was going to go at some stage, we couldn't have stopped him. The boy was so miserable on the farm and desperate to join the air force. At least he's happy up there in the clouds. Every time the planes go over us, I look up and wonder if Basil is flying and if he can see us down here.'

'Yes, I do the same,' Clara lied, swallowing down a hard lump of grief that had lodged in her throat. When the planes flew over, it wasn't Basil she thought of. It was Rosemary, shot down in the lane by a German pilot and bleeding to her death.

'Will supper be long?' Will asked.

'Ten minutes.'

'I'll take it in the snug this evening.'

'Oh, Will, you're not going to sit by the wireless again, are you?'

'I like to know what's happening.'

'I'll tell you what's happening,' Clara yelled angrily. 'Those planes will be reaching London soon. They'll be dropping incendiary devices and setting buildings alight, and they'll be letting their bombs land on innocent people, killing women and children, destroying peoples' homes. That's what will be happening, and I can't bear to hear it!'

Will seemed taken aback by Clara's outburst. 'I'm sorry. I'll, erm, I'll eat my supper at the table in here.'

'Yes, you will, and I'll thank you to take that wireless back to the barn. Katy has her ear glued to it every chance she gets. It's not good for her to be continually hearing about the tragedy that's going on this world.'

'All right, I'll take it out to the barn right now.'

The war raged around them, and Clara couldn't bury her head and pretend it wasn't happening. But she didn't want constant reminders. As it was, she looked forward to Penny's letters, but it was upsetting to read about the horrendous details of the Blitz. And she really didn't want to listen to bulletins about troop movements and the heroic efforts of the Royal Air Force. Clara had already buried one child. She didn't want to think about losing another.

Penny sat at a bench in a factory that had been requisitioned by the government to produce components for aircraft. The factory operated day and night, churning out much-needed parts for military planes. The pay was basic, and the workers didn't earn any overtime. But most were content to put in the extra hours as they felt they were doing their bit to help with the war effort.

Penny stifled a yawn, yearning for the day to pass quickly. She'd been at work since seven-thirty that morning. And like everyone in London, she felt tired and worn out. The nightly bombing raids were taking their toll. But disturbed sleep was nothing to complain about compared to what some folk were enduring. Only yesterday, Penny had learned that Lizbeth, a young woman who worked in the factory, had been killed in an explosion. The bomb had flattened Lizbeth's house and taken the lives of her mother and father too. And last week, Nora, a mother of six who lived on the same street as Penny, she'd been thrown through the air. The woman had been buying her groceries when the air raid warning had sounded. She'd rushed to a public shelter with two of her young children in a pram, but they hadn't made it to safety in time. Poor Nora had been left paralysed and now only had four children. Indeed, feeling tired was nothing to complain about.

'Will you come to the dance on Saturday?' Maggie asked.

Penny turned to the woman who worked beside her. 'No, I don't think I will.'

'Go on, Penny, you'll enjoy it. And, oh boy, we need to have some fun, especially after the week we've had! I can't believe we've got through unscathed these past months. But I ain't going to sit indoors waiting for the bombs. Nope, not me. I'm going dancing and I'm going to dance until I've got blisters on my feet.'

Penny wished she was more like Maggie. Though both eighteen, Maggie had an hour-glass figure and was far more worldly-wise than Penny, especially when it came to men. Her vivacious personality and blonde, waved hair attracted a lot of attention. Penny felt like a shrinking violet in comparison.

'Phil said he's going to the dance,' Maggie teased.

Penny could feel herself blushing. Phil worked in the factory too and he'd made no secret of his feelings towards her. 'I don't like Phil,' she said, embarrassed.

'He likes you, and he'll be disappointed if you don't come.'

'He'll get over it.'

'You could do a lot worse than Phil, you know. Most of the men are away fighting, there's not many around to choose from. I know you're still holding a torch for that farmer boy, but when was the last time you saw him?'

'Basil's not a farmer, he's in the Royal Air Force now.'

'Stop splitting hairs, you know what I mean. Face it, Penny, you're not likely to see him any time soon. Whereas Phil...'

'I'm not interested in Phil.'

'You need to let your hair down. We could be dead tomorrow. Do you really want to die a virgin?'

'Shush,' Penny hissed, looking around at the other woman working on the row. She hoped they weren't listening to the inappropriate conversation.

'I'm just saying. Live for today, that's all. And Phil is *today*.'

'Why hasn't Phil signed up with the army?' Penny asked. As far as she could see, the young man was fit and healthy.

'Flat feet and asthma. Phil was really upset when he was rejected, but he's our hero. If it wasn't for Phil doing his fire watching duties, the factory would have burned down.'

Penny hadn't heard the story of Phil being a hero and wanted to know more. 'What happened?' she asked.

'Ask him. He loves to tell his story,' Maggie grinned.

It was a relief when the bell rang through the factory to signify the working day had finally ended. As Penny made her way through the gates, the night shift began to arrive, and she had to dodge the stream of bicycles flowing in.

'Are you sure you won't change your mind about the dance?' Maggie pushed.

'Maybe next time,' Penny placated her.

'Huh, if there is a *next time*. I'm sick to death of sleeping in my clothes and getting woken up in the middle of the night by the sirens. And don't get me started on the Anderson in the backyard. I wish we lived nearer to an underground train station. I'd much rather spend the night on a platform than in that damp and stinking corrugated iron thing.'

'We just get under our beds.'

'I suggested that to mum, but when that bomb landed at the end of my street, those who'd stayed in their houses were all killed. I don't like the Anderson, but it might save my life. You're not safe under your bed, Penny.'

'I know, but we don't have a shelter and I don't like the public one. I can't see how it's any safer than the house.'

'You can always come to mine. My mum won't mind.'

Twenty-two-year-old Phil pushed in between Penny and Maggie and draped an arm over each of their shoulders, greeting them. 'Ladies.'

'I bet you think you look good with your arms over us two beauties,' Maggie chortled.

'All the fellas will be jealous,' he grinned.

Penny felt uncomfortable and shrugged him off.

'She won't come to the dance,' Maggie said, nodding her head towards Penny.

'Have you got something better to do?' Phil asked.

'I'm busy,' Penny answered, trying to think of a plausible excuse.

'Not with another fella, I hope?'

'Maybe,' Penny answered. *Maybe* wasn't entirely a fib. She intended to spend Saturday evening writing a letter to Basil. She hadn't heard from him since he'd joined the air force. Katy wrote weekly and Clara sent a letter every month or so, but it was Basil's letters that she looked forward to receiving the most.

Phil waved goodbye, saying as he went, 'I'll do whatever it takes to win your heart, Penny. You'll be my wife one day, mark my words.'

'He's cocksure of himself,' Maggie said. 'But like I said, you could do worse than Phil. He's a smashing fella and quite a dish, too.'

Penny agreed, Phil was nice, albeit a flirt, and she found him quite handsome. He had a good build with broad shoulders and a slim waist, greased-back blonde hair and the brightest of blue eyes. She liked the dimples in his cheeks when he smiled, and the swagger in his confident walk. But for all of Phil's qualities, he wasn't Basil.

'If you want my opinion,' Maggie said, 'Forget about *farmer boy*. I think you're mad to save yourself for a man who doesn't even know that you're in love with him.'

Penny couldn't forget about *farmer boy*. She'd tried. But every morning when she woke, she missed the welcoming aroma of fresh bread baking in Clara's kitchen... and she missed Basil, too.

After saying farewell to Maggie, Penny picked up her pace in a rush to get home. She hoped Jimmy would be there and that he'd be sober. Her brother had found solace in the bottle. *Drowning his sorrows*, Florence had said. But his heavy drinking was affecting his health and Jimmy's moods had gone to a very dark place.

Nearing home, Penny saw Mrs Darwin coming out of her front door. There was no way to avoid the woman, but Penny didn't want to speak to her.

'Hello, Penny, you're looking well. Have you heard from Katy?'

'Yes, thanks,' Penny replied, tersely. Mrs Darwin always asked after Katy and it felt awkward.

'How is she?'

'She seems happy enough.'

'Good. And is she enjoying school?'

'I should think so, but now she's fourteen, she won't be at school for much longer.'

'Will you be writing to her soon?'

'Yeah, probably.'

'Please, send her my love. Tell her she's always on my mind.'

Penny nodded, thinking *tell her your bleedin' self!* She'd never get her head around the reason why Mrs Darwin hadn't contacted Katy.

Indoors, Penny threw her coat over the banisters and walked into the front room. Looking around, there was no sign of Jimmy, but she spotted an empty bottle of brandy on the sideboard.

She found Florence in the kitchen sitting at the table, her face grim as she pulled hard on the cigarette in her thin lips.

'Is Jimmy out again?' Penny asked.

'Do you see him here? No. Then he's out,' Florence snapped. 'I should imagine he's pinching stuff to fund his drinking. Seems he took after your father after all.'

Penny wanted to make herself a cup of tea and a bite to eat, but she couldn't stand to be in the same room as Florence. She felt intimidated by the woman and preferred to keep out of her way. Instead, she went to go to her bedroom, but as she walked away Florence's bullying voice followed her.

'Don't leave your coat over the banisters. My passageway ain't a bleedin' coat stand!'

Penny breathed in deeply, biting her tongue. How could

Florence refer to the passageway as her own when it was Penny who worked six days a week to pay the rent! And she did the cleaning too. Florence claimed to be busy looking after Jimmy, but Jimmy was rarely home, and when he was, he'd be unconscious from booze.

'And another thing, get your ugly backside in here... NOW!'

Penny spun on her heel, her heart racing, and she hurried back into the kitchen.

Florence's eyes looked her up and down with disdain. 'You make me sick,' she snarled. 'I brought you up to be respectable, so why I am hearing tales about you and some bloke at the factory, eh?'

'I – I – I don't know what you mean,' Penny stuttered, nervously and licked her dry lips.

'Don't play sweet and innocent with me. I heard you've been messing about with some bloke called Phil. I don't know what you think you're playing at, but I won't have it! Your responsibilities are here, to this house and to your brother. You can't afford to get yourself in the family way, do you hear me?'

Penny shook her head, arguing, 'There's nothing going on with me and Phil.'

'You'd better be telling me the truth, or are you a slut like your mother was?'

'I'm not lying,' Penny insisted.

'Good. I'm glad to hear it. Now clear off.'

Penny fled the kitchen and up the stairs. Her bedroom had been one larger room that had been partitioned into two, Jimmy having the other half. She threw herself onto her thin mattress and buried her head in the pillow, muffling the sound of her sobs. *I'm eighteen, a grown woman* she thought, yet Florence made her feel like a helpless and scared child. She wanted to stand up to the woman, but she didn't have the guts.

Reaching under the bed for a notepad and pencil, Penny wiped away her tears and began to write.

Dear Katy
I hate being here and I wish I could come home to Kent, but Jimmy needs me more than ever. I'm trapped with a woman I fear and despise, and with a brother who is in such a drunken stupor most of the time, he barely knows what day it is or where he is. God, I miss my life on the farm!

Sorry, I know I'm ranting, but you're my best friend and the only person I can really speak to. It's so miserable here, the only light in my life are my thoughts of Basil, but he's probably forgotten all about me now that he's realising his dreams and flying planes...

Penny jolted and her pulse quickened when the air raid siren suddenly wailed out. She ran down the stairs and out the front door, leaving it wide open behind her. Standing in the middle of the street, Penny threw back her head and looked skyward. She couldn't see the German bombers yet, but she knew they were on their way to rain terror on London, peppering death and destruction under their paths. *Oh, Basil,* she thought, *I hope you're up there somewhere ready to protect us. Take care, my love, stay alive!*

41

March 1942
One year later

Florence had left the house early in the hope that the corner shop where her ration book was registered might have some decent stock. Alas, the shelves had been almost empty, and she walked back home with a meagre amount of groceries in her basket. Even soap was rationed now! At least they had made it through the colder winter months so she no longer had to stand in queues for coal to warm the house. It saddened Florence to see piles of bricks and rubble where houses had once stood. Children played on the bombsites, though they weren't supposed to. Ruined homes littered the streets, a constant reminder that Hitler wasn't finished with them yet. There hadn't been any nightly raids for a while, but the threat of death was never far away.

Indoors, Florence stood outside the front room, glaring harshly at Jimmy who was still slumped on the sofa and snoring. He'd passed out there last night in a drunken daze. She shook her head in disapproval and wrinkled her nose at the foul-smelling stench of stale beer.

'Get up, Jimmy,' she boomed, 'I won't have you sleeping all day on my sofa.'

Jimmy grunted.

'Get up. Do you hear me?'

'YES, *Mother*, I can hear you.'

'Good. Then move your lazy arse and go and have a wash. You smell rotten and you're stinking out my front room.'

Marching into the kitchen, Florence ignored Penny and placed her basket on the table.

'I've made a fresh pot of tea. Would you like a cup?' Penny asked, sniffing, and then she blew her snotty nose into a handkerchief.

Florence glanced at the girl with disgust. 'No, I wouldn't like a cup of tea. I'd like you to bugger off back to your bedroom and stop infecting us with your germs. That's what I'd like!'

'Sorry,' Penny croaked, her voice hoarse. 'I needed something to drink.'

'If you're well enough to come downstairs and make yourself a drink, then you're well enough to go to work.'

'My head is pounding and I ache all over,' Penny moaned.

Jimmy trudged in and poured himself a glass of water. Florence noticed his hand was shaking as he drank thirstily. And she knew that he'd soon be looking for his next beer.

'Look at the bleedin' state of the pair of you. This is what I'm lumbered with. A son who is a thief and can't live without a belly full of booze, and you,' Florence scathed, looking down her nose at Penny, 'you, the child of a whore.'

'Don't start on Penny,' Jimmy warned, growling his words through gritted teeth.

'I ain't starting nothing, Son. You'll know it when I do. I'm just fed up with this war. And I'm fed up with you drinking.

And I'm fed up with you stealing to pay for your drink. And I'm fed up with looking at her ugly face!'

'Well, I'm fed up with you moaning and complaining all the flippin' time!' Jimmy barked. 'I'm a man, Mother. I might not be a whole man, but I'm a man nonetheless. If I want to drink, I will, and where I get the money from has got nothing to do with you. And you seem to forget that it's Penny who pays the rent on this house. Do you know what, you 'orrible, nasty, miserable cow...'

Florence backed away as Jimmy stepped towards her with a look of twisted hatred on his face.

'If I was Penny,' he continued, 'I would have thrown you out ages ago. Why are you here, eh? I don't need you. She don't need you. We'd be better off without you, so shut your vile fucking mouth!' he snarled, jabbing his finger in her cheek.

Florence held her hand over her chest. Her heart was beating rapidly. She'd never seen Jimmy like this before and it scared her. Turning on her heel, Florence fled the kitchen and hurried up the stairs. Running into her bedroom, she slammed the door closed and breathed in several long, deep breaths. *It must be the drinking*, she thought, trying to reason why her son had been so threatening. But his words got Florence thinking. Jimmy had made her realise that there was nothing to stop Penny from throwing her out onto the streets. *I'd better start being nicer to the girl*, she thought. After all, Florence enjoyed being a kept woman, and Penny was the breadwinner. But just in case she ended up homeless, Florence thought she should have a contingency plan in place. She needed to have something to fall back on, some savings. The money she'd blackmailed out of Mrs Darwin had dried up, but Florence knew where she could lay her hands on cash... And hopefully, Penny wouldn't notice her wages being skimmed.

'I don't know why you put up with her,' Jimmy said as he pulled his coat on.

'She's your mum,' Penny replied with a shrug of her shoulders. But the truth was, Penny tolerated Florence because she was too afraid to stand up to the woman.

'I'm going out. If she gives you any lip, tell her to sling her hook.'

Penny nodded, but she knew she'd never have the courage to speak in that way to Florence. She watched the front door close behind Jimmy, her heart sinking. Her brother was off to find booze and to drink himself into oblivion. Moments later, she heard Florence padding down the stairs.

'I'm sorry,' the woman said. 'It's not often Jimmy loses his temper, but when he does, he really blows. He's just like your father. Cyril was the same.'

Penny couldn't believe her ears. Florence had said sorry. She'd never heard the woman apologise for anything before.

'How are you feeling?' Florence asked.

Penny wasn't sure how to answer. Surely the woman wasn't asking after her health.

'There's a newspaper in my basket. Put your feet up and read it. I'll bring you a cuppa... Go on then, don't just stand there looking gormless. Go and sit down in the front room.'

She didn't argue. Florence was being nice for a change, but Penny didn't trust her. She'd seen the wrath of the woman on too many occasions, and she feared she was being led into a false sense of security.

When Florence fetched her the newspaper and a cup of tea, Penny thanked her, but braced herself for a verbal onslaught. Nothing. The woman smiled and left the room. *This is weird*, Penny thought.

The warm tea soothed her painful throat. And as she sipped on the drink, Penny glanced at the newspaper headlines. Her stomach flipped. The front page was splattered with news about the Royal Air Force attacking German cities. Her eyes quickly scanned the article, her heart racing when she read that British planes were lost. Tears stung her eyes and the words became a blur. Bile burned the back of her already sore throat. *Oh God*, she thought, worrying that Basil might have been involved in the bombing of the enemy, and terrified at the idea of his plane being downed. When she'd lived in Kent, she'd seen first-hand the aftermath of a plane falling out of the sky. Had the same happened to Basil? It was too horrific to contemplate.

42

Two weeks later

'Will you marry me?' Phil asked, down on his bended knee in the factory.

Penny could feel her cheeks flaming red. 'Get up, you daft bugger,' she said, feeling everyone watching.

'Go on, Penny, say yes,' Maggie squalled.

'I know this ain't the most romantic of proposals, but be my wife and I'll spend the rest of my life wooing you with romance,' Phil smiled.

A silence fell on the factory as everyone waited for Penny to answer. 'We've not even been out on a date,' she whispered. 'What are you playing at, Phil?'

'He wants his leg over,' an older woman laughed crudely.

'He ain't courted her 'cos he's saving his money, the tight git,' another joked.

Phil stared deeply into Penny's eyes. 'We've been mates for a long time now. I love you, Penny, plain and simple. Say yes. Say you'll marry me.'

Penny had dreamed of hearing those words, though not from Phil. She didn't want to humiliate the man in front of the whole factory, but she couldn't accept his marriage proposal. 'I'm sorry, Phil, but I can't marry you,' she said quietly.

Phil looked hurt as he climbed back to his feet and snapped shut the lid of the box that held an engagement ring. 'I hope I can get my money back on this,' he said, smiling, though the smile didn't reach his eyes.

Maggie pretended to play a violin and hummed a sad tune.

'You're a fool, Phil, but I still love you,' the older woman shouted.

'Yeah, Phil, I'll marry you if she won't,' another called in jest. 'But I'll want a bigger diamond than that!'

As Phil wandered off with his tail between his legs, Penny looked at Maggie, saying, 'I feel awful.'

'You shouldn't. I told him not to do it, but he's an idiot and wouldn't listen. I reckon he thought you'd say yes in front of all of us.'

'Do you think he will still want to be friends?'

'Course he will, he's besotted with you, Penny.'

Penny sighed and glanced around at her fellow workers, happy to see they'd all resumed work. She didn't like to be the centre of attention.

'Have you heard anything from *farmer boy*?' Maggie asked.

Penny's face broke into a spontaneous smile. 'Yes. He sent a letter last week.'

'And did he declare his undying love for you?'

'No, but he said he missed me.'

'Huh,' Maggie scoffed, 'Well, I hope you haven't just let a good man get away because you're too wrapped up in dreaming about a fella who's never made you any promises.'

Penny sneaked a look behind her and saw Phil oiling a machine and having a laugh with the woman who worked the equipment. She was pleased to see that he didn't look too upset. *He deserves a woman who really loves him*, she thought, *in the same was as I love Basil.*

Clara was waiting desperately for news of Basil. Every mother and wife in Britain dreaded a telegram arriving, or uniformed men knocking on their door. The coming of either meant one thing: notification of the death of a husband or son. But it was Mary, the pretty Land Army girl, who came to Clara's door.

'Mr Gaston asked if I could take the lunch to the fields,' she requested.

'Yes, of course. Come in,' Clara said. 'Lambing season is always a busy time for farmers. It'll quieten down soon. Thankfully, we don't have a large flock of ewes.'

In the kitchen Clara wrapped bread, cheese and hard-boiled eggs. As she bottled fresh milk poured from a jug, she studied Mary's delicate features. The girl's hair was dark, mostly hidden under a turban-style scarf. Her pale green eyes were deep and wide, and she had a sprinkling of freckles across her small, upturned nose. Will had been right, Basil probably would have been rather enamoured by Mary, though Clara believed her son still had a crush on Penny. And Katy had hinted that the feelings were reciprocated.

'How are you finding life on the farm?' Clara asked.

'It's hard and mucky, but I'm enjoying it. I can't keep up with Bet though, she works like a machine.'

'Just go at your own pace and you'll be fine.'

'Thanks. I don't want to let Mr Gaston down.'

'Has he complained?' Clara asked.

'No, but he hasn't said much of anything.'

Clara smiled. 'Then you must be doing well. My husband would be quick to let you know if he wasn't happy with your work. He's quiet, and he can seem stand-offish, but once he gets to know you, you'll see a different side to him.'

'I'm so glad you said that! I thought he didn't like me.'

'Far from it, Mary.'

Clara suddenly felt weak-kneed and dizzy as she handed the packed basket of food to Mary, and she quickly sat down at the table.

'Are you all right, Mrs Gaston?' Mary asked.

'Yes, I'm fine. I'm just tired, that's all.'

'Shall I fetch Mr Gaston?'

'No, no, no, honestly, it's just tiredness. I haven't slept very well since my son joined the RAF. I'm too much of a worrier.'

'My mum's the same. I don't think she's had a wink of sleep since my brother was conscripted. He's in the Navy, on a big boat somewhere up near Scotland. I don't know why he joined the Navy, he can't swim. I hope his boat doesn't get sunk!'

'Goodness! I should hope not.'

'Thanks for this. If you're sure you're all right, I'd better get this lunch to the hungry workers.'

'Yes, Mary, I'm fine. Off you go. And please pass my regards to Joan. I hope Mrs Savage is making sure you're comfortable in her boarding house?'

'Oh, yes, it's smashing. Thank you, I will.'

Clara began to feel better and wandered through to the snug, catching her reflection in the mirror over the hearth. She looked just as tired as she felt. Dark circles ringed her eyes and her complexion appeared dull and sallow. She sat on the sofa, resting for a while. She must have nodded off, and woke with a start to the sound of someone hammering on the front door.

Darting to the door, there was an urgency to the knocking which made Clara fear there was an emergency. She was relieved to see Mary standing there, though the girl was gasping for breath.

'We have to fetch Mr Hamble from the nurseries,' Mary blurted. 'Or the police... or the army!'

'All right, Mary, calm down and tell me what's happened.'

'There's no time! Mr Gaston said to run and tell Mr Hamble to bring the Home Guard.'

'Why? Why do you need to bring the Home Guard to Gaston Farm?'

'We've caught a German spy!'

Clara wondered if the girl had lost her marbles. 'Come in, sit down and tell me how you caught a German spy,' she insisted, calmly.

'No, Mrs Gaston, I must fetch the army, but I don't know where the nurseries are or who Mr Hamble is. Please, you've got to help me!'

'I will, but first tell me how you captured a German spy.'

'He parachuted out of the sky and landed in the back field. Mr Gaston and Bet are holding him down. Hurry, Mrs Gaston, in case he escapes.'

Clara could see in Mary's eyes that the girl was telling the truth. Panic set in, but she knew what she had to do. 'Follow me,' she said, and ran along the drive and towards the nurseries.

She often walked along the lane and laid freshly picked wildflowers on the roadside near the spot where Rosemary had been killed. But there was no time to think about her daughter now. Fear drove her to run faster. Will was holding a German prisoner. Her husband's life could be in danger!

Clara found Mr Hamble who'd said that he would rally the troops. Rushing back to the farm, she instructed Mary to wait at the gates to show the Home Guard where they should go. Running through the fields, Clara had to slow down to catch her breath. Her heart was racing and she wanted to cry. Stretching her neck, she saw her husband in the back field where Mary had said he would be. Thank goodness he was on his feet and alive!

'Are the army coming?' Will asked.

'The Home Guard,' Clara answered.

Her eyes stared at the young man sat on the ground who still had his parachute and harness attached. 'Is he all right? He looks to be in pain,' she asked.

'I think his leg is broken,' Bet replied. 'He won't be running off anywhere.'

Clara pulled her eyes away from the injured German and noticed blood on Will's shirt. 'You're hurt!' she cried.

'It's nothing, just a nick.'

'What happened?'

'He had a penknife,' Will explained, holding the knife aloft. 'And we had a bit of a wrestle.'

The German prisoner groaned.

Clara could see that his skin looked clammy. 'He needs medical attention,' she said.

'Let the army deal with him.'

'No, Will, he needs help now.'

'Leave off, Clara. He's a German.'

'So? Look at the state of him, he isn't going to be a danger to any of us. We can't just leave him sat there in pain. I think he's going into shock.'

'What do you want me to do about it?' Will asked, irately.

'Pick him up and bring him to the house. You and Bet can manage.'

'A German... in our house?'

'Yes, Will, a German in our house!' Clara said, heatedly.

'Have you lost your head, woman?'

'No. Our son is up there in the sky somewhere, possibly flying over enemy grounds. I'd like to believe that if Basil had to parachute into a foreign land, and if he was injured, that some kind people would take care of him.'

Will sighed. 'Grab his good leg,' he directed Bet. 'I'll get him under the arms.'

The man screamed when they lifted him from the ground.

'It's all right,' Clara soothed, and took his hand in hers. 'We are going to look after you.'

The man peered into her eyes and she saw his fear.

'Do you understand me? Do you speak English?'

'Yes,' he cried. 'Thank you.'

43

Nearly a week later, on Sunday morning, Clara carefully pulled the dressing from her husband's shoulder and checked the knife wound. 'It looks clean,' she said, before dabbing it with iodine. 'You're lucky to be alive,' she tutted.

'I told you, it's only a little nick,' Will said.

'It could have been worse. Please don't ever try to be a hero again, Will. You're a farmer, not a spy catcher!'

'He wasn't much more than a kid.'

'Will they hang him?'

'I don't know, probably. This damn war, its such a waste of life!' Will griped.

'I wish we hadn't sent for the army and had kept him hidden here. I know he stabbed you, but he was only trying to avoid capture. Once he realised that we were helping him, he seemed, I don't know... nice. I thought I hated all Germans, and with good reason after what happened to Rosemary, but I didn't see that man as the enemy. I just saw a frightened and injured boy who needed our help. '

'We couldn't have harboured an enemy spy, Clara. If we'd been found out, we all would have been charged with treason.'

'Hmm, I suppose you're right. I just don't like to think of that poor young man being imprisoned or executed.' Clara knew the agony of losing a child, and when she thought of the death of the German spy, she could feel the pain of his mother.

It was a lazy Sunday morning and Penny sat on her bed reading again the letter she'd received from Basil. She'd read it so many times she could recite it word for word.

'Who's that from?' Jimmy asked, leaning against the bedroom doorframe.

Penny looked up at her brother, shocked to see the state of him. His unkempt hair needed washing, as did his stained and grubby shirt. He hadn't shaved in weeks and now sported an untidy ginger beard, only it was patchy and hadn't grown on the side where his face had been burned.

'Judging by the soppy smile on your face, I'm guessing the letter is from someone special,' he mused.

'It's from Basil.'

'I didn't know you had feelings for Basil.'

Penny sighed. 'I've loved him for years.'

'Does he love you back?'

She shrugged. 'I doubt it.'

'Why do you doubt it?'

'I dunno. I thought maybe he liked me, but look at me, Jimmy, I'm nothing like Maggie. She's a stunner.'

'And so are you.'

'No, I'm not, I'm ugly.'

'Take no notice of anything *she* says,' Jimmy said, wagging his finger. 'You're very pretty, Penny. I've seen the way blokes look at you.'

'Clara said I'm pretty and so did Vera Hamble, but I don't think I am.'

'So, we're all liars, are we?'

'No, but I'm not tall like Maggie, or shapely, and I don't look womanly.'

'Maggie is attractive but in an obvious sort of way. Not all blokes like that. Some prefer a more *homely* looking girl, like you. Trust me, Munchkin, you're the prettiest girl I know.'

'Do you really think so?'

'Yeah, I do. And if this Basil bloke breaks your heart, he'll have me to deal with. I can still swing a good punch with only one arm.'

Penny smiled. 'Thanks. You're the best big brother. But… I don't know how to say this…'

'Spit it out,' Jimmy coaxed.

'I wish you'd stop drinking.'

'Here we go. You're as bad as *her*,' Jimmy hissed, irritably.

As he turned to walk away, Penny heard him mumble, 'What's the point of living like this. I might as well drink meself to death.'

Penny wanted to chase after him, but she knew he'd push her away. Florence had tried reasoning with him too, but Jimmy had become angry and smashed his fist through the door. There seemed to be no way to reach her brother and drag him out of his depression. Occasionally, she'd see glimmers of the *old* Jimmy, moments like just now, but most of the time, Jimmy was either drunk or moody and enraged. Penny often hoped that he'd get caught stealing. At least he wouldn't be able to drink if he was locked up behind bars.

She heard the front door slam. Jimmy had gone out. She prayed he'd come home tonight, but her brother had been spending many nights away. Penny didn't know where he slept, but she suspected, sadly, that it was on a park bench. Her brother caused her so much worry. Penny would have loved to return to Gaston Farm, even if only for a short visit, but she didn't feel she could turn her back on Jimmy.

Folding away the letter from Basil, she reached under the bed for a small box in which she kept her most important things. Lifting the lid, she flicked through the numerous letters from Katy and Clara. She kept her Penny Black stamp in the box too, but she couldn't see it. She searched meticulously in every envelope and between each sheet of paper, but the stamp had gone. *Strange*, she thought, knowing that she couldn't have lost it. Jumping off the bed, Penny lifted the mattress and pulled out a sizable cloth bag she'd sewn for herself. She emptied the contents onto the bed and stared aghast. Her savings, the small amount of money she'd managed to keep to one side, most of it had gone!

Florence called up the stairs, 'There's some breakfast down here for you.'

Penny gathered the few remaining coins and quickly stuffed them back into the bag. There were only two people who could have stolen her hard-earned cash: Florence or Jimmy, neither of whom Penny wanted to confront!

Florence had found that her charade of being more affable with Penny was surprisingly paying dividends. With Jimmy away from home for long periods, and Florence being alone for much of the time, she'd come to enjoy the girl's company. Penny was quite the little chatterbox, sharing tales and gossip from the factory and talking about Katy and Gaston Farm. It whiled away some of the hours that Florence would otherwise have been sat lonely. She'd never hold any affection for the girl, but the hatred that had once consumed her was slowly diminishing.

'Tea and toast,' Florence said, flicking her head towards the kitchen table.

Penny sat down, a frown on her face.

'Why the face like a smacked arse?' Florence asked.

Penny chewed on her thumbnail, a sure sign the girl was nervous or upset about something.

'Out with it. What's bothering you?' Florence pressed. 'Is it Jimmy?'

Penny shrugged. 'My savings are gone.'

'What savings?' Florence asked, her heart skipping a beat. She'd wondered how long it would be before Penny noticed her money was missing.

'Money I've been putting by. There's only a few bob left.'

'What, you think someone has stolen it?'

Penny nodded, 'Yeah.'

'Oh no, that's awful. I knew Jimmy was in a bad way, but I never thought he'd stoop so low to steal from his own sister!'

'You think Jimmy stole my money?'

'Well, who else could it have been?' Florence said with a voice of innocence.

'Oh, gawd,' Penny moaned.

'I don't suppose there's any point in confronting him about it. He'll only deny it or not even remember that he's pinched it. I suggest you hide your money or give it to me to look after. Jimmy wouldn't dare to try and steal from me.'

'I can't believe he'd steal from me,' Penny said indignantly.

'What a bleedin' waste, eh. All that cash, just thrown down his neck. I know it ain't a good time, but I was going to ask if you could up the housekeeping money. Jimmy's supposed to be helping with the food and bills, but he ain't given me any money in ages.'

Penny nodded.

'I'm sorry, I hate to ask, especially now, but I can't make the housekeeping you give me stretch to what we need.'

'It's fine,' Penny said. 'But we've got to stop Jimmy from drinking.'

'I know, but how?'

'I dunno. It breaks my heart to see him destroying himself.'

'Me an' all, Penny, me an' all.'

Florence poured herself a cup of weak tea, silently sighing with relief. She'd managed to deflect the theft of Penny's savings to Jimmy, and she'd also swindled more of the girl's wages from her. With the money that Jimmy was handing over for his keep, Florence was building herself a comfortable little nest egg.

44

June 1944
More than two years later

Penny disembarked the carriage and as the steam from the train cleared, she looked along the short platform. She sucked in the deepest breath. Ah, she'd missed the fresh country air of Kent.

'There she is!' Katy exclaimed.

Penny smiled and dropped her small suitcase to the ground as Katy ran towards her with open arms.

'It's so good to see you,' Penny cooed, holding her dear friend closely.

'I can't believe you're here,' Katy cried. 'I've missed you so much!'

'Hello, Penny,' Clara greeted, warmly. 'You've hardly changed.'

'The same can't be said for this one,' Penny smiled, eyeing Katy from head to toe. 'She's at least a foot and a half taller than me now and she looks so grown-up.'

'Yes, Katy has blossomed into a fine young woman. Working on the farm with the Land Girls and all that fresh air has done her the world of good. Come on, Will has the cart waiting.'

'How do?' Mr Gaston asked.

Penny grinned and climbed up on to the cart beside him. Taking the man by surprise, she planted a kiss on his cheek. 'It's good to be back, Mr Gaston.'

'I'll say,' he chuckled.

After clambering into the back of the cart and taking her suitcase from Katy, she said proudly, 'I've got presents for everyone in here. And a special one for you,' she told her friend.

The cart trundled along the lanes towards Gaston Farm with Penny relishing every sight. She'd missed the green fields, the big skies and the long views. It all looked so much brighter than she'd remembered. Even the birds' song sounded chirpier.

In the farmhouse, Penny was greeted by the welcoming smell of Clara's fresh bread which made her stomach growl. 'I'm looking forward to meeting Mary and Bet,' she said as she removed her felt beret hat and handed it to Katy.

'You'll like them, especially Mary. Bet is rather a *jolly hockey sticks* type and I swear she's twice as strong as Mr Gaston!' Katy popped Penny's hat on her head. 'What do you think?' she asked, doing a twirl.

'It looks better on you than it does on me.'

'I don't think so, Penny. You're so fashionable now.'

'Clothes are hard to come by in London. We mostly make our own or put up with utility clothing. And high heels are virtually impossible to buy.'

'Ha, you won't be needing high heels here,' Katy grinned.

The afternoon passed quickly with Penny, Katy and Clara sitting around the kitchen table, talking and drinking tea.

'Your mum sends her love,' Penny said, awkwardly.

Katy didn't look impressed.

'Do you think you can ever forgive her?' Clara asked.

'I don't know. I want to, she's my mum, but...'

Penny didn't want to rake up painful memories for Katy, and quickly changed the subject. 'I wish I could have been here when Basil visited,' she said, blushing.

'Oh, Penny, you should have seen him. He looked so handsome, my heart melted,' Clara smiled. 'He asked after you and was disappointed that you weren't here.'

Penny sighed deeply. 'It's been impossible to leave Jimmy. Honestly, I'm at my wits' end with him. He's been arrested several times for being drunk, he's been in hospital twice after injuring himself falling over and he's always getting into fights that he can't possibly win.'

'The poor man,' Clara sympathised. 'He's never adjusted to losing his arm, has he?'

'It's more than that. He's lost his confidence and his will to live. But I don't want to dwell on that today. So, tell me more about Basil,' Penny grinned.

She noticed that Clara and Katy exchanged a strange, awkward look. And then Clara quickly jumped up to bring cake to the table while Katy fiddled with a lock of her hair and averted her eyes. Penny had the impression that there was something about Basil that they weren't telling her. And each time she mentioned his name, they skirted around talking about him. Nevertheless, the afternoon passed quickly, and Penny enjoyed meeting Mary and Bet. As the night drew in, she retired to her old bedroom with Katy. Standing beside Rosemary's bed, the memories of the girl's tragic death flooded her mind. 'Do you mind if I get in with you?' she asked her friend. 'I can't bring myself to sleep in Rosemary's bed.'

Katy held the covers up. 'Climb in,' she said, 'It'll be just like the old days when we were kids.'

Penny's two-day visit flew by, and it was soon time to return her to the train station. Katy waved them goodbye from the front door. The girl had said she couldn't cope with a tearful farewell at the station. Clara was sad to see Penny leave too and wished she could have stayed longer. Having Penny around had been good for Katy and Clara had noticed a marked difference in the young woman's mood. Where Katy was normally quiet and sullen, she'd been more animated with Penny. Yet Clara felt awful for keeping news of Basil from Penny. It had been clear to see that the girl still held a torch for him. But Katy had begged her not so say anything, and though Clara didn't feel it was right, she'd agreed to Katy's request.

Sitting on Will's cart with him at the reins, Clara reached for Penny's hand. 'You will come back to see us as soon as you can, won't you?'

'Yes, most definitely. From what you'd said in your letters to me, I was expecting to find Katy in a bad way, but she was ever so cheerful, and it was smashing to see her looking so well.'

'Funny, I was just thinking the same. Seeing you has been good for Katy. I worry about her though. I don't believe she's ever truly recovered from what happened that night when Will went to London to fetch her home.'

They arrived at the train station and Clara waited on the

platform with Penny. 'You're a very brave and accomplished young lady,' she said.

Penny looked surprised.

'It's true. You're working to support your family, you've lived through unthinkable conditions in London under constant threat from Germany and you're travelling the country alone on a train. I'm very proud of you, Penny.'

'Thank you. But I do get scared sometimes.'

'We all feel scared from time to time, but your fear doesn't hold you back.'

The brakes of the train screeched as it pulled alongside the platform.

Hugging Penny, Clara whispered in her ear, 'Write soon.'

She watched the train leave. The thought of Penny returning to Battersea caused a knot of worry to gripe in the pit of Clara's stomach. The war hadn't yet been won, though since the British and allied troops had landed on the beaches of Normandy in France, talk of victory was on most people's lips. But Clara feared that Adolf wouldn't surrender easily. There were already whispers of a retaliation attack from Germany. Flying bombs were rumoured to have hit London. Churchill and his government hadn't yet confirmed the reports of deadly rockets being launched from Holland. The notion was unimaginable, but Clara believed it was probably true. And she also knew that it would be the civilians of London who would bear the brunt of the German vengeance.

Florence hadn't seen Jimmy since Penny had left to visit Gaston Farm. The summer sun meant longer days and two days alone in the house had dragged by. She couldn't say that she was looking forward to Penny's return, but she did crave the company.

Sitting on the edge of her bed, bored and fed up, Florence knew what to do to cheer herself up. She pulled out a small drawer from the bedside cupboard where she kept her under-garments. Removing her spare underwear revealed a concealed layer that she'd fashioned from a piece of sturdy cardboard. Florence carefully took out the false bottom of the drawer and clapped her hands together with glee. Her nest egg was looking very healthy! She counted the money, stacking it in neat piles on top of the cupboard. Then she placed the Penny Black stamp beside her small fortune. Florence had no clue of the stamp's value, though she assumed it must be worth money and planned to sell it once the war had ended. If visiting Gaston Farm had given Penny a craving to move back to Kent, at least Florence had secured her own future and wouldn't be left destitute.

Her ears pricked when she heard the front door close. Florence wasn't expecting Penny home just yet and she didn't think that Jimmy would bother showing his face. 'Hello,' she called, going to the bedroom door.

'Hello, I'm back,' Penny shouted up the stairs.

Florence's pulse quickened. 'I'll be down in a tick,' she said, and quickly closed the door. Scurrying to the cupboard, she threw her money back in the drawer and covered it with her underwear.

Penny knocked, asking, 'Can I come in?'

'Just a minute,' Florence answered, shoving the drawer back into the cupboard. Straightening herself, and blowing out a long breath of air, she swallowed hard, and then called, 'Come in.'

Penny opened the door with gusto, smiling broadly. 'Sorry to disturb you, but I wanted to give you this,' she said, holding a package wrapped in newspaper towards Florence. 'It's not much, but I thought you might like it.'

Florence gazed at the package, gobsmacked. Granted, her relationship with Penny had improved in recent years, but she'd never have anticipated that the girl would offer her a gift! 'It's heavy,' Florence said, smiling uneasily when she took the package from Penny. And slowly unwrapping it, she gawped at the large block of cheese.

'It's fresh from the farm and I know you like cheese.'

'I don't know what to say,' Florence mumbled, gazing at it. She was rarely lost for words and felt humbled by Penny's generosity. 'I do like cheese, very much, but haven't had a decent bit of cheese on toast since it's been rationed. Thank you, Penny, this is very thoughtful of you.'

Lifting her eyes from the cheese and looking back at Penny, she gulped when she realised that Penny was staring at the stamp on top of the bedside cupboard. Florence had failed to put it away with the stolen money and could have kicked herself. She'd have to think fast.

'That's... that's my Penny Black stamp,' Penny said, pointing to it.

'Oh, I wondered what it was. I, erm, I found it when I was cleaning Jimmy's room. It was between the floorboards under his bed,' Florence lied. She was feeling clever with her cover story until she saw the accusing look in Penny's eyes.

'You've *never* cleaned Jimmy's room. You don't do the cleaning, I do.'

'Yes, but you weren't here, and Jimmy's room needed cleaning.'

'No, it didn't. I did it before I left.'

'Jimmy had thrown up. It was stinking, so I cleaned it.'

Penny didn't look convinced.

'What are you accusing me of, Penny?' Florence challenged, hoping that the girl would back down. After all, Penny had never had much of a spine.

'Nothing... but that stamp was stolen from me.'

'Well, lucky for you I found it then. Take the bloody thing, it's only a stamp for gawd's sake, not the crown jewels.'

Penny's eyebrows knitted together as she picked up the stamp and studied it closely. 'I've cleaned Jimmy's room many, many times. How did you find this, and I didn't?' she asked.

'I dunno, perhaps I'm more thorough than you,' Florence replied. It was then that she noticed that, in her panic, she hadn't closed the drawer properly or put the false bottom back in, and Florence could see several coins on display.

She looked at Penny. The girl was peering down into the drawer too.

'Did... did you steal this from me?' Penny asked, sounding nervous. 'And my money?'

'How dare you suggest such a thing!' Florence barked.

Penny recoiled, and then stuttered, 'You – you – you did! I should have known that Jimmy would never have stolen from me.'

Before Florence could protest further, a strange, chugging sound reached her ears. The noise was coming from above the house, in the sky, a pulsing, rasping drone, like a locomotive train engine struggling up a hill.

'What's that?' Penny gasped, staring at the ceiling.

'Shush,' Florence ordered.

The noise had stopped and there was silence.

Florence sighed with relief, but then screamed in terror as a terrific blast boomed through the house, blowing the windows in and throwing her off her feet. She landed on the other side of the room with a thud, her head crashing into the wall. Laying dazed and staring up, as the dust settled, Florence felt confused – she could see the sky where a ceiling should have been. She lifted her head and looked along her twisted body that was scattered with bricks and debris. Her foot seemed to be facing the wrong way and blood seeped where she'd been showered with broken glass. Yet she felt no pain.

'Florence... Florence...' Penny gasped.

The girl's hair and face were white with dust. She looked like an angel peering down.

'What happened?' Florence asked. 'Was it a bomb?'

'Yes, it must have been.'

'I can't move,' Florence moaned, trying to lift her arms and shift her legs.

Penny, her eyes wide and wild, spat, 'Don't try to move! Stay exactly where you are! Don't move even an inch.'

Florence could hear panic in Penny's voice and wondered why. 'We're alive. A bit battered, but we'll live to tell the tale.'

Pink skin streaked down Penny's cheeks where her tears washed away the dust. 'I, erm... I'm going to need help to get you out,' she cried.

There was a dreadful fear in Penny's eyes that unnerved Florence. She lifted her head again and looked down at her broken body. It was then that she saw the jagged edge of a piece of wood sticking out through her midriff. How hadn't she noticed it before? She felt she was laying on something damp and warm, and it dawned on her with horror that the damp beneath was her own blood. 'Oh my God,' she screamed, 'I'm impaled!'

'It's all right, Florence, I can fetch help. We'll get you out of here. Just, please, do not move.'

Florence's jaw clenched and she nodded, terrified. Her life was in Penny's hands, and the girl was willing to save her even though Florence had robbed her. Penny could flee and leave her to die where she lay, trapped yet numb. 'I'm sorry,' she said, a tear slipping from her gritty eyes. 'Please ... help me.'

Penny's dress had been ripped off her back, and she'd lost a shoe. Her hair was thick with dust and caked in blood from a wound at the back of her head. Her elbow throbbed, her shins bled, her shoulder was in agony and she thought a couple of her fingers were broken. But staring down at Florence, her bottom lip quivered and she supressed a scream of horror. The sight of Florence skewered on what looked to be a broken floorboard was too much to contemplate. Penny knew that her own injuries weren't nearly as severe, and it was down to her to recue the woman.

A draught from behind blew against Penny's aching body. It was coming from where the front of the house was now exposed to the street. Two walls had collapsed, and Penny could see into the house next door which had taken the brunt of the explosion. All that stood of the neighbour's home was the chimney stack.

Penny's whole body trembled. She willed her legs to work. If she didn't fetch help, Florence would die. Looking around, she knew that something wasn't right, but her brain wasn't thinking clearly. What was it? What was missing apart from the ceiling and walls? The staircase! A gaping hole was in its place and Penny could see down to the wreckage-filled passageway. She edged away from the hole, afraid that the floor beneath her feet would give way.

Moving towards the front of the house, she peered out onto the street. Four houses on the opposite side of the road had gone. Men, women and children were wandering around, some bewildered and wounded, others trying to help. An ambulance drove along and stopped in the street by the debris littering the road. Volunteers wearing tin hats and armbands began scrambling over the fallen houses, searching for survivors. People came out of their homes carrying blankets, flasks and bandages. For a short moment, Penny felt as though she was watching everything before her play out on a movie screen like she'd seen at the picture house twice before. She watched, looking down from Florence's upstairs bedroom fascinated, until she heard raspy breathing.

Penny glanced over her shoulder to Florence. The woman had always been a formidable bully, towering over Penny and with powerful fists. But now she looked so small, weak and vulnerable.

'Help,' Penny croaked, calling out onto the street below, but her voice was a whisper. Her throat felt parched, the brick dust drying her mouth. 'Help!' she tried to shout again, a little louder this time. 'HELP!'

A man looked up. 'I see you. Move back, Miss. That floor isn't stable. Move back, slowly, like, slowly.'

'I need help up here,' Penny called.

'Don't worry, Miss. We'll get you down.'

'There's someone else up here with me... she's trapped... she's going to die. Please, hurry.'

Florence's feeble voice cried out to Penny. 'Don't...leave... me...alone,' she husked, slowly.

Penny looked around at the woman and then back to the man below. 'You have to help us!' she shouted.

Dropping to her knees on the rickety floor, Penny crawled over the fallen roof tiles and wooden rafters and back to Florence's side. She grabbed the woman's hand, noticing that Florence had no grip. 'I'm here,' she reassured.

Florence's eyes rolled into the back of her head, and Penny knew the woman's life was ebbing away. Help wouldn't come in time. It was too late for Florence. She was dead.

45

It had been three weeks since Florence's death. Penny sat on a bench in Battersea Park with Maggie to one side of her and Phil on the other. She gazed up at the huge barrage balloon, wondering how it was supposed to stop the V1 rockets. The 'doodlebugs' were the newest threat from Adolf Hitler. The rockets were even more terrifying than living with the constant fear of bomber aircraft flying overhead, as well Penny knew. When the V1 engine would cut out, the missile would fall from the sky, packed with at least a ton of deadly explosives. Penny would never forget the silence after the doodlebug's engine had stopped and before the bomb had detonated. In those few silent, tense seconds, it had felt as though the world had been about to end.

'What are your new lodgings like?' Maggie asked.

'All right, I suppose,' Penny replied with a sigh. 'I've got the two rooms upstairs, one for me and one for Jimmy. It's a nice enough house and it's close to the factory which is handy.'

'Have you seen your brother?'

'Only the once since I told him about Florence. I also told him about how she'd been stealing from me and had tried to blame him. I'm not sure I should have said anything. I don't think he's taken it well. Jimmy was in a right mess when he last came home.'

'You're not alone, Penny,' Phil assured. 'We're your mates and we're here for you. I hope you're not thinking about moving back to Kent?'

'I'd love to, but I feel I need to be here for Jimmy. I know he's lost in the bottle now, but I can't abandon him. And thanks, I don't know what I'd do without you both.'

'You could still marry me and let me take proper care of you,' Phil said, with a gentle nudge to her ribs.

'You already take care of me,' Penny smiled.

'Will you two stop flirting,' Maggie moaned. 'I feel like a spare part.'

'We're not flirting,' Penny argued, but she had to admit, her and Phil had become close in the past couple of weeks. He'd helped her to look for somewhere to live, had taken her shopping for second-hand clothes and had managed to talk his mum and three of his cousins into donating furniture for her new rooms. And she could still feel the comfort she'd felt when he'd held her in his arms as she'd cried. There'd been no tears shed for Florence, but the shock of witnessing such horrific injuries to the woman and of coming so close to death herself had been upsetting and had rattled her nerves.

'If I'm flirting with Penny, you're only jealous,' Phil said with a cheeky wink to Maggie.

'In your dreams,' Maggie scoffed. 'I've only got eyes for Hank.'

'Are you going to marry your Yankee G.I.?' Phil asked.

'I might, if he asks, which I think he will. Can you imagine how my Uncle Charlie would react though?'

'He's a bit overprotective of you,' Phil said, pulling a worried face. 'I wouldn't want to be in Hank's boots if Charlie finds out you're seeing a Yank.'

'I've kept it quiet from him.'

'I don't blame you. Your Uncle Charlie scares the life out of me, and the fella thinks highly of me. I wouldn't like to think what he'd do to Hank the Yank.'

'*Hank the Yank,*' Penny parroted, chuckling. 'Will you marry him?' she pushed.

'Probably,' Maggie answered, 'But I'm not sure that I want to move to America. It would break my mother's heart.'

'And mine,' Phil said.

'Leave off,' Maggie smiled. 'You ain't got a heart. You're like the tin man in that film with Judy Garland.'

'*The Wizard of Oz,*' Phil said, and leapt to his feet. 'Now you know that's not true, Mags. I've got a very big heart and it belongs to Penny. But brains, well, I can't swear to have a brain. That makes me like the scarecrow,' he said, and began falling over deliberately, just as the actor had done in the film.

Maggie also jumped up, and she linked her arm through Phil's. 'If only I had a pair of ruby red slippers,' she said, and began to skip along, yanking Phil with her as she sang, *We're off to see the Wizard*...

Penny enjoyed listening to the banter and laughter between her friends. It made her feel normal in a world that was mad. As Phil and Maggie joked with each other, for just a few moments Penny could forget about the war, bombs and death. And she could forget about the man she loved who hadn't written to her in months.

46

*Christmas Day 1944
Six months later*

There was no joy in Christmas for Clara. There hadn't been since Rosemary's death. Christmas was just another cruel reminder that her dear, beautiful daughter was missing, her life cut short because of war. And Basil's absence added to Clara's misery. But she tried to make an effort for Will and Katy's sake. Though there were no early morning games around the kitchen table, and she hadn't made a Christmas cake. The two lonely stockings hanging over the hearth looked as sad as Clara felt.

'I wish Penny had come for Christmas,' Katy mumbled. 'Though it would have been difficult to explain this away,' she added, rubbing her swollen stomach.

Clara didn't acknowledge Katy's comment about the baby she was carrying. She still believed that it was wrong to keep the news from Penny. 'I can understand why she'd want to stay in Battersea for her brother.'

Katy shrugged. 'I don't see the point. She hardly sees Jimmy. I reckon Penny will end up spending today alone.'

'I hope not,' Clara said, 'after all, she has friends in Battersea.'

'Yeah, but Maggie and Phil will be busy with their own families.'

'We can only hope they think of Penny.'

Will came into the lounge, still wearing his coat and rubbing his hands together. 'It's bitter out there today,' he grumbled, walking over to the fire and holding his palms towards the flames.

Katy heaved her heavy body off the sofa. 'Excuse me,' she said, 'I need the loo again.'

'It'll be the baby pressing on your bladder,' Clara explained. Then turning to Will, she said, 'You'll miss Mary and Bet this Christmas.'

'I will. I've come to rely on those girls more than I'd like to admit.'

'Well, they'll be back soon enough. It's only right that they should spend time with their loved ones.'

'We should bring the wireless in from the barn to listen to the King's Christmas message, what do you say, Clara?'

'Yes, Will, of course. In fact, I think the wireless should remain in the snug. I believe this war will be won soon and when it is, I want to hear the announcement.'

'There will be victory in forty-five, I'm sure of it,' Will smiled.

'I hope so, Will, I really do. I want our son home more than anything in the world, and I'm sure Katy does too.'

'Let's hope it's not too long until he meets his child.'

'I still can't believe we're going to be grandparents,' Clara said, shaking her head.

'Well, it all happened so fast. Basil has a few days leave, then the next thing we know Katy announces she's in the family way. Then Basil has another flying visit and the two of them get married. I can tell you, Clara, I never saw that one coming. Between you and me, I always thought that Basil was sweet on Penny.'

'He was,' Clara whispered. 'But he did the right thing and married Katy.'

'He didn't have a choice.'

'No, I suppose not, but I'm sure they'll be happy together. I just wish that Katy would tell Penny.'

Penny picked up the Christmas present that she'd bought for Jimmy and went to his door, knocking lightly. But she knew he wasn't in there. She'd stayed awake until late, listening for sounds of him coming home, and she was sure he hadn't. Returning to her own room, she scribbled a quick note, pulled on her coat, and then left the gift and the note on the floor outside of Jimmy's door. If he came home, he'd know that she'd gone to look for him.

Outside the streets were quiet. Penny could imagine families behind the street doors, opening gifts, sharing Christmas cheer and missing their men folk. Her mind wandered back to the best Christmas day she'd ever had, at Gaston Farm. She'd have liked to have been there today, but she didn't feel it was right to leave Jimmy alone, not today of all days.

A thin layer of morning frost sparkled under the light from the early morning sun. There was a chill in the air, making Penny shiver. Buttoning up her coat, she headed towards the Latchmere public baths and Culvert Road. Jimmy had a friend, Benji, who lived there, and Penny hoped that Benji might be able to shed some light on her brother's whereabouts.

Passing the Battersea Tavern pub, Penny paused outside the door. She could hear fun and laughter on the other side and knew that Winnie Berry would be throwing one of her famous Christmas parties. Much of the street was in ruins, destroyed by German bombs, yet the Battersea Tavern stood tall and proud and invited in the locals. Penny was pleased to hear folk enjoying themselves, even during the hardest and most austere of times. But the joy of others was a stark contrast to the loneliness that weighed heavy in her heart. She hoped she could find Jimmy. After all, it was Christmas day and family should be sharing the festivities together.

She eventually arrived at Culvert Road, a small street of just twenty or so houses with a strong sense of community, tucked away in an almost forgotten corner of Battersea. Not a soul could be seen. The place felt eerily quiet. Knocking on Benji's door, Penny crossed her fingers and shoved her hands into her coat pockets.

Benji came to the door wearing a dirty vest, a roll-up stuck on his lips and his hair a mess. Like Jimmy, he'd retuned from war an injured and broken man and had quickly become Jimmy's drinking buddy. Even from a couple of feet away, Penny could smell Benji's foul body odour and tried not to heave at the sight of his brown, rotten teeth.

Benji tried to focus his bleary eyes. 'Penny, ain't it?' he asked.

'Yeah, hello, Benji. I was looking for Jimmy. Have you seen him?'

Benji snorted and ran a grubby hand through his dark, greasy hair. 'He was here last night. Do you wanna come in?'

'Er, no, thanks, Benji,' Penny answered, politely. She dreaded to think how filthy Benji's home would be. 'I want to find Jimmy. He didn't come home last night. Have you got any idea where he could be?'

'I dunno, love, sorry. He was here when I fell asleep but gone when I woke up.'

'And you don't know where he might have gone?'

'No, love,' Benji answered, and scratched his head. 'Is it Christmas today?'

'Yes, Merry Christmas.'

'Yeah, thanks, and to you. Do you know what, I'm sure I can remember Jimmy saying that he wanted to be with you today... Yeah, that's right, he did. And he had sumfink for you an' all, a Christmas present. Are you sure he ain't at home?'

'I'm sure,' Penny replied.

She felt better knowing that Jimmy intended to be with her today and hoped he was at home by now. As she went to thank Benji and say goodbye, a young child's scream echoed through an uninviting tunnel that connected Culvert Road to Culvert Place. Penny stood outside Benji's door and watched a mother run from a house at the end of the road and towards the screaming child in the tunnel.

'What the bloomin' 'eck is that all about?' Benji said, leaning out to look.

The mother came running from the tunnel with the child in her arms. 'Fetch an ambulance,' she yelled. 'There's a bloke in the tunnel frozen half to death!'

'Oh no... please, no,' Penny uttered, her blood running ice cold.

Benji pushed past her and ran barefoot towards the tunnel.

Penny followed. She hurried into the gloomy darkness, her heart racing. *Please don't let it be Jimmy*, she prayed. But when she saw Benji pulling at his hair and heard him cursing angrily to God, Penny knew that her brother was dead.

47

Four weeks had passed since Jimmy had tragically frozen to death in the tunnel. Penny's grief was raw, but she tried to maintain a *stiff upper lip*, especially at work in the factory. As Maggie had reminded her, *we just have to get on with it*. There were many words that had become commonplace in the language of Londoners since the war had begun. *Make do and mend, dig for victory, look out in the blackout*... And the *Blitz spirit*. While pilotless rockets were blowing up London and other cities across the country, maiming and killing innocent people, destroying homes and businesses, the civilians of Britain were supposed to be stoic. Penny tried to muster that stoicism. She tried to be strong. But most nights, she cried herself to sleep.

Another long day in the factory ended. Penny was on her way through the factory gates when Maggie fell into step beside her.

'Do you want to come to mine for your dinner tonight?' Maggie asked.

'No, thanks. It's been a month today since Jimmy passed away. I'm going to the tunnel to pay my respects.'

'Oh, Penny, I'm sorry, I hadn't realised. I've got to get home to see to my mum. She's laid up in bed with the flu. If I could, I would have come with you.'

Phil ran up to them and caught the end of the conversation. 'Where are you going?' he asked.

'Penny's going to the tunnel,' Maggie mouthed in a whisper. Then turning back to Penny, she added, 'I've got to dash, sorry, but I'll be thinking of you, and of your brother of course.'

Phil walked beside Penny, both silent, but she was grateful for the comfort he offered when she felt his hand slip into hers.

As they passed the Battersea Tavern, the door opened and a policeman walked out.

'Evening,' the copper greeted Phil. 'How are you, lad?'

'Hello, Tommy,' Phil smiled. 'I'm all right, thanks. I thought you had a desk job. Are you back on the beat again?'

'Yes, lad. With so many of the younger men signing up to fight, it left us short-staffed, so I've had to oil my old bicycle and bring it back to life. I can't complain, it's done me good. So, who is your lady friend?'

'This is Penny. We work together.'

'Nice to meet you, Penny. I'm Sergeant Bradbury, Tommy to my friends and family, and I consider Philip to be family.'

'Tommy saw me into the world,' Phil explained. 'My mum was in the baker's shop when she went into labour and I'm told that I made a very quick appearance, too quick for me mother to get home. So I was born in the back of the shop, my mum leaning on a sack of flour, with Tommy at the helm.'

'Cor, I'll never forget that day. Your mother was a lot braver than me. And I'm not ashamed to admit that in all of my career, it was the one and only time I shed a tear. I'd never seen a baby being born, and thank gawd, I've never seen one since. But it was a very special moment.'

'My mum was going to call me Tommy, but there were already three in the family. So, instead, Tommy picked my name.'

'That's a lovely story,' Penny smiled.

'Are you going in the pub for a drink?' Tommy asked.

'No, we're on our way to Culvert Road.'

'That's a long way from home for you, Philip. Is that where you live, Penny?'

Penny shook her head and looked down at the pavement. She couldn't explain for fear of crying.

'No,' Phil replied. 'Penny lives near me. We're going to Culvert Road because Penny's brother died there in the tunnel recently.'

'I'm sorry to hear that. I didn't know your brother but I heard about his death. You must be Cyril's girl then, is that right?'

Penny nodded.

'I've felt your dad's collar a few times. In fact, it was me who arrested him a few months ago. Has he calmed down yet?'

'What do you mean?' Penny asked.

'Well, he was drunk but he was going on and on about someone who was supposed to be dead who wasn't really dead, and he kept telling us we had to dig up the grave. Cyril seemed very upset about it. We didn't know if he should be hauled before a judge and sent to prison or to a lunatic asylum. Is he still making outlandish claims about the undead?'

'I – I don't know. I haven't seen my dad for a few years.'

'Probably for the best. The gaols are no place for a young lady to be visiting. Anyway, I must get going. Stay out of trouble, the pair of you.'

'Always,' Phil answered. 'See you around, Tommy.'

As they carried on their way to Culvert Road, Penny wasn't surprised to have heard that her father was behind bars again. She reckoned it was no better than he deserved. She didn't give the man a second thought, instead remembering Jimmy with affection.

In the tunnel, Penny stood over the spot where her brother's body had laid. Crouching down, she lightly touched the ground. Then, reaching into her pocket, she pulled out a stamp and gently kissed it. 'Thank you, Jimmy,' she sniffed, 'I'll always treasure it.'

She felt Phil's hand on her shoulder and she rose to her feet, turning and throwing herself into his arms. Phil held her close as her body jerked with harrowing sobs.

'What was that in your hand that you kissed?' he asked softly, handing her a handkerchief.

Penny drew in a juddering breath. 'My Christmas present from Jimmy,' she answered, uncurling her fingers, and showing Phil the stamp.

'What is it?'

'It's a Penny Black. My dad gave me one but Florence stole it and then it was destroyed when our house was blown up. After Jimmy died, the police gave me a folded piece of paper they'd found in Jimmy's pocket. The paper was addressed to me, and Jimmy had written *Merry Christmas, Munchkin*. The stamp was stuck inside. It looks a bit different from the one my dad gave me. I don't think the police knew that there was a stamp. Jimmy must have stolen it from somewhere, but I'll treasure it all the same.'

'It's a shame that Jimmy never got to give it to you in person.'

'Yes, it is, but he's at peace now.'

'Come on, let's get you home.'

It took them half an hour to stroll to the house that Penny lived in.

'Thank you for coming with me and walking me home,' she said.

'Can I ask you a question?'

'Yeah, as long as you're not going to ask me to marry you,' she smiled.

'I will ask you again one day, but not tonight.'

'Go on then, ask me what it is you want to know.'

'Now that Jimmy's gone, are you considering moving back to Kent?'

Penny sighed. 'I'd like to, and I probably will, but not until after the war. Everyone thinks it will be over soon. And when it is, I'll leave the factory and hopefully get my old job back at the nurseries.'

Phil looked down and scuffed the ground with the toe of his boot. 'I wish I could talk you into staying in Battersea. I'll miss you, Penny.'

'I've not left yet,' she said, and gave the top of his arm a friendly punch. But since Jimmy's death, Penny had thought of little else except returning to Gaston Farm. After all, she had no reason to stay in Battersea now, and she couldn't wait to see Basil.

48

7 May 1945
Over four months later

It was late in the evening. Clara sat in stunned silence as she listened to the wireless. The BBC program had been interrupted with a newsflash, announcing that Germany had surrendered, and tomorrow, Victory in Europe Day, would be a national holiday. A time for celebration.

'It's over... it's bloody well over,' Will said, leaping to his feet and punching the air. 'We've won! Do you hear that, Clara? We've won the war!'

Will grabbed her hands and pulled her up from the sofa, spinning her around and dancing. But Clara didn't feel like celebrating. She didn't want to dance. The victory felt small. Yes, she was relieved that the war was over, but it had claimed the life of her daughter.

'Basil will be coming home!' Katy exclaimed, excitedly. 'He'll finally get to meet his son.'

Yes, he would, and though Clara couldn't find it within herself to be joyful, she was grateful that her son would be returning soon.

'Yep,' Will laughed, 'Basil will be coming home. No more blackouts across the country. No more rationing. No more

Land Army girls on my farm and no more bombs! It's taken nearly six years to defeat the Nazis, but we've finally done it.'

'I'll make us a cup of tea,' Clara offered, feeling that she was dampening her husband's joviality.

'*Tea?*' Will parroted. 'Don't bother with the tea. Open a bottle of brandy and let's drink to victory and freedom!'

Clara trudged through to the kitchen and took the bottle of brandy down from a shelf in the Welsh dresser. She placed it on a tray with three glasses, then holding on to the kitchen table, she drew in a long breath and closed her eyes. The image of Rosemary's beautiful face floated in front of her. *My dear girl*, Clara thought, her heart aching.

Will's voice carried through from the snug. 'Where's that brandy, woman?'

Clara cleared her throat and dashed away a tear. 'Coming,' she called, trying to sound happy.

In the snug, Will poured three very large glasses. 'Cheers,' he said, clinking his glass with Clara's and then Katy's. 'To our Rosemary and to all those who fought for our freedom.'

'To Rosemary,' Katy echoed.

Clara liked that Rosemary had been remembered. Will rarely spoke about their girl. She understood that her husband found it too difficult to share his grief. He'd buried it deep inside, but he often called Rosemary's name in his sleep, and it would sound anguished, tearing Clara's heart apart.

'I'm so pleased that my son won't know the ravages of war,' Katy sighed, her tone melancholy.

'I second that,' Will agreed as he poured himself another large brandy.

'Careful, Will,' Clara warned. 'It's a national holiday tomorrow but not for us. The cows, sheep and chickens will still need seeing to.'

'Then I shall see to them with a sore head,' Will chuckled. 'But tonight, tonight we party. Who's with me?'

'Me!' Katy squealed and held out her glass for a top up.

'And me,' Clara said with reluctance and forced a smile.

Will took Clara's glass and placed it beside his own on the sideboard. Then, he cupped Clara's face in his huge hands and looked deeply into her eyes. 'Now, listen to me, woman. You've grieved every day for Rosemary and I've no doubt that you'll grieve every day for the rest of your life. But you are allowed to be happy, too. Rosemary wouldn't want you to be sad on a night like tonight. She'd be telling you that you've a good reason to celebrate: Basil is alive and well and will be coming home soon. The war is over, Clara. Life for us will never be the same, but the damned war is over.'

Clara bit on her bottom lip and tried not to cry. Her husband had seen that her mood was low, even though she'd tried to hide it. The man could read her like a book. But Will was right. Rosemary wouldn't want sadness to abound. In fact, if Rosemary had been here to celebrate with them, she'd have been boisterous and loud and would have infected them all with her cheerful spirit. Clara smiled, thinking, *I'll be the happiness that my girl would have spread.* She felt that it would keep Rosemary's memory alive. 'Give me my brandy,' she said, determinedly, 'I intend to get very drunk and very silly!' Taking her glass from Will, she held it aloft and chimed, 'To victory and to our beautiful Rosemary.'

★

On the day of the official national holiday to celebrate Victory in Europe, Penny sat on her bed with Maggie yanking on one of her arms and Phil on the other.

'You've got to come with us,' Maggie urged. 'You'll have so much fun!'

'We won't enjoy the party without you,' Phil coaxed.

'All right, all right, you win,' Penny sighed. 'But let me put my lipstick on first.'

As Penny swept a soft red colour over her lips, in the reflection of the mirror she saw that Phil had noticed her half-packed suitcase on a chair in the corner of the room.

'You're going to Kent, aren't you?' he asked.

Penny gulped and snapped the lid of her lipstick back on. Spinning on her heel, she met Phil's hurt eyes. 'Yes, I will be leaving as soon as I can.'

'I see. When was you going to tell us? Or was you just gonna leave without saying goodbye?'

'To be honest,' Penny said, nervously, 'I was hoping to slip away unnoticed.'

'I suppose you can't wait to go back to *farmer boy*,' Phil spat, and stamped out of the room.

Penny heard him pound down the stairs and out of the house.

Maggie picked up her cardigan and draped it over her shoulders. 'He loves you, Penny. He's upset, but he won't stay angry with you. And today isn't a day for arguing. Today is for celebrating, so let's go, we'll find Phil or I'm sure he'll find us.'

Outside, bunting decorated the busy street and it was lined with tables and chairs. Housewives came out from their homes carrying plates of food and cakes. Children waved flags and music could be heard all around. An old woman from the end of the street had lifted her skirts to her knees and was doing a jig on a chair to the sound of her husband blowing into his harmonica. People had gathered around her and were clapping and cheering. Penny couldn't help getting caught up in the party atmosphere, and with her arm linked through Maggie's, they danced their way along the street. The next street was the same and the one after that.

'Where are we going?' Penny asked.

'To find Phil. He'll be licking his wounds and I think I know where he'll be.'

'Ah,' Penny said, as it struck her that Phil would likely have retreated to his house. 'But do you really think he's gone home and will miss the parties?'

'I don't think he was much in the mood for a party. You've broken his heart, Penny.'

'Gawd, I feel terrible. I think the world of Phil, but as a friend.'

'I know. We can't help who we fall in love with. I mean, look at me, I've fallen for an American.'

'He'll be returning to America now. I should imagine that you're gonna miss him.'

Maggie stopped walking and turned to face Penny. 'I won't miss him,' she said, and placed her hand on her stomach.

'Won't you?' Penny asked.

'No, 'cos I'm going to America to be with him. I'm having a baby, Penny. And me mum said I've either got to get rid of it, give it away or marry Hank... so, I got married!'

'What?' Penny spluttered. 'Oh... congratulations. I take it that this is what you want?'

'Yeah, it is. I love him. I'm scared out of my wits, but Hank reckons I'll love New York State, though he said it's blinkin' cold there in the winter.'

'I can't believe it! You're married, having a baby and moving to the other side of the world!'

'All right, Penny, thanks. That's quite a statement and it doesn't help with my nerves when you put it like that,' Maggie chortled. 'I won't be able to go to America straight away. Hank has got to save up the fare and then he'll send for me.'

'When did you get married? Why didn't you tell me?'

'We got married two weeks ago. I wanted to tell you, but me mum begged me to keep it a secret. She was worried that my Uncle Charlie would hear about it and turn up at the wedding and put a stop to it. There's no way Charlie would let me go to America. Mum will tell him once I'm on the boat and gone.'

'Yeah, I suppose that's for the best. I reckon Charlie would do some serious damage to Hank if he knew that you were in the family way.'

'Exactly.'

'Have you told Phil?'

'No, not yet. I was going to tell him today, but I don't think I will now, not seeing how upset he was about you leaving an' all. You won't say anything, will you?'

'No, of course not,' Penny promised.

Standing outside Phil's house, Maggie strode to the door and knocked loudly.

Phil opened it and rolled his eyes when he saw them. 'I should have guessed that you'd come looking for me,' he said.

'Well, we couldn't enjoy ourselves without you,' Maggie smiled. 'Come on, Phil, you can't miss the biggest party that

Britain has ever seen. It sounds like all of London is singing and dancing!'

'I can't have you ladies being miserable without me,' he smiled. 'It's a hard life, but I suppose I've got a responsibility to make sure the pair of you have a good time.'

Now it was Maggie who rolled her eyes. 'Put your dancing boots on then, Phil, and let's go and set Battersea alight!'

As the jubilant day passed and the sun began to set, Penny felt exhausted from laughing and making merry. She also felt a tad dizzy which she blamed the beer for. It wasn't a beverage that she'd normally drink, but several bottles had been shoved into her hands throughout the day.

The three friends were sat on a garden wall in the light of a bonfire, and grinned when they saw Maggie's Uncle Charlie staggering towards them, holding a bottle of beer in one hand, a cigarette in the other and crooning a badly-sung song.

'My favourite niece,' Charlie said, swaying. 'How are you, kids? Have you had a good day?'

'It's been smashing, Charlie. Looks like you've had fun an' all,' Phil replied.

'I have, mate, the best. Penny, love, if Phil here gives you any trouble, you let me know and I'll sort him out.'

'He's all right, Charlie,' Penny smiled.

'I know he is. But I won't have no blokes messing with you or my Mags.'

Maggie jumped down from the wall. 'I've had a smashing day but I'm tired now. I should go. I'll see you tomorrow,' she said. Then gabbing her Uncle Charlie's arm, she added, 'Come on, you can walk me home.'

'I've had the best day too,' Penny told Phil, 'But I should

probably get home an' all.' As her feet landed on the pavement, she felt herself wobble unsteadily.

'I'll come with you and make sure you get home all right,' Phil offered, and slipped his arm around her waist. 'Lean on me. I think you've had one too many.'

'I think you might be right,' Penny said, feeling sick and putting her hand over her mouth.

As they made their way through the streets, the celebrations were still going strong with no sign of them ending any time soon.

'There'll be a lot of headaches tomorrow,' Phil chortled, 'including yours.'

'Yeah, probably,' Penny said, fighting the urge to throw up.

Outside Penny's house, Phil insisted on seeing her up the stairs and to her room. Penny didn't argue. He opened the door for her, and when she saw her bed, she thought it had never looked so welcoming.

'Are you sure you're going to be all right?' he asked.

Penny slumped onto her bed and laid back with her legs dangling over the edge. The room was spinning as she felt Phil remove her shoes.

'Come on, sleeping beauty,' he said, and picked her up in his arms, hitching her up the bed. 'Get under the covers.'

After tucking her in, fully dressed, he leaned over her. Penny gazed into his eyes, trying to focus but she could see two of him. 'You're a good friend,' she said, jabbing his chest with her finger.

'You know I want more than that, Penny,' he husked.

'I know you do, but I love Basil.'

'Basil isn't here. I am.'

Penny saw Phil's face coming closer and then his lips were

on hers. His kiss was soft and tender, and Penny found herself lost in the moment. She'd never been kissed before. Her pulse began to quicken. Phil's kiss became deeper, more passionate. Her body responded. Penny didn't want to stop, but she knew this wasn't right.

'No,' she said, pulling away and turning her face. 'I can't.'

'Didn't you like it?' Phil asked.

'Yes, but... but I can't.'

'Forget him, Penny. He'll never love you like I do.'

A tear fell from Penny's eye. 'He might, one day.'

'When was the last time you heard from him, eh? Face it, Penny, you're not in his thoughts. He doesn't think about you all the time like I do. He doesn't care about you.'

Penny had been having the same doubts, but she didn't want to hear them from Phil. 'Shut up!' she yelled. 'Go, please. Just leave.'

Phil closed his eyes and drew in a sharp breath. 'I'll always love you, Penny, but I can't wait forever. I hope *farmer boy* doesn't disappoint you. Good luck. You won't be seeing me again,' he said, and stomped off.

The door closed behind Phil, leaving Penny laying in the darkness. The way Phil had left, she could tell that their friendship was finished. She rolled over, upset, curling herself into a ball. The war in Europe had ended and now there was nothing to stay in Battersea for. Jimmy was dead. Phil had given up on their relationship. Maggie would be leaving shortly for a new life in America. The sooner Penny returned to Gaston Farm, the better it would be. And as she slid into slumber, she imagined running into Basil's open and waiting arms.

49

The next morning, Clara sat at the kitchen table and read the words she'd penned. Even having drunk several glasses of brandy, she'd still struggled to sleep and had spent most of the night worrying about Penny and how the girl would react to coming to Gaston Farm and discovering that her best friend had been keeping a secret.

Katy came into the room and poured herself a glass of water at the sink. 'What are you doing?'

Clara turned in her seat and looked at the girl. Her voice firm, she replied, 'I'm writing to Penny and I'm telling her everything.'

Katy slammed down the glass beside the sink. Her eyes wide, she said, 'No, Clara. No, please don't tell her!'

Clara didn't want to be the one to tell Penny the truth, but she'd been left with no choice. 'I must tell her, Katy. If you won't, then I will. The war in Europe is over and with Jimmy gone, I think Penny will want to come back to us.'

'But she'll hate me!'

'I'm sure she'll understand. It's better that Penny knows all the facts before she gives up her life in Battersea. This way,

Penny will be fully armed to make the decision that is right for her, don't you agree?'

Katy shrugged. 'I suppose so.'

'I still think it would be better coming from you,' Clara suggested.

'No. I can't tell her. I wouldn't know what to say.'

'That's fine. But you understand that I'm doing the right thing, don't you?'

Katy nodded. 'Do you think she'll ever forgive me?'

'I couldn't say, but I hope so. Make yourself some lunch, and for Will too. I'm going to the village to post this letter. And try not to worry. I'm sure Penny won't take the news as badly as you're assuming she will.'

'You're looking a bit green around the gills,' Maggie said.

The noise from the machines in the factory were rattling Penny's head and waves of nausea washed over her. 'I feel terrible,' she moaned.

'Yeah, well, half a dozen or more bottles of beer will have that effect on you.'

'Have you seen Phil?' Penny asked, discreetly glancing around the factory floor.

'No, not this morning. Why?'

Penny shrugged.

'Did something happen with you two after I left last night?'

Penny could feel herself blushing.

Maggie gasped. 'It did, didn't it?' she asked.

'No, not really.'

'*Not really,*' Maggie repeated incredulously. 'That means it did. Tell me, then.'

Penny sighed. 'Oh, Maggie, it was awful. I don't think Phil wants to be friends anymore.'

'Why? What was so awful?'

'He ... he, erm, he kissed me.'

Maggie's eyebrows shot up. 'And did you kiss him back?'

'A little bit, but then I stopped him and he went off with the right 'ump.'

'Don't worry. He'll get over it. You know what Phil's like.'

'I don't think so. There was something different about him. He said I wouldn't be seeing him again.'

'That's daft. You can't avoid seeing him here.'

'Then where is he?' Penny asked.

Maggie stood up from her stool. 'Has anyone seen Phil this morning?' she shouted across the factory.

Everyone shook their heads, some called back *no*.

'Told you,' Penny said.

'We'll go round his house after work. He had a fair bit to drink yesterday. I bet he's in his bed nursing a sore head.'

Penny hoped it was as simple as that, though she suspected that she'd never see Phil again. She felt terrible for rejecting him and knew that she'd miss his friendship. But she couldn't love him, not in the way that she loved Basil.

'You do look ever so pale. Are you sure you're all right?' Maggie asked.

'Yeah, I'll get through today, but this is going to be my last day here. I've already told our supervisor that I won't be back.'

'So you're definitely moving back to Kent, then?'

'Yes. I think I'll catch a train tomorrow and surprise them all on the farm.'

'Well, it won't be the same here without you,' Maggie said, sincerely, then lowering her voice she added, 'Though with the baby on the way, I don't know how much longer I'll be here. I think I'll tell Phil this evening when we see him. And you can say a proper goodbye to him.'

Penny knew that Phil wouldn't be pleased to see her, and she didn't feel that she should be there as Maggie knocked on his front door.

Phil's mum answered. 'Hello, Maggie, Penny.'

'Hello Mrs Miner. Is Phil home?' Maggie asked.

'No, dear, he's gone. Didn't he tell you?'

'Gone where?'

'To stay with his brother in Crystal Palace. Mind you, I'm not surprised that he never mentioned anything to you. The first I knew about it was when I found a note he'd left beside the kettle this morning. He'd packed a bag and gone before I was out of bed.'

'Oh. How long has he gone for?'

'For good, he reckons. I'm sure he'll be back to visit me soon, but his note said that he's going to find work in that part of London.'

Penny felt a stab of guilt cutting through her heart. Phil had left because of her.

'Blimey, he never said a word to either of us. When you see him, will you ask him to write to us?'

'Yes, of course, dear.'

As they strolled away, Maggie shook her head. 'The daft idiot. Fancy running off like that and not saying anything. Well, I hope Hank can save up quickly. With Phil gone and you leaving tomorrow, I think I'm quite looking forward to going to America now.'

They rounded the corner to the street that Maggie lived on and Maggie's six-year-old sister, Susan, ran towards them.

'Mum said you've got to come home right now,' Susan blurted, sounding serious.

'Yeah, yeah, I'm coming.'

Susan ran back home and Maggie asked Penny, 'Will you come in for a cuppa?'

'I could do with one.'

Penny liked Maggie's house. It was untidy but always felt warm and homely. Maggie's dad had been away at war leaving Maggie's mum run ragged caring for four young girls. Susan and Milly had both been born before the war, but June had come along just after the war had started and Sarah, the youngest, was born mid-way through. Maggie had wrinkled her nose with disgust when she'd told Penny that her mother was expecting again, and that the baby must have been conceived when her father had been home on leave. *I thought they were too old for all that malarky* Maggie had said.

Indoors, Maggie invited Penny to sit at the kitchen table while they waited for the kettle to boil. Maggie's mother came into the room, wringing her hands, her brow creased with concern.

'Oh, I'm glad you're home,' Vi said, her lips pursed.

'What's wrong, Mum?' Maggie asked.

'That church in Tooting who look in on your grandad, they sent someone round here today. He's had a bad fall and has damaged his leg pretty badly. He can't walk. So while he's laid up, I'm going to have to look after him for a while.'

'Oh, are you fetching him here?'

'No, there's no room. He won't manage on that sofa, it's only sits two.'

'Then how are you gonna look after him?' Maggie asked.

'I'll have to go and stay with him. The community hospital can't keep him in, and we can't afford for a nurse or anything. So, it's down to me.'

'And how's that going to work? What about the girls?'

'You'll have to watch them.'

'How am I gonna do that and work at the factory at the same time?'

'I don't know, Maggie, but I can't leave your grandad to take care of himself, can I? I'm sorry, but you'll have to take the time off work.'

'Can't my sisters go with you?' Maggie pleaded.

'No, course they can't. Your grandad lives in one room. He needs rest, not four noisy kids badgering him. For gawd's sake, Maggie, don't be so selfish. Your grandad is seventy-nine, he's got emphysema and is riddled with arthritis and now he's messed up his leg an' all. It won't hurt you to take a few weeks off work.'

'Blinkin' brilliant!' Maggie grumbled.

'I, erm... I could help,' Penny offered.

'You're leaving tomorrow,' Maggie reminded her.

'I can put that off for a while. You can go to work and I'll stay here with the kids, if you like?'

'Really? You wouldn't mind?'

Penny shook her head.

Maggie grabbed her into an embrace. 'Thank you, Penny, thank you so much. I'll split me wages with you, and don't say no, it's only fair.'

'All right,' Penny agreed. It felt good to help when it was needed, and she didn't mind waiting a short while to return to Gaston Farm. There wasn't any need to rush to Kent, especially as it was unlikely that Basil would be home yet.

50

June 1945
Three weeks later

Penny sat in Maggie's house, enjoying that the lights were switched on and the curtains open. After years of blackouts, it had felt strange at first, but now, three weeks after Victory in Europe had been declared, all of London was lit up.

'Thanks for staying, Penny,' Maggie smiled. 'Are you sure you're happy with what I've paid you?'

'Yes, I'm sure. Half of your wages is more than enough. And it's been a pleasure.'

'You've jacked in your job at the factory but you've still got the rent to pay on your room. I don't want you out of pocket because you've been staying here to look after my mother's brood.'

'My rent is all paid up. I've only got the room until Monday and then someone else is moving in. Anyway, I've been happy to help you out. But I wish Phil was here too. I didn't realise how much I'd miss him.'

'I know what you mean. It's quiet without him. I doubt we'll ever see him again.'

'It's my fault,' Penny mumbled.

'No, Penny. You never led him on or nothing. You've always been straight with him.'

'I know, but I can't help feeling responsible for him running off to Crystal Palace.'

'Don't feel bad. I reckon he'll be all right. He's got his brother living there and I'm sure he's found himself a decent job.'

'It's his mum I feel sorry for,' Penny said and sighed. 'She must miss him too.'

'Talking of mums, mine rang the factory today and said that she will be home tomorrow by midday, so you know what that means, don't you?'

Penny grinned. 'I've loved staying here and helping to look after your sisters while your mum has been away, but I'm really looking forward to going to Kent.'

'I can't tell you how much I appreciate you putting off leaving for a while. If you hadn't've of stayed with me, gawd knows how I would have coped.'

'You'd have managed.'

'I doubt it. Four children are quite a handful. You've been a godsend. Have you told Katy that you're coming?'

'No, not yet. I wrote to Clara and said that I'd be there as soon as your mum was back. I've not heard anything, but the post takes a while to arrive.'

'Well, don't get your hopes up too high. You know that Basil won't have been demobbed yet, don't you? My dad will be home earlier than lots of others. They're sending the married men back first.'

'Yeah, I know. It's funny, I thought all the soldiers would be arriving back in their hordes, but it's taking ages to get the men home. And some are being reassigned to duties in the Pacific. I hope Basil ain't sent off to the other side of the world to fight the Japs.'

'We should get some sleep,' Maggie advised. 'Mum won't be back until tomorrow afternoon, and in the meantime, the little monsters will be up at the crack of dawn. Are you coming up to bed?'

'Yeah, I'm shattered,' Penny said and yawned.

Climbing into bed beside Maggie, Penny smiled. It reminded her of good times spent at Gaston Farm when she'd shared a bed with Katy. She longed to return, and not just to see Basil. Katy, Clara and Mr Gaston – they were her family now. Kent was where her heart was which meant it was her home.

The following morning, Penny woke to the sound of girls screaming and someone jumping on the end of the bed.

'What's going on?' Maggie moaned, sitting up.

Susan bounced up and down on her knees as she explained, 'June has bwoken Sarah's doll. Milly smacked June.'

Maggie looked furious. She wasn't much of a morning person. 'For gawd's sake, you lot. It ain't even light yet. Get off the bed and go and tell your sisters to keep the noise down,' she growled.

Susan's bottom lip began to quiver. 'I want Mummy,' she bawled. 'I want my mum.'

Penny knew there wasn't any chance of getting back to sleep. Throwing off the bed covers, she picked up Susan, assuring the child, 'Mummy will be home today. Now, what shall we have for our breakfast?'

Thankfully, the girl quietened.

'So much for having a lie-in,' Maggie grumbled as she pulled on her dressing gown.

'Ain't you going to work today?' Penny asked. 'I'll be here for the kids.'

'I thought I'd throw a sicky, but thanks. Your duties here are officially finished.'

'In that case, if you're sure you'll manage, I'll get off home. I've still got packing to do and I'd like to leave the place nice and clean.'

'You've done more than enough here, Penny. Go and enjoy some peace and quiet and get your packing and cleaning done. Will you come for your Sunday dinner tomorrow?'

'I'd love to, thanks. And then on Monday, I shall be on my merry way to Kent.'

Penny washed and dressed, gathered her clothes and then said goodbye to Maggie's young sisters. She'd enjoyed her time at Maggie's house but was pleased that it was over so that she could move on with her life. 'I'll see you tomorrow,' she said cheerily to Maggie as she left.

The sun had risen by the time Penny arrived home. Walking in, she passed a door on the left where another young woman lived then climbed the stairs to her own room. A couple had moved into the room next door which had once been Jimmy's. It was Saturday and the house felt so quiet compared to the morning mayhem at Maggie's.

As Penny opened her door, she saw a letter had been pushed underneath. Bending down to pick it up, she instantly recognised Clara's writing on the envelope. With a wide smile, Penny dropped her bag and eagerly ripped open the envelope, keen to read what Clara had written.

Dearest Penny

Penny read quickly. She always did, and then she would re-read the letters, savouring every word.

Basil won't be home until the Japanese have been defeated. He tells me that he is boarding a ship from Liverpool to India, and from there he will be joining other squadrons in Malaya. To say I'm devastated is an understatement, I was looking forward to him returning home to us.

Just as Penny had feared, the war wasn't yet over for Basil and thousands of British troops. Her heart lurched, but she continued reading.

I have exciting news. I do hope you will be as happy as I am. Basil and Katy are married! They do make such a handsome couple...

The letter went on for another two pages, but Penny couldn't see the words through her tears. She felt as though a sledgehammer had thumped her in the stomach, taking all the wind out of her. Sitting on the edge of her bed, she read the words again. *Basil and Katy are married.* She hadn't been mistaken in what she'd read. It was there, in black and white, written by Clara's hand. But how could this be true? How could her best friend be married to the man who Penny loved with all her heart? And Katy knew how Penny felt about Basil. As it began to sink in, Penny felt incredibly hurt by Katy. It was the most horrid of betrayals.

She thought back to the last time she'd been at Gaston

Farm. It had been shortly after Basil had been home on leave. Katy and Clara had been acting in a peculiar way. They'd avoided any conversations about Basil. Now Penny understood the reason why. Katy must have been with Basil at that time, yet she hadn't said a word! And neither had Clara. They must have known that this would break her heart. How cowardly of them to inform her with a letter. Penny gritted her teeth and suppressed a scream as she thought bitterly, *I hate you Katy Darwin and I'll never forgive you, never!*

Throwing herself onto the bed, sobbing, muffling her cries in the pillow, Penny's heart broke. In just one letter, her whole life had changed. She'd lost both her best friend and the love of her life. And she'd lost her home too. She could never return to Gaston Farm now. She couldn't bear the thought of seeing Katy and Basil together. *Oh, Basil*, she cried, *I loved you so much.*

51

The next day, Penny couldn't face getting out of bed. She heard someone knocking on her door. Burying her head under the blankets, she hoped whoever it was would soon go away.

'Penny... Penny... It's me, Maggie. Are you all right?'

Penny pulled the covers further over her head.

'Penny... please, I'm worried about you. Are you in there?'

She didn't want to see Maggie or anyone, but she couldn't leave her friend to worry. Feeling exhausted, Penny forced herself out of the bed and went to the door. When she pulled it open, Maggie gasped.

'Good grief, what's happened?' Maggie asked.

Penny didn't answer. She left the door open for Maggie to come in and went to the table beside her bed. Picking up the letter from Clara, she turned and handed it to Maggie.

Maggie looked worried. 'Your eyes... have you been crying all night?'

Penny nodded.

'What's this?' Maggie asked, holding the letter.

'Read it,' Penny instructed.

She watched Maggie's eyes widen as she read the lines about Katy and Basil's marriage.

'Oh no, I'm so sorry, Penny. This must have been an awful shock for you.'

'I still can't quite believe it. Katy was supposed to be my best friend.'

'Huh, some friend, eh. What are you going to do?'

'What can I do? I can't go back to Kent now. That's it, my life is over.'

'I know it's rough, lovey, but your life ain't over.'

Tears pricked Penny's eyes again. 'I've got no one, Maggie, no one. I never want to see Katy again, Basil doesn't love me, he loves *her*. Jimmy is dead. My dad doesn't give two hoots about me and is in prison. Phil has left because I drove him away and you'll be moving to America.'

'Oh, darling,' Maggie cooed, opening her arms to Penny. 'You'll find happiness, I'm sure you will.'

Penny fell into Maggie's arms. 'I have to face facts. I'm all alone in this world.'

As she cried, Maggie seemed to have a light-bulb moment. 'Hang on a minute,' she said, sounding pleased.

Maggie's enthusiasm felt inappropriate to Penny, given the circumstances. 'What?' she asked, sullenly.

'Didn't you tell me once that your dad said you've got a grandad in Battersea?'

'Yeah. So?'

'Well, maybe if you found him you wouldn't feel so alone. And who knows, if you find your grandad, you might discover that you've got a whole a lot more family who you've never met.'

'But what if my grandad doesn't want to know me?'

'And what if he does? You won't know unless you meet him.'

'How? I don't know anything about him.'

'Do you know his name?' Maggie asked.

'Only that it's Archie.'

'What else? What was your mum's name?'

'Jill. I can't remember her last name, but I'm sure it began with a *D*.'

'There you go. We're looking for an old bloke called Archie who had a daughter called Jill *D* who died twenty-two years ago. That's quite a lot to go on. Someone will know him.'

'What, we just start asking around?' Penny asked, unsure of Maggie's plan.

'Yes, and I know where to start... The Battersea Tavern. Winnie Berry might have heard of him and if she hasn't, she might know who to ask.'

Penny wasn't convinced that she wanted to find her grandad. She risked being rejected and she wasn't sure that she was strong enough to cope with anymore heartache. But the notion of having a family of her own gave her a warm and fuzzy feeling inside.

'Come on,' Maggie encouraged. 'What have you got to lose?'

'Nothing, I suppose,' Penny answered. 'All right. Will you help me find him?'

'Do monkeys like bananas?'

Penny looked at her friend curiously. 'Yes, monkeys like bananas.'

'Then there's your answer – yes!'

Penny stood outside the Battersea Tavern biting on her bottom lip.

'Don't look so worried,' Maggie said. 'That cold water has

helped to take the swelling out of your eyes. You don't look quite as bad as you did.'

'I've never been in a pub before.'

'Me neither, except with Hank a few times. But loads of the women from the factory go into pubs now. Come on, what's the worst that can happen?'

Maggie went in, looking confident, with Penny following closely in her shadow. She didn't like the smoky atmosphere or the smell of beer. Neither did she like being aware of all heads turning to look at them. It made her feel very self-conscious. She was glad when she saw Winnie Berry behind the bar with a welcoming smile.

'Hello, ladies. What can I get you?' Mrs Berry asked.

'We've come to pick your brain,' Maggie replied.

Carmen, a barmaid, chuckled as she interrupted saying, 'Good luck with that, but you'll have to find Winnie's brain first.'

'Oi, cheeky,' Winnie smiled at Carmen. Then she turned back to Maggie. 'Go on, love, pick away.'

Penny felt Maggie nudge her.

'Ask her, then,' Maggie encouraged.

Glancing around nervously, Penny spoke in little more than a whisper. 'I'm, erm, I'm looking for someone,' she mumbled.

'Do what?' Mrs Berry asked, leaning closer over the brown painted bar.

Penny stared at the woman and couldn't find her voice.

'What's the matter, love? Has the cat got your tongue?'

Thankfully, Maggie spoke on Penny's behalf. 'We're trying to find a fella called Archie. He had a daughter named Jill who died over twenty years ago.'

'Oh, right. And may I ask what your business is with Archie?'

'He's Penny's grandad.'

Mrs Berry placed her hands on her wide hips. 'I see,' she said knowingly, then looking at Penny warmly, she added, 'Well, love, it's none of my business, but I know you've had a hard time. I heard that your father is banged up again, and I was sorry to hear about Jimmy. I haven't seen Archie for a few years, but last I knew, he was living on the Shaftesbury Park Estate on Tyneham Road. Luckily for him he lives up the top end of the street. Good job an' all 'cos the bottom part has been pretty much blown up.'

'That's smashing, thank you, Mrs Berry,' Maggie gushed. 'See, Penny, I told you that we'd find him. And I said that Mrs Berry would know where to look.'

'Glad I could help,' the landlady said. 'He's a nice old boy, you'll like him.'

Outside, Penny gazed at Maggie with wide eyes. 'That was easy! What do we do now?'

'We go to Tyneham Road and introduce you to your grandad.'

Eighty-year-old Archie Durrant folded his newspaper and added it to a pile beside his armchair. It was only June, but come the winter, the newspaper would make good firelighters for the coals.

Resting his head back and sucking on his pipe, Archie savoured the flavour of the tobacco. He looked around his small front room. It wasn't much, but the bricks and mortar of the cottage-style house belonged to him. And thankfully, unlike at the other end of the street, the Hun hadn't destroyed his home. Archie was proud of being a homeowner. Most folk on the estate rented their houses. But Archie, in 1884, had moved to *The Workmen's City* and had purchased the three-bedroomed house for two-hundred and ten pounds with a mortgage from the Southern Co-operative Permanent Building Society. The mortgage had long been paid off, but those first ten years of finding six shillings and one penny a week had been a struggle, especially as his wife, Daisy, had pushed out one kid after another. Archie's memories drifted back to his beloved wife. She had been so proud of their home and had kept it pristine. But Daisy had passed away thirty years earlier, leaving Archie a lonely man. He'd outlived seven of his nine children. He had disowned his one remaining daughter and she'd moved out of London. His youngest son, Larry, had joined the Merchant Navy. 'But I've got you for company, eh, Winston,' Archie smiled and stroked the big ginger cat that had jumped up on his lap. Archie had no idea where Winston had come from. The cat had turned up a few years ago and made himself at home. Archie assumed that Winston had lived in one of the houses on the street before it had been bombed. 'Come on, down you get. I need to see to the birds.'

Winston jumped down as Archie pushed himself up from the armchair. Then in his small kitchen, he scooped birdseed into a large metal bowl. Carrying it out into the backyard, he placed the bowl in the 'V' of a branch in a small, dead tree, and then he sat on a rickety wooden chair by the back door and waited. It didn't take long for the sparrows and pigeons to find their lunch. Archie took great pleasure in watching the birds feeding. He was sure that they waited somewhere nearby for him to appear with their food. Looking over to the kitchen window, Archie smiled. Winston was staring out, his eyes transfixed on the wild birds. 'You're not coming out, Winston,' Archie admonished. Thankfully, as far as Archie knew, Winston hadn't yet caught any wildlife. He knew it was nature's way, but Archie loved animals and didn't like to see them harmed.

After half an hour, Archie went back inside and put the kettle on to boil. As he spooned tea leaves into the teapot, he heard someone knocking on the front door. 'I wonder who that can be?' he said to Winston. 'We don't often get visitors.'

Although Archie was a man in his dotage, he still felt sprightly for his age. The odd ache bothered him now and then, and he couldn't easily bend down. But his eyes were bright and his hearing was fine. He'd often say to Winston *there must be a good reason for God to keep me on this earth, I just don't know what that reason is.* And it was truly what Archie believed. He'd wanted to die when Daisy had been taken so cruelly from him by cancer. But all these years later and still going strong, Archie knew there was a purpose for his long life, and once he'd fulfilled that purpose, he hoped to be reunited with his wife in heaven.

As he opened the door, Winston rubbed around his ankles. The cat never wandered far and only left the house to do his business, and Winston enjoyed the company of visitors just as much as Archie did.

Two young ladies stood on his step. The taller blonde woman, the more striking of the two, smiled broadly. But Archie's eyes fell on the slightly-built woman with red hair. He looked at her eyes and instantly recognised them, feeling that Daisy was staring back at him.

'Sorry to bother you,' the blonde woman said, 'but are you Archie?'

'Yes, I'm Archie,' he replied, his eyes still fixed on the smaller woman. 'And I know exactly who you are.'

'This is Penny... she thinks that you might be her grandad.'

'I am, and I'm over the moon to finally meet you. Come in, mind Winston, he's a bugger for getting under your feet. Excuse me language, ladies, I do apologise.'

Archie held the front door open wider and the blonde woman pushed Penny through. 'Go on,' she urged.

Penny looked terrified.

'It's all right, me and Winston don't bite, pet. Come in and go through to the front room. I would think that you've got a hundred questions for me,' he chuckled.

Archie invited the women to take a seat on his very old sofa. 'Sorry about the hairs. Winston likes to sleep on it. Can I get you a cup of tea? The kettle is just boiling.'

'I'd love one, thank you,' the blonde woman replied. 'Sorry, I'm Maggie, Penny's friend.'

Penny shook her head. 'Just a glass of water, please,' she said, timidly.

Archie couldn't take his eyes off her and hoped he wasn't making her feel even more uncomfortable than she already looked.

'I'll be back in a jiffy,' he said.

'Can I help?' Maggie offered.

'No, pet, just give Winston a stroke. He likes a fuss, especially from a pretty young lady,' he smiled.

In the kitchen, Archie drew in a long breath and gathered his thoughts. He'd known that his daughter, Jill, had birthed a child and had given the girl away, and looking at Penny, he was sure that she was Jill's daughter. Jill had been the spit of Daisy, taller and wider but her features had mirrored her mother's. And now Penny looked like her too. The hair was different, no doubt from her father's side of the family, but the eyes, the nose, the lips and even her tiny frame were almost identical to Daisy. Archie had never given much thought to Jill's daughter. He hadn't believed that he'd ever get to meet her, and Jill had never said what had become of her daughter. Yet here she was, sitting in his front room, and he couldn't have been happier! Family meant everything to Archie. It had broken his heart to have buried so many of his loved ones. Four of his kids hadn't made it past their tenth birthdays. Two of his sons had died in the trenches in France during the Great War. And Alice, his favourite and eldest daughter, had succumbed to the same fate as her mother, cancer taking her far too young. Penny was his only grandchild and he wished that Daisy could have been here to share this joyous day.

Penny's eyes fell on a black and white framed photograph that sat on top of the hearth. 'I look like her,' she whispered to Maggie.

Maggie walked over to the photo and picked it up. 'Blimey, it's uncanny.'

'That's Daisy,' Archie said, coming into the room with a tray. 'She would have been Penny's grandmother. Sadly, my wife died many, many years ago. But you can see the family resemblance. You look just like my Daisy, pet.'

Penny smiled. She hadn't known what to expect from Archie and was pleased with his warm reception. Winston jumped onto her lap and nudged her hand with his large head. As she stroked him and tickled behind his ears, the cat purred the loudest purr that she'd ever heard.

'I see that Winston has taken a shine to you. He's a good judge of character.'

Penny immediately liked Archie, though she still felt nervous.

'So, pet, how did you find me?' Archie asked as he handed her a glass of water.

'We asked Mrs Berry in the Battersea Tavern and she told us what road you live on. And then me and Maggie knocked on a door and a woman sent us here.'

Archie laughed. 'I meant, how did you know that I'm your grandad? I would have come searching for you if I'd know where to look.'

'My dad told me that I had a grandad in Battersea called Archie and that my mum, Jill, died soon after I was born. But that's all I knew.'

'You knew more than me. Who raised you, pet?'

'Florence Black.'

Archie's eyes looked as though they were popping out of his head on stalks as he gawped at Penny. 'Are you Cyril's girl? Of course you are, I've only got to look at your hair to know that! Well, I'll be buggered! Oops, sorry, excuse me language again, pet. I just can't believe it. Cyril's girl, my granddaughter. All these years you've been right under my nose and I never knew it.'

'You know my dad then?'

'Yeah, I know Cyril well, though not as well as I thought, it seems,' Archie said, shaking his head. 'I can't believe that he never said a word to me about you. I can't lie, pet, I'm disappointed in your father. He should have told me about you.'

Penny shrugged. 'He's always been a disappointment to me.'

'Yeah, well, I can understand that. I can't find a good word to say about the man. He's a lying thief and wouldn't know what honesty was even if it jumped up and punched him square between the eyes. Sorry, pet, I know he's your father, but Cyril has done wrong by me on one too many occasions. And this, keeping you from me, this is just about as wicked as it gets.'

Penny agreed and didn't feel a need to defend her father.

'Anyway, enough about him,' Archie said, smiling again. 'I expect there's plenty you want to know.'

'Can you tell me about my mum, please,' Penny asked.

Archie blew out a long breath. 'What can I say about Jill... Well, she was what we called the black sheep of the family. Me and her clashed something terrible. Her trouble was, she was too strong willed and didn't like to be told what to do. I suppose, if you was being generous, you'd call her a free spirit. Your mother left home when she was very young and she wanted to make her own way in life. Her path took her down a dark road and she did what she had to do to get by. But she was stubborn, so stubborn, and wouldn't accept any help from me. I've always admired Jill's strength, but it often worked against her. She was her own worst enemy. Sorry, pet, I haven't painted a nice picture of your mum, but you deserve the truth.'

'My dad said that Jill was an entertainer.'

'Ha,' Archie scoffed, 'I suppose she was, of sorts. An entertainer,' he laughed, 'that's one way to put it.'

Penny threw a confused look at Maggie who shrugged her shoulders.

'I'll be frank with you, pet. Your mother made some bad choices, but like I said, she wouldn't accept any help from me. She did well to support herself and get by, but she did it by selling herself... to men.'

'She was a prostitute?' Penny spluttered, almost choking on the water she'd just sipped.

'Yes, pet, I'm sorry to say she was. She did what she felt she had to do in the only way she knew how to do it. I can't say I was happy about it, mind. I dragged her home here loads of times, but your mother made her own rules and would soon be off and back to her old ways. To be honest, I was ashamed of her. Even more so when I saw she was carrying you. I should be ashamed of myself though. 'Cos when I realised that she was in the family way, I turned me back on her. And that's when she probably needed me the most.'

'I, erm, I don't know what to say.'

'This must all be a lot to take in.'

'Yeah, it is. Have I got any other family?'

'You've got an uncle, Larry. He's in the Merchant Navy. He travels all over the world and rarely comes back to Battersea. But he sends me postcards, here...' Archie walked over to a drawer and pulled it open. Taking out a large pile of cards, he handed them to Penny. 'See, postcards from every corner of the globe. There's some proper exotic places there, countries I've never even heard of,' Archie chuckled. 'I couldn't be prouder of him. The British Merchant Navy kept our country and our armies supplied with food, ammunition, all sorts. But they took a hell of a thrashing from the Hun. Many ships were sunk, but my Larry pulled through.'

'And Larry is your son?'

'Yeah, that's right, Jill's younger brother.'

'So, it's just you and Larry, no one else?'

Archie looked down at the threadbare rug. 'Er, yeah, that's right, pet.'

Penny wasn't sure what to say next. After a moment of awkward silence, Archie asked, 'Do you live in Battersea?'

'Yes, near Plough Road, but I'm supposed to be moving out tomorrow.'

'You're not moving away, are you?' Archie asked.

'No. I was, but I'm not now. I just hope my landlord will let me stay on, but I think he's already found someone to rent the room and paying more than I do. I've got to find a job too.'

'You're always welcome here, pet. I've got three bedrooms upstairs, and I only use one of them. It won't cost you nothing.'

'Oh, that's, erm, that's very, erm, kind of you ... thank you,' Penny replied, clumsily.

'That's what family are for.'

Penny smiled and felt that warm and fuzzy feeling inside again. *Family.* She had a family of her own. A grandad who was willing to take her in and an uncle who sailed the seas.

Maggie stood up. 'Excuse me,' she said. 'Thanks for the tea, but I think I'll get off and let you two catch up.'

Penny stood too. 'I should probably be on my way an' all,' she said, not wanting to outstay her welcome.

'So soon?' Archie said, sounding disappointed. 'Wouldn't you like to stay for lunch? I ain't got much in, but I'm sure I could rustle up something.'

'I wouldn't want to put you to any trouble,' Penny answered, though she liked the idea of having lunch with her grandad.

'It wouldn't be any trouble, pet. You'd be making an old

man very happy. As much as I enjoy sharing a piece of fish with Winston, he lacks conversation.'

'In that case, I'd love to stay for lunch, thank you.'

'And what about you, Maggie? The more the merrier.'

'No, thanks, Archie. My mum will be wondering where on earth I am. It was nice meeting you. Ta ta.'

Penny walked her friend to the door as Archie busied himself in the kitchen. 'What do you think of him?' she asked in a whisper.

Maggie placed her hand on Penny's shoulder. 'He's a smashing fella. You should think about taking him up on his offer to stay here. It sounds like he could do with the company, and it'll take the pressure off you to find a decent job to pay your rent. That's if you've even got a room to live in after tomorrow.'

'But I don't really know him. It would feel odd.'

'You don't know the people you're sharing the house with now. At least Archie is your family. How about that, eh? And he seems overjoyed to have met you.'

Penny closed the door after Maggie and went into the kitchen to find Archie. 'Are you sure you wouldn't mind me moving in for a while? Just until I get back on my feet.'

'Mind? No, pet, I'd be over the moon.'

'Then in that case, you'd better let me muck in. Sit down, *Grandad*, and I'll make us our lunch.'

It felt strange to call the man *Grandad*, but they looked at each other with a genuine affection. Penny smiled. She had a family. A real, blood family. And she wasn't alone in the world anymore.

52

Archie woke up tired. He'd hardly slept since Penny had moved in a week ago. He enjoyed having his granddaughter around and the more he came to know her, the more he liked the girl. She reminded him so much of Daisy, not just in the way she looked, but in some of her mannerisms too. *Oh, my Daisy, you would have loved our granddaughter to the moon and back* he thought, saddened that his wife had never enjoyed the pleasures of being a grandma. But Archie had vowed to himself that he'd be the best grandad he could be and would make up for the time he'd lost with Penny and for her rotten start in life. And because of his desire to do right by the girl, he'd been left with a shocking dilemma. There was a deep secret that he hadn't shared with Penny. And the worry of it had been disturbing his sleep.

'Good morning,' Penny greeted him cheerily in the kitchen.

'Morning, pet. What's all this?' he asked, pointing to the pile of clothes on the table.

'I've washed and dried all your shirts and mended your clothes, including your socks.'

'You didn't have to do that, but thanks. I suppose I needed

smartening up a bit and it'll be nice to wear me socks without me toes poking through the ends.'

'There's fresh tea in the pot. Would you like one?'

'I could get used to this,' Archie laughed. 'Once you've got yourself a job, don't you dare go rushing off to find somewhere else to live.'

'I like it here, Grandad. It's much nicer to share a house with family instead of strangers.'

'This ain't a *house*, pet, it's a home. Your home.'

'Thank you. Maggie said there's no vacancies in the factory where I used to work so I thought I might see if there are any jobs going in the shops at Clapham Junction. I might try in Arding and Hobbs.'

'The back of that department store took a bit of bomb damage during the Blitz, but if my memory serves me right, it didn't close its doors to the public. Cor, they've got some fancy things in that shop. I'd be proper proud to see you working in there. Good luck, pet.'

Archie's mind was turning as he spoke. With Penny out of the house, it would give him a chance to nip out and have a discreet word with his good friend, Smithy. He'd known Smithy his whole life. They'd been at school together and had then gone on to be taxi cabbies. Back in those days, Archie had worked the horse-drawn cab by day, and then they'd swapped, and Smithy had worked the night shift. They'd earned a reasonable living ferrying the gentlemen and ladies of London through the busy streets. But with the advent of the motorised cabs in the 1920s, Archie and Smithy's horse and cab were forced into retirement. Up until this day, the men had remained firm friends and Smithy was the only person alive who knew Archie's secret.

★

Penny liked the bustle of Clapham Junction. She could lose herself in the crowds and go unnoticed. Standing outside the large department store, her confidence plummeted and she couldn't find the nerve to go inside to enquire about a job. She'd been much better suited to working in Mr Hamble's greenhouses in the Kent countryside, or even in the factory. Realistically, Penny knew that she wasn't suited to retail work in such a prestigious store such as Arding and Hobbs. But with little money left, she had to find a job and soon. As kind as her grandad had been, Penny didn't want to rely on the charity of an old man.

She meandered around the shops, looking at all the things she couldn't afford. Without feeding from Maggie's confidence and missing Phil's cheeky banter, Penny felt she wanted to hide away. She'd once been a brave girl, excited for a new life when she'd run away from Florence to Gaston Farm. But now that Katy had betrayed her and she'd lost Basil, Penny felt her personality retreating inwards.

The world felt a scary and threatening place. But she had her grandad and Penny suddenly felt the need to rush back home to him and the comfort he offered. It was her place of safety.

Smithy's door was never locked, and Archie let himself in, calling, 'It's only me, mate.'

Smithy, as usual, was sat in a rocking chair in front of the front room window. The man would sit there all day just watching the world go by.

'I knew it was you,' Smithy said, 'I saw you coming.'

Archie tried not to show any concern on his face, but he thought Smithy looked dreadful. His lifelong friend hadn't aged as well as Archie had, and it didn't appear that Smithy had been taking good care of himself. The man was wearing the same clothes he'd worn two weeks ago when Archie had last visited. Even from the other side of the room, Archie could smell Smithy's musty body odour. He looked thin too, and Archie wondered if Smithy had been eating properly. 'Are you all right, mate?' he asked.

'I'm still here,' Smithy replied, grumpily.

'Ain't you going to offer me a cuppa?'

'Help yourself, you know where the kitchen is.'

'I'll make us both a hot drink. Have you had any breakfast? Shall I do you something to eat an' all?'

'You ain't me missus, Archie, so stop talking to me like you are.'

Archie smiled. His friend had become rather cantankerous these past few years, though Archie couldn't blame the man for his bad moods. Smithy could barely walk, even with the aid of a walking stick. He was trapped in a ground floor flat with only a good neighbour who would call in and bring him his shopping. Like Archie, Smithy was a widower. His wife had passed away ten years ago, and though they had wanted a large family, the marriage had been childless.

In the small kitchenette, Archie was shocked to find that the milk had curdled, the bread had grown green mould and the cupboards were almost bare. He didn't bother with the tea and went back into the front room. 'Hasn't Mrs Bailey been getting your groceries for you?' Archie asked.

Smithy looked out of the window.

'Oi, Smithy, what's going on?' Archie demanded to know.

'Mrs Bailey has gawn to stay with her sister and she won't be returning. Good luck to her, that's what I say. The woman was dreading her old man being demobbed. He's always knocked her about. I used to hear it through the walls. Well, with him away these past five years, she's enjoyed her life without him, so she's gawn to start a new one.'

Archie felt awful for not calling in on Smithy sooner. A thick layer of dust covered the furniture and he could see bugs climbing the walls. Smithy was a proud man; he'd never ask for help. But Archie couldn't stand by and watch his friend deteriorate. 'You're coming with me,' he said, decisively.

'Eh?'

'You heard me, mate. I'm going to pack up your stuff and you're moving in with me. No arguments.'

'I bloody well ain't, thank you very much!'

'Yeah, you are, and you'll be doing me a favour.'

'How?' Smithy asked, his rheumy eyes narrowing.

'You ain't going to believe this, mate, but Jill's daughter has turned up and now she's living with me.'

'Jill's daughter, you say?'

'Yeah. I couldn't believe it. But you wait until you see her. I swear, she's the double of Daisy.'

'Well, I'll be buggered!'

'I always wondered why God kept me on this earth. I knew there had to be a reason for me being here. And this is it, Smithy. I'm still here so that Penny could find me.'

'Gawd knows why I'm still alive. I reckon if there is a God, he don't like me much and that's why he's left me here.'

'God wouldn't put up with your moods like I do, that's why he ain't taken your soul yet,' Archie chuckled.

'So what's your granddaughter like?'

'She's a smashing girl, mate, really sweet. But she's out of work which means I'm supporting her,' Archie fibbed. 'So, I could do with a few extra few pennies. Like I said, you moving in with me will be doing me a favour 'cos you can pay me a bit of rent money instead of paying for this place.' Archie didn't like to lie to his friend, but he'd had to think quickly. Smithy was a proud man and would never accept charity.

'I ain't as stupid as I look,' Smithy snapped. '*Doing you a favour*, my arse.'

'You would be. But at the end of the day, mate, I can't leave you living like this.'

'This is my home and I won't leave it.'

Archie drew in a long breath, and then a thought struck him. 'My granddaughter needs work, and you need looking after. I know you've got plenty of money stashed away, you tight old git. You can't take it with you and you ain't got anyone to leave it to, so now is the time to spend it. I'm gonna send my Penny round to shop, cook and clean for you, and you can pay her for her time.'

Smithy slowly nodded. 'All right,' he agreed, 'I'm happy with that, just as long as she ain't as mouthy as you,' he smiled.

'The thing is, she asked about her mother, but I ain't told her *everything*, so watch what you say in front of her.'

Smithy's eyes widened. 'Oh, right, so she doesn't know the whole story about Jill. Are you going to tell her?'

'I dunno, mate. I really don't know. I keep turning it over and over in my head. I can't think what to do for the best. I don't want to lie to the girl, but I can't see what it will achieve by telling her the truth. What do you reckon?'

'Hmm,' Smithy said, as he thought. 'What she doesn't know can't hurt her. I'd leave things be. Let sleeping dogs lie.'

Archie agreed. 'Yeah, that's what I thought an' all. I just hope she never finds out the truth and ends up hating me for keeping it from her.'

53

June 1946
One year later

Clara held her grandson close, singly softly as she swayed from side to side, comforting the baby as best she could. She hoped that little Lawrence couldn't hear his parents arguing again. Night and day, Basil and Katy seemed to be constantly at each other's throats. It was clear that Basil wasn't happy working on the farm, and Katy was struggling with just about everything. Even before Basil and Katy had married, Clara had harboured concerns. She'd suspected that Katy was secretly drinking, and as it turned out she'd been right, only now, it wasn't a secret any longer. Katy openly downed bottles of brandy, whisky, gin – anything she could get her hands on. They'd all tried to stop the girl. Will had thrown the contents of countless bottles of booze down the sink, yet Katy always managed to find more. When she was drunk, Katy seemed to forget her sorrows and would be gregarious, though loud and annoying and often turning nasty with Basil. The sober Katy was mostly sullen, locked in a world where her traumatic past haunted her mind.

Basil stamped into the kitchen, his face twisted with rage.

'I don't know what to do with her!' he screeched. 'I'm at my wits' end.'

'Shush, darling, you'll upset Lawrence.'

'Katy should be looking after our baby, not you!'

'I know, and she will once she's feeling better,' Clara assured him, trying to placate her enraged son.

'*Feeling better* – she's not ill, Mum, she's bloody drunk again! Where did she get the alcohol from? I've already spoken to the landlord of the pub who swore blind that he wouldn't sell Katy any booze. No one in the village shops will either. So, where is she buying it from?'

'I don't know, Basil,' Clara said, exasperated. 'Someone must be buying it for her. But I've no idea who.'

'I know who,' Basil snarled. 'Alfred Johnson. I'd lay money on it being him.'

'Oh, I don't think so, Basil. Alfred is a married man.'

'So? You've seen the way he is around Katy. He can't keep his eyes off her. Married or not, I'm telling you, Mum, he's trying to win favours with *my* wife.'

'If that's what you really believe, then I shall have a word with your father. He'll have to sack Alfred and find another farmhand.'

'Dad won't be happy about that. Alfred is a good worker.'

'I couldn't care less if he ran the whole farm single-handed. If the man has been supplying Katy with alcohol, then he must be sacked at once.'

Basil sighed heavily and pulled out a seat at the table. 'How's Lawrence?'

'He's fine. But I worry what effect all the arguing and shouting will have on him.'

Running a hand through his hair, Basil sighed again. 'Maybe I should take Katy and Lawrence away from this and start a new life. Perhaps she'd be able to forget about her past.'

'I'm afraid her memories would move with her wherever she goes.'

'I don't know, Mum. But at least one of us would be happy. I didn't enjoy farm work before the war, and now I like it even less.'

'I know, Basil, but this farm is your legacy. It will belong to you one day.'

Basil hung his head. 'I don't want it. I don't want any of this life.'

Katy's voice came from the doorway. 'Does that include me?' she asked, bitterly.

Basil turned and glared at his wife. Clara could see the contempt in her son's eyes, and she worried that they were going to start fighting again.

'Well... does it?' Katy hissed. 'You don't want *any* of this life... does that include me?'

'Sometimes, Katy, yes, it does.'

'Well tough! You're stuck with me and Lawrence and this farm. *Poor Basil*. Life is so difficult for you. A big house, a farm that makes money, a beautiful son, a mother who adores you, oh dear, what a hard life you have,' she mocked.

'And a wife who drinks herself into oblivion and doesn't take care of her son!' Basil spat.

Clara stepped back, pulling Lawrence closer. The baby was becoming agitated, upset by the raised voices.

'Is it such a sin that I drink sometimes? If you'd had the life I did, then maybe you'd drink too!'

Clara was relieved when Katy stomped away.

'See, Mum, there's no talking to her. How did it get to this?'

'I suspect that when Katy had a drink on V.E. day, it made her feel good. And I think she's been drinking ever since.'

'I don't know what I'm going to do, but I can't take much more of this.'

'Marriage isn't always easy, but if you love her, you'll get through it. Do you love her, Basil?'

'Yes,' Basil said, quickly. 'I thought I did.'

'You don't sound sure,' Clara challenged.

'Katy always seemed... vulnerable. I wanted to take care of her.'

'That's not the same as loving someone.'

Basil scraped back the seat, stood and leaned down to kiss Clara's cheek. 'I'd better get back to work. See you later.'

Clara gazed after her son in his wake. His marriage to Katy was not a happy one and she feared that it was doomed. 'I wonder what will happen to you, my little one,' she cooed, stroking Lawrence's soft cheek. 'But don't you worry. Your nana will always look after you.'

In Smithy's flat, Penny washed up the dinner plate and made a fresh pot of tea. She enjoyed taking care of the old man and had soon learned that he wasn't quite as grouchy as he'd first led her to believe. In fact, she liked his company and always looked forward to playing cards with him and her grandad. The job didn't feel like a job. It didn't pay much either, but Penny was happy with her lot.

'I had a letter from Maggie,' she told Smithy as she handed him a cup of tea. 'She's not happy in America, which doesn't surprise me because I didn't think she would settle over there.

She said she feels trapped and now her husband is already talking about having another baby.'

'What about you?' Smithy asked. 'You ought to be thinking about marrying and starting a family. Most women are married by the time they're your age.'

'I'm only twenty-three, Smithy, and not quite an old spinster yet.'

'But you haven't even got yourself a fella. You should get out more.'

'I'm happy enough,' Penny fibbed. The truth was, as much as she loved her grandad and thought the world of Smithy, she missed friends of her own age.

'Are you going up town to the Victory Celebrations? You'll get to see all the famous military commanders that you've read about in the papers, like General Montgomery and Eisenhower.'

'No, I'm not bothered about standing in huge crowds to watch a military parade.'

'It's not just the British armed forces taking part, you know. They'll be units from all over the Commonwealth and the allied forces. I reckon it will be spectacular.'

'I'm sure it will, Smithy, but I won't be going.'

'Is that 'cos you ain't got anyone to go with?'

Penny shook her head as she pulled on her cardigan. 'No, it's because I'm not interested in seeing tanks and guns and what have you.'

''Ere, before you leave, I want to show you something,' Smithy smiled. Then using his walking stick to steady himself, the old man pushed himself up from his rocking chair.

'Careful,' Penny warned, stretching out her arm towards him.

'Watch this,' he said, and walked across the room, albeit slowly.

'That's wonderful!'

'I know. I've not been able to get to my bed without help for the last six months but look at me now. I'll be entering the two-hundred-metre sprint at the Olympics if I carry on at this rate,' he chortled.

'Well, I don't know about that, but you're doing ever so well.'

'Thanks to you, Penny. I'd just about given up on life 'til you came along.'

'Just doing my job,' Penny said. 'I'll see you later. It's card night.'

Penny walked home feeling pleased with herself. It felt good to have made such a vast difference in Smithy's life. Good food, a clean bed and cheery company had perked the old fella up no end.

'I'm home, Grandad,' Penny called as she trotted along the passageway and into the kitchen. But there wasn't the usual cup of tea waiting for her.

The back door was open. She assumed her grandad was outside soaking up the warm sun and, knowing him, watching the birds or finding a hedgehog to feed. She looked down when she felt Winston rubbing against her legs. 'Where is he?' she asked the cat.

'Grandad,' she called again as she stepped into the backyard.

And then her heart plummeted when she saw him. Archie was on the ground, lying on his side. Penny could see that his face was grey, and he looked to be struggling for breath.

She dashed to his side, panic twisting her stomach. 'Grandad... Grandad...'

'Argh,' Archie groaned.

'What happened? Can you move?'

Archie managed to roll over onto his back. It was then that Penny saw the extent of how deathly ill he looked. She grabbed his hand. It felt cold but clammy, and she could see that he was sweating.

'It's me old ticker, pet, it's worn out,' he wheezed.

'I'll fetch the doctor.'

Archie's eyes squeezed shut and he yelled in pain, grabbing his chest. And then he was very, very still.

'Grandad! Grandad!' Penny cried. 'Please, Grandad, wake up. Don't leave me ... you're my family ...'

As Archie's heart stopped beating, Penny's broke. 'Oh, Grandad,' she sobbed. 'I'm all alone again.'

54

Archie Durrant had bequeathed his house to Penny. She hadn't thought that it was right. After all, her grandad had a son, Larry, and Penny felt the house should have been left to him. Larry hadn't come to his father's funeral. He'd been stuck at sea midway between oceans. But after arriving in port, Larry had sent a letter in which he'd stated that he had no desire to put down roots on land, and he'd conveyed his best wishes to Penny.

For weeks Penny had rattled around in the house until, after much persuasion, Smithy had eventually agreed to move in with her.

'This makes so much more sense,' Penny chirped. 'I can take care of you without having to traipse around to your flat twice a day.'

'I'm not happy about taking your front room as my bedroom, but I won't manage to get up the stairs.'

'I've got three rooms up there. I don't need the front room too.'

Smithy was sat in his rocking chair near the window.

'There's someone coming to the door,' he said, stretching his neck for a better look.

'Who is it?'

'I don't know. A woman, but she's wearing glasses and a scarf.'

Penny went to the door as the woman banged on it heavily. Pulling it open, the woman looked Penny up and down before barging in.

'Excuse me,' Penny said, shocked at the intrusion, 'What do you think you're doing?'

The woman ignored Penny and marched into the front room. She stood, peering around. 'Nothing much has changed in here,' she said, before turning her focus to Smithy. 'I see you've got your feet under the table too. Huh, that's not a surprise. You always did sponge off my dad.'

'Now listen here,' Smithy barked.

'Who are you?' Penny questioned, annoyed at the uninvited guest.

'I'm the rightful owner of this house,' the woman answered, smugly.

'No, you ain't,' Smithy insisted. 'Your father disowned you years ago, as well you know. You've no right to this house or anything else that belonged to Archie.'

'Keep your beak out, Smithy, it's got nothing to do with you. This is a family matter, and you're not family.'

None of this was making any sense to Penny. As far as she had been made aware, Archie only had one living son and that was Larry. 'Who are you?' she asked again.

The woman, her nose held high, announced, 'I'm Archie's daughter, Ruth.'

'Who are you trying to kid,' Smithy derided. 'You and me both know full well that *Ruth* died over twenty years ago.'

'Is she an imposter?' Penny asked, confused.

'Yeah, you could say that,' Smithy replied. 'She ain't Ruth, that's for sure. Ruth was a lovely, kind young woman.' And then his eyes blazing, he looked back at the woman, and hissed, 'It should have been you that died, not your dear sister... it should have been you!'

The woman stepped towards Smithy and pushed her face close to his as she jabbed her finger in his chest and warned, 'Shut your mouth, Smithy, or I'll shut it for you.'

'Don't threaten Smithy,' Penny snapped, her heart pounding. 'Your business is with me, not him.'

The woman turned and sneered, 'That's right, it is, and I will have what should be mine. And by the way, thank you for informing me of my father's death.'

'I – I – I didn't.'

'No, you didn't. I expect you were hoping that I'd never find out and you could keep his house all for yourself. Well, unfortunately for you, Larry had the good mind to tell me. My brother might be stupid enough to roll over and let you take what's ours, but I'm not.'

'I don't know who you are... My grandad never said anything about having a daughter.'

Smithy pushed himself up, balancing on his walking stick. 'You've no rights to this house, and as far as Archie was concerned, you weren't his daughter. You've always been trouble and a nasty piece of work which is why your father turned his back on you. This is Penny's house and you ain't welcome in it. Clear off, sling your hook and don't show your face round here again.'

'Who do you think you're scaring, Smithy? Look at you, you can't even stand up straight.'

'I know things about you, and I'll shout out the truth from the rooftops,' he threatened.

'Old news, Smithy. No one cares anymore. All that is in the past. It's over. Finished with. Tell whoever you want, it makes no odds to me.'

Penny rushed to Smithy's side. 'Please, sit down,' she encouraged. 'I can sort this all out. It will be all right.'

Smithy peered back at Penny, 'She's your mother,' he blurted. 'That's Jill Durrant.'

Penny, gobsmacked, slowly turned to look at the woman. 'Is that true?' she asked.

Jill shrugged. 'Well, if Smithy says so then it must be.'

Penny staggered to the sofa and flopped down. 'You're my mother,' she croaked, staring disbelievingly at the woman.

'Yes, I'm your mother, but as far as the authorities and anyone else is concerned, I'm Ruth, Ruth Durrant. And you and Smithy can't prove otherwise.'

'I don't understand...' Penny said, looking from Jill to Smithy for clarification.

As Jill pulled a cigarette from her bag and lit it, Smithy explained. 'Jill, your mother there, she got herself into serious trouble with some rough blokes from the West End of London. They were after her blood and were going to kill her. Around that same time, Ruth, who was Jill's younger sister, she died suddenly. They reckon she had a weak heart, God rest her soul. Jill begged your grandad to claim it was her who'd died and then she would take on Ruth's name and be free of the men who were after her. Archie didn't want to do it, but he'd just lost Ruth and he didn't want to see

Jill hurt. So, *Jill* was buried, and *Ruth* lived on. Archie never forgave himself for Ruth being denied a proper grave in her own name.'

'The sentimental fool,' Jill sniped, and blew smoke towards Smithy's face.

'Why didn't my grandad tell me?' Penny asked in a whisper.

'He was going to, but he wanted to protect you... from *her*,' Smithy said, eyeing Jill with disdain. 'She's wicked to the core, and Archie believed you was better off without her.'

'Right, that's the happy family reunion done, now can we get down to business. As Archie's daughter, I'm entitled to his house. I'm sure the courts will agree. And don't think for a moment that anyone outside of these four walls will believe that cock and bull story about me swapping identity with Ruth. I *am* Ruth, Jill is a skeleton six foot under.'

'Archie left this house to Penny in his will. You can try and fight it, Jill, but the court won't go against a legal will. You're flogging a dead horse,' Smithy said, smugly.

'There was a will?' Jill asked, sounding surprised. 'Larry didn't mention a will.'

'Penny, show your mother a copy of the will.'

Penny sat staring at the woman. She'd always imagined that if she'd met her mother, she'd have felt an instant rush of love. But she'd taken an instant dislike to Jill and found it difficult to comprehend that the hard-faced, bullying woman had birthed her.

'Penny, show Jill the will,' Smithy urged.

'Don't bother,' Jill snapped. 'If there's a will, then that throws a whole new light on the situation.'

'Well, there is, and now you know you can bugger off!'

Jill looked down at Penny, a wry smile on her face. 'Give

your father my regards. He saw me once a year or two ago. You should have seen the look on his face. He must have thought that he was seeing at a ghost,' she laughed. 'Congratulations, Penny, you have a lovely home.'

Jill flounced out, leaving Penny's mind spinning. 'Should I chase after her?' she mumbled.

'No, please don't. The woman is trouble. She always was and always will be. If you chase after her, she'll end up bringing you down with her. Stay well clear. Archie had good reason to keep you away from her.'

Penny understood. *I've come from bad stock*, she thought. Her father was a reprobate and her mother, well, Penny didn't have the words to describe Jill. She wasn't angry with her grandad for keeping Jill's secret. Having met the woman, Penny could see why he had. *I'm better off without my mum and dad*, she reasoned. Having no family was better than having family like the pair of them.

55

'Where is he?' Katy screamed.

It was mid-afternoon, yet the girl had only just crawled out of bed.

Clara popped a bottle into Lawrence's mouth, and calmly replied to Katy. 'I think you should have a wash, brush your teeth and run a comb through your hair. I shan't dilute the truth; you look and smell horrid.'

'Tell me where Basil has gone,' Katy seethed.

Clara had hoped that Katy wouldn't have even noticed that Basil was gone, but she had and was now demanding an answer that Clara didn't want to give her.

'If you don't tell me where my husband is, I swear, Clara, I'll walk out of this house and I'll take Lawrence with me. You'll never see your grandson again.'

'Now you're just being ridiculous, Katy. Where would you go? How would you live?'

'I'd find a way. Huh, that would kill you, wouldn't it? I see how you are with Lawrence. I might be drunk a lot of the time, but I ain't daft! You want *my* son for yourself. But let me remind you of something... you *ain't* his mother, I am. So, tell me where Basil has gone, or I'll take Lawrence away from you.'

Clara didn't believe that Katy was fit to be a mother in the state that she was in, and she had to bite her tongue. Though some of what the girl had said hit a raw nerve. Clara did feel like Lawrence's mother and dreamed of raising him as her own. The idea of Katy running away with him sent a shudder of fear down her spine. 'Basil has gone to London,' Clara blurted.

Katy looked unsure at first but then a bitter expression crossed her face. 'Why?' she asked, her jaw clenched.

'I don't know, Katy. That is a question that you will have to ask him when he comes home.'

'You must know why? You wouldn't have let him go to London without asking him his reason for going.'

'Like I said, you can talk to him when he returns. It has nothing to do with me.'

Katy threw her arms in the air. 'He's gone to see Penny!' Then pacing around the kitchen like a woman possessed, she started rambling. 'I knew it... I knew it was *her* that he wanted... He's a coward... He's run off behind my back... Oh, he denies that he loves Penny, but I've always known it...'

Clara worried about Katy's state of mind and what she was capable of. While Katy marched up and down, seething all sorts of crazy theories about Basil and Penny, Clara edged towards the door. Slipping out, she ran into the snug and carefully placed Lawrence on the sofa, piling cushions beside him. 'Mummy's not very well, darling,' she whispered, 'but you're safe here.'

Closing the snug door quietly behind her, Clara dashed back to the kitchen. Katy had quietened and was standing at the sink. Clara sighed with relief, but then she spotted a knife in Katy's trembling hand. The girl was holding the blade to her wrist over the scars from her previous wounds.

'No, Katy, NO!' Clara screamed and ran towards Katy.

As Clara grabbed Katy's forearm, Katy lashed out, and the knife sliced across Clara's face. She staggered backward, holding her hand over her bleeding cheek.

Katy stared, looking horrified, and dropped the bloodied knife to the floor.

'What have you done?' Clara asked, as warm, wet blood gushed from her face.

'I – I – I didn't mean to… Oh, gawd, Clara… I'm so sorry.'

Katy ran from the room leaving Clara reeling in shock. She stumbled towards the sink and picked up a towel, holding it to her cheek.

'What the hell?' Will asked, hurrying towards his wife.

'I'm fine… it probably looks worse than it is.'

Will eased Clara onto a chair and gently pulled away the towel to look at the cut.

'Christ, Clara, how did this happen?'

Clara gulped, tears pricking her eyes. 'It was Katy… but she didn't mean to do it.'

'Katy did this to you?'

Clara nodded.

'That's it. We've put up with enough from her. She'll have to go. I'm not having my wife attacked in her own home.'

Panic surged through Clara. 'No, Will,' she protested. 'If you throw Katy out, she'll take Lawrence with her. Please, Will, don't do it, don't throw her out!'

'All right, all right, calm down. I won't throw her out, but she can't get away with this.'

'I know. Go and fetch Lawrence from the snug. And then we'll have to find Katy.'

Clara felt dizzy as she sat holding the towel to her face. She assumed it was probably the shock. Thankfully, the bleeding had slowed.

Will rushed back into the kitchen, his arms empty. 'Lawrence isn't in the snug.'

'Yes, he is, on the sofa.'

'No, Clara, he's gone.'

Clara's blood ran cold. 'Oh, dear Lord,' she muttered, 'Katy has taken him!'

Clara ran out of the farmhouse with Will, desperate to find Katy before she did any harm to herself or Lawrence. 'You check the barn and the fields. I'll go to the stream,' she said with urgency.

'We'll find her and they'll both be all right,' Will assured her before taking off.

Clara forgot about the gaping wound on her face as she hurried around the back of the house. The wound had opened again and blood ran down her neck and into the collar of her white dress. As she raced towards the stream, relief flooded over her when she saw Katy sat beside the trickling water, cradling the baby.

Clara slowed her pace to a rapid walk. She didn't want to scare the girl. The long grass rustled as she walked through it and Katy looked over her shoulder. Clara could see she looked distressed and had tearful eyes.

Standing close by, she said softly, 'It's going to be all right, Katy.'

Katy shook her head. 'It's not. Look what I've done to you. I'm so sorry, Clara, I never meant to hurt you.'

'I know. Come home, please, and we can work this all out.'

'I can't. I've ruined everything.'

'No, Katy, you haven't. There's nothing that can't be mended.'

'My marriage can't be. Basil has never loved me. I tried to make him love me, but I knew he had feelings for Penny. And now he's gone to her.'

'You don't understand, Katy. He's gone to see Penny to ask her to come here, for you, to help you.'

Katy sobbed harder. 'I don't deserve him, or you or any of this,' she cried. 'I don't think I can stay here.'

Clara panicked. She couldn't allow Katy to take Lawrence away. 'You *must* stay here. This is your home, and we are your family,' she pleaded.

'No, Clara, it ain't. My home and my family are in Battersea... I want my mum.'

'But... but... your father.'

'I know what you're thinking. He's dead. My mum wrote to me a few weeks ago. She begged me to forgive her and said how sorry she was. I couldn't, not at first. But I'm a mum now, and I've really messed it up. I love Lawrence though, I swear I do. But I ain't been good to him. It's made me think about my mum. She made mistakes, but she loves me, I know she does.'

'I'm sure she does, and I'm glad you've found it in your heart to forgive her, but please, Katy, reconsider your decision to return there. You must see that life here will be better for Lawrence. And as his mother, I know you will only want what is best for your son.'

Katy clambered to her feet, gazing adoringly at Lawrence. She walked towards Clara, and to Clara's surprise, Katy gently placed the baby in her arms.

'You raise him,' she sobbed. 'You're better at it than me... it'll break my heart to leave him, but you're right; I will do what is best for my son.'

Lawrence gurgled happily in Clara's arms as she stood speechless and watched Katy walk away. 'What about Basil?' she called.

When Katy turned, Clara saw a new strength in the girl's eyes. 'You can let him know that he's free now. If he doesn't find Penny, remind him that he's better off alone rather than in a loveless marriage.'

Clara drew in a juddering breath, her tears flowing. She was grateful to have her grandson in her arms but she felt she was losing a daughter again.

'I will get better, Clara. It's going to take a long time to fix me. But one day, when I'm mended, I'll be back. Please tell Lawrence I love him. Tell him I was a good mum because I did what was best for him. You will tell him that, won't you?'

'I'll tell him,' she wept. 'I promise, Katy, I'll tell Lawrence that you're the greatest mother he could have wished for. But, please, reconsider. Stay here. Let me help to mend you. Lawrence needs you.'

Katy fell to her knees, sobbing into her hands. 'Look at the state of me. What if I can't be mended?'

'You can and you will get better, for the sake of Lawrence.'

Lifting her tear-streaked face, Katy cried, 'I wanted to be a better mother than the one I had. But I can't even look after myself, let alone my son.'

'I'll help you, Katy. But you must stop drinking. Do you think you can do that?'

Katy shrugged.

'I know the alcohol helps you to forget your pain, but it's ruining your marriage and you're neglecting Lawrence. I *know* you can do better. Will you try?'

'I'd like to... But I'm scared. Lawrence and Basil will be better off without me. Basil never loved me. He only married me because I was in the family way.'

'That's not true. They need you, Katy. But they need you to be sober. You're a married woman and a mother, loved by your husband and your son. I won't allow you to walk away from your responsibilities, and deep down, I don't believe you want to, do you?'

Katy shook her head.

'Good. We're a family, Katy. We'll get through this together. You're not going anywhere, and Basil would never forgive me if I stood by and let you leave.'

'But what if I can't do it? I don't know how to be a mother or a wife.'

'No one does, Katy. We learn as we go. You'll make mistakes, God, I made plenty. But I muddled through and so will you. But first we need to concentrate on you. Are you ready to start mending?'

'Yes, I think so. Do you really believe I can do it?'

Clara nodded as she held her hand towards the young woman. 'Come on, let's go home. And you can put Lawrence down for his afternoon nap.'

'I wanted to protect my son from the horrors of the world, but it's me who Lawrence needs protecting from.'

With Lawrence in the crook of her harm, Clara gently

squeezed Katy's hand as they headed towards the farmhouse. 'That's not entirely true. You've hit rock bottom, but we'll build you up again. Being a mother will give you strength that you didn't know you had within yourself. You *will* protect Lawrence. From this day on and every day, look at your child and remind yourself of how strong you are. You're fierce, Katy, a mother lioness.'

Katy half-smiled. 'Thank you. I'm going to really try. No more booze... I'm a mother lioness.'

56

Penny sat beside Smithy's bed in the front room, worried about the man's lack of energy and pallid skin. He hadn't been well since Jill had turned up at the house two days earlier.

'I'm going to fetch the doctor,' she told him.

'No need. I'm all right. I reckon all that excitement with your mother must have taken it out of me.'

'Yeah, well, she's enough to bring down the biggest and bravest of men. And please don't call her my mother.'

'It must have been a shock for you to find out like that.'

'You can say that again,' Penny replied. 'It's strange. I'm not upset. Should I be?'

'You've never knew her or had her in your life, so you ain't lost nothing.'

'Yeah, I suppose so.'

'But you do need people around you, Penny. My days are numbered, and I'll be gone soon.'

'Don't talk like that, Smithy.'

'It's fact. I'm not bothered about meeting me maker, but I am worried about you.'

'Why are you worried about me?' Penny asked.

'Because you haven't got a fella or any friends. You haven't even got a proper job where you'd meet people. Stuck home here all day caring for me is no life for a young woman. So, I'm putting me foot down. I want you to go out there today and you're not to come home until you've found work.'

Penny could tell by Smithy's tone that he was serious. But her life had become so insular, the thought of working with lots of people made her feel uncomfortable. 'But I like being home with you,' she argued.

'I can cope all day without you. To be honest, you get on my nerves. I'd like a bit of peace and quiet. So, go on, put your smart clobber on and find yourself a job.'

'I'm sorry,' she said, quietly, feeling awful. 'I didn't realise that I get on your nerves.'

'You don't really, you daft moo. But you really need to get out of this house more.'

Penny thought for a moment. Smithy was probably right, though she wished he wasn't. 'Are you sure you're going to be all right?' she asked as she stood up.

'Yes, I'm sure.'

Upstairs, Penny changed into a smart, deep blue dress that tied in a bow loosely below her neck. She pinned back her hair, making a curl at the front, and swept a bit of colour onto her lips.

'You look smashing,' Smithy said. 'Now, get out there and knock 'em dead.'

Fighting back tears, Penny smiled at Smithy and left the house. She'd come to love the old man and dreaded losing him. And she also dreaded being alone again.

★

Penny had been in this scenario before: standing outside Arding and Hobbs department store and trying to pluck up the courage to go inside to inquire about vacancies. And the same as last time, she turned and marched away, feeling like a failure.

'You're back early,' Smithy said when she arrived home. 'Any luck?'

Penny threw herself down onto the chair beside the old man's bed. 'I couldn't do it, Smithy. My nerve went.'

'Dear oh dear,' Smithy tutted. 'Right, let's forget about working in fancy department stores, and I know you're not keen to work in a factory again, so have a think, what suits you?'

'I don't know,' Penny shrugged. 'I really liked working in the nurseries in Kent.'

'What did you like about it?'

'Growing things. I enjoyed working with the plants. And I liked being my own boss. Mr Hamble trusted me to get on with my work.'

'Right, now we're getting somewhere. What about working in a flower shop?'

'Funny you should say that. I was looking at the woman who sits along Station Approach with her baskets of flowers, and I thought to meself, I could do that.'

'I don't think you want to be out in all weathers selling flowers, Penny. But working in a nice, warm shop, well, that's a different kettle of fish. There's some proper fancy flower shops over the river, especially round Mayfair and Berkeley Square.'

The idea of a flower shop appealed to Penny, though she didn't think she spoke well enough to work in a posh,

London florists. But thinking of selling flowers had grabbed her imagination. 'I wish I could open my own shop,' she mused.

'What's stopping you?' Smithy asked.

'Money. And I wouldn't know the first thing about running my own business.'

'Money is an obstacle, but don't let anything else hold you back. You're a bright girl, you'd soon learn the trade. If it's what you really want, there's nothing to stop you selling this house and buying a shop, maybe with a flat above.'

'Oh no, I couldn't sell my grandad's house. This was his pride and joy.'

'I can't see how else you'd raise the money. You could rent a shop, but you'd still need money upfront and some for stock, too. Anyway, your grandad wouldn't have wanted you to hold on to this house in his memory. Yes, it was his pride and joy, but he would have been even prouder to know that his legacy had set you up in a new business. It makes sense. Or have you got anything worth selling?'

'No,' Penny answered. 'All I've got to my name are my clothes and an old stamp, nothing worth money.'

Smithy looked curiously at Penny. 'An old stamp... what old stamp?'

'A Penny Black, obviously,' Penny laughed.

'A Penny Black. Well, it could be worth a few bob,' Smithy said, his eyebrows raised.

'I doubt it.'

'You might be surprised. I know a bloke who has got a shop in Hatton Garden. He's a jeweller but he knows about stamps. I reckon you should show him yours.'

'Why? You don't really think it might be valuable, do you?'

Smithy tapped the end of his bulbous nose. 'Who knows. You could be sitting on a small fortune. But even if you ain't, you've still got money tied up in these bricks and mortar.'

Penny couldn't believe that a stamp Jimmy had gifted her would have any value. And even if it was worth anything, she wasn't sure that she'd be willing to sell it. It was all she had to remind her of her brother. But if Jimmy were still alive, she believed he'd tell her that she was a fool if she didn't sell the stamp. He would have wanted her to be happy and he'd have been proud to see her in business.

'I'll write the address down for you. When you get there, ask for Mr Letterman and tell him Smithy sent you. He'll remember me.'

'What, go now?'

'Yes, Penny. Strike while the iron is hot.'

Penny huffed. She supposed she might as well catch a bus up to town. She didn't have much else to do. After carefully wrapping the stamp, she tucked it into her purse before heading out.

'Good luck,' Smithy called as she closed the front door.

As Penny walked along the street and past the bomb-damaged houses, she squinted her eyes against the sun when she saw a man coming towards her. He looked familiar, and her stomach flipped, but she knew he couldn't possibly be Basil. Though as he drew nearer, Penny was sure it was him and her pulse raced.

'Penny,' he smiled, 'I've been looking everywhere for you.'

Penny stared back at him, unsure of what to say. He looked even more handsome than she remembered. It had been years since she'd seen Basil and he'd filled out into a muscular man, his shoulders broad and his jaw strong.

'How are you?' he asked.

Penny stared, speechless.

'You look fabulous,' he said, his hazel eyes boring deeply into hers.

'What are you doing here?' she managed to splutter.

'Looking for you,' he answered. 'I didn't know where to find you. I only had Katy's mum's address. She sent me this way.'

'Why? What do you want?' Penny snapped. Anger burned in her chest, and so did an overwhelming desire to be in his arms.

'Sorry to just turn up like this. Is there somewhere we can go to talk?'

'You still haven't told me why you're here.'

'Christ, I don't know where to start,' he said, drawing in a long breath. 'I know I've no right, but I came here to ask you to help with Katy. She's in a bad way. I don't know what to do with her.'

'You're not making any sense, Basil. What's wrong with Katy?'

'She's drinking... a lot. When she's not drunk, she's moody. My mum is having to care for our son.'

'You – you have a son?'

'Yes, Lawrence.'

Penny looked down at the ground so that Basil wouldn't see the pain in her eyes.

'I've tried everything, and so has Mum. But we can't get through to her. She'll listen to you. I know she misses you... and so do I.'

Penny's face shot up and she could see in Basil's eyes that he had feelings for her.

'Don't. Don't you dare,' Penny whispered.

'I should never have married Katy. It was a mistake. I always knew it was the wrong thing to do.'

'So why did you?'

'Because Katy was having my child. But you've got to understand... Katy threw herself at me.'

'And you couldn't resist,' Penny spat.

'It wasn't like that, Penny. She needed me. I felt I had to look after her. Katy's never been strong like you.'

Strong, Penny thought, incredulously. That wasn't how she saw herself.

Basil sighed heavily. 'I shouldn't be talking like this. It feels disloyal to Katy. She's my wife and the mother to my son. Please, Penny, can we put the past behind us, and will you help her?'

'Katy ended our friendship when she *threw* herself at you.'

Penny found it difficult to turn her back on her friend when Katy was clearly struggling, but she couldn't find it in her heart to forgive the girl's betrayal. She went to step around Basil, but he blocked her path and grabbed her arm.

'Please, Penny, don't walk away from me. Katy needs you... and I don't know what else I can do or how much more I can take.'

'What do you mean?'

'I mean, I don't think I can face returning home to Katy, not without you.'

'I won't be coming with you, Basil. You and Katy made your bed, and you can lie in it. Go back to Gaston Farm and look after your wife and son.'

'I can't, Penny. I never wanted the farm, you know it's never made me happy. And now it's even more miserable than ever. I don't want to be there, and I don't want to deal with Katy's problems.'

'What are you saying?'

'That I want out. I've tried, Penny, Lord knows I've tried. I feel trapped on the farm and tied to a deranged woman. I can't take it. What about me and what I want? No one cares about what I want!'

Penny looked up into his eyes and wondered if she'd ever really truly loved him. Because now, all she saw was a weak man who was willing to walk out on his wife in her hour of need. He had everything: a good home, a comfortable income, loving parents and a child of his own. Yet Penny could see that Basil had been spoiled and would never be happy with his lot. He was nothing like his father. 'Let go of my arm,' she sneered through gritted teeth. 'You can't run at the first sign of trouble. You should be with Katy and your child.'

Basil pulled her closer towards him. She could feel his breath on her cheek.

'I'm a desperate man, Penny. Desperately unhappy.'

'Poor you,' Penny said, her tone heavy with sarcasm.

'I thought you loved me. If you did, then you'd help me.'

'I. Don't. Love. You,' she said firmly and slowly. 'I had a crush on you, Basil. I was a young girl who fell for a young boy. But I don't like the man that you've grown into. Now, let go of me or I'll scream.'

He tried to plead with his eyes, but Penny yanked her arm free of his grip.

'Is this man bothering you?' a deep voice asked.

Looking over her shoulder, Penny saw Maggie's Uncle Charlie. The man, though in his late fifties, still had a violent reputation. His cauliflower ears and broken nose added to the menace of his threatening snarl.

'This is my business,' Basil said, 'Move on, if you will, sir.'

'I'm talking to the lady,' Charlie growled. 'Are you all right, Penny?'

'Yes, thanks, Charlie. Would you walk me to the bus stop, please?'

'My pleasure,' Charlie said with a wink.

'Please, Penny, Katy needs you…'

'Go home, Basil. I hope Katy gets better soon.' Then smiling at Charlie, she said, 'Great timing,' and walked away with him, her heart thumping hard.

'What was that about?' Charlie asked. 'Do I need to go back and give him a good hiding?'

'No, it's fine, thanks. He won't be bothering me again.'

57

Penny found the scenery passing by her in a blur. Her mind was still reeling from her encounter with Basil. Seeing the man had shaken her. She sat on the bus trembling and fighting the urge to cry. It had been a shock to realise that the love she thought she held for him had been nothing more than a young girl's foolish dream and had never been real. And though she couldn't forgive Katy, it upset Penny to think of her being in a bad way. But reaching her destination, she got off the bus, determined to push thoughts of Basil and Katy out of her head. They had their life, and she had a new one to build. She wanted to leave the man and her treacherous best friend in the past where they belonged.

Strolling through Hatton Garden, Penny was amazed at the riches on display in the goldsmith's windows. *How the other half live*, she thought. Stopping briefly, she glanced at a ring, the most opulent she'd ever seen with a diamond the size of a kidney bean! She couldn't imagine who would wear a ring like that, except for maybe Princess Elizabeth. Penny doubted that she'd ever wear an engagement ring, let alone one with a huge diamond. Not that she expected diamonds.

A sudden sadness washed over her. The illusion of Basil and her feelings for him had been shattered. But she wanted love in her life. Smithy's time in the world was limited, and then she'd be left with no one. She could feel her insides churning with anxiety and wished she could shrink to the size of an ant and disappear down a crack in the pavement.

Come on Penny, you can do this she reminded herself. As much as Penny would like to hide away in the sanctuary of her grandad's house, she knew she had to carve out a life for herself. And working with flowers in her own shop was the life she wanted. She just needed the courage and the belief in herself to make it happen. Biting on her bottom lip, Penny carried on walking until she found Mr Letterman's jewellers. She pulled out a slip of paper from her bag and looked again at the address Smithy had written. Then glancing up, she saw that the number in gold paint displayed above the shop corresponded. 'This is it,' she said to herself, 'be brave, Penny, be strong and brave.'

Taking a deep breath, Penny walked in with trepidation. Tall glass cabinets showing off twinkling jewels lined one wall. And behind a marble counter, she saw a young man wearing glasses perched on the end of his nose and a crooked bow-tie around his neck. He eyed her up and down as if giving her the once over.

'Can I help you?' he asked.

His tone suggested to Penny that she shouldn't be in the shop. She felt out of place and almost ran back out. 'I'd like to see Mr Letterman,' she said, her voice shaking.

'*I* am Mr Letterman,' the young man replied.

'Oh, I thought you'd be older. Sorry, erm, Smithy sent me.'

Acknowledgements

Thank you to my and mum's wonderful readers. Losing my mum has been heartbreaking, but your kind words and support have helped me through the tough times. I'm truly grateful.

Thank you to my wonderful team at Orion, especially my editor, Rhea Kurien.

Thank you to my agent, Judith Murdoch.

For the first time in as long as she could remember, she was overjoyed to look forward without any nervousness.

'Once I'm living back in Battersea, I ain't never leaving again,' Phil said, soberly. 'I've missed the place, and I've missed you an' all. You're stuck with me forever now, Penny, and with Eleanor too. And I hope you're up for babysitting 'cos we're planning on having a big family,' he chuckled. 'You'll be their *Aunty* Penny.'

'And their Godmother,' Eleanor added.

Penny's smile widened as she looked from Phil to Eleanor. She felt as though she was walking ten feet tall. They gave her confidence, and a feeling that even when Smithy passed, she wouldn't be alone again. So what if she didn't have a family? She didn't need Jill, her heartless mother, or her uncaring father. Penny would always have her friends. And she would treasure them forever.

'Hardly,' Eleanor said.

'I'm only kidding. I think I'd like the name to mean something dear to me. Maybe Daisy's Blooms, after my grandmother. Or something like Jimmy's Jasmine, in memory of my brother. But Rosy Rosemary would be nice too, in honour of my friend Rosemary. And there's my grandad, Archie. I'd like to remember him too.'

Eleanor spoke softly, her tone caring. 'With all your departed loved ones in mind, may I suggest a name ... Forget Me Not Florals.'

'Perfect! That's blinkin' perfect. Thank you,' Penny gushed.

She was pleased to see Phil so happy and had instantly warmed to his fiancée. As they walked together and chatted easily, seeing how Phil and Eleanor looked at each other, Penny hoped that one day she would meet someone special, too. Maybe get married and have children. But first, she had a new business to open. Forget Me Not Florals, the proprietor Penny Black. Her pulse raced at the notion of it!

'I'm proud of you, Penny. Your flower shop will be a success, I know it will. And me and Eleanor will do anything we can to help you set it up.'

'I'd love to help,' Eleanor confirmed. 'If you'd like?'

'I would appreciate that, thank you. I'm going to need all the help I can get.'

Phil placed his arm over Penny's shoulder and the other over Eleanor's, just like he used to with Maggie. 'You can count on us. That's what friends are for, ain't that right,' he said, giving them both a gentle squeeze.

Penny was on the verge of embarking on a new business. And she had the promise of support from Phil and his fiancée.

Penny hadn't contemplated courting anyone, and her stomach flipped at the notion of meeting a man. Though she was surprised to find herself thrilled at the thought. 'I think I'd like to meet your brother,' she said, returning Eleanor's smile.

'I can't tell you how happy I am to see you, Penny. Me and Eleanor are coming over to Battersea and taking my mum out tomorrow night. Will you join us?'

'I don't know...'

'Go on. We're going down the Labour Club. You know the one, on Falcon Road. There'll be plenty of familiar faces from the factory. It'll be a laugh, say you'll come.'

'All right, then, I will,' Penny agreed, surprising herself.

'My feet have had enough of window shopping,' Eleanor said. 'I noticed a café near the station. I don't know about you, Penny, but I'm gasping. Shall we go for a cuppa?'

'I'd like that,' Penny replied, happily.

'And you can tell me the long story about your grandad,' Phil said with a wink.

'Me and Phil are looking at moving to Battersea. We might be neighbours,' Eleanor beamed.

'Yeah, wouldn't that be good, Penny. It would be just like the old days with you, me and Maggie but with Eleanor instead of Mags,' Phil said excitedly. 'Best of mates.'

'Yes, it really would be good,' Penny answered, and she meant it.

'What are you going to call your shop?' Eleanor asked.

'Oh, I don't know. I haven't thought of that yet... I could name it after me.'

'What, Penny Black?' Phil asked.

'No, The Shrinking Violet,' Penny giggled.

Penny smiled back, awkwardly, but she felt quite bowled over at seeing Phil. She hadn't realised how much she'd missed her friend.

'Phil is such a braggart. We're only looking in the shop windows at rings. He couldn't possibly afford to buy me one from here.'

'I would if I could, sweetheart,' Phil said, looking at Eleanor with loving eyes. Then facing Penny, he asked, 'How's life been treating you? Did you move back to Kent?'

'No, I'm still in Battersea.'

'Are you working in the factory?'

'No, I haven't been there for ages now. At the moment I'm looking after someone, but once I've sold a property left to me by my grandad, I'll be opening my own business.'

'That's exciting. Your grandad?'

'Yes, it's a long story.'

'What sort of business are you opening?'

'A flower shop.'

'Well, that's a coincidence!' Phil grinned.

'What is?' Penny asked.

Eleanor answered, 'My dad sells flowers wholesale that are grown in Cornwall.'

'Really?'

'Yes,' Phil said, 'You should speak to him.'

'I'd love to. I'm new to flower selling. I've got a lot to learn.'

'We're having a party on Saturday. Come along, my dad will be there,' Eleanor suggested.

'Oh, that sounds smashing, thank you.'

'And my brother,' Eleanor smiled, 'He'll be at the party. I think you and him might like each other.'

that counted. Still, her hopes weren't dashed. She would sell her grandad's house and as London was desperate for housing stock, she felt sure that a buyer would quickly snap it up.

Walking back through Hatton Garden, Penny gripped her bag closely. Though worried about how she'd make her dreams of owning a flower shop come true, and scared of only having herself to rely on, Penny was also filled with a new-found optimism for her future. In a way, she was glad she'd had the encounter with Basil earlier. It meant that she could truly put the past behind her and focus on what was ahead.

'Penny... Penny...'

She heard someone calling her name and turned around. She couldn't believe it when she saw Phil waving at her. He had an attractive, raven-haired woman on his arm who smiled at Penny too, with bright red lips and twinkling dark eyes.

'Fancy bumping into you here!' Phil enthused. 'I knew it was you as soon as I saw your red hair. It's really good to see you. How are you?'

'Yeah, I'm all right,' Penny answered, amazed to see him. She had that warm, fuzzy feeling inside, just the same as she'd felt when she'd met her grandad for the first time. 'And you, how are you?'

'Good. Better than good, actually. Sorry, let me introduce you. Penny, this is Eleanor, my fiancée! We're here now looking at engagement rings.'

'Hello, Penny,' Eleanor said with a genuine smile. 'It's nice to meet you. I've heard so much about you, I feel that we're already friends.'

contorting his lips into the strangest of shapes as he made a closer inspection. 'Interesting... the stamp is in mint condition... the margins are good.'

Taking his eye away from the stamp, he looked at Penny and explained, 'The stamps came off the printing press in unperforated sheets, hence, collectors always look for good, cut margins.' Then returning his attention to the stamp, he said, 'I'm afraid your stamp is worthless.'

'But it can't be... My brother gave it to me. It must be worth something.'

Mr Letterman smiled. 'Your stamp isn't a stamp, my dear. This Penny Black may look like one of the rarer samples. I can confirm that if it were a stamp, then it would have been from printing plate number eleven, from which only one hundred and sixty-eight thousand stamps were produced. Unfortunately, this is a picture of one, cut from a reference book and stuck down onto the paper.'

Penny stood, flabbergasted, but she wasn't disappointed. Jimmy's gift was worthless, but it was priceless to her.

'Thank you for coming in and please pass my warmest regards to Smithy. I do apologise, I didn't ask your name?'

'It's Penny,' she smiled as she carefully placed the fake stamp into her purse. 'Penny Black.'

Mr Letterman roared with laughter. 'If you say so. Well, good day to you, *Penny Black*... Penny Black, indeed. Hilarious!'

Penny left the shop in a hurry and smiled to herself, thinking that Jimmy was probably looking down on her from heaven and laughing at her. She should have realised the stamp wasn't a stamp, but as Jimmy would have told her if he had lived to give her the Christmas gift, *it was the thought*

'*Smithy*,' he repeated, wrinkling his nose as if there was a bad smell underneath it.

Another man came out through a door behind the counter, much older and with a huge stomach that hung below his waistcoat. Penny thought his buttons might pop off!

'Did you say that Smithy sent you?' the older chap asked.

Penny nodded.

'Is he still alive?'

'Yes.'

'Knock me down with a feather! What can I do for you, young lady?'

'I've got a stamp,' she said, rummaging in her bag before pulling out the paper that the stamp was glued to, and holding it aloft.

'Bring it here, my eyes are good but they're not that good,' he laughed.

Penny approached the counter, glancing sideways at the younger man who was still looking down his nose at her.

'Don't worry about my grandson,' the old man said. 'He's a terrible snob,' and then he pretended to whisper when he added, 'I blame his mother.'

Penny smiled. She preferred the older Mr Letterman to the younger one.

'Right, what have we got here then,' Mr Letterman Senior said as he studied the stamp. 'Ah, I see, a Penny Black. A most enviable stamp to have in every schoolboy's collection, but there are few that are of much value.'

Penny wasn't disappointed. She hadn't got her hopes up and allowed herself to believe that the stamp was valuable.

Mr Letterman put a peculiar-looking eyeglass to one eye and held the small piece of paper in a pair of tweezers,